The Prophecy of the Codex

Melissa Frey

Independently Published
in the United States of America

www.melissafrey.com

Book Layout © 2017 BookDesignTemplates.com

The Prophecy of the Codex / by Melissa Frey. —1st ed.

Summary: With the Secret of the Codex revealed, archaeologists Kayla, Grady, Mandy, and Justin are attacked on all sides by a ruthless enemy determined to stop them from fulfilling the prophecies detailed in the Codex while stealing the Power for themselves.

ISBN 978-1-7324335-4-0

For my husband, Andrew,
who will forever be my Grady

The Prophecy of the Codex

Glowing

Harrington McGready Central American Exhibit Hall,
Central Florida Natural History Museum, Gainesville,
Florida, United States

IF THERE'D BEEN ANYONE ELSE around, the incessant click-clacking of the security guard's nightstick against the marble walls would have been irritating. But instead, the museum's sole defender dragged his nightstick at knee level, not caring about the sound. Sometimes that was the only way to stay sane on the night shift: manufacture a distraction to make your mind believe someone else was there. Lonely job.

He really didn't mind it, most nights. He liked the solitude, the lack of micromanaging, and the pay. Plus, he got to carry a gun. Oh, he wasn't stupid about it. He knew how to handle it—in a word, *carefully*—but he liked how it made him feel: powerful. Strong.

Not that he'd admit that to anyone. Least of all, his infuriating ex-girlfriend. He wondered what she was doing right now. Probably asleep next to her new *fiancé* . . .

He smacked the nightstick into his left palm a little harder than he intended. "Ow!"

The nightstick tumbled to the marble floor, sending a clatter reverberating throughout the entire marble-clad museum. He quickly stepped on it to make it stop bouncing and froze.

Because he'd heard something.

With the echoes dissipating, he leaned down slowly, so slowly, and gently lifted the nightstick off the ground, his navy-blue security uniform crinkling. He tilted his head, still bent over. What was that?

He carefully straightened, taking his time to make sure he wouldn't make any extra noise. He gazed across the darkened Incan exhibit, looking for something, anything that could've made the sound he'd heard. Or thought he'd heard.

He shook his head, blinking. Sometimes the mind played tricks on you at—he checked his phone—three in the morning. Probably just a fluorescent light on somewhere.

His shoulders heaved. Five more hours until the day shift got here. *They're all probably home, still asleep,* he thought. *Must be nice.*

There it was again.

He froze, every muscle in his body tensing. He turned to the left, toward the room around the corner that housed the rest of the Central American exhibits. Did something flash in the Mayan wing? He supposed he should go find out.

He tiptoed around the Incan pyramid replica, the collection of ancient burial masks, and a ceremonial bridal dress before finally spying the doorway to the Mayan collection. Truth be told, this was his favorite room in the whole museum. The curator here had received a generous donation of

Mayan artifacts just this past summer—they'd even renamed this section of the museum after the benefactor, though he didn't know who Harrington McGready was—and now it was all on display. Beautiful gems, smooth stones, colorful pottery—it was all here, in living color, and was honestly breathtaking.

And this was for a guy with a high school education.

He rounded the corner, and his view of the entire room opened up. Amid the seemingly endless parade of miscellaneous artifacts, one piece always stood out. It caught his eye whenever he entered the room. *There it is.*

Standing in its own display case, visible from nearly every corner of the L-shaped room, was the most fascinating thing he'd ever seen. And that was saying something, given that he spent his nights surrounded by the curious and interesting.

A sphere, probably less than a foot in diameter and made up of what looked like solid rock, commanded his attention. He wasn't really sure what made the object so fascinating, but he found himself drawn to it.

He came up to the display case and saw his dark, buzzed hair and square jaw briefly reflected in the glass, then his light-blue eyes found and fixed on the globe. As he did, his eyes widened. "What the—"

The sphere had started glowing.

That was the last thing he remembered.

Twelve Hours Earlier, Central Florida Natural History Museum

The olive-skinned, dark-haired woman stepped into the lobby, tossing her long hair to the side as she pulled her handbag to her shoulder. Simón Cortez, the museum's curator, adjusted his thin knit tie and smoothed his gelled, jet-black hair as he scurried through the glass door that had the single word "Offices" painted across it in a muted yellow. He indulged himself a look back through the clouded glass, catching a glimpse of the thin, petite outline of his fiancée. The same thin, petite outline he'd just become intimately reacquainted with in the janitor's closet. For the fifth time this week.

The attractive woman's dark-brown eyes searched the cavernous lobby, and Simón tugged at his light-gray, perfectly tailored suit jacket as he hurried toward her. He didn't know why, but this woman just screamed VIP.

And he was nothing if he wasn't accommodating.

Her eyes found his dark-brown ones, and he stumbled slightly as he approached. *How is she doing tha—* The thought died in his brain, and he suddenly forgot how to speak. The woman's eyes held his with the power of a thousand chains, and he tried to swallow without being too obvious. "H-hello, Miss, may I help you?" Simón clasped his hands in front of him to remind them to be still.

"Yes, thank you." Her voice was as sultry as the summer nights he spent as a child on the Riviera Maya. "I am here to view the Mayan exhibit."

Simón exhaled as she broke their gaze, and his mind was suddenly clear once again. He blinked once then directed her toward the Mayan wing with a flourish of his right arm. "Of course! Right this way." His quick, staccato steps echoed in the marble lobby as he followed her toward the hall immediately to her left. He tried not to notice the way her mid-length, forest-green wrap dress swayed around her perfect calves as she walked.

Simón hurried through the Incan and Aztec exhibits, moving ahead of her as soon as he noticed she was staring past all the eye-catching artifacts surrounding her. Once they passed through the large, rectangular opening and into the long, L-shaped room that made up the Mayan exhibit hall, Simón launched into curator mode. Force of habit.

"To your left is a photographic display of the people from Lamanai, an archaeological dig in northern Belize, and the artifacts they found and cataloged. It was said that this particular dig was only open a short time before they found a large number of items with significant value. And next to these photographs"—Simón continued down the wall—"are reproductions of some of the hieroglyphs they found underground at the same site."

The woman was staring intently at the first display. "Are these reproductions a full representation of all the hieroglyphs they found?"

Astute question, Simón thought. *Beautiful and smart.* "These reproductions simply give us a taste of what they found. The full text is still being analyzed and transcribed. We hope it will be available in the coming months."

The woman was frowning, so Simón quickly changed the subject, pivoting ninety degrees to show the next collection. "And these items are actual artifacts unearthed at the dig." He motioned to the large glass display case behind her. "They found a burial chamber with several pieces of pottery and other items used in the burial process." The case was inhabited by all manner of clay pieces, most only part of their former selves.

Simón turned, moving further into the room toward another display case on their right—this time, one with some textiles in it. "The articles seen here are reproductions of period tapestries and garments worn by the native Mayans during the eighth and ninth centuries, just before their civilization realized a drastic decrease in their native peoples. The cause of the Mayan demise has never been determined and is a heavily debated topic among academics."

He glanced at the woman again, whose gaze was fixed on the beige wall on the far side of the room. The plain, empty wall.

Time to move on.

As they neared the center of the room, Simón sensed that this would be a short tour today. "Along this other wall"—he indicated the other part of the "L" in the room, to their left —"are some rare stones they discovered as well as other pictures of the modern dig, showing the archaeologists who made this discovery and who also donated all the artifacts you see here." He swept his arm in a wide arc but then noticed the woman was frowning again. Definitely time to wrap it up.

They had reached the center of the room, and now he stopped. "And this, our final stop, is the *crème de la crème*." He moved to stand beside a smaller display standing proudly in the middle of the room. "This is a globe they found underground at Lamanai. It's said to contain a light source from within, though that is simply conjecture at this point—*I've* never actually seen it light up." Simón offered the requisite smile then fell silent. Though the other cases dwarfed it in size, there was something otherworldly about this piece that gave it the most presence in the room. Simón loved to bring patrons in for a tour and watch their reactions.

And he wasn't disappointed. The dark-haired woman leaned in toward the piece, her eyes widening. Simón even thought he saw them sparkle.

"Incredible," the woman breathed, and Simón followed her gaze, staring at the artifact next to him. Atop a marble pedestal, at just about chest height and behind four walls— and a ceiling—of glass, a curious globe sat. Simón had always wondered what made this piece so special; it honestly looked like a spherical piece of tan rock. It didn't even have any writing on it.

But as he watched the globe, he noticed something start to happen. As the woman stared into its center, Simón could've sworn the globe was lighting up—*reacting* to her.

No, that would be ridiculous. Simón straightened his back and adjusted his suit jacket again then cleared his throat. "Would you like to stay here a little longer?"

The woman never took her eyes off the subtly glowing sphere. "Yes, I would like that very much."

Simón nodded once. "Very good." Then he turned on his heels and had to remind himself not to run through the gallery. He suddenly didn't want to be in the same room with that woman or that globe another minute.

CHAPTER 1

The Globe

Anthropology Department, University of Central Florida, Orlando

"Okay, so what's the first step in excavating an archaeological site?"

Dr. Kayla Harrington glanced around at her freshman class, the only class of bright-eyed newbies she had this year, as she tucked her long, dark-brown hair behind one ear. Her students sat in black, wheeled office chairs behind long, off-white tables on four tiered, burgundy-carpeted rows. This was her largest class, and the classroom was cramped; she'd taken to leaving her warmer clothes at home on Tuesdays and Thursdays for this very reason. As her hands smoothed over her royal-blue silk tank top and light-gray dress pants, she made a mental note again to talk to Dean Stewart about changing rooms before the next semester began.

Because the fall semester was almost over—the closer they got to Thanksgiving then Christmas break, she could see the students' attentiveness exponentially decrease—and she was grateful. She loved to teach, even freshmen, but their naïveté sometimes frustrated her. She much rather enjoyed the masters' students. Not that she'd ever admit that aloud. Probably not even to Grady. Of course, he would know anyway . . .

A tiny, bespectacled girl in the second row raised her hand. Kayla nodded at her. "Gretchen?"

The girl swallowed before answering. "We use radar and/or land surveys to find where the artifacts are placed . . . ?" She let the statement hang, ending the sentence with a question.

Kayla nodded once. *At least she was listening at some point this semester . . .* "Very good. Next?" She glanced around the room.

A dark-haired boy named Tommy answered from the fourth row. "We map the site."

Kayla nodded again. "And how do we do that?"

Tommy continued. "We place stakes and twine in a grid pattern, noting the location of every stake."

Kayla smiled. "Very thorough. Someone else want to take the next step?"

Blonde Holly in the back spoke up, glancing at her notes. "We start excavation. Tools and methods will vary depending on the type of soil, weather conditions, and state of the artifacts."

Kayla clasped her hands in front of her, nodding once again. "Good." She glanced at the clock on the wall to her left that faced the row of windows to her right. "Looks like that's all the time we have for today. The final is two weeks from today. And remember: Your semester paper is due Tuesday."

She always thought it was cruel to have a paper due *after* Thanksgiving, so she liked to collect them from the class before the students left for the break.

"I will finish up my lectures in the next class, then we'll have a few of you present your papers the following week. We're in the home stretch." She smiled, and most of the students grinned back. She walked back to her lectern. "See you Tuesday."

Kayla collected her things as her students did the same, but not as quietly. She smiled to herself. These young kids sure did have a lot of life in them.

Her phone buzzed on the desk next to her. She glanced over, her smile widening as she read the text that'd just come through. Grady, wanting to meet for lunch. As always.

She packed her things more quickly.

"Hey, beautiful." The brown-haired, blue-eyed Dr. Grady McGready stood to pull out a wrought iron bistro chair for Kayla as she approached. He'd picked this place specifically for her; he knew it was her favorite restaurant on campus.

"You're crazy," she shot back with a smile on her face as she scooted in toward the table.

Grady sat down and reached for her hand, smiling. "Crazy about you." He knew his response was cheesy, but he couldn't help himself. Kayla made him feel alive, almost like he hadn't really been living before her. And besides, Grady knew she didn't mind.

Since this past summer, when their relationship started, things had been moving quickly. And given all that had happened this summer—finding the Codex and receiving its Power, namely—their swift romance made sense.

I love you, Grady McGready. Always will.

Grady grinned at Kayla's thoughts in his head. They'd been able to hear each other's thoughts for several months now, and he honestly loved it. But as his mind started down a path he knew she wasn't ready for yet, he had the realization that sometimes it could be a little problematic . . .

He quickly spoke, pushing the thoughts from his mind. The last five or so months had given him a little practice in being able to surprise Kayla—not a small feat when the woman could hear his thoughts. "So what sounds good today?"

Kayla gave a perfunctory glance at the menu. They came here almost every day, and every day the same song and dance. She'd peruse the menu, pretend to want to try something new, then always settle on one of the three dishes she ordered here. Fish sandwich, soup of the day, or . . .

"Probably the barbecue bacon burger."

Grady grinned. Yep, that was the third one.

"How about you?" Kayla took a sip of her ice water, her eyes smiling at his thoughts in her head.

Grady reached for his own ice water, taking a big gulp, and relished the feel of the cold liquid flowing down his throat. He found himself wishing he'd opted for a short-sleeved shirt today. He'd rolled up the sleeves of his light-blue button-up shirt, but still, November in Florida was always pretty toasty. After over a decade of living here, he should've known better.

He reached for the menu, scanning it. Grady did his best to try new things whenever he had the chance, but sometimes it was exhausting. That's when he decided today was going to be a boring day. "Chicken tenders basket."

Kayla scrunched her nose, smiling, and Grady knew why. Fried food didn't agree with her. Neither did dairy, and she didn't like mushrooms. Or kale. She hated kale.

He loved that he knew nearly everything about her.

Their favorite waiter stepped up to their small, jet-black table in his signature gray high-top sneakers. "Grady, Kayla, hi! How are you both this fine Florida day?"

They smiled up at the skinny young man with vintage, horn-rimmed glasses dressed all in black from his neck to his ankles, his shoes the one aberration management allowed. That and the multiple tattoos exposed by the rolled sleeves of his button-up shirt. "Glen, hi! How are your classes going?" Grady knew from their previous conversations that he was a junior economics major with a minor in statistics. The guy loved business and numbers. Grady's polar opposite.

Glen rested his forearm against his notepad, pen in hand. "Oh, they're going well. Next semester's gonna be crazy, but I'll figure it out." He turned to Kayla. "How are you?"

Kayla smiled up at him. "I'll be glad when this semester's over." She grinned. "And also hungry."

Glen chuckled. "What can I get for you?"

"Barbecue bacon burger, how it comes. With a side salad instead of fries. Olive oil and lemon for the dressing." She handed Glen her menu, who took it and turned to Grady.

"Chicken tenders basket for me, with sweet potato fries. And honey mustard."

Glen nodded, taking Grady's offered menu. He turned to walk away then quickly flipped back around. "Hey . . . you both were the ones who donated all those artifacts to the Natural History Museum in Gainesville, right?"

Grady and Kayla nodded in unison.

"It's on the news." He nodded toward the ceiling-mounted flat screen just inside the open-air restaurant. "Mysterious disappearance, I think."

The three of them stared at the screen, trying to piece together the story from the subtitles on the silent news piece.

After about a minute, Grady asked, "Do you know what happened?"

Glen shrugged. "Not really. I just remembered the name of the museum from that news story last summer, where they interviewed the two of you about all that stuff you'd found in —where was it—Belize?" Kayla nodded, and Glen shrugged. "Sorry, that's all I know." He offered a half smile then walked away to put their order in.

Grady caught Kayla's gaze and held it. *I wonder . . .*

Grady, that's insane. How could anything possibly go wrong?

Kayla, you know better than I do the crazy things that globe did to you.

So you think it's the globe?

I don't know what else it could be. Grady sighed, combing his short hair back with his fingers. Then he reached in the pocket of his khakis for his phone. *I know we promised to keep these away at meals, but . . .*

Kayla nodded once. *We need to find out what happened. This could be nothing—or it could be very bad.*

Grady nodded back, unlocking his phone and quickly searching for and finding the story. He could hear Kayla in his head, trying to understand what he was reading but apparently having little success.

"Grady? What does it say?"

Grady cleared his throat. "The story I found doesn't say much, just that a night guard disappeared early this morning. His nightstick was on the ground . . . in the middle of the Mayan exhibit."

Kayla gasped.

"They didn't find any other evidence, and the museum was still locked when his relief got in this morning."

Grady felt Kayla freeze across from him, and he could sense why. He took a deep breath. "Look . . . our classes are out for the day. I can let the department admin know that we'll be out the rest of the day if you'd like to drive to Gainesville."

Kayla's eyes flew to his. "Really?"

Grady attempted what he hoped was a reassuring smile. "Of course. You won't have peace of mind until we check it out."

Kayla's face relaxed as her shoulders released. She mouthed a quick "thank you" as he dialed the anthropology department.

Wyatt's Sports Bar and Tavern, Miami, Florida

Fridays were always busy here, but the young man with long, dark hair pulled back in a loose ponytail hadn't been able to figure out why. He grabbed up yet another plate of half-eaten hot wings and tossed it into the black bin he carried around. He was barely making enough to keep himself fed, but these jokers wasted food every time they ate. It made him sick.

He paused for a moment to look around, setting his bin on the table. Roger didn't like him to do that, but his boss was two minutes into his every-two-hours twenty-minute smoke break. He'd never know.

Surrounding him and the more than a dozen flat-screen TVs mounted high on the walls were men of varying ages and sizes, all wearing some manner of suit and tie in stark contrast to his all-black uniform. This was the financial district, after all—the young man supposed it made sense. "Important" men drowning their sorrows and yet another soul-sucking workweek in bar food and whatever alcohol they could afford.

He felt sad for them.

But was he really better off? Here, away from any family he had ever known? His existence had become extremely lonely of late with no end in sight.

He sighed and reached for the bin, wiping the table down with a quick swipe of his used-to-be-white rag then starting back toward the kitchen as he thought about the events of this summer, about the four Americans he'd helped. He wondered what they were doing right now . . .

The young man froze, and the black bin fell from his hands, the contents of it clattering to the tile floor. It was happening again.

"You okay, man?" His favorite coworker, Antonio, whispered as he hurried past with a huge platter of nachos, slowing only slightly as he passed. The young man barely heard him but couldn't move.

The platter abandoned at its proper table, Antonio returned to the young man's side. He grabbed his shoulder, but the youth couldn't even feel it. He'd been transported somewhere else.

After another fifteen seconds had passed, the teenaged boy blinked several times, his dark-brown eyes slowly adjusting to the dimly lit dining room. His gaze finally found his friend, and he smiled slightly. "I am okay, Antonio. Thank you for checking."

The other man smiled, shaking his head and bending down to help the kid pick up the discarded plates and silverware and put them back in the bin. He blew out a gust of air as they finished. "You're a little weird, dude, but I still like ya." He patted him on the back.

The boy straightened and smiled back, shrugging as Antonio walked back into the kitchen.

As soon as Antonio was out of sight, the young man stalked toward the far entrance to the kitchen, toward the back where their aprons and the time clock were stored. He hurriedly tossed the black bin on the stainless steel counter near the dishwashing station and yanked his black apron over his head, hooking it on one of the dozen pegs on the wall before reaching for a piece of paper. His boss wouldn't like him quitting without notice, but he hoped the note would smooth things over a little bit. Not that it mattered—he wasn't staying in town.

His friends needed his help.

After the quickest lunch they'd had in a while, Grady and Kayla hopped in Kayla's Jeep and headed north, out of Orlando. Once they got on the interstate, Kayla gazed out the windshield at the sky, where dark clouds were forming. She hoped they wouldn't get stuck in a bad storm.

"So why are you still teaching Arc 101?" Grady's voice interrupted her thoughts.

Kayla shrugged, reaching for Grady's hand from the passenger seat. "I'm not sure . . . sometimes those kids drive me crazy, but there are always a few of them who fall in love with archaeology in that class. It's really amazing to see that spark being lit and to be a part of that."

Grady glanced over at her with a smile and squeezed her hand.

"How are your classes going?" Kayla asked, knowing most of what had transpired this semester anyway. Though they could read each other's thoughts, they both recognized the value of conversation and showing interest in the other. She hoped that would never change.

"I'm glad the semester's almost over, too." He grinned. "Looks like we'll both be busy over Thanksgiving. I have two classes turning in papers next Wednesday."

Kayla nodded. "I just have the one, but there are forty students in that class. *Freshman*. Ugh."

Grady laughed aloud, throwing his head back. "You crack me up." He lifted her hand to his mouth and kissed it.

"At least you have all grad students in your classes. And Justin."

Grady nodded. "True, but Justin always seems to think he has some sort of pass in my class." He smirked, glancing sideways across the front seat.

"That jerk," Kayla shot back, grinning. "I'm sure he's upset with me for keeping Mandy busy all the time."

Justin's longtime girlfriend, Mandy, was heading up the translation and transcription of the Codex—the ancient Mayan book they'd discovered in the Belize rainforest and beyond this past summer—which took most of her nights and weekends. But Kayla knew Justin frequently spent most of his time there with her anyway—and was actually learning a little K'iche along the way.

Mandy Carlson and Justin Stanford had recently become their close friends, just a few months ago. They had joined Kayla and Grady at the Lamanai dig after the two professors had gone missing. Once Mandy and Justin rescued them, the Four had gone on a monthlong quest to find the Codex, a secret book guarded by a ruthless group of mercenaries—and one that gave the four of them supernatural powers. They each now controlled one of the four elements—earth, water, fire, and air—and Kayla suspected their power would only increase as time went on.

Though they'd ultimately found the Codex, received its Power, and defeated the Mercenaries, their journey was not without a cost. Like their good friend and Lamanai's handy-man, Jack, and Justin's parents . . .

Kayla had no intention of adding any more to that list.

"Have you spoken with Jack's family?" Kayla asked aloud, knowing Grady had been listening to everything running through her head and had kept up with her chaotic train of thought.

Grady shook his head. "Unfortunately, no. Haven't taken the time." He took a breath. "But I think Mandy and Justin are fine. Isn't Mandy set to graduate in the spring? I think Justin may be up in the summer."

Kayla nodded absently. "I'm just glad we can't hear them all the time. As long as they keep their distance . . ." Kayla fleetingly remembered the night they'd gotten back to Lamanai after they'd defeated the Mercenaries, how they could hear Mandy and Justin in their tent . . .

Grady cringed. "Yeah. Super grateful for *that*." Then he smiled again. "But it does help in class. I can yell at Justin without disturbing the rest of the students."

Kayla laughed then glanced over at a passing road sign. "Oh, good. Probably only half an hour left."

"You sick of being stuck in the car with me, Harrington?"

Kayla playfully hit his arm as she crinkled her nose. "Of course."

Central Florida Natural History Museum, Gainesville

Steven didn't understand what was happening. Why was everyone ignoring him? He'd tried to say something to the first person he saw, but as soon as he'd opened his mouth, the middle-aged man had taken off running—full speed—out of the exhibit hall and into the parking lot. He wanted to punch the marble wall but stopped himself just before he broke his hand. Why was no one listening to him?

But wait . . . that man hadn't really looked *at* him, did he?

Slowly, very slowly, Steven stuck his hands out in front of him then forced his eyes toward the floor. His stomach rolled.

His hands were missing.

He stared down at his body. His hands felt him touch his chest repeatedly, but his eyes saw nothing. His breath came more quickly, and he felt his heartbeat speed up. He reached up and touched his face. Everything *felt* perfectly fine, and for a second he thought he'd been imagining the whole thing.

Then he put his hands in front of his eyes. He blinked. Then blinked again.

Nothing. His hands were just *gone*.

He started breathing faster, harder, his breaths more shallow. The room was starting to spin; he needed to get out of here. He walked through the exhibit hall—careful to avoid the displays—and into the employee break room. On the wall to his left stood a mirror. He took several slow steps toward it.

He knew he was in front of it—he couldn't have been anywhere else—but the reflection in the mirror was completely . . . well, *empty*. The glass simply showed the gray lockers on the wall behind him, the well-worn tables and chairs set up for employee lunchtime, the three vending machines—but not him.

His knees buckled and he stumbled, reaching for the closest orange plastic chair and crashing into it. He started gasping, putting his hands on his knees and leaning forward. Wasn't that what you were supposed to do when you couldn't breathe?

Steven?

What the— Steven whipped his head around the room. He didn't see anyone. What was happening? Was someone in his head?

Steven? I'd like to talk to you if that's okay.

Steven swallowed hard. Was he hearing voices now? He supposed it made sense. He was invisible, after all—nothing was impossible anymore.

So he decided to talk back, though he wasn't quite sure how, then figured aloud would be as good a way as any. "Sure." He was surprised how comforting hearing his own voice was. Almost like a reminder that he still existed. "Where are you?"

Just then, the other door to the room—the one in the back that led to the loading docks, the door opposite the one he'd come through—opened and a dark-haired beauty, adorned in a red sleeveless wrap dress that hugged her incredible curves, glided in. Steven thought she might've been the most beautiful woman he'd ever seen.

As soon as the door fell shut behind her, the mysterious woman closed her eyes. Steven felt his skin start to crawl before she opened her piercing brown eyes and headed straight to his table.

Steven's jaw dropped. "You can see me?"

The woman shook her head as she stopped just in front of him. "No, but I can feel your thoughts. It's how I knew where you were."

Steven shivered though he wasn't cold. "What do you want?"

She smiled. "To help you."

"With what?" It was an automatic question that seemed idiotic once he'd spoken it aloud. But he'd utter nonsense if it kept this woman talking to him.

"Your . . . sit-u-a-tion." She carefully pronounced each syllable as if mulling over each one.

Steven nodded automatically, forgetting she couldn't see him. "This is all too weird."

The beautiful woman just nodded, her dress swishing slightly in the near-silent room.

"Why would you want to help me?"

A little edge crept into the woman's grin. "I have my reasons, which will become clear soon enough."

Steven hesitated, though he didn't know why. The woman spoke again before he could. "I will not expect you to do anything you're not comfortable with. You can always say no to anything I ask."

Again, Steven paused. Then: "Okay."

The woman clasped her hands together, pressing them against her ample chest. "Oh, excellent! I'll tell you what I'd like you to do, then you can tell me if it sounds okay with you. But before that, I'm sure you have some scores to settle on your own, am I right?"

He nodded again. *She can't see you, Steven.*

The woman continued anyway. "You can certainly get that out of the way. Whatever you want to do, you should go do that first. I encourage that—no sense being invisible if you can't have a little fun with it, right?"

"Yeah." Steven had found his voice, and he didn't mind at all what this lady was saying. Come to think of it, that little liar and her new *fiancé* could use a lesson . . .

The woman started laying out her plans, and Steven, invisible though he was, sat and listened to every word coming out of this intoxicating creature's mouth. As she spoke, he felt himself being pulled toward her, drawn in, agreeing to everything she was saying.

And he just kept nodding like an idiot.

Central Florida Natural History Museum

The rain was just beginning to fall as they pulled into the museum parking lot. Kayla flipped up the collar of the light jacket she had in her car for just such an occasion as she and Grady jogged toward the entrance, hand in hand.

"Dr. McGready! Dr. Harrington! How nice of you to visit!" The dark-haired, well-dressed curator, Simón Cortez, met them just inside the second set of glass doors as Kayla and Grady shook out their clothes, which had become quite wet on the jog in.

"Simón, how are you?" Grady extended his hand.

"Well, thank you. How are you both? Come to visit your collection?"

Kayla noticed a glint in his eye as she shook his offered hand. "In a way. We heard about the disappearance last night."

The curator's face fell. "It's horrible. Steven was one of our best employees. The police can't figure out what happened. All the doors were locked from the inside! He's just gone."

Grady nodded. "Could we see where it happened?"

Simón extended his arm to their left, out of the large lobby toward the Central American exhibits. "Of course."

Kayla had always loved museums, even as a child. She supposed the many trips to museums with her father growing up was what made her fall in love with archaeology in the first place. Her chocolate-brown eyes took in everything as they passed through the Incan and Aztec collections, critiquing artifact placement, display finesse, exhibit descriptions—she was just too much of a perfectionist. Character flaw.

They stepped into the Mayan exhibit hall, an L-shaped room near the front of the museum that displayed most of the artifacts they'd found at Lamanai in brilliant fashion. The clay pots from the burial chamber, pieces of some of the skeletons they'd found, even a piece of the stone that had broken off when the globe had given way atop the boulder . . .

That's when her eyes found it, the reason she knew they were here: the globe, sitting unassumingly in the middle of the room.

Unassumingly? Kayla chastised herself. *You're giving the globe powers, now, Kayla. Get it together.*

You may not be too far off, sweetie, Grady's voice echoed in her head. *We need a closer look, but not with Simón here. Too many questions . . .*

Kayla caught his gaze, then she turned to their friend. "Simón, where did it happen? Didn't the news say they found the guard's nightstick in here?"

Simón nodded emphatically. "Yes, right over there." He pointed to the base of the globe's case. "The nightstick is with the police now."

Kayla and Grady stayed glued to their spots. "Perhaps Grady and I could look around for a little while? We'd like to see how everything turned out in person, since we're here."

Simón nodded again, backing away with a smile. "Certainly. If not for the two of you, this room would not exist." He turned and headed back the way they'd come, smoothing his suit jacket as he went.

Grady released his breath. "Let's go check it out. Quickly."

Kayla nodded and hurried toward the globe. As soon as she was just a few feet from it, it started to glow. She tried not to look straight into it—that was how all the trouble had started last summer—but she couldn't help it. It was calling her, drawing her in . . . perhaps this would be how they'd find out what happened.

Grady's voice came from right beside her. "Kayla, honey, be careful. You haven't had any seizures since . . ."

Kayla nodded. He didn't have to say any more. She'd gotten a clean bill of health, but the toll the globe had taken on her body was substantial, and it seemed she'd just recently fully recovered. She remembered it all too well.

The problem was that she simply couldn't look away.

Suddenly she was back in this room, but everything was dark, and the moon was shining through the high window on the far side of the room. She turned and saw a dark-haired guard coming toward her, shaking his hand as if he'd hurt it. He was staring now, and she could sense it wasn't at her but *through* her, at the shining globe behind her. She stepped out of the way as the wide-eyed apparition approached.

"What the—" she heard him mutter, then a light brighter than the sun shone in the room, and Kayla squeezed her eyes shut. She heard the guard's nightstick clatter to the floor. When she opened her eyes, she was back in the room today, right now, and Grady was still beside her, staring at her, holding her arm.

"Kayla!"

She blinked, coming back to reality. "Grady?"

Grady sighed. *Don't scare me like that.*

I'm sorry, sweetie. Kayla put a hand on his cheek. *I'm okay. It was just a small one.*

What did you see?

Kayla swallowed hard. *I saw the man last night—Steven? The globe lit up and swallowed him whole.*

Grady's eyes widened abruptly. "What?!"

"Shh!" Kayla put a finger over her mouth, leading him further into the room, away from any curious onlookers. *I didn't see it happen per se—the light was too bright for me to see—but the globe lit up, then he was gone.*

Grady crossed his arms. *What do you suppose that means? What happened? Did it move him somewhere? Or is he going to be getting visions now?*

Kayla shook her head. *I don't think so. This feels like something entirely different. Like . . . I'm not sure. Maybe the globe did something to him.*

Grady shuddered. This was not good. They couldn't have the globe disappearing people. At the very least, that would draw way too much unwanted attention.

"So what do we do?" he whispered.

Kayla shrugged then ran her fingers through her hair. "I'm really not sure."

The two of them stood in silence for a minute.

"Maybe . . ." Kayla started.

"What?"

Maybe he didn't just disappear. If he's still alive—and he may be—perhaps the globe altered him in some way.

In what way?

Kayla glanced around the room. *Like maybe he's still here.*

Grady froze. *Are you kidding?*

Kayla shook her head ever so slightly. *It makes sense, Grady. Think about it—the doors were still locked, so maybe he's . . .*

Invisible?!

Kayla nodded slowly.

I don't see how the globe could do that. How . . . that can't be possible, Grady objected.

I don't know how else to explain what happened.

Just then, a bloodcurdling scream sounded from the other room then abruptly cut off. Kayla's eyes grew wide. "Did that sound like Simón to you?"

Grady met her gaze and nodded.

They both took off for the lobby in a dead run, and as they entered the vast space, Grady got the distinct impression that he'd brushed past someone—or something. But he didn't see anyone there.

CHAPTER 2

The Invisible Man

Main Visitor Lobby, Central Florida Natural History Museum

SIMÓN CORTEZ WAS LYING in the middle of the grand lobby near the immaculately groomed planter box, extremities twisted and mangled, blood splattered everywhere—on his impeccable gray suit, his mutilated face, the marble floor . . .

Kayla gasped and put a hand to her mouth. "Oh, Grady . . ."

Grady stepped in front of her as they carefully approached the handful of onlookers who'd made it to the body just before they did. *How could this have happened?* He looked over at Kayla.

She was frowning, fighting back tears. *I don't know, Grady. This is terrible. He didn't deserve this. No one does.*

He nodded as EMTs entered the lobby through the main doors, not hurrying like Grady thought they should be. He supposed they already knew Simón was gone.

They had been working on Simón for several minutes when another group showed up and started pushing the crowd back, taping off a perimeter, getting statements from the onlookers closest to the scene. Grady stepped away to let the police do their job then turned to the group that had moved to another part of the lobby, farther away. "Did anyone see what happened?"

A young, dark-haired woman who couldn't have been more than twenty-five stepped out from the crowd dressed in a modern-cut black suit that flattered her petite curves. "I was here." She still hadn't taken her eyes off the body.

Grady walked up to her with Kayla just behind him. "What's your name?"

The woman only met Grady's gaze when he positioned himself between her and Simón's body. Her dark-brown eyes were rimmed with threatening tears. "Hannah . . . Hannah Loya."

"Tell me, Hannah—what did you see?"

Unable to see the body, she stared down at the floor. "I . . ." She glanced around at the people who were still gathering, her right hand covering her left and fidgeting with something Grady couldn't see.

He reached an arm out toward her but was careful not to touch her. He didn't want to scare her any more than she already was. "Let's go somewhere we can talk."

Hannah nodded slowly and let him and Kayla lead her away from the crowd. When they reached a soft black leather bench between the restrooms and the water feature at the back of the lobby, she sat and looked up at him slowly. "Is . . . is he really . . . gone?"

Grady squatted until he was at eye level then nodded. "Yes. I'm so sorry for your loss."

The young woman started sobbing. Kayla moved to sit next to her and put an arm around her shoulders. Hannah covered her face with her right hand, her body shaking.

Once she started to quiet down, Kayla asked Grady's question again. "Hannah, what did you see?"

The woman's tearstained face turned toward her. "You wouldn't believe what I saw."

Kayla glanced over at Grady briefly, who turned his attention solely to the girl. "Try us."

Hannah licked her lips. "He . . . I was in my office over there"—she pointed toward the front of the lobby where a glass door clearly marked "Offices" stood beside a small, half-moon reception desk—"and I heard him enter the lobby. He talks loud, and it echoes." She was still staring at the office door. "I jumped up to go see him—uh, ask him a question—and that's when I saw . . ."

"Go on," Kayla prodded.

Hannah swallowed again. "It was almost as if . . . as if a . . . *force* or something was attacking him."

Grady's eyes shot to Kayla's, but he was careful to keep his mouth shut.

Hannah continued, her back straightening, her voice sounding a little stronger. "He was up in the air, and it looked like someone was punching him, tearing at him, breaking . . ." She sniffed. "I waited until it stopped, then I ran to him, but I could tell he wasn't breathing, so I called 911. He . . . we . . ." She started crying again, her right hand once more fidgeting with something on her left . . . oh.

Kayla, look. Grady nodded at Hannah's left hand. The diamond glinted in the light, and Kayla nodded at him.

"Hannah, were you and Simón engaged?"

Hannah's crying stopped abruptly, and her watery eyes widened as they met Kayla's. "How . . . how did you know that?"

Kayla looked down at her left hand.

Hannah tucked her hand under her thigh. "Oh. It just happened a few nights ago; not very many people around here know yet. Just Simón, of course, and . . ." She froze, and her eyes grew wide. "And Steven."

"Why would Steven have known?" Grady asked.

Hannah was staring toward the dispersing crowd as the EMTs lifted her fiancé's body onto the stretcher. The vacant, detached stare in her eyes made Grady's stomach clench. "Steven and I . . . we were together for a long time. Simón and I started dating soon after Steven and I broke up, but Steven found out about it really quickly, so I'm pretty sure he thinks I was with Simón before I left him. He wasn't too happy about it, of course."

Grady didn't like the sound of that. And with the way Simón ended up . . . "Hannah, be very careful, please. Your life may be in danger."

"How?"

Grady looked to Kayla for a little help.

Kayla took a breath before answering. "Steven may have been the one who hurt Simón."

"That's insane. I was there, and Steven wasn't!" Hannah was yelling, and it was echoing in the now nearly empty room where the EMTs and only a few police department lab techs remained, collecting samples and documenting the scene. A few of them looked over upon hearing her screams.

Grady eyed them before turning back to Hannah. Time to wrap this up. "We're so sorry, Hannah, really. Just please, be careful." Grady straightened and reached for Kayla's hand to pull her to her feet as Hannah dropped her face into her hands and sobbed.

Kayla took Grady's hand and walked a short distance away, toward the water feature at the back of the lobby.

My theory doesn't sound so weird now, does it? Kayla asked as she shoved her hands in her pockets.

Grady stared as the last of the lab techs disappeared and the EMTs rolled the stretcher out the front doors. He watched Hannah first address the lingering crowd—who promptly dispersed—then head off toward the exhibits on the far side of the lobby and disappear into the Mayan wing. He sighed. *I should have known, given what the four of us can do . . .* He crossed his arms over his chest. *So what do we do about it?*

Kayla's eyes surveyed the now-empty lobby. *We fight. We were given powers for a reason, and maybe initially it was to stop the Mercenaries, but what if we can do more with them? What if we can stop this guy before he hurts anyone else?*

Grady bit his lip. *It's worth a shot. We can't let this guy keep killing people because of the globe we found, the globe we put here.*

Kayla nodded. *Should we call Mandy and Justin?*

Grady glanced at the enormous, faceless wall clock on the left wall of the lobby. *They're still in class. Let's see what we can find out, then we'll bring them in.*

Bring us in on what?

Grady's mouth fell open. *Justin, is that you?*

At your service. Are you close?

We're in Gainesville, at the museum where we donated the artifacts from Lamanai.

Whoa! So not close at all then. How am I hearing you? And what are you doing there?

We . . . wait, we should tell Mandy, too.

31

I'm here, too, boss. Reporting for duty!

Ha! Impending finals are turning your brains into mush.
Grady grinned. Kayla gave him a look. *The* look. He wiped
the grin off his face.

Okay, Kayla started, *here's what we know. Looks like the
globe has given a security guard here named Steven some sort of
invisibility power.*

Cool!

Stop it, Justin, Kayla interjected. *Someone's dead.*

They could all hear Mandy gasp. *What? Who?*

Grady took over. *The curator here, Simón. He was . . . a
friend.*

Justin spoke up. *So what can we do? What do you need from
us, Grady?*

Kayla and I think we can stop him.

How on earth would you be able to do that? Mandy asked.

Grady paused for a brief moment and stared at the white
marble wall next to the giant clock. *Our powers.*

The group was silent for a split second, then from Justin:
Awesome.

Kayla and Grady both rolled their eyes, then Kayla
jumped in. *We should have this covered for now. Mandy, when
you get out of class, can you get back to the Codex? For some
reason, I feel like there may be answers in it. Maybe something
that explains what's happening.* Grady looked over at her, and
Kayla just shrugged. *It's worth a try.*

The Four could feel Mandy nodding. *Of course. Justin,
meet me in the anthro lab as soon as you're out of class.*

*Yes, ma'am, will do. Kayla, Grady, are you sure you don't
need our help?*

Looks like we'll be able to reach you if we do. Kayla
shrugged. *Just let me know if you find anything, okay? Anything
at all that might help us.*

Silence followed for a few seconds, then Mandy chimed in. *I remember reading something last night that might help you, but I'm not sure I remember exactly what it said. I'll let you know, okay?*

Kayla and Grady both nodded, knowing the others could somehow sense it. This telepathy was still a lot to get used to.

Steven slid to the cold cement floor in the corner of the back storage area, near the loading docks, and dropped his head in his hands. He wasn't feeling too good right about now; he was soaked in blood and sweat, and he couldn't seem to stop shaking.

Where was that woman? He wasn't sure where she'd gone; she'd only said that she would find him when she needed him. But what if he needed her? He was tired, sore, and had never killed someone before. What did he do now?

Oh, he was certain that Simón had deserved it. Hannah could deny it all day long, but Simón had to have been sleeping with her when she was still with him—and that couldn't stand. He'd deserved what he'd gotten, that was for sure.

At least that's what he kept telling himself.

So where was the woman? He didn't even have a name to call her—"the woman" was starting to sound stupid, even just in his head. He needed someone to tell him that this nagging feeling in the pit of his stomach would go away soon, that what he'd done had been completely deserved and he'd been completely in the right.

He cursed to himself. This was all Hannah's fault! If she hadn't been sleeping around, he wouldn't have had to kill Simón.

Then he felt it, what he'd felt not too long ago in the break room, a feeling of being drawn toward someone, a blissful longing to be with another. A sort of calming intoxication seemed to settle his uneasy stomach, and he realized that the woman was nearby, drawing him to her. He didn't mind, not one bit. The pit in his stomach was a distant memory, and whatever she was doing that had taken it away was just fine by him.

In that moment, as she came into view, he realized that he would do anything she asked, follow her anywhere. He didn't care about himself any longer; he lived only to please her.

She kept him in that state of perfect bliss for several minutes as Steven's breathing slowed, his hands stopped shaking, and he could finally think clearly once again. He owed this woman his very life.

So when she told him what was coming next, he agreed without question.

Kayla wasn't really sure what their next step should be. The globe gave some random guy superpowers . . . but how did they stop him? Did they need to figure out how the globe did this? Or who Steven was? Despite their curious natures, they weren't detectives.

But she knew in her heart that the police couldn't help, not really. Not against a man with powers, and an invisible one at that. It would be up to them to stop him.

They would have to learn how to do so quickly, and hope against hope that Mandy would find something soon.

Let's find Hannah and ask about the globe. I have an idea. Grady's voice interrupted her thoughts.

Kayla nodded at the plan she heard in his head. It was a solid one.

Grady was gone and back in a matter of minutes. "We're all set. Hannah's having someone take the globe downstairs so we can examine it."

Kayla offered a half smile. "Perfect. What did you tell her?"

Grady replied with a half shrug. "Not much. Didn't really *have* to say much of anything; I just said that we wanted to check it out. She was still dazed, but she knew we were the ones who donated it, so she was happy to do it." He reached an arm around Kayla's shoulders, pulling her to his side. "I also recommended she close the museum; almost everyone left after what happened to Simón anyway, so she's getting the rest of them out and locking up." He kissed Kayla's hair. "She'll be back in a minute when she's ready for us."

Just as Grady'd said, the grieving curator's assistant—perhaps now the acting curator—was back momentarily, and Kayla and Grady followed her to the basement and through a pair of metal doors that led them into an artificially lit, army-green room that reminded Kayla curiously of a morgue. At least the ones she'd seen on TV.

She spied the globe sitting in its holder atop a large metal table in the middle of the room. To their left, stacks upon stacks of metal shelving stood guard, housing boxes of various sizes as well as artifacts that were too big to box or simply didn't need it. A few open crates sat on the floor surrounding the three long stainless steel tables in the middle of the room. Several computer stations stood along the far wall, near the end of the long tables.

Hannah stopped just inside the door and spoke softly. "Please make yourself at home—you are welcome to use whatever you need."

Grady smiled her direction. "Thank you, Hannah. We really appreciate the favor."

The young woman nodded once then headed out the sterile metal doors.

Kayla took a deep breath as soon as the doors swung shut and looked at Grady. "Shall we begin?"

Grady approached the globe carefully, knowing what would happen when they got close. True to form, it started glowing as soon as they were within a few feet of it. He glanced back at the matching small square windows in the metal doors, making sure Hannah was out of sight. She appeared to be.

"So how should we check this thing out? It's a little hard to see at the moment."

Kayla stepped closer, peering intently into the globe's center. "Your eyes adjust." She shrugged. "But I honestly don't even know what we're looking for . . ." Her voice trailed off as the astounding yet not entirely unexpected happened.

The globe started to show her pictures, images, people—much like it had happened this past summer—scenes playing out before her eyes but entirely in her head. But this time, unlike the visions she'd seen this past summer, the vision carried her through several locations nearby in an odd, disjointed order.

First, she saw inside what appeared to be a gas station where people were strewn about the junk-food-lined shelves, unmoving, their bodies contorted in painful ways. The clerk lay haphazardly across the counter, lying in a pool of his own blood.

Then she saw the outside of a gas station she recognized from their drive here, the gas pumps outside the building she'd just seen, a sea-foam, older-model hatchback driving of its own accord, people staring wide-eyed at it, those same people flying backward one by one as if by an unseen force, falling to the ground, bleeding, bruised, and broken. Dying.

Then the museum lobby, the museum offices, Hannah screaming, Hannah pleading with a void that Kayla couldn't see but knew was there, Hannah lifeless. And she knew that these last images, ones of someone she'd actually met and spoken with, would stay with her a very long time. She fought the nausea forming in her stomach.

Kayla could feel Grady in her mind, taking in everything she was seeing. That would definitely save them some time— she'd always had trouble explaining this part. And just as soon as she realized that, she also realized the vision was a little, well, off. Different than before. Out of order, maybe, or . . . backward?

Then the vision finished, and Kayla stumbled back half a step. Grady led her to a nearby computer chair.

"What did that all mean?" Grady ventured.

Kayla swallowed hard, her hands on her knees, still trying to recover. She didn't miss this part.

When Kayla didn't answer, Grady asked a different question. "So was that like what you saw at Lamanai?" The first vision given to her by the globe had been atop a large boulder in an underground cavern they'd unearthed. That vision had led them on a quest to find the Codex, though they hadn't known it then.

Kayla shook her head. "No." She took another breath. "This was different."

"How?" Grady wheeled over another computer chair and sat.

Kayla stared off into space. "Those *scenes*"—she shuddered at the too-fresh memory of the bloody bodies littering the ground—"I know it was because of Steven. All those people . . . he killed them—or *will* kill them. I know that somewhere deep in my gut. He's going to kill them all." Her eyes met Grady's. "We have to stop him, Grady. We may be the only hope those people have."

Grady nodded, reaching for her hand. "How long do we have?"

Kayla briefly flashed back to Hannah, who she'd seen butchered, bloody, and left behind in this very building. He'd kill her first, she was sure of it. "If Hannah's still alive, we still have time."

Just then the fire alarm sounded, jolting Kayla and Grady to their feet. Kayla caught Grady's frenzied gaze before sprinting for the doors.

University of Central Florida, Main Anthropology Lab

"Justin, could you grab me a water?" Mandy Carlson tucked her shoulder-length, strawberry-blonde hair behind her ears as she leaned over the giant tome known as the Codex amid stacks of artifacts and reference books, display cases, and a few wide tables. The long, narrow room boasted state-of-the-art equipment—including a magnifying camera and flat-screen monitor—the latest reference books in the field, and an extensive collection of artifacts always on hand. "The stacks," as Mandy called them, fanned out from the center main table on both sides and held one of the most impressive undisplayed collections in the anthropological world. She always thought the anthro lab—UCF's students' term of endearment for the university's largest anthropology lab—looked more like a library or museum than a sterile science lab, and for that she was grateful.

She'd been hunched over the Codex for the past hour, and her back was starting to hurt. She could probably have gotten a water herself—and goodness knew she wouldn't drink it near the book anyway—but sometimes she just liked to think of Justin as her assistant.

I heard that.

Mandy froze, her hand stuck in midair over the book. Then she glanced at Justin sideways and offered an apologetic smile. *Sorry.* She straightened, stretching out her back, and her flowy, pink blouse fluttered down around the top of her skintight jeans. "I need a break, anyway."

Justin, Mandy's blond-haired, blue-eyed boyfriend for the past three-plus years, stepped out of the way so she could get to the mini-fridge tucked under the long counter against the back wall. Mandy bent down to grab a water, opened it, then leaned against the counter as she took a drink.

Justin perused the giant book lying open on the large table, and Mandy, not for the first time, appreciated how good his backside looked in his khakis. Justin smirked at her thought in his head but didn't look up. "I still have a hard time reading this stuff."

Mandy screwed the lid on the water and set it on the long counter then walked back to stand next to Justin. "It's not that hard, really." She moved the camera into position above the book, and the flat-screen monitor next to her showed an extreme close-up of the tip of her finger and the symbol she now pointed to. She was pleased that she'd learned so much in such little time—she was basically useless with this language just this past summer.

"This symbol here means 'eternity,' or 'eternal life,'" Mandy started. "This page tells a story about the Old Ones and how they lived forever—or would have, if they'd kept the powers of the Codex. Kayla and I assumed that somehow—

probably supernaturally—the stories of the Old Ones were added to this book after they separated it, effectively removing their powers. Almost like the book updated itself."

She shook her head as if to clear it then took a breath and adjusted the camera again, pointing to the next symbol. "This one is the symbol Alexia and I translated as the Old Ones." Mandy had a graduate student helping her translate the text, vetted and approved by Kayla, of course. After what had happened at Lamanai last summer, they couldn't be too careful. "We couldn't be one-hundred-percent certain, but the symbol literally means 'ancient people,' which we inferred meant the Old Ones."

She looked over at Justin, whose eyes were trained on the monitor. She smiled. "Then this symbol here—"

Justin interjected. "That means 'Codex', right? I recognize it from the front of the book."

Mandy grinned. "Yes! It's just about recognizing the symbols and putting them in a logical order."

Justin pointed to a symbol on the right page. "What does this one mean?"

Mandy stared at it more closely. "I'm not sure . . . wait."

Justin leaned in. "What?"

Mandy grabbed the camera arm, trained it on the symbol, and adjusted the magnification so she could examine the enlarged image on the screen more closely. "We weren't sure what this one meant. But now, maybe . . ." Mandy swallowed hard. "I think we should call Kayla."

"What is it?"

Mandy slowly stood up straight and looked over at him, her eyes wide. "I think I know what the globe's new mission is."

"New mission?"

What new mission?

Kayla, is that you? Mandy still found it odd that their friends could hear their thoughts at seemingly random times. Perhaps Kayla felt Mandy calling for her?

Yes, and Grady, too. What did you find? And quickly—we've got some issues here.

Mandy swallowed hard. *I think the globe's new mission is to activate powers in certain people.*

An odd silence fell over the group, then Kayla's voice sounded. *I think you're right.* A brief pause. *Thanks, Mandy. See what else you can find out, maybe how the globe chooses those certain people? Or maybe its purpose in doing this—the why?*

Mandy nodded, knowing they would understand.

Just let us know if you find anything else. We— Kayla's voice abruptly cut off, and Mandy could suddenly only hear Justin inside her head once again.

"What was that about?" Justin crossed his arms over his forest-green t-shirt.

Mandy shrugged. "They must be busy. I could hear their anxiety below the surface—did you sense that, too?"

Justin cocked his head to the left then nodded. "Yeah, I guess so." He glanced down at the open Codex in front of them, grabbing two stools and dragging them closer.

Mandy took the one he offered her and pulled herself up close to the table.

"So can you decipher anything else?" Justin asked from her left.

Mandy scrunched up her nose and leaned closer to the screen directly to her side, adjusting the magnifying camera slightly on the page. "Maybe." She glanced at the clock on the nearby wall. "Geez. Looks like we'll be here all night."

"How can I help?"

Mandy paused then nodded once toward the phone sitting on the counter beside them. "You could order delivery?"

Justin grinned. "Of course."

Kayla and Grady burst through the stairwell door at the back of the lobby. Kayla couldn't believe that, just a few minutes ago, the lobby was the scene of a horrific crime. Now it stood empty, evidence of the murder still smeared on the white marble floor.

The fire alarm kept pulsing through Kayla's head.

Hannah must've pulled the alarm.

Kayla nodded once at him. *Check the offices?* Kayla eyed the door on the far side of the lobby. Grady nodded back then sprinted away.

Kayla froze in place, her eyes scanning the empty room. Although . . . it didn't feel empty. Perhaps Steven was here. But how did she locate the invisible?

Kayla closed her eyes, tried to drown out the deafening alarm. If Steven was here—and her subconscious was telling her he was—she should be able to find him. She had super-powers, right? She just had to figure out how to use them . . .

Like stretching a muscle that hadn't been used in a while, Kayla reached deep inside her, reached for her power, the power to control the earth. But there wasn't much earth in here. Except . . .

She remembered the rectangular planter box in the middle of the lobby, saw the sole tree and the black dirt in her mind's eye . . . at once, she opened her eyes, lighting immediately on that single tree then the dirt. She stretched her hands out toward it, coaxing the dirt into the air. Soon a dust storm of her own making was swirling in the wide lobby. Kayla stared through the haze, scanning for any aberration.

Then she saw him.

Against the wall to her right, far closer than Kayla would have imagined, the swirling dirt was being deflected by what seemed like nothing at all—but Kayla knew what that meant. Steven was right there, right next to her.

She froze, the dirt still swirling. Could he see her?

Of course he can see you, Kayla, she thought to herself. *Come on.*

The shapeless form started moving toward her, faster and faster . . . Kayla yelped and jumped aside as she let go of the dirt, which immediately fell like a dark, heavy blanket as it spattered to the marble floor. She felt a body rush past her, barely missing contact with her skin. She turned and sprinted toward the front doors.

Grady was just coming out of the office when Kayla reached him, out of breath. "Kayla, honey, what happened?" He glanced around at the dirt-coated lobby. "Did he . . . ?"

Kayla swallowed hard, leaning up against the marble wall as she tried to start breathing normally again. "Grady . . ." she choked. "Steven is . . . he's here."

Grady's eyes narrowed as he glared through the still-dusty lobby. Suddenly, right next to him, he heard Kayla cry out and turned to see her double over in pain, holding her stomach. "Kayla!"

She groaned. "Gra . . ."

Grady reached for her as she sunk to the ground along the wall. "Kayla! What happened? Are you okay?" He felt the panic rising in his throat and tried to swallow it down, but to no avail.

Kayla was reaching for him with one arm, the other arm still clutching her stomach. Her mouth was moving, but no sound was coming out. Grady's heart started beating erratically. He was bent over beside her, arm around her shoulders, eyes scanning the room when he finally heard her. *Grady, Steven hit . . . I can't . . . it's hard to . . . think.*

Kayla, sweetie, he soothed as he pulled her head to his chest. *Where is he?*

I . . . I'm not sure. Use the water, Grady. Find him.

Water? Grady glanced around the room. How would he use water? What water?

Then it hit him. The fire alarm was sounding; shouldn't the sprinklers be going off right about now?

Grady kissed Kayla's forehead, propped her up against the wall, then stood. He stretched his arms out toward the high ceiling, staring at the first sprinkler head he found. Then his eyes slid shut.

Calling the water in the pipes, he pushed the water through the sprinkler head until it broke off and crashed to the floor. Water started spraying into the room in a waterfall. He opened his eyes at the sound, pushing the water through the rest of the pipes in the ceiling until all the sprinkler heads started tumbling to the floor one by one. For good measure, he even forced water through the water fountain at the far end of the lobby, near the bathrooms, until the stainless steel fountain went crashing across the marble floor. A fresh gush of water sprayed through the newly formed hole in the wall where the water fountain had been.

He didn't stop there. The water feature in the back corner of the lobby became a torrent, splashing into the room until it coated the floor. The lobby was awash in glistening rainbows of misty color.

Grady spotted Steven a few yards away, heading back toward them, presumably toward the office. Grady hadn't found Hannah in there, but Steven didn't know that.

"Steven, stop!" Grady's voice boomed through the torrential downpour, his wet hair dripping down his forehead in tiny streaks. He saw the negative space in front of him freeze, the water dripping off it. "Steven, please . . . why are you doing this?"

The figure moved toward him slowly, deliberately. It was soon only a foot from Grady. Then, impossibly, the void spoke. "Because no one can stop me."

In a rush, the figure called Steven whooshed past Grady and through the swinging office door. Before Grady could even reach the door, he heard Hannah scream.

CHAPTER 3

A Little Help

University of Central Florida, Main Anthropology Lab
JUSTIN WAS A LITTLE TIRED of feeling completely un-
helpful. After a quick dinner out of white cardboard cartons,
Mandy was back to translating. Their most dedicated grad
student, Alexia—the blonde-haired, brown-eyed student Kayla had handpicked herself to help them—had shown up over
an hour ago, and she was currently helping Mandy transcribe
the words Mandy was translating. Justin could've done that if
she'd asked.

I'm sorry, Justin. I didn't mean to exclude you.

Justin's eyes shot to Mandy's from his chair off to the side.
Despite the last few months of being able to communicate
with Mandy telepathically, he sometimes still forgot she
could access pretty much every thought he had. Sometimes it
was a little irritating.

Hey! Mandy's eyes narrowed at him before going back to the book.

Sorry. Are you sure there's nothing I can do to help?

Mandy shook her head without looking up from the Codex. Justin didn't think Alexia noticed. *Maybe you should check in with Grady and Kayla? See if they need help in Gainesville with Steven?*

Justin sighed then reached in his pocket for his phone.

Hello? Justin jumped to his feet when Grady's thoughts broke into his, and his chair went flying. The grad student turned at the noise, brow furrowing in his direction. "S-sorry," Justin stammered as he reached to upright the metal chair.

Mandy's voice sounded in his head. *Grady, please give Justin something to do.*

They all heard Grady's chuckle echo through their thoughts, though it seemed to Justin that there was an underlying sadness hiding beneath the surface. What was that about? *There's probably not much you can do up here. We're going to track Steven down and hopefully stop him. Plus, it would be awhile before you got here; we're hoping to have him contained before then. Thanks, though.* A brief pause. *We'll definitely let you both know if anything changes.*

Mandy sighed audibly as Kayla and Grady's voices suddenly left their minds. *Justin, you can help me transcribe then. I'll send Alexia home.*

Are you sure? I don't know how much help I'll be.

Mandy smiled without looking up. *Then I'll teach you. It'll be good practice. If I can teach you, I can teach anyone!*

Justin threw her a dirty look.

"Alexia, would you mind heading home? I think we'll be able to manage for the rest of the night."

Alexia flipped her long hair behind her shoulder as she looked up from her work, gave Mandy a side smile, then started to pack up her things. "Sure. Have a good night."

After they said goodbye, Mandy turned to Justin. "I'm sorry. I just—"

"Mandy," Justin interrupted, "it's okay. I know I can be frustrating to work with sometimes. I love archaeology, but languages are hard for me to comprehend."

Mandy nodded. "I know, babe." She leaned in for a quick kiss then handed him the notepad Alexia had been using. "Okay, let's get started. Just write down the words in English I tell you, okay? If there's something I'm struggling with, I'll let you know, and maybe we can decipher it together."

Justin took the offered notebook with a grin. "Sure!"

Mandy smiled as she bent back over the book. *Love you, Justin.*

Love you, baby, Justin responded quickly, thinking that she never said that aloud anymore. It sure would be nice to hear out loud again.

The thought had passed through his mind so quickly—and he could hear that Mandy was already back to concentrating fully on the Codex—that he doubted Mandy even heard it.

Kayla's breath was just now returning to normal. If she ever got her hands on Steven . . .

Then the door marked "Offices" opened, and Kayla braced herself before seeing Grady exit, his head low. He glanced up, meeting her gaze, then shook his head, his eyes drooping.

Kayla's stomach dropped. First Simón, now Hannah. She thought she might be sick.

Grady dropped to her side, squatting down and tucking her hair behind her ear. "It's okay, sweetie. It'll be okay."

Kayla swallowed hard, sitting up straighter against the marble lobby wall, shoving his hand away without really meaning to. "How will it be okay, Grady? Simón is dead, Hannah is dead, and Steven is loose out there, probably killing people!"

Grady straightened, sighing, and offered her his hand. After a moment's hesitation, Kayla took it and let Grady pull her to her feet. "You'll figure it out. We all will."

Kayla shook her head as if to clear it, the wet ends of her hair sending a spray through the muddy lobby. It looked like a bomb went off in here. "Grady, I . . ." *What Steven did, is still doing . . . it makes me sick. We let this happen; I let this happen. I made this happen.*

Grady pulled her head to his chest. "No, Kayla, none of us could have foreseen this. We will deal with this quickly. We will stop him."

Kayla nodded against Grady's wet chest, feeling her anger dissipate at his touch. *Thank you, Grady.*

Any time, sweetie. He stroked her hair with his hand.

Kayla lifted her head to catch Grady's gaze. "We have to get the globe back to Orlando."

He nodded at once. "I agree. Until we know what's going on with it, we should take it home with us."

Kayla glanced at the destroyed lobby. "But who should . . . is there anyone left to ask?"

Grady followed her gaze. "I guess we just take it. Our contract says we retain ownership, so technically we can take it back at any time. Since we can't report it to the curator . . ."

Kayla nodded. "Let's go get it."

She led the way to the basement, where they quickly retrieved the globe. Kayla grabbed a black cloth bag she found nearby—presumably to transport items just like this—and carefully placed the globe inside, zipping up the bag before following Grady back upstairs.

When they reached the lobby and Kayla saw again the mess Steven had caused, she sighed. "So what do we do next? I'm sure Steven will leave a wave of destruction in his wake, but how can we get ahead of him? How do we stop him?"

Grady paused for a moment. "Your vision—maybe we start there."

Kayla swallowed hard then nodded. As they passed through the front doors and into the parking lot, she could feel a pit growing in her stomach.

"Why didn't you tell me?!" Steven was back in the break room, inches from the face of the beautiful woman he'd met only a few hours ago. But her beauty didn't temper his rage in the slightest.

"Tell you what?" The innocent words dripped from her tongue like honey, her lilting accent sending a calming effect through the air.

Steven shrugged it off. "You didn't tell me they had powers!"

The woman sighed then took a seat, her red dress cascading over the sides of the chair. "Steven, please sit."

"I don't want to sit!"

Despite his invisibility, the woman somehow caught his gaze, and Steven started to squirm. Though he knew he didn't want to, he found himself pulling out a nearby chair and dropping into the plastic seat.

"Steven, I need to explain some things to you. Are you ready to listen?"

Steven didn't appreciate her patronizing tone but still nodded without intending to.

"You are invisible because I allowed you to be."

"What?!" Steven couldn't help the interruption.

The woman eyed him again, and Steven shut his mouth. "I activated that globe to give you powers. You are this way because I allowed the globe to give you this ability." She paused. "And as such, you are now under my control. You will do as I request. I have allowed you to take revenge in your personal dealings, but now you will do as I say."

Steven's eyes were wide, but he couldn't seem to open his mouth to speak. What right did she have . . .

Then his thoughts cut off, and he felt that warming, calming sensation again. *She's using that to control me,* he realized. Yet, somehow, he couldn't summon the will to fight her off.

Once he had calmed down, he found his voice again. "What should I call you? What's your name?"

The woman stared at him with impossibly large, beautiful eyes. "You may call me Shani."

Gas Station on SW 34th St., Just off NE State Road 24

Kayla and Grady were currently sitting in Kayla's Jeep in the parking lot of the gas station they'd seen in Kayla's vision, no nearer to a workable plan than when they'd left the museum. There'd been no sign of Steven yet—Kayla tried to tell herself this was a good thing.

"Grady, I'm sorry about all this."

Grady reached for her hand, looking over at her. "Nothing to be sorry about. Things happen. Lately, the crazy things seem to happen to *us*, but . . ." He grinned.

Kayla got all warm and fuzzy every time he smiled at her. Sometimes she tried to suppress it so Grady didn't know all her secrets, but today, she let him hear it in her thoughts.

I didn't know I had such an effect on you.

Kayla playfully shoved his upper arm, his long-sleeved shirt still slightly damp but returning to its normal sky-blue color. *Of course you did.* She chuckled, thinking that it felt really good just to laugh, just to forget about everything else for even only a second.

Grady nodded then leaned over to steal a kiss, his hand grazing the bottom hem of her silky blouse. Kayla lingered for an extra second before he pulled away. *I don't mind that at all.*

Grady, just inches from her face, grinned again. Kayla felt the butterflies in her stomach start swarming. He just laughed.

"Moving on . . ." Kayla straightened in her seat, the smile fading from her lips. "Where is Steven? And how are we going to stop him?"

Grady turned to look out the windshield. "Not entirely sure. Maybe our powers?"

Kayla shrugged. "Worth a shot."

Just then, a sea-foam green, beat-up hatchback drove into the gas station parking lot and pulled up to lane twelve. The same lane that same car had been in her vision. The same car that had seemed to drive up on its own.

This was going to be a massacre.

CHAPTER 4

Gone Missing

STEVEN'S CAR STOPPED at the gas pump, and the front door opened then shut seemingly of its own accord. The guy manning his pump in lane eleven craned his neck to try to see what had happened. The woman in lane thirteen peered timidly over the hood of her minivan then hid behind it.

Kayla looked over at Grady. *My vision, Grady. We have to stop him from hurting these people.*

Grady nodded beside her, and Kayla reached for the door handle and jumped out before she could talk herself out of it. "Steven!" she yelled as loudly as she could, hoping she'd distract him enough that he'd forget about hurting that guy on lane eleven, that young mother on lane thirteen.

She sensed her distraction had worked. Suddenly, she felt a gust of air fly past her, toward the gas station. The bell dinged over the door, and Kayla looked over at Grady, who was standing on the other side of the Jeep.

Showtime. Let's hope this goes well.

Grady nodded at her as she came around the front of the car and reached for his hand. *Yes. And I think we should hold off using our powers unless we have to.*

But . . .

Grady cut her off as they headed for the station door. *We shouldn't risk others finding out about our powers.*

Kayla was surprised the topic hadn't come up for discussion yet. She supposed it was because they hadn't needed to use their powers before now. An empty museum lobby was one thing, but here . . . Kayla glanced around at the busy gas station, right at rush hour. She nodded. *I'll keep it under wraps as best I can.*

Grady smiled tentatively as they approached the station entrance. He reached for the glass door.

The bell chimed as they entered. The attendant was still standing at the front counter to their right, but his eyes were wide, and he was barely moving. *Heads up,* Grady thought, *he's still here.*

Kayla nodded.

Any ideas?

Kayla glanced over at Grady's question and looked at the attendant. The attendant just stared at her for a moment then looked toward the soda machine pointedly. That's when Grady noticed a plastic cup mysteriously hovering under the ice machine. The ice crashed into the cup, shattering the silence in the deathly quiet store.

Grady wasn't sure what to say but thought he should at least try to talk him down. "Steven, you need to stop."

The cup froze in midair then slowly moved to the counter.

A voice came out of the emptiness. "I don't want to stop. And you can't stop me."

Grady could almost feel Steven's gaze boring holes into him. "Actually, we can. And that's what we're here to do."

The blank void that was Steven just laughed. Grady waved toward the group of wide-eyed people huddled at the back of the store. *Get them out of here. I will hold him off until you get back.*

Grady, no!

Kayla, their safety is our priority.

But what about your *safety?*

I will be fine. He is only invisible, and we figured out a way around that at the museum, right?

Kayla sighed but moved to lead the other patrons and the attendant toward the back door.

A can of something that was supposed to pass as edible flew across the room toward where Kayla had just been and crashed through the glass door of refrigerated drinks right behind her.

Kayla! Grady rushed to her side, but it seemed the projectile had just missed her.

Just hold him off, Grady, like we talked about. She kept corralling the others toward the back hallway that led to the exit.

Grady turned and froze, facing where he thought Steven might be. Just then, an invisible force connected with his right jaw, sending him crashing into the shelf to his left.

Kayla had just come back in the store and now ran to him. *Grady!*

Grady straightened beside her, determined to face Steven, wherever he was.

What do we do? Kayla's eyes searched the room.

Grady glanced at her for a split second, but another invisible force kicked the side of his leg, forcing him to his knees.

"No!" Kayla dropped to his side. *Where is he, Grady? What do we do?*

Grady felt so unprepared for this, and his jaw and leg hurt. What did they do? What *could* they do? There wasn't any dirt or water around here for them to use like there had been at the museum.

Kayla suddenly went tumbling down the aisle, and Grady felt himself being lifted into the air. He could hear Kayla screaming, but she sounded so far away. *What—*

Then he was flying, and he stuck his hands out in front of him before he hit the far wall, sliding down it. Fortunately, he'd found the one spot to land that wasn't crowded with merchandise. Or unfortunately . . . he moaned, wincing.

Kayla?

Grady was still on the ground, slumped against the wall, but his eyes searched the place he'd last seen her. Nothing.

Then an eerie voice sounded. "If you want her back, you'll let me leave."

Grady's stomach dropped. "What? Where is she?" He struggled to his feet and hurried up the aisle, limping but moving. *Kayla, answer me!*

No response. Grady heard the bell above the front door ding, then the store was silent once again.

Kayla? Please, sweetie, answer me. Where are you?

She didn't answer. He couldn't hear her at all.

"Kayla!" Grady yelled as he ran out of the store, eyes searching for anything out of the ordinary. He scoured the parking lot, finding Kayla's Jeep still intact.

But the sea-foam green hatchback was gone.

Mandy? Justin? Grady tried to reach his friends on their supernatural frequency. *Can you hear me?*

No response. He grabbed his phone and quickly found Mandy's number. He hadn't needed it in forever.

"Hello?"

"Mandy? Thank God! Is Justin there with you?"

"Grady?"

"Yes! Is Justin there with you?"

There was a pause on the other end of the line. "Um, yes . . . uh, Grady . . . why can't we hear you?"

Grady ran a hand through his hair then started a brisk walk toward the Jeep. "No clue. Can you hear Kayla?"

Mandy paused again. "I . . . there! I hear her! But she sounds so distant."

"What is she thinking?"

"She . . . uh, she sounds really scared, Grady. Is she not there with you? Why can't you hear her?"

Grady unlocked the Jeep and climbed inside. "I don't know. Can she hear you? Please ask her where she is so I can go get her."

Another pause. Grady drummed his fingers on the steering wheel while he waited. "She—she doesn't know where she is. Somewhere dark. And she's moving. She thinks maybe the back of Steven's car? Something heavy is on top of her, but her hands are tied."

Steven sure does quick work. "Okay, thank you, Mandy. Please tell her I'm coming."

"Of course. But Grady, why can't you hear her? Or us?"

Grady swallowed hard, his brow furrowing to the empty car. "I'm not sure. It's almost like something's blocking . . ." Then he froze.

He didn't really know why, but he sensed something familiar in what was happening. Déjà vu, maybe, or just a similarity he remembered from his encounter with someone who could control minds at Lamanai, someone dangerous, terrifying. Someone who was strong enough to pull this off.

And if that same someone was blocking him now, it could only mean one thing.

Shani was here.

CHAPTER 5

Old Friends and Enemies

"GRADY?"

Mandy was expecting an answer, so he gave it. "I think Shani's nearby."

Mandy gasped, and Grady heard Justin ask if she was okay. Then Justin came on the line. "What happened? Grady?"

Grady gave Justin a quick rundown on Kayla's abduction, Grady not being able to hear her, Shani's likely presence. Grady could almost hear Justin going pale as he explained. "What do we do?" Always the pragmatic one when he needed to be, for which Grady was extremely grateful at this moment. He wasn't exactly thinking straight.

"Try to contact Kayla for me, see if she has any idea where she is or where she's going. Then call me back."

"Will do." Justin paused, and Grady wasn't quite sure why. "Okay, we'll call when we know anything. Stay safe."

The line went dead.

Justin set Mandy's phone on the table next to the Codex and pulled Mandy behind him, his eyes trained on the window-less door to the lab. "Hello?"

Another knock sounded, more insistent this time. Justin caught Mandy's gaze then ventured toward the door. Mandy pushed up against his back.

"Hello?" The voice on the other side of the door sounded a little familiar, albeit muffled.

Who is . . . oh! Justin placed the voice, reaching for the door and throwing it open. "Holun!"

Mandy stared at their guest, the slightly older, slightly taller, slightly, er, more-than-slightly *stronger* version of the boy they'd met this summer. "Holun!" She wrapped him in a tight hug—where had those muscles come from?—then ushered him in the room and toward the center table. "What are you doing here?"

Holun flipped his long, black hair behind his shoulders and took the chair Mandy offered him. "I saw you were about to have some problems. With the globe?"

Mandy stared at him, wide-eyed. "Holun—your English!"

Holun grinned at her—even seated, his dark-brown eyes were nearly at eye level—and a little of the youth she remembered came through. Had it really only been a few months? "I have been practicing."

Justin put his hand on the kid's shoulder. "It shows, man! Good job!"

Holun was beaming but quickly got down to business. "So the globe—it did something, right?"

Mandy nodded at him. "Kayla and Grady are trying to track down a man who came in contact with it. Apparently, the globe made him invisible."

Holun furrowed his brow, but Mandy noticed he didn't seem surprised.

So she continued. "Then he started killing people. We're not sure if it's him or the globe causing him to do that."

Holun was frowning. "I do not think it is the globe. It can give powers to certain people, but I do not think it can make people kill."

Justin pulled up a chair next to him. "You've heard of this?"

Holun looked over at him. "Yes, some. I have been researching it since this summer; there were old stories about it in our ancient writings. But the Elders hide the writings very well, so I did not find much helpful information."

Mandy nodded. "So where have you been since we saw you last?" Mandy knew he wasn't welcome at home any longer, not after the events of this past summer.

Holun smiled at her. "I have traveled a lot, some here in the States, some in Belize, all over. Mostly staying away from Na-um and my—the Clan." Mandy saw his eyes droop, just a little.

"You miss them, your family."

Holun nodded. "They *were* my family, and I betrayed them." Then he cleared his throat, blinking and shaking his head. "But it was the right thing to do, and I will never regret helping all of you." He smiled as if to underline his words.

Mandy nodded, not sure what to say.

Justin, true to form, picked up the conversation. "So what did you learn about the globe? How did you know it had been activated? Are you still getting your visions?"

Holun nodded. "Yes, it was how I knew you would need my help. So I came right away. I was not far, anyway."

Mandy, still standing, walked over to the table that held the Codex. "I think we could use your help translating this."

Holun seemed to see the book lying on the table nearby for the first time. He gasped, eyes wide. He muttered something in K'iche.

Mandy smiled. "Yes, Holun, that's the Codex."

Holun nodded, slowly standing to his feet and walking over to it, eyes trained on the book the whole time. He leaned over it reverently, careful not to touch it. "Yes, yes . . ." Then he abruptly straightened and looked at Mandy. "I will help you translate this." He scanned the open page quickly, and his eyes lit up. "I see you have found some information about the globe."

Mandy nodded, coming to his side and pointing at the page. "Yes, but I'm having a hard time translating this part. Kayla hasn't been available much to help."

Holun nodded back at her. "Do you have a pen?"

Mandy grinned at Justin, who grinned right back. He handed her the pen and paper then stepped back.

As Holun began to translate the book aloud, Mandy began furiously recording everything he was saying, interrupting at various intervals to confirm something he'd said, get him to slow down, or ask him a question about the nature of the symbol on the page. Justin knew they'd be busy for a while, so he decided to start listening for Kayla. The second he did, he could hear her again.

Grady?

No, Kayla, it's Justin.

Why can't I hear Grady? Her voice was shaking, even in her thoughts.

We don't know for sure, but Grady thinks maybe Shani is nearby.

What?!? He could almost hear her breathing speed up.

Yeah, he thinks that's why he can't hear you anymore. Justin paused to take a breath. *And something else—Holun just showed up here.*

Holun? A pause. *Where is 'here'? And where is Grady?*

I think he's still in Gainesville, waiting to hear where you are, and we're at UCF in the anthro lab. Holun's helping Mandy translate the book. He doesn't think the globe is what made Steven start killing people. Hopefully, we'll know more once they get this passage about the globe translated. Where are you?

Kayla didn't answer right away. *It's dark, but the heavy thing—probably a thick blanket—isn't on me anymore. Is it dark outside?*

No, not yet. It's still early in the evening.

Kayla paused again. *Man, my time must be all screwed up. Or maybe he knocked me out for a little bit, and I don't remember it. Or maybe . . .* She stopped, then her voice came out a bit more rushed. *Maybe Shani's messing with my head, too.*

Justin thought about it. Made sense. Shani could be up in Gainesville near Kayla and Grady, affecting their powers. He didn't know what kind of range she had, but clearly it was affecting Grady, and if Kayla was affected, too . . . Shani may be more powerful than they knew.

Shani was the sister of Na-um, the leader of the mercenary army who'd tried to kill them last summer, tried to stop them from finding the Codex. She'd not been an active part of their Clan for some time—she'd spent years in the archaeology program at UCF under a different name just to spy on the four of them—but they found out she'd been working with the Elders of the Clan nearly the whole time; even Naum hadn't known she'd been helping them all along.

She'd rejoined the Clan in person and used her position and powers—which they didn't know much about; they just assumed she had the powers of the Clan, including their superspeed, and knew that she somehow manipulated their minds to get away from them this past summer—to help them carry out their mission just as the Four had found the book and received their own powers. She'd gotten away from them, just barely, and they hadn't heard from her since.

Until now, presumably.

Kayla, can you tell me anything about where you are? Can you see anything?

No, everything's dark. Maybe he blindfolded me?

Justin drew a breath. Grady would not like that. *Okay. Then what do you hear? Smell? Or do you feel anything nearby that could give us a clue where you are?*

Justin waited for her response. He could tell she was surveying her situation. *Oh! I hear . . . wait . . . I hear water dripping. And it smells . . . um, wet. Maybe like dirt or clay, too? Oh, I don't know. And it's dark, really dark, but I don't feel a blindfold over my eyes. Weird . . .* Justin could hear her trying to move. *Seems like my hands are tied behind me, too. Been here before.*

He cringed. He remembered all too well.

And I feel like I'm sitting on rocks. Justin, where on earth am I?

He didn't know what to tell her.

Yeah, I know. How on earth will you guys find me if I can't figure out where I am? I—

Her voice abruptly cut off. *Kayla? Are you there?*

But no matter how hard he tried, he couldn't reach her.

Underground Caves, Location Unknown

"Steven?" The woman named Shani, now in fitted jeans and a lavender cotton tank top, stepped out of the waning light of the warm Florida evening and into the cool cave where Steven sat guarding Kayla, not that she needed it. She'd been pretty out of it—and it wasn't like her cage had a door.

When Shani was gone, he'd started to question her motives again. But as soon as she'd come back, all dissenting thoughts disintegrated. "Yes, Shani?" Steven looked up, feeling eager to please.

Shani flicked her long, straight hair behind her back and pulled up a nearby chair. "How is our hostage?"

Steven straightened in his chair and faced her more directly. "She seems utterly confused."

Shani grinned, a humorless smile that showed all her teeth. "Good."

After a few minutes of silence, she stood and started pacing in the small space. "Has she said anything?"

"Just a few grunts and moans, nothing else. I must've worked her over good." Steven grinned at his own prowess.

Shani crossed her arms but otherwise didn't move. "Yes, I suppose you did." Then she fell silent again.

Steven had to ask the question that had been wearing on him since she'd told him this plan at the museum—the first part of it, anyway. "So what do we do next?"

Shani straightened. "You do nothing. You are to stay here and keep watch." She headed back toward the cave's exit. "I will be back shortly." She glanced back over her shoulder before she stepped outside. "You may want to ready yourself for another prisoner."

Just before she stepped out of view, she turned back around. "And make sure she doesn't wake up for a while."

Steven just grinned as the captivating woman walked out of sight.

CHAPTER 6

The Crash

JUSTIN REACHED FOR HIS PHONE to call Grady, but the phone rang in his hand before he could make the call. Maybe their telepathy was still working on some level, a level Shani couldn't touch. "Grady?"

"Justin! Do you have something new on Kayla?"

Justin chuckled a little, a laugh tainted by sorrow. "Yes, I heard from her." He paused. "But Grady, I'm sorry; she doesn't know where she is. She said she heard water dripping, that it smelled wet and like dirt or clay, and she thought she was sitting on rocks or something hard. She didn't seem to be blindfolded, but she couldn't see anything in the pitch black, and her hands are tied behind her back."

As he expected, Grady did not like this news, and his words came out strangled. "No . . . Kayla."

"Grady, she's alive. That much we *do* know. And it doesn't sound like Steven wants to hurt her," Justin reasoned.

Grady sighed on the other end of the line. "You're right. I just hate this. I'm cut off from you guys, but I don't want to head home in case she's close." Grady paused. "Have you guys made any progress with the Codex? Anything about the globe?"

"Funny you should mention that . . ."

"Yes?"

Justin took a breath. "We had a friend show up. Holun's here."

"Really?!" Justin winced and held the phone away from his ear.

He waited until Grady was quiet. "Yeah. He's helping Mandy translate the section about the globe, so we should know something very soon."

"Great!" He could practically feel Grady's elation through the phone. "Let me know the second he does. Was there anything else?"

Justin hesitated, not wanting to say anything but knowing he must. "Grady . . . I was talking to Kayla, and then we got cut off. I tried to get her back, but I haven't been able to. Can you hear her at all?"

Grady was quiet for a moment. "No, I still can't. If Shani hurts her . . ."

"I know, Grady."

Grady fell silent, and Justin wasn't sure what to say.

Then Grady broke into his thoughts, sounding almost hopeful. "I think I have an idea of where to look. Just let me know if you guys find anything else. *Please.*"

This mental whiplash was tiring Justin out. "Of course. And Grady . . . be careful."

Grady paused. "Justin—it's Kayla." Then he was gone.

Justin nodded, because he completely understood. If it was Mandy . . .

The voice of the woman he loved cut through his thoughts. "Justin, we have it."

He turned toward her quickly, crossing the room in a few steps. "What did you find?"

Holun spoke up. "The globe is definitely doing this to this man. And, according to this, it is not going to stop."

Justin's mouth fell open. "What's it doing?"

Mandy took over. "The globe has the ability to transform someone by giving them a special power."

Justin had a thought. "But why Steven and not anyone else? At least, not yet . . ."

"We think the globe somehow chooses who to turn," Holun began, "or there are certain people who are susceptible to the globe's power. The Codex does not really say. Or . . ." Holun's eyes got wide. "The globe has always had this power, but this has not happened in a very long time. What if someone activated the globe? And that person is using it to make Steven do what they want?"

Justin heard the thought pass through Mandy's head just as it passed through his. Mandy's mouth dropped open as he said what they were both thinking. "Shani."

Holun gasped. "Shani?" Justin watched him swallow hard. "She is *here*?"

Justin nodded. "We think so. We can't communicate telepathically with Grady, so we suspect she's blocking us."

Holun, who had turned white, nodded slowly.

Then, after a few moments, Justin saw the color start to return to Holun's face. The young man blinked, shaking his head. "Either way, the globe *will* turn more people whether Shani is involved or not. I am certain of that." He looked over at Mandy with wide eyes.

Mandy nodded, looking first at Holun then over at Justin. "Yes. We somehow need to contain it. If we don't, we could have a lot worse than Steven on our hands."

Justin nodded back at her. "Right."

Silence fell in the room before Mandy broke it. "So what did Grady say?"

Justin pulled up a stool. "He has a lead on where Kayla might be. He's headed there now."

Mandy's eyes were wide. "Has he seen Shani yet?"

Justin shook his head. "No, but she may be affecting Kayla's mind, too." He crossed his arms. "Was there anything else about the globe?"

Mandy shrugged. "Not really, except what we already knew, that it would help those destined to find the Codex to discover it."

Justin nodded once then looked at Holun's back as the kid-who-wasn't-much-of-a-kid-anymore started reading the Codex again. Justin watched as he flipped one page, scanned it quickly, then flipped another page, scanned that as well, and kept repeating the process. After several pages, Justin had to ask. "Holun? What is it?"

Holun kept going, flipping pages and reading them quickly. Then he froze, and Justin and Mandy came around to either side of him. Mandy put a hand on his shoulder and repeated what Justin had said, more urgently this time. "Holun, what is it?"

Holun straightened, eyes wide, but didn't speak.

Justin swallowed hard. "You found something." It wasn't a question.

Holun, still staring at the open book, nodded slowly.

"What is it?" Justin asked again, catching Mandy's gaze. *This can't be good.*

Mandy shook her head. *No, not good at all. I'm a little afraid to find out what he read.*

We have to know. Justin tried again. "Please, Holun. What did you find?"

Holun turned to Justin as Mandy moved closer. "This book gives so much more of the Codex story than I could have imagined." Holun glanced over at the Codex before continuing. "This tells of prophecies about the Codex."

Mandy leaned against the table. "We know, Holun. Prophecies about how 'four people from the North'"—she added air quotes for effect—"would find the Codex . . ."

"No." Holun's word hung in the air, and Justin felt a knot forming in his stomach. "This details prophecies about what happens *after* the Codex is found."

University Coffeehouse Parking Lot, Gainesville, Florida

Grady wasn't exactly sure what he was doing. He'd been going crazy over the past couple of hours—he couldn't exactly go back to Orlando and leave Kayla here, but he couldn't just sit around and do nothing, even though the sun had set thirty minutes ago and she'd be nearly impossible to find in the dark. He just didn't have it in him to give up. Not when it came to Kayla.

He'd thought he'd had a lead on Kayla's location—he figured a cave fit the description she'd given Justin—but he didn't have a clue where to even start with that. There was one cave system nearby, Warren's Cave, but that system covered at least four miles of underground caverns, and he couldn't be sure Kayla was in any of them. That could take weeks to search, and Kayla would certainly not have that long. He needed her back *now*.

He growled as he threw his empty coffee cup a little too harshly in the outdoor recycling bin and headed to Kayla's Jeep. Once inside with seatbelt fastened, he turned the key in the ignition and reached to put it into drive though he had no clue where he was going.

But he didn't make it to the gear shift. He saw a blurry hand from the backseat swing toward his face just in time for him to duck out of the way. The horn sounded as Grady strained for the gearshift, then he finally threw it into drive. He rammed his foot on the gas, and the car lurched forward, sending his attacker in the backseat flying into the closed door. Grady careened out of the lot, barely missing the front bumper of an oncoming car as he flew out into the evening traffic.

The person in the back reached between the front seats and tried to grab the steering wheel. Grady jerked the wheel suddenly to the right, swerving onto the shoulder, tires screeching. The assailant fell against the side of Grady's seat, then the passenger seat, then reached for Grady. The car started swerving dangerously close to the other cars in the road as Grady tried to jump away from the hands reaching for him.

The attacker was now halfway in the front seat, and Grady's heart stopped at the sight of long, black hair. Just like . . .

Shani sneered at him from inches away just before she yanked the steering wheel, sending the car onto the shoulder once again, but this time, Grady had no control. He caught a glimpse of a brightly lit, larger-than-life steel telephone pole just before glass from every window in the car shattered inward, and the hood crushed like an accordion. Grady's head snapped forward before slamming into the headrest behind him, the airbag deploying in his face with a power that took his breath away.

It was the last thing he remembered.

Mandy just stared at Holun. She'd heard what he said, but she couldn't believe it. From the moment she'd heard of the Codex—even before that, when she knew they were looking for something but didn't know what—she'd unswervingly believed that the Codex was the end result of their search. That once they'd found it, they would go back to their normal lives—albeit with superpowers—and things would return to normal, mostly.

But if what Holun was saying turned out to be true—and she suspected it was—their lives would never be the same. Sure, never aging would take some getting used to, and hearing Justin in her head all the time could definitely be disconcerting, but those were minor details in the thread of her life. If there was more to the story, she would never go back to her old life again. And it scared her.

"Holun, why do you think that?" Justin broke the thick silence before Mandy could even collect her thoughts into a coherent sentence.

Holun pointed to the open page. "Here it talks about four prophecies."

Mandy's heart skipped. "Four?"

Holun nodded. "Yes, four." He looked her way. Once he saw her, he turned away from the book and grabbed a free stool. "Mandy, sit, please."

She must have looked terrible. She never did have much of a poker face.

Mandy took her seat next to Justin, reaching for her near-by water and taking a slow, deliberate drink before turning back to Holun. "Okay, I'm ready. What does it say?"

Holun gave her one last look then turned back. "Mandy, I will need your help translating into English; mine still is not perfect. Justin, can you transcribe what we give you?"

"Sure."

Mandy took another swig from her water bottle, finishing it off. "Okay, Holun." She tossed the empty bottle into the nearby recycling bin. "Let's figure out what this says."

It took all night for Mandy, Justin, and Holun to get every-thing down on paper and in English. Mandy suggested they head home for some sleep before they tried to make sense of everything they'd written down; she was going cross-eyed looking at the book anyway.

The sun was rising just as the three of them left the an-thro lab and headed toward the parking lot, feet dragging. Mandy was glad neither she nor Justin had classes in the morning; they would've most certainly slept right through them.

As they stepped outside, Mandy grabbed her phone to try Grady again. It rang four times, then . . . no answer. *Hope he's okay.*

Maybe he's underground looking for her and doesn't have a signal, Justin's thoughts interrupted her own. *Or maybe he already found her, and they're on their way back home.* Mandy frowned—that would be too easy.

"Holun, where are you staying?" Justin asked as they crossed the lot to their car.

Mandy saw Holun shrug out of the corner of her half-closed eye. "I float around. Depends on if I have found work and can pay for a hotel—the Clan does not really use money, so I did not come here with much of anything."

Mandy came up beside him. "You can stay with us."

Holun looked over at her. "Are you sure?" He glanced over at Justin.

Justin came up on his other side and put an arm around his shoulder. "Of course, man. Our couch is pretty comfortable."

You would know, Mandy thought.

Ouch! Justin grinned over at Mandy, who just rolled her eyes with a barely concealed smile.

Holun smiled widely. "It would be nice to have somewhere to stay. It has been hard to find a place."

"Then it's settled." Mandy reached the car first and handed her keys to Justin. Mandy always had hers out before he even remembered he needed them. He smiled his thanks.

Holun headed for the back door of the car. "Thank you."

Mandy smiled back at him from the passenger seat. "Of course." Then her stomach growled. "How about some pancakes first?"

Holun nodded quickly.

CHAPTER 7

Forgotten

KAYLA BLINKED AS SHE woke up. She'd been here for—well, she didn't know how long, but probably only a couple of hours . . . or was it morning already?—a little while now, but she still hadn't quite figured out where she was. Given what she'd told Justin, maybe she was underground? That might fit.

She couldn't see a thing. She blinked again. Yup, her eyes were definitely open, and her eyelashes weren't rubbing against anything as she would have expected with a blindfold. She'd been right about the lack of one—it was so dark down here, she couldn't tell the difference.

Grady? Justin? She took a breath. *Mandy?* When no one answered, Kayla sighed, realizing she was still cut off from everyone. Was Shani still here, messing with their heads? Sure seemed likely.

Then she heard something move beside her, way too close. What on earth was that? Her mind instantly flew to the most extreme, most unlikely possibility: an underground monster of some sort, one only imagined by the most creative of Hollywood directors. She jumped away from the sound, bumping her head on something sharp. Great. She winced at the pain radiating through her skull, hoping a knot wasn't growing underneath her hair. With her hands tied behind her back, she couldn't tell.

She heard the sound again and moved farther away from it, more carefully this time. She didn't need a bleeding head wound down here.

Then the sound changed. It sounded almost like . . . was that a person?

"Hello?" She wasn't sure if calling out was the best idea but figured it was worth a shot. She hoped.

A sound came again, this time as a groan. Yes, it was definitely a person. Was Steven down here with her?

"Who's there?" She felt like she was talking to herself in this pitch-black prison.

Kayla heard some rustling, some movement, then an "ow!"

Instantly, her stomach erupted in butterflies. "Grady!"

"Kayla?"

Kayla moved toward him, crawling awkwardly on her knees with her hands still tied behind her back, careful to avoid the sharp object hanging from what had to be a low ceiling. "Grady, sweetie, are you okay?"

She heard movement headed her direction. Certainly they would find each other soon . . . Suddenly, she felt him right in front of her.

"Grady?"

"Kayla, where are you?"

Kayla moved closer to him, wishing her hands were free so she could touch him. Then suddenly she felt his hand on her shoulder, and she leaned closer. Grady pulled her into a hug, holding her tightly for several moments. In that moment, Kayla didn't care that her hands were tied behind her back or that she had a headache that felt like an anvil had been dropped on her head; she just needed Grady close to her. And he finally was.

Grady pulled away slightly, moving to untie her hands. They must not have been tied very well as he made quick work of it, even in the dark. She touched her wrists where the ropes had rubbed them raw then reached to find Grady's hand and intertwined her fingers with his.

"Grady." That one word held all the emotion she'd felt since Steven had torn her away from the man she loved. She pulled herself closer to him, felt him moving to put his arms around her again.

"Oh, Kayla. I didn't know if I would ever see you again." His voice broke as his arms encircled her, and suddenly everything was okay. It didn't matter if they were trapped underground—or wherever they were—because they were together. He pulled her close to his chest, not an inch between them. For the longest time, they just held each other. And Kayla was more than okay with that.

When they finally pulled away, it was only a few inches, and Kayla found Grady's hand once again. She couldn't let go of him in this impossibly dark, scary place. He was her anchor, the reason she would get through this, the reason they would get out of here. She felt that truth in her very soul.

"Kayla, how are you feeling? Are you hurt? What did Steven do to you?" Kayla could hear Grady's voice drop with his last question.

She swallowed once. "I'm fine, really. Steven just brought me here, after he took me from the gas station." She didn't mention that Steven must've knocked her out pretty good, since she didn't know how long she'd been here once she woke up.

Kayla reached up for Grady's face, exploring it with her hands. She'd memorized every part of his face by sight, but exploring it with her hands was a completely new and intimate experience. She cringed as she noticed several scrapes across his forehead, his cheeks. What had happened?

She felt Grady reach for her and do the same. She leaned in to his touch, comforted by the closeness of the man she'd fallen completely in love with. She'd only ever felt this connected to him when they could hear each other's thoughts—she loved every minute of it, despite the situation.

But, at some point, they would have to address the issue at hand and find a way out of here. "Grady," she began, her hands still on his face, "how did you get here?"

She felt Grady's face fall, just a little. "Shani."

Kayla gasped; she couldn't help it. "You saw Shani?"

Grady nodded against her hands. "She ran me off the road with her in the backseat."

"Are you okay?"

She felt the corners of his mouth turn up. "I'm okay. It's okay, really. She brought me to you."

Kayla smiled, knowing Grady would feel it through his hands. "Very true. But as far as I can tell, we're still trapped down here."

Grady's voice changed suddenly. "Down where?"

Kayla frowned. "I'm not sure, but I was thinking that we might be underground."

Grady nodded again. "From what you told Justin, I thought you might be in a cave of some sort."

"That makes sense. It would explain why we can't see one speck of light." Kayla shifted to save her leg from falling asleep, but she kept her hands on Grady's face. "So the question now is: How do we get out?"

Grady moved closer to her, his hands still on her face. "First, what do we have? Did Steven take your phone?"

Kayla shrugged in the darkness. "I don't have it; I already checked. He either took it, or it may have fallen out at the gas station."

Grady removed his hands from her face, and Kayla heard some shuffling around. Then a light brighter than the sun blinded her. "Grady!"

"Sorry." He covered up the phone's face with his hand, but even the little bit of reddish light showing through his fingers pierced the darkness surrounding them. He gradually removed his hands, and Kayla's eyes adjusted slowly. "No signal. We couldn't possibly be that lucky."

Kayla noticed a smile in Grady's voice. "What?"

Yes, he definitely was grinning. "This just reminded me of that time in the cave where you shined your flashlight right in my face. When you didn't want me to know you liked falling into my arms."

Kayla clearly remembered their first adventure together, when they discovered the cavern at Lamanai, the one that contained the globe and started them on the path to discovering the Codex. She'd been scared in the pitch black—much like now, she realized—and had fallen from some hanging roots into Grady's arms. It was just like he'd said: She hadn't wanted him to know how good it felt. And it had felt *really* good.

She grinned back. "True." She leaned forward, pulling him closer. "Can't say I mind if you know now."

Grady wrapped his arms around her, revealing the blinding light once again. The light shook her out of her reverie, and Kayla stared at the phone on the ground next to them like she'd never seen one before. It felt foreign in their current state. "We could at least use the flashlight to explore where we are?"

Grady nodded in the spooky light. "Good idea." He turned the flashlight on and pointed it to Kayla's right. "Let's find out what's down here."

Kayla's eyes followed Grady's light, but she only saw the gray stone floor and more darkness. She started to stand up, then she remembered the sharp object she'd hit her still-throbbing head on. "Grady, shine the light up."

The white light hit the ceiling in a hurry—the ceiling was only a few feet above their heads, punctuated with sharp stalactites every few feet. Kayla must've hit her head on one of them. "Oh, great." Grady swung the light back and forth across the low ceiling. "We're not going to get anywhere fast without being able to walk upright."

Kayla sighed. "Right." Still seated, she scooted closer to Grady. He reached for her hand and sat down beside her before aiming the light away from them into the black expanse beyond.

What they saw scared Kayla more than the darkness.

Mandy and Justin's Apartment, Orlando

Mandy slept until ten, and the boys were still asleep when she rose, wrapping a thin, yellow robe around her and heading to the kitchen to make some coffee.

Must. Have. Coffee.

What a long night. She was grateful for Holun's help—and even Justin's—but she needed her beauty sleep. She considered going back to bed after her coffee for a split second before she heard Holun stirring on the couch.

"Mandy?" The coffee pot gurgled beside her as Holun padded into the kitchen. "That smells good."

"You drink coffee, Holun?"

"Oh, yes."

Mandy smiled, pulling two mugs from the cupboard next to her. She grabbed the pot and started pouring before the carafe was even full, handing the first cup to Holun.

Holun breathed in the aroma before sipping from the cup Mandy'd given him. "This is what I think heaven must be like."

Mandy laughed quietly. She didn't want to wake Justin up until he was ready. "Yes, I think you're probably right." She nodded to the kitchen table.

Holun grabbed a chair and sat down, placing his cup on the table. "Mandy? Can I ask you a question?"

Mandy nodded over her cup just before her first sip. "Of course, Holun."

"What is it like here? At the university, I mean, and here with Justin?"

Mandy swallowed. "It's . . . nice. Comforting. I like the university, and I love Justin."

Holun grinned. "I know."

Mandy smiled a little, hiding behind her cup as she sipped again. "It's a nice, normal life so far. Just how I like it."

Holun set his cup down and looked her straight in the eye, so directly that Mandy shifted in her seat. "But you discovered the Codex. You have the Power of the Codex and are destined to start using it."

Mandy glanced past her hanging plants and out the window over the kitchen sink. "Holun . . . we never asked for this. Not really. We don't have some noble quest to go on now that the Codex gave us superpowers. We're just everyday people that—"

"—can hear the thoughts of another person? Talk with her boyfriend through her mind, even miles away? Use wind to knock someone over or steal their breath? Live to be a thousand, even ten thousand years old?"

Mandy held up her hand. "I get it, Holun."

Holun was still staring at her. "I do not think you do, Mandy. This Power is part of you now, and it was given to you for a reason. I think that reason is to fulfill the prophecies we translated last night."

Mandy was so tired last night, she wasn't really sure *what* the prophecies had even said. "That may be true, Holun, but don't the four of us get a say in the matter?"

"I do not think so."

Holun took another sip of his coffee while Mandy stared off into space. Could Holun be right? Could discovering the Codex have so irreparably changed them that they no longer had any choice in the matter? She certainly hoped not.

Holun got up for a refill, and Mandy noticed he was wearing the clothes he showed up in. "Holun, is that all you have to wear?"

Holun turned, glancing down at his threadbare, light-blue t-shirt, faded khaki pants, and beat-up sandals, then nodded. "Mostly, yes."

Mandy stood and walked over to him, putting a hand on his shoulder. "Looks like I'm taking you shopping."

Location Unknown, Somewhere Near Gainesville

Kayla and Grady were staring at a wall. But not just any wall —one that completely surrounded them on all sides in a rough square. Kayla suddenly felt claustrophobic and could feel her breathing start to pick up.

Grady noticed it, too. "Kayla, honey, it's okay. Just breathe." He hadn't let go of her hand, but now he rubbed his other hand on hers. "We're going to get out of here."

Kayla tried to steady her breathing. "I know, Grady, but I just don't see how. I don't see any door or exit of any kind."

Grady nodded at her but didn't say anything. She wished again that she could hear what he was thinking until a sound echoed from the far side of the room. Something was happening.

What could only have been described as a door was opening on the wall farthest away from them, though it hardly resembled any door Grady had ever seen. It looked like the wall had simply opened up and created an empty space. Given all they'd seen over the summer, though, maybe it had.

Shani stood in shadow at the opening, light pouring in the room from behind her and falling on the two prisoners. "Kayla, Grady, welcome. I trust Steven has been a good host."

Grady scowled at her.

"Now, Grady, don't be like that. I just need you here for a little while longer, then I'll let you both go. I promise."

"Yeah, right" came from Kayla.

"No, really! On my family's honor, I will be releasing you both soon."

Grady snorted; he couldn't help it. He'd never known Shani to be altruistic—or merciful. "What are you planning? Why do you need us down here?" He wanted to ask how she was blocking their telepathy, but he didn't want to alert her to that fact in the off chance she didn't know she was doing it.

Though they couldn't see Shani's face, Grady sensed her wide grin. "Oh, come now, Grady. It wouldn't be fun to give away all my secrets, would it?"

"Shani, let us out!" Kayla yelled from beside him.

"Soon, Professor Harrington. Very soon." Then Shani suddenly disappeared, and the opening closed. They were in the dark—save Grady's phone light—once again.

Shani walked back to the cave's entrance where Steven was sitting, waiting for her.

"You're just going to let them go?" Steven asked as soon as she appeared.

Shani pinched the bridge of her nose. "Yes, *Steven*." She spat his name at him. She didn't have time for his inane questions.

"Why?"

"Steven! Do not question me!" Shani's patience was growing thin with this one. She'd have to be more careful who she selected next—one without so many issues. If she could even control it.

But right now she needed to focus. Blocking Grady and Kayla's telepathy barely required any effort, but what she had planned next would take all her concentration. She hadn't even been certain she could use her power this way until a few years ago when Alex, her lover, had discovered something about her she couldn't stand letting him know.

This would be an even bigger undertaking than that, but she could do it. After all, Grady and Kayla both deserved this. They'd been getting in her way for years—it was time for the shoe to be on the other foot. They needed to feel the pain she'd felt, the pain of losing someone close to them. They needed to *suffer*.

Shani took a seat on the ground, crossing her legs and letting her eyes fall shut. She steadied her breathing then felt her power start coursing through her veins.

Suddenly, her eyes flew open. As though she'd created an aura of her power that was now expanding beyond her, she could sense it was working—it wouldn't be long now.

She felt a satisfied grin spread across her face.

"What did she mean by that?" Kayla ventured.

Grady shuddered, pulling Kayla closer to him. "I'm not sure." Whatever Shani had planned, it wasn't good. And with every second that passed, Grady was getting more worried.

"Grady, I . . ." Kayla started, her voice dry and cracking. "What does Shani want with us?"

"I don't . . ."

Suddenly, Grady couldn't remember what he was saying. He couldn't think . . . what was he doing here? Where was he? He took the phone he held in his hand and surveyed the space around him. Was he in a cave? Underground somewhere? What on earth was going on?

And who . . . he noticed someone next to him, someone he had an arm around. For a moment, he just stared at the woman sitting close to him.

Who was she?

CHAPTER 8

The Return

KAYLA'S EYES GREW WIDE, and her stomach dropped as Grady's whole countenance changed. What was happening? One second, he was here with her, then the next . . . clearly something was wrong. "Grady? What's going on?"

Grady backed away from her as his eyes widened and swept the room, back and forth. "Who . . . who are you?"

Kayla's heart stopped. "Grady? It's me, Kayla."

"Kayla?" For a split second, Kayla let herself hope. Then: "I'm sorry, I don't know who you are."

Kayla's stomach knotted up, and she thought she might be sick as the truth settled into her gut with devastating clarity. With everything they'd been through, all they'd fought together, she'd counted on the fact that they would be living out the rest of their life together. That no matter what would come their way, they would go through it together. But now, he didn't even recognize her.

Their life together was gone in an instant—if Grady couldn't remember her, couldn't remember *them*, how would their life ever be the same? Tears welled up in her eyes, and she looked away.

"Why are you crying? Are you hurt?"

The truth behind his questions cut through her very core, and Kayla couldn't control the tears any longer. She began sobbing.

Grady, but not Grady, reached for her. "I'm sorry, did I do something to hurt you?"

Kayla was still sobbing, couldn't even catch her breath to respond. She didn't know how she could live through this, how she could go on without him when he was still right in front of her.

The door opened again, but this time no one was there to greet them. And Kayla knew this was what Shani had been waiting for, what she'd been planning all along. Kayla'd known Shani was powerful and could manipulate the minds of others, but she didn't—couldn't—know the awful extent of her power until now.

As she and Grady crawled toward the open door, tears still streaming down her cheeks, any hope Kayla'd felt when she'd realized Grady was down here with her had evaporated into this terrifyingly dark, dank cave. Shani had tried to take the Codex from them before—and that had felt like it would've been an unbearable loss—but they'd ultimately prevailed. Now she'd revealed a more insidious plan, and it was working like a charm.

In one horrible instant, Shani had finally succeeded in taking everything from her.

Mandy left Justin a note on the fridge—right where she knew he'd see it—and took Holun to the nearest clothing store. She looked away from the other shoppers who were not-so-discretely staring at them as they walked in. She imagined they made a strange couple.

Though Holun wasn't young enough to be her son, Mandy felt a strong nurturing instinct toward him. She wanted to make sure he was well taken care of, dressed properly, eating enough, stable and safe—though nothing about Holun's life was safe, and probably never would be. The Mercenaries and Na-um were likely still looking for him, and they wouldn't play nice if they ever found him. But Mandy still felt a strong need to protect him; he was in this situation because of them, after all. Though he'd never admit that.

"What do you think?" Holun came out of the fitting room in a pair of shorts and a Hawaiian shirt.

Mandy stifled a grin. "Um, let's try something else." She was giggling as she reached for a nearby dark-gray polo shirt. "Here; try this."

Holun took the shirt, nodding, then headed back to the fitting room. He emerged moments later with the shirt on, stretched over his muscular chest. A trio of teenage girls walked by and first stared then started giggling amongst themselves. Mandy smiled and nodded at Holun once they'd walked past. "I think we have a winner." Holun didn't seem to have noticed the attention—he just furrowed his brow then walked back into the dressing room with a shrug.

Mandy's phone went off in her pocket. She answered it without looking. "Hello?"

Kayla's voice came through loud and clear. "Mandy?"

"Kayla! Thank God you're okay!"

"Yes. Grady's here with me, too."

"Oh, Kayla—I'm so happy you're safe."

"Uh, Mandy . . ."

"Are you headed back to Orlando?" Holun came out of the fitting room in another dark-colored shirt—a navy t-shirt this time—and a light pair of khakis, and Mandy nodded with a thumbs up. Holun sauntered back into the fitting room.

"Yes . . . wait—we don't have a car."

Then Mandy really heard Kayla, and something in her voice made her stop. "Kayla—are you guys okay? Do you need us to pick you up?"

Kayla didn't answer, and Mandy's stomach fluttered. She turned away from the fitting room and instinctively ducked behind a display, lowering her voice. "Kayla? What's wrong? Is Grady okay?"

Kayla paused, but Mandy was determined to let her answer. "Grady . . . he's alive, he's not hurt, but he's . . . not himself. Mandy, I . . . we have to see you and Justin ASAP."

"Of course. I'm out shopping with Holun. Justin told you he was here, right?"

Kayla's voice lifted only slightly. "Yes. That's great, Mandy."

Now Mandy was certain something was drastically wrong. "Kayla . . . are you still in Gainesville? Do you need us to come get you?"

Kayla paused for a moment. "Um . . . we can rent a car."

"Don't be silly, Kayla. We'll come get you."

"It's okay, Mandy, really. I could use the time to think."

"Are you sure?"

"Yeah. We'll be home soon." Kayla's voice was soft, and Mandy couldn't miss the underlying distress she heard in it. What on earth was wrong?

Mandy frowned as Holun came out of the dressing room with armloads of new clothes. She motioned for him to take them up front—they were paying and leaving.

"Okay. We'll be at our apartment waiting for you. And Kayla—please be safe."

Mandy heard her friend sigh through the phone. "It's too late for that now." Her stomach dropped as the line went dead.

Once Shani could feel her plan was working, she had Steven quickly grab up their folding chairs while she opened the door to the cave. They then ran for their SUV and took off for Orlando before Kayla and Grady even made it outside. Shani knew that's where the couple would be headed next, headed back home.

Now, as they drove out of Gainesville, Shani took her eyes off the road for a second to eye the globe that was sitting on the floor behind the passenger seat. She'd thought Steven might protest leaving his hometown, but perhaps she'd yelled at him enough that now he knew better. She honestly hated bringing him with her, but he could be useful, at least until she could find another candidate to accept the globe's powers.

Shani wasn't entirely sure how the globe decided who would receive powers, but she quickly realized it didn't really matter. She just needed her unwitting recruits to *think* she knew, think she controlled it somehow. It didn't have to be true, they just had to believe it—but that was the easy part. She'd spent a lifetime weaving deceptions and lies, so much so that it was second nature to her now.

Kayla was reaching out to Mandy again; she could feel it. She steeled herself against it, making sure nothing got through. A bead of sweat broke out on her forehead, and she wiped it away. It would only get harder to keep all these plates spinning, but for her plan to work, she needed Grady's memory to stay gone.

Which gave her an idea.

All those years she'd spent training under Kayla and Grady masquerading as a sweet, innocent archaeology student, she'd spent her free time studying the legends of her Clan. She knew that one day she would be able to return to her people and use the knowledge she'd gained during that time against the new keepers of the Codex, which had turned out to be, not surprisingly, her professors and fellow students.

She remembered one legend she'd studied, several years ago, about a treasure trove of artifacts that the Elders kept close to ward off various powers, especially those of the Codex if it came to that—which now it had. She hadn't discovered their true purpose, or how the Elders came to have them, but their power was unquestioned. And if she couldn't have the Power of the Codex—though she still considered stealing that Power away from the Four a viable option—this was an excellent second choice. Stealing those artifacts may actually help her steal the Power of the Codex in the end.

Shani found herself grinning. She knew the Clan was still in Belize but had moved, closer to Lamanai. So that's where she would go.

But she had a few things to take care of first.

Mandy and Justin's Apartment, Orlando

Mandy joined Justin and Holun on the two bright-blue easy chairs facing her and Justin's stylishly worn brown leather couch—Mandy sunk down to the arm of Justin's chair—just as Kayla and Grady entered the room behind her and inched toward the couch. Mandy was convinced something weird was going on. Grady just didn't seem to be himself, and Kayla seemed . . . off. Her friend's face was sunken, her eyes were empty, and Mandy could tell she'd been crying, a lot.

Even though her friends were now back in Orlando safe and sound, no one seemed to want to speak first. In the nearly two hours since Kayla had called, Mandy's mind had been conjuring up all sorts of heinous scenarios for what had happened to Grady. Justin just kept thinking she should stop imagining the worst. Though she usually put on a positive face for everyone else, she was never good at actually holding out hope.

Mandy eyed Kayla and Grady again, who'd both sat down on the couch across from her, a greater distance between them than usual, their clothes from yesterday grimy and disheveled. She couldn't understand the look she saw on Grady's face. It almost looked, well, blank. Plus, she still couldn't hear anyone's thoughts but Justin's. That was probably the most concerning part.

She'd told Justin what Kayla had told her over the phone, which was precious little. She and Justin had been discussing the situation in their thoughts ever since, avoiding bringing Holun in on it—though Mandy sensed he was about to find out anyway.

"Kayla . . ." Mandy started but didn't know how to finish, so her single word hung thick in the air. She saw Kayla fidget in her seat and noticed Grady watch her, then do the same. Mandy thought Grady seemed like he wasn't sure what he was supposed to be doing and was simply following Kayla's lead. Grady had never been unsure of anything since she'd known him. Her stomach knotted.

Justin attempted to restart the conversation. "Kayla, Grady, we're so glad you're okay." Mandy thought even Justin seemed guarded, which was completely unlike him.

I'm scared, Justin. What's wrong with them?

I don't know, Mandy. I'm scared, too.

Kayla was the one to speak first. "Do you have any water?" She glanced over at Grady, and Mandy noticed she didn't really make eye contact. "Are you thirsty, too?"

Grady nodded once, shifting in his seat on the couch, moving even farther away from Kayla than he should've been.

Holun, closest to the kitchen, jumped up and hurried out of the room for some water. He came back a moment later carrying two full glasses.

Kayla took a large gulp then set the glass on a coaster on the glass-topped coffee table. Mandy looked on as Grady again watched what she did first then mimicked her. Mandy shivered.

"What's going on?" Holun broke the silence, the only one brave enough to actually ask the question.

Kayla's shoulders dropped. "We . . . um . . . Steven, the night guard from the museum, captured me when Grady and I"—she glanced over at Grady as she said his name—"confronted him at a gas station near the museum. He took me to a place underground where I must've been overnight. Grady showed up this morning, stating that Shani had attacked him and brought him there." They all cringed at Shani's name, but Mandy noticed Holun jerk at the sound from the corner of her eye, almost as if he'd been slapped. Perhaps he felt her betrayal even more sharply than the four of them did—she was one of the main reasons he'd lost his family, after all.

Justin took over. "How did you get out?"

Kayla took another sip of her water. "Shani came in to see us, taunted us, then said she'd let us go soon after that. She left, but then something happened."

"What?" Mandy needed to know, now.

Kayla frowned. "Grady . . ." Her voice cracked as her chest heaved in quick spurts. "One second, he was fine, but the next . . ." Tears threatened to break through, and one escaped down her cheek before she caught Mandy's gaze and held it. "Mandy—he doesn't recognize me anymore." The tears finally came, flooding her eyes instantly and spilling down her cheeks. She turned away from Grady, who just looked at her curiously, albeit compassionately, but with the compassion one would have for a stray animal, not the woman he loved.

Mandy's heart stopped. She couldn't even imagine . . . Grady and Kayla's love was the stuff of legend, and to have that ripped away in an instant . . . Mandy was finding it hard to breathe. She didn't know how Kayla was doing it.

Mandy stood and walked over to her friend, sitting down and wrapping an arm around her. Kayla's head fell to her shoulder as sobs wracked her body.

Rest Area off Interstate 75, Just North of Orlando

Shani was getting a headache. She pressed her thumb and index finger to the bridge of her nose as she sat in the hot car, the A/C barely making a dent in the one-hundred-degrees-plus weather. Steven's presence was insufferable—first, it was the not talking at all that got to her. So she'd tried to make conversation. That's when he'd started talking, and now he wouldn't stop. Blah, blah, his ex who'd cheated on him, blah, blah, her and her lover had gotten it now . . .

She'd never really connected with normal humans—they just seemed so . . . *ordinary*. Certainly not worth wasting her time on.

Alex—her Alex, the one she missed so dearly every single day—wasn't like the rest, and she'd known that right away. He'd been intelligent, well-spoken, and adventurous; she'd always loved that about him. Though he'd had a promising career in Belize, he'd given it up for a few years to live with her in Florida. Once she started to suspect her end game was drawing near, she'd encouraged him to get his job back with the Central American Institute of Archaeology to help her carry out her plan.

She was always careful to let him in on just enough of the plan to keep him on board. He'd only discovered one of her most heavily guarded secrets once, but she'd easily blocked the realization from his mind and halted any further inquiries before they could get out of control. Before he could learn the truth she didn't want him to know. Before he could learn who she *truly* was, deep inside.

Shani sighed and opened the car door, jumping out onto the hot pavement in the sweltering sun. She wished she'd opted for something cooler than jeans—this was one of those days where the waterparks would be full just as soon as school let out. She slammed the driver door shut and leaned against the side of the car, facing away from Steven. Intentionally.

As she suspected would happen, Steven followed her out of the car, talking all the way. He leaned his invisible elbows on the hood before yelping and jumping back. Idiot. He couldn't figure out that the hood of a recently running car would be hot in this blistering sun? She really needed a new sidekick. Someone who had a little more class, was a little more refined.

She eyed the globe through the backseat window. It was still glowing, just a little, so she was able to find it easily through the tinted glass.

She stared at it for a few moments then glanced over at the carloads of tourists and travelers milling around who had stopped, like them, for a brief reprieve. Could it be possible that her next perfect mark was here, waiting for her, waiting for the power the globe would give them?

Maybe she should just pick someone at random, cross her fingers, and hope for the best. That would be wonderful; she could let Steven loose and send him on his way. The globe was a very special, very specific type of artifact, and its powers were not to be taken for granted—of course, she knew that—but that didn't mean selecting the next person she saw and ditching Steven wasn't an attractive option. And getting more attractive by the minute.

If it even worked that way.

Steven's mouth was still going, still spewing out anything and everything that crossed his mind. And Shani had finally had enough.

"Steven, shut UP!" She didn't like yelling, but she couldn't figure out another way to get him to stop talking. Several necks of passersby craned in her direction. "Your incessant prattling is grating on my nerves!"

She felt Steven freeze, immediately shamed into silence. She could sense him and his expressions and emotions, which made their proximity even more frustratingly intimate.

"Thank you," Shani trilled, her sincerity sounding utterly questionable though she really didn't care. Steven wouldn't be able to figure that out anyway. He wasn't smart enough. "We have work to do." She moved toward the back of the SUV, but a voice stopped her just before she reached the rear door's handle.

"Uh . . . Miss? Are you okay?"

Shani looked over at the guy in a yellow polo shirt with a popped collar and khaki shorts who had just stopped at their SUV. What did this jerk want? "Yes?" Shani asked as sweetly as she could muster.

The young man, a tall, probably college-aged kid with short, light-brown hair and chiseled features was looking around, trying to get a glimpse inside the tinted windows of the SUV without looking like he was trying to. He was utterly failing in the attempt. "Um . . . I just heard you talking to someone—are you sure you're okay?"

Shani pointed at her ear, which was fully covered by her long hair, then started speaking again. "I'm sorry, Steven, continue. What happened next?" She offered her best sheepish smile to the young man as she shrugged then continued her imaginary conversation.

"Oh, I see. Well, we'll have to change our plans then," Shani stated to no one at all, finding that she rather enjoyed the make believe. Her smile had become genuine right around the "what happened next?" question.

But then the smile froze on her lips. Because she felt it; something was happening. What, she couldn't quite be sure, but she could sense something coming.

And her heart stopped. *No.*

She lurched toward the door handle, trying to get to the globe. But it was too late.

A light brighter than the sun blinded her just before she hit the pavement.

Mandy and Justin's Apartment, Orlando

Justin couldn't believe what he was hearing. How could Grady just forget Kayla? He wouldn't have thought it possible. How does someone forget the most important person to him in the entire world? His stomach dropped as another, more foreboding thought occurred to him: Could he ever forget Mandy?

He decided to address the issue head on. "Grady, what *do* you remember?"

Grady, sipping his water, looked up upon hearing his name. The glass in his hand and the water in it was shaking. "I remember you, Justin. I remember Mandy, too, and Holun. Even that horrible woman, Shani. But this woman, Kayla, is a stranger to me."

Justin caught his gaze and held it. "You remember everything about this past summer?"

Grady nodded, setting his glass on a coaster. "Yes, most of it. Certain parts are hazy, but I seem to remember us finding something underground . . ."

"The Codex," Justin offered.

Grady glanced over at Mandy and the woman he didn't recognize. "I don't really remember that part."

Justin had to fight hard to keep from yelling. "That's because Kayla was there with us. Every step of the way."

Grady leaned back, swiping his hand down his face. "I'm sorry, I just don't remember."

Justin was seething. Shani had to be messing with his mind again, but this was nothing as trivial as blocking their telepathy. This was something much bigger. He didn't think she was so powerful, but it seemed they'd been underestimating her all along.

Mandy spoke up. "Grady, you don't even recognize Kayla from UCF?"

Grady stared at the woman next to Mandy then shook his head. "Her name doesn't even sound familiar."

"Dr. Kayla Harrington, tenured archaeology professor at the University of Central Florida, where you are also a tenured professor in the same department?"

Grady stared at the floor in response to Mandy's question. "I remember all of that, where I work and what I do, but to my recollection no one named Kayla has ever worked there."

Kayla started sobbing again. Mandy held her while Justin tried to bring the conversation back around to what they could actually fight. They had to find Shani—she was the only one who could make this right.

"Grady, do you remember your power?"

Grady nodded. "I control water."

Justin nodded back. "Good, we can use that. Can you help us fight Shani? Defeating her is the only thing I can think of that might get your memory of Kayla back."

Grady looked over at Kayla again, lingering for a moment, then turned back to Justin. "I know now that I should know Kayla. I don't feel it now, but I understand that I loved—love—her. What we have must have been special."

Mandy nodded from Kayla's other side. "It was—it is."

Grady turned back to Justin, and Justin could see the determination in his eyes. "We have to find Shani. We have to fight, force her to give me my memories of Kayla back. If this is all true, and I sense that it is, she stole my life—our lives—from us. We deserve to have that back, and she deserves no mercy."

Kayla wiped her eyes and sat up next to him, nodding and sniffling, tears subsiding. "Do we have a plan?"

Justin spoke up. "Not yet, but we found something last night. Holun, Mandy, and I were working on the translation of the Codex, and Holun discovered four prophecies about the Codex, prophecies about what is going to happen after the Codex is found."

Justin noticed Kayla freeze in her seat. "What?"

Holun nodded from the easy chair where he'd been sitting silently, almost casually, taking everything in. "We have not put it all together in English yet, but we have it all translated."

Kayla stood. "Then I say we go to campus and find out what they said. After a quick shower, of course." She glanced down at her visibly dirty clothes pointedly, and Grady nodded beside her. Justin figured a quick stop at their respective condos wouldn't hurt.

Mandy joined her, nodding. "And Shani?"

As the others also stood to their feet, Justin looked over at his girlfriend. "We're not even sure how to find her. At least this gives us something productive to do. We'll figure out how to find her and deal with her very soon."

Mandy nodded at him.

Justin looked over at Grady. "You okay, man? You up for this?"

Grady shook his head as if to clear it. "Yeah, it's just really weird—it's like part of my life is just missing. I had no idea Shani could do something like this."

Mandy stepped to the door and grabbed her keys then opened the door to usher everyone out. "Yeah, she hid everything scarily well. She's even more dangerous than we realized."

Justin couldn't have agreed more.

CHAPTER 9

The Four Prophecies

Just North of Orlando, Off Interstate 75

IT TOOK SEVERAL MINUTES for Shani to regain full use of her eyes—that globe was *blinding*. But when she had, she pushed herself up and stood. And immediately, her stomach dropped.

The young man before her, the one who had casually approached their SUV, appeared to be the same person she'd met only moments ago. But her other senses told her a different story.

The tall, college-aged man stood before Shani with eyes wide. "What . . ." He seemed to be having trouble forming sentences. "What . . . did you do to me?" he rasped, his voice barely above a hoarse whisper.

Shani just stared, not even sure what to tell this kid. That his life had been irrevocably changed in an instant?

"What did you do to me??" The man was getting louder, and the other patrons at the rest area were starting to stare.

Shani waved him off frantically, shushing him, trying to quiet him down. She sensed what his power was, and it definitely should not be released here.

But the young man was not having it. "I said, WHAT DID YOU DO TO ME?!"

Shani tensed as a rush of power burst from the man's lungs and toward the SUV. As soon as the wave hit, the vehicle—along with Shani and Steven—went flying across the pavement. The SUV slammed into a car ten spaces down. Shani landed in the grass next to the parking lot on her back, her skin scraped and bruised. She winced as she lay there; every part of her body stung. Steven moaned from a few feet away. *What a child.*

As soon as she'd caught her breath, she attempted to raise up on her elbows. She winced again, sensing she would need a great deal of disinfectant to clean up all the wounds she'd just been given, but managed to sit up.

She struggled to her feet and headed back toward the young man. He was just staring at the SUV, mouth and eyes wide, as she approached.

Shani reached him quickly, despite her injuries and slight limp, and put a hand on his shoulder. "I think we need to talk."

The man slowly looked over at her and simply nodded, looking like he didn't dare utter a word.

Maybe this one would be smarter than Steven after all.

UCF Main Anthropology Lab

The anthro lab was quiet, even for midafternoon on a Friday. The five of them filed in quietly, almost reverently. Kayla grabbed the locker key from her keychain and retrieved their book from where she knew Mandy would have placed it when she left—they didn't dare leave the Codex out and accessible—then set it on the main table.

They'd just upgraded the lab last year and their center, main table boasted a backlight. Kayla turned it on, lighting up the Codex from behind. She grabbed the moveable camera that was attached to the side of the table—the same one Mandy had probably been using to examine the ancient pages earlier—and slid it into place above the book. Kayla clicked on the adjoining monitor as well, which flickered to life and began showing the magnified image of the book's worn, dark-brown cover with only half a second's delay. She grabbed a spotlight attached to a long, pliable neck and clipped it on the side of the desk, switching it on. Everything finally in place, she motioned the others to surround her.

Kayla was glad to be back in the lab, because here she could ignore all the problems of life for a short period of time and focus completely on work. She needed that desperately right now. She couldn't think about Grady . . .

No, she yelled at herself, *just focus.*

You don't have to be strong for us, Kayla. We're here for you.

The sound of another person's thoughts in her mind once again was startling, and Kayla jumped. *Mandy? Is that you?*

Mandy smiled at her across the table, nodding. *It's good to finally hear you again, Kayla.*

Kayla grinned back at her. *You as well. Justin?*

Here and accounted for, ma'am.

Kayla wanted to smack him. Justin just grinned.

Grady? Kayla didn't dare to let herself hope that he could hear her. Undoubtedly, Shani had corrupted his mind so much that he was lost to them, at least for now.

As she'd come to expect, Grady offered no response.

Mandy's smile turned sad. *We'll get him back, Kayla. He'll come back to you.*

Kayla just nodded then turned back to the book. "So where are these notes you all took last night?"

Justin reached behind him to a desk pushed up against the end of a set of bookshelves, opened the top drawer, and pulled out a large handful of loose papers. He handed them to Kayla. "Here."

Kayla took the offered papers and started spreading them out on the lighted table. It took a little bit of time, but the five of them worked to get them laid out in a logical order. At first, Grady stayed back, but by the end, he was working right alongside them. Kayla took this as a good sign.

"Okay," Kayla started once everything was in order, "let's figure out what we've got here." She looked at their young friend. "Holun, you can start."

Holun grinned, and stepped up to the table. He read from the page to himself first then summarized it out loud for the rest of them. "The Codex was destined to be found by four from the North"—he looked around at the four of them—"but that was only the beginning of the story. There is so much more. This talks about why the Codex would be discovered now, how it will help usher in the end of the world."

Kayla's heart dropped.

Mandy gasped. "What?"

Holun nodded somberly. He pointed at the second page. "Here it talks about the end of the world. The Age of the Codex was ushered in when the Codex was found and signifies that the end of the world is coming." He stopped to find his place and read from the page. "Literally, 'the end of the world as it stands.' Or the end of the world as we know it."

Justin was uncharacteristically reserved. "So we're going to destroy the world?"

Holun shook his head. "No, I do not think so. Given all we have been through, we know that the Codex was destined for all of you, but I do not think it was for evil. I think the Codex will help you stop evil in this new world."

"But doesn't a 'new world' mean that the current world will be destroyed?" Grady spoke up from his side of the room as he crossed his arms, drawing Kayla's eyes to the red t-shirt that stretched across his chest.

Holun shook his head again. "No—again, I do not think so. Or maybe in a way, but not like what you are thinking. 'The end of the world' could mean a number of things. It could mean that the world will be destroyed, but I think it is more likely that it means the end of the way the world currently works, the end of the way we currently think about the world."

Justin looked over at Kayla. "Does this make sense to you? Is there a precedent for what he's saying?"

Kayla leaned over the Codex, translating the words for herself. After a few minutes, she murmured a quiet "mm-hmm" then looked at Justin. "I think Holun's right. The connotation of the ancient language doesn't always translate well into English. I think Holun may be on to something. And . . ." She cut herself off. "Wait—what if what we're seeing the globe do is the beginning of that? Maybe the globe is destined to give a lot of people superpowers, and maybe only the powers of the Codex can keep them in check?"

Mandy stepped toward the table. "So we're going to have a world full of psychopaths on our hands?"

Holun took over. "Probably not, though it is possible. I think it turned Steven evil because he was already that way, or maybe Shani used her mind control on him. It certainly seems possible. It is more likely that we would be dealing with a world full of people with powers that do not know

how to use them correctly and may accidentally hurt someone. Potentially dangerous but not evil."

Kayla nodded absently. Grady's voice broke into her
thoughts. "Kayla, what else does the Codex say?"

She looked up at his question and met his gaze. He looked
back into her eyes, with little recognition of her but what
looked like a determination to understand what was happening to him with a drive to fix it. The look gave Kayla the
smallest sliver of hope, and she could hardly keep a smile
from her face as she began reading where Holun left off. "The
end of the world is just the first part of the first prophecy.
The rest talks about an inevitable Battle, and the beginning of
the end of the world will be brought about based on the re-
sults of that battle."

"What does that mean?" Grady was still looking right at
her.

Kayla shifted her weight, tucking her long hair behind one
ear. "It means that there are still battles left to fight, namely
this important one, and that we must win it. I don't know if it
means literal battles or something else, but we must be prepared."

Justin nodded beside her. "We need to train ourselves on
how to use our powers. We're all rusty on using them. We
won't be as lucky as we were the first time, I'm sure." The
first battle they'd fought against the Mercenaries was just
after they'd received their powers. They'd made it out alive
but just barely.

"Agreed." Kayla nodded at him.

Mandy stepped up to the table and started making sense
of the second prophecy. After a minute, she began. "Okay . . .
this mentions someone who is to save the entire human race,
someone called the 'Monarch.' They must not die in that im-

portant battle or the world will not be saved." Mandy visibly shuddered. "These are really dark."

Kayla nodded at her. *Are you okay, Mandy?*

Mandy just caught her gaze and nodded once. *We have to know.*

I agree, Justin piped up. *Let's figure this out so we can focus on finding Shani and getting her to reverse her mind games on Grady.*

Kayla swallowed hard, nodding to the two of them but trying to remain subtle. She didn't think it'd be helpful for Grady to know they were having a conversation about this without him. "Justin? Would you take the next one?"

Justin nodded at her, stepping forward. "This one talks about us, the Four. It says . . ." He stopped, and Kayla saw his Adam's apple bob up and down. "'The Four will be substantially and irreversibly transformed as a result of the Battle, and survival is unlikely.'"

The room fell silent. Kayla couldn't conceive of them losing the battle, much less losing one—or more—of them in the battle. They couldn't die, right?

Right, we're not supposed to be able to die.

I know, Justin, but this seems pretty clear, Kayla shot back.

Mandy chimed in. *Maybe it's like the first prophecy, where it's not so literal? Maybe survival of the people we are now is unlikely?*

Kayla shrugged, ever so slightly. *Maybe. We can hope.*

Grady cleared his throat and stood up from his perch on a stool against the end of a bookshelf, taking a few steps toward the table. "Even though my memory of Kayla is gone, I still remember you guys can hear each other's thoughts. It's pretty obvious you're having a conversation without us." He nodded over at Holun.

Kayla's stomach dropped, and she turned to him, facing him head on. "We're sorry, Grady. We didn't mean to exclude you. It's just . . ."

Justin finished her sentence for her. ". . . natural. We can't help it. You remember, right?"

Grady looked at each of them closely then finally nodded. "Anything we need to know?"

Mandy spoke up. "Just that we think the prophecy about us not surviving may not be literal, like the first one."

Grady offered a half smile, a smile that reminded Kayla of the man she'd lost, and her heart broke. "We can hope."

Maybe Grady had somehow heard her after all.

Grady knew the other three didn't mean to exclude him, but he couldn't help but feel left out. Yet he knew Shani was the one that had done this to him, and she would pay for it. Dearly.

At the moment, though, there were more pressing issues at hand, like deciphering the final prophecy. He stepped to the table in front of the remaining pages. "Mind if I take the last one?"

Kayla smiled at him, one he noticed didn't quite reach her eyes. "Go ahead."

Grady looked over the final pages, tried to make sense of the words he saw, then started reading the translation word for word. "'The Final Truth will be revealed upon the Monarch saving the world, and that Truth will change life on the planet forever.'"

Grady didn't know what that meant—none of them *could* know—but it scared him. Life wasn't perfect, but what if this change wasn't for the better? What would happen if they didn't win, and Shani or the Mercenaries did? What would happen to them—or worse, what would happen to the human race?

Grady needed Kayla back, now. He sensed the strong connection they'd had, though his mind told him it wasn't real. But she was here, right in front of him—he couldn't deny that. And he could feel something pulling him toward her, something his fractured mind couldn't fight. Something innate and strong, something unmistakable.

"Kayla, can I talk to you for a minute?"

Kayla looked up at his question then quickly nodded and followed him out the door.

Rest Stop North of Orlando

After running over to hurriedly snatch the black bag that held the still-glowing globe from the crashed SUV, Shani ushered the young man up the walkway. She pulled him behind the rest stop's sole building, sliding between it and a row of tall bushes. She sensed Steven was close by but could barely bring herself to care. "What's your name?"

The young man just stared.

Shani had to tell herself not to roll her eyes. *Be nice . . .* "It's okay to speak; just be quiet."

The man swallowed hard then stuttered as he whispered, "T-Tyler."

Shani nodded. "Nice to meet you, Tyler. I'm Shani. But we have to get out of here."

Tyler nodded, his eyes darting around, but he didn't speak.

"Did you come here alone?"

Tyler looked back at her, eyes wide, but nodded again.

"Is your car here?" she asked, but Tyler's eyes had drifted away from her again. She snapped her fingers in front of him. "Tyler!"

The young man's eyes whipped back to hers, then he whispered a question. "What . . . what happened?"

Shani placed a hand on his shoulder and ushered him back to the parking lot. The police would surely be here soon—one of the nosy patrons had certainly called them. They had to get out of here. "I will explain later. Which car is yours?"

Tyler nodded toward the middle of the parking lot at a sporty red coupe.

Shani put her hand out. "Keys? I don't think you're ready to drive right now."

Tyler just nodded again then dug his keys out of his pocket and handed them over.

"Thank you." Shani unlocked the doors with the key fob and nodded for the men to climb in. She tossed the black bag behind the driver's seat before climbing in herself. "Steven, sit in the back."

"Steven?" Though his question was quiet, Tyler's whisper still conveyed his shock. He pulled the passenger door shut. "I thought you were talking to a Steven on the phone?"

Shani flicked back her hair to reveal her naked ear. "I lied." She smiled at Tyler and snapped on her seatbelt as she threw the car into drive. She slammed her foot on the gas, and they lurched out of the parking lot and back onto the interstate just as Shani heard the sirens.

Outside the UCF Main Anthropology Lab

Kayla wasn't sure what Grady wanted, but she was willing—perhaps even eager—to find out. She wondered what was going on in his head. She'd taken the fact that she could hear his thoughts for granted too many times, and now she was paying for it. She'd give anything to hear him in her head again.

"Grady," she began once they were out in the empty hallway. Shadows lengthened around them as the sun started to set beyond the floor-to-ceiling windows to their side. "What is it?"

Grady shoved his hands into his pockets and looked away. She hated how nervous he was around her now—just yesterday, there were no secrets between them. "I needed to talk to you."

"Okay." She didn't know what else to say.

"I just . . ." Grady put a hand to the back of his neck and caught her gaze. "I wanted to let you know what's going on inside my head. I remember Justin and Mandy and almost everything that happened this summer, and I trust what they've told me—and what you've told me—about us."

Kayla's heart skipped a beat involuntarily, but she quickly got her emotions back under control. She knew he didn't really remember her, *couldn't* remember their history, the things she liked, didn't like, the way they'd been when they were together. At least he wasn't denying that it ever happened; he just couldn't remember any of it.

Grady dropped his hands to his sides. "I was thinking in there . . . Shani's stolen so much from us."

Kayla nodded.

"We can't let her win."

"No, we can't."

Grady smiled warmly then slowly, tentatively, reached to tuck her hair behind her ear. Kayla instantly felt the warmth of his touch radiate throughout her entire body, heating her up despite the purple tank top and khaki shorts she wore. "Kayla," he breathed, his fingers still grazing her ear, "I know

I have to fight this. Even if I never get my memories of you back, I'll still have the ones we're making now."

Kayla swallowed hard, no clue what to do next. This was all new territory for her, for them, and she was determined to let Grady take the lead.

Then, in the next moment, he did. "I know I need you in my life."

Kayla nodded slowly. "Whatever that looks like, whatever you need, I'll be here. I need you in my life, too, Grady. I can't do any of this without you."

Grady nodded, sliding his hand down to cup her cheek. He leaned in ever so slowly, carefully, eyes searching Kayla's as he closed the distance between them. She urged him closer, hoping he'd understand what she was thinking. And though she knew he couldn't hear her thoughts, she sensed he could *feel* them.

Grady closed the distance between them, and their lips touched for what felt to Grady like the first time. He breathed in her scent, the taste of her lips, the way her lips felt on his, begging his mind to remember this. He moaned slightly, quietly, and drew her closer to him. And from what he could tell through his confused thoughts, she wanted him to continue, wanted him closer, wanted his lips on hers.

He felt Kayla's hands reach up into his hair, and the slightest inkling of a memory struggled to break through. Did she always do that when they kissed?

He pulled away slightly to catch his breath, the breath that had sped up and become shallow. Having her close was intoxicating, and he wanted more, so much more.

His jumbled thoughts could wait.

He kissed her again, harder this time, pulling her even closer. With not an inch between them, he could really feel her. He wanted her, yes, but it was more than that. He was a part of her, and she of him; he knew that now, though he didn't know how.

"Kayla," he whispered as they pulled away for only an instant. "I need you."

Kayla pulled him to her, and their lips connected once again.

After what felt like many glorious minutes, Kayla pulled away and smiled at him. She touched the side of his face, rubbing her thumb along his cheek. She wanted to ask him if that was okay, but she could sense that it was—it most *definitely* was. She stared into his eyes to see if anything had changed for him, if he remembered her.

Grady was smiling back at her, but his eyes told the real story. He very much needed her, very much wanted her, but their history together was still missing. Kayla's smile faltered slightly before she pasted it back on, choosing to be grateful that he was willing to be close to her again.

Like he'd said, even if Shani never gave him his memories back, they still had the here and now. And that was going to be okay with her if it killed her.

CHAPTER 10

Memory Is
Not Exact

KAYLA AND GRADY RETURNED to the others a few minutes later, only when Kayla was sure their appearance wouldn't give them away. Falling in love with Grady the first time with Justin watching their every move had been hard enough; having to go through that a second time would be unbearable.

She sensed Grady would need time to process everything anyway. Best to keep it quiet, if they didn't know already.

Mandy was grinning at her as soon as she entered the room. Yup, they definitely knew. *Were you guys listening in? Not cool.*

Mandy just kept grinning. *I'm just happy for you, Kayla.*

He still doesn't have his memories back. I feel like we're starting from the beginning. Kayla felt herself frowning as she dropped to a stool beside Grady and tried to quickly rearrange her features before Grady noticed. Then his voice sounded in her ear, barely a whisper. "You're doing it again, aren't you? Do they know?"

Kayla looked over at him and nodded slowly. "Sorry."

Grady shifted in his seat then made an announcement to the group. "Yes, Kayla and I are getting to know each other. At least, I am. Or again? Ugh, this is so confusing. Let's just find Shani and be done with this. Any leads?"

Mandy spoke up. "Well, since you guys were out there *forever* . . ." She grinned their direction again, and Kayla hid her eyes. "We thought maybe we should try to track Steven. Maybe he will lead us to her."

Holun chimed in. "I have tried to see her, but she has been blocking me. I think certain things take a lot more brain power for her than others, and blocking others out of her brain may be easy for her. Making Grady forget Kayla—that has got to be draining her."

Grady sat up straight. "That's it!"

Kayla started to reach out for him but pulled her hand back before it reached the leg of his light-colored khakis. "What's it?"

"Shani! If doing this to me is draining her, I don't imagine she'll be able to maintain this forever." Grady looked over at Kayla and reached for her hand. Kayla squeezed his automatically. "And even if she *can* maintain it, in her weakened state, she'll be that much easier to defeat. Either way, this means I'll come back to you."

Kayla thought about it; it made a lot of sense. All at once, she felt a burden lift off her shoulders. Grady would soon return to her, and they would be whole once again.

Unless they were missing something . . .

"So what do we do until then? Should we still track down Steven?" Mandy leaned against the main table, the Codex inches from her elbow. As she did, the book began to glow. Kayla jumped to her feet.

"Mandy!" At Kayla's outburst, Mandy followed her gaze. The book was glowing, a clear but subtle yellow light.

Mandy jerked away, but the light persisted. "What is *that?*"

Kayla ventured closer. It reminded her of something very familiar, almost like . . . "The globe!" she shouted, making everyone jump. She turned to the man she still loved. "Grady, do we still have the globe?"

Grady's eyes shot wide for a split second then turned sad as his shoulders drooped. "Nope. It was in your Jeep, which is probably at a junkyard since Shani wrecked it. Shani has to have it now."

Kayla sighed. "Does that change our game plan?"

Justin shook his head. "Not really, but we should split duties. Mandy, can you work with Holun on translating as much of the Codex as you can as quickly as you can? Maybe we'll get lucky and it will reference something that can combat mind control. It would certainly come in handy with Shani."

Mandy and Holun both nodded as Mandy answered back. "I think I saw a part where it referenced the Clan, so maybe it talks about their powers, too."

Justin nodded once at her then turned to Kayla. "Do you think there might be a way to track the globe? I figured if anyone could, you could, since you've been the one most strongly connected to it."

Kayla thought about it. It just might work. "Sure, I can try."

Grady spoke up from beside her. "What can I do?"

Justin cocked his head to the side. "We need to find Steven, track him down."

Grady nodded.

"There's a TV in the lounge around the corner, right? You're on media duty. See if you can find him or the bodies he's left in his wake. My guess is that some media outlet somewhere is reporting the museum disaster, maybe even the gas station. Maybe he's hit somewhere else since then."

"Of course."

"What are you gonna do?" Mandy asked Justin as Grady headed toward the lab door. Kayla jumped up and followed him.

"I'm staying with you and Holun. I figure I can be the most help here." Justin glanced back at Grady and Kayla. "You guys gonna be okay?"

Kayla nodded. "It'll be quieter in the lounge anyway." She glanced pointedly at Mandy and Justin. Mandy was laughing as they walked out the door.

UCF Anthropology Department Lounge

The anthropology building's main floor lounge was one Kayla'd been in a million times, but this time it felt completely foreign to her. This wasn't really the first time she'd been alone with Grady since he'd lost his memory of her, but this felt different, and her heart was breaking.

Neither of them seemed to know what to say as they entered the unoccupied room that had a kitchenette tucked between two long, floor-to-ceiling windows, a couple of round tables with plastic chairs, and a comfortable seating area against the far wall to their right. Kayla took the black leather couch facing the wall near the door, and Grady sat in a matching chair facing the blank TV, both avoiding eye contact for what seemed like a full minute. Then Grady spoke.

"This is silly."

"What is?" Kayla's eyes found his.

"Being this uncomfortable around each other."

Kayla nodded. Couldn't argue with that.

"We were definitely in love, right?"

"Yes." Her voice cracked, just a little.

"How long have we been together?"

"Since this past summer."

"When we found the Codex?"

"A little before, but basically, yes."

"How can we be so in love in that short amount of time?"

Kayla sighed, her eyes dropping. "I don't know, Grady. Some might say love at first sight? We knew each other here, at UCF, but never on a personal level. We didn't really have any meaningful conversations before Lamanai. But this summer, in Belize, something changed—or, rather, everything changed. We had a connection from the moment we found the passageway that led to the first cavern, the cavern where we found the globe."

Grady stared at her blankly.

"You don't remember the cavern?"

Grady cocked his head to one side.

Kayla thought explaining might somehow trigger a memory; she figured it was at least worth a try. "The Lamanai crew uncovered a large hole in the ground. You and I explored it on our own, after the rest of the crew had gone to their tents. The hole dropped us into a room with the Mercenaries' symbol all over the walls, floor, and ceiling."

"Lightning, right?" Grady interjected.

"Yes! Exactly." Kayla nodded. "There was a passageway off that room, which we explored. It took us further underground. We even crossed a room where the floor . . ."

"It was missing, wasn't it?"

"You remember?" Kayla was too spent to let herself hope.

But Grady nodded. "Yes, some. I—we—had to cross the room by swinging from something . . . ropes? Or vines?"

Kayla smiled sweetly at him. "Roots, actually. That was the first time you teased me, flirted with me."

"Really?"

Kayla was still smiling as she nodded. "Yeah. Then on the other side of the room, I couldn't find the entrance back into the tunnel . . ."

". . . so I reached out and pulled you in. And you stumbled into my chest."

Kayla's mouth fell open. "You remember that?"

Grady nodded slowly, almost cautiously. "A little. It seems like a dream."

Kayla shook her head. "That was no dream, Grady; we lived that. That was where our love started."

"In a dark tunnel underground?"

Kayla chuckled. "Yes. I fell against you and remember thinking how good it felt then tried to recover so you wouldn't guess what I was thinking. I figured you were just being kind."

"Oh, it was probably more than that."

Kayla laughed. It felt good to let some of her true self show with Grady again.

After she quieted, she asked a more serious question. "Do you remember anything else? Anything that might seem like a dream to you, hazy?"

Grady's brow furrowed. She'd seen him do that many times, but now, today, it looked a little bit different. "Again, very little. The farther back the memories are, the easier they are to access."

"So the new stuff, that's just completely gone." Not a question.

Grady nodded.

Silence followed, so long that Kayla almost suggested they start looking for the globe and Steven, but then Grady broke the silence with a question of his own.

"Do I still have my condo?"

"What?" Where was he going with this?

"My condo. I remember it, but I feel like I don't spend much time there. I'm just not sure *where* I spend most of my time—it's all hazy, so I assume it would be with you."

Kayla smiled to herself, nodding. "Yes, we spend nearly every free moment together."

"Are we living together?"

Kayla shook her head then looked away. "No." She didn't offer any further explanation, though she had a feeling she would need to in the next ten seconds or so.

"Why not?"

Kayla paused, not quite sure how to answer. If he didn't remember her, didn't remember their relationship, he wouldn't know that they'd never had sex. Great. That conversation was certainly hard enough the first time. She prayed she wouldn't have to go into any more detail, then prayed that if she did, he would understand. Again.

"We just . . . still need our own space."

"Then we haven't slept together." It was a statement, which surprised her.

"No. How do you know that?"

"Oh, I'm sure I would remember that."

Kayla wanted to smack him. Instead, she just shot him a disapproving look, fighting back the satisfied grin that threatened to rise to the surface and mostly losing.

Grady chuckled. "Hey, I'm kidding." He got up and joined her on the couch. "Sorry, just trying to lighten the mood." He reached for her hand, and Kayla let him take it. "Given the way you've talked about us, I think you know I would never take advantage of you, would never ask that of you until you were ready. You're safe with me—when I remember you, and even when I don't."

Kayla felt tears threatening, but she turned to Grady anyway. "That's almost exactly what you told me before."

Grady smiled sweetly at her. "Really? Tell me."

Kayla started relaying moment after moment of their own love story, Grady hearing them as if for the first time. She was sure she was forgetting some of the moments, but she hit on all the important ones, at least to her.

When she was done, she sat silently and let Grady digest all the information she'd given him. After several moments, he spoke. "Wow."

"And that's what you said when we really kissed for the first time. Admittedly, it was pretty intense."

Grady chuckled. "I bet it was, if today was any indication."

Kayla wouldn't have thought it possible, but she actually thought she might have blushed.

They fell silent again, Grady's hand still holding hers, then: "This must be horrible for you."

Kayla nodded. "I just feel like Shani took everything from us, all at once."

Grady frowned then stared off into space. "She did. But you just told me several of our stories, and now those I will remember."

"But not like you were there, which you were."

He looked back at her, caught her gaze. "True. But the more I hear about us, the more I feel for you, Kayla. The stronger I feel for you. With everything you've told me, I know our love was strong, maybe even stronger than most, and that bond can't easily be broken or forgotten. Shani won't be able to fight my subconscious much longer—I can sense it. And I think it's because our love was—is—so strong."

Kayla smiled at him, but she could feel the sadness reach her eyes. "I hope you're right, Grady."

Grady held her gaze for a few moments then stood up to move back to the chair, reaching into his pocket for his phone as he did. "I'm going to check the internet for reports of Steven. Maybe you can try to find the globe?"

Kayla shrugged. "I'll try, but if Shani is blocking our telepathy and your memory, there's a good chance she's blocking us from finding that, too."

"Or she's already stretched too thin, and it'll lead us right to her."

Kayla smirked at him. "Good point. Can't hurt to try."

CHAPTER 11

Hope, Finally

FORTY MINUTES, THREE SOCIAL MEDIA outlets, and five
TV stations later, Grady was about to give up. Maybe Steven
was done? He had attacked and killed Simón and Hannah—
maybe the revenge he wanted had been satisfied.

Didn't seem likely. It never was that easy, was it? Even if
Steven's personal vendettas had been appeased, Shani's
weren't. Her determination to make the four of them suffer
was readily apparent, and he suspected she'd barely gotten
started.

Grady sighed, muting the TV and leaning back in the
cushioned chair. He glanced over at Kayla. Her eyes were
gently closed, her legs were crossed on the couch beneath
her, and her hands rested on her knees, palms up. Did she do
this often? She was clearly meditating—did it help her focus
somehow? For the millionth time today, he wished he could
remember.

Then something on the TV caught his eye. He reached for the remote and turned up the sound.

"—five, where a crash of unknown origin has occurred at a rest stop just north of Orlando. It appears an SUV crashed into the side of a parked car." An aerial video of the crash site played, and Grady sat up straighter. The SUV almost looked like it had been *pushed* into the other car . . .

"What happened?" Kayla uncrossed her legs and pulled them up beside her on the couch as she spoke, eyeing the TV.

Grady nodded toward the screen. "Something strange." The news station moved on to the next story, so Grady muted the TV and turned to Kayla. "Looks like an SUV crashed into another car—but they appear to have hit each other from the side." He swallowed hard, still staring at the TV, then looked over at Kayla. "It couldn't be Steven, but it still doesn't sit well with me. My gut tells me that Shani or the globe—or both—is involved here."

Kayla nodded, but Grady thought her eyes looked a little sad. "You're probably right." Kayla unfolded her legs and stood up. "But we have to go." Grady followed suit, though he wasn't entirely sure why.

"What's up?" he asked, turning off the TV and setting the remote on the coffee table in front of him.

"They've found something. We've got to get back to the lab."

Warehouse Near the University of Central Florida

Shani drove the boys to an abandoned warehouse she'd procured just after she'd come here. She'd sensed she would eventually need a quiet, hidden place to crash. She'd been right.

Now she sat across from Tyler in two beat-up folding chairs they'd found stashed inside the warehouse. She'd driven Tyler's sporty coupe right inside when they'd arrived and left the headlights on to give them a little light to talk—there weren't many windows in here, and it was dark outside, anyway. Steven had dutifully closed the garage door behind them before wandering around the warehouse perimeter. Shani didn't really care what he did as long as he didn't draw any attention to himself.

"Tyler, there are some things I need to explain to you," Shani began, trying to catch his gaze.

Tyler's eyes were darting around the darkened warehouse, looking for all the world like a scared little boy who'd been kidnapped.

"Tyler!" Shani was careful not to yell too loudly, but she needed his attention. This young man's life had changed in an instant, and he deserved to know what was going on. And the quicker he understood and accepted it, the quicker she could use him to execute her plans.

Tyler finally looked at her, and she held his gaze. She paused, then she sighed; best to rip off the bandage. "You were given a power back at the rest stop." She paused, watching his face. She supposed, under normal circumstances, that Tyler would have laughed off what she'd just said and dismissed it as a fairy tale, but feeling the power release from you was hard to ignore. She would know.

Tyler's eyes grew wide, and he looked like he was about to throw up. Shani sure hoped not.

She continued. "It appears you were given the power to release energy from your mouth when you yell. That bright light you saw—right before you were given this power—came from a powerful globe. That globe gives people powers. People who have a connection to it somewhere in their history.

My guess is that somewhere in your family tree is someone of Mayan descent."

The blood had drained from Tyler's face, and now he *really* looked like he was about to vomit. Shani didn't like that at all. "If you're going to be sick, please do it back there." She nodded past him, into the darkness. Tyler nodded quickly then stood and ran.

Shani rolled her eyes, leaning back in her chair and crossing her arms. Then she saw a small flash and heard some scraps of metal scatter across the ground as the sound of Tyler losing his last meal reached her ears. "Could you please do that more quietly?" she called. "We can't have you putting a hole in the cement."

After a moment, Tyler came back into the light, wiping his mouth. Shani squinted, curling her lips and pulling back slightly. *Disgusting.* "Are you finished?"

Tyler nodded.

"Are you okay?"

Again, a nod.

"Okay, here's how I'm thinking your power works. You can whisper, and probably even talk in a somewhat-normal tone of voice, but I wouldn't recommend raising your voice or getting angry. It could be your emotions that trigger this power, so I'd try to stay as even-keeled as possible until you get it under control."

Tyler swallowed then attempted a question at a low volume. "What . . . why did this happen to me? How do we fix it?"

Shani leaned forward, placing her elbows on her knees. She sighed again. "I'm sorry, Tyler, but this is irreversible. You will always have this power."

For the first time since she'd met him, Tyler looked like he was about to cry. Shani sensed he needed a sympathetic shoulder more than a drill sergeant, so she acquiesced. She scratched her chair across the gray cement to sit next to him then reached to put a hand on his shoulder.

"I'm so sorry, Tyler." Shani rubbed his shoulder as his tears fell. She let him cry. Sorrow was an important part of the grief process, and this was another step in the right direction. *Let him get there, Shani,* she reminded herself. *Patience.*

Shani wasn't used to comforting others, but she supposed this little escapade with the globe was changing more than just other people—she was changing, too, though she fought it. She was having to do things she would never normally have done, fake who she was, and it was exhausting.

Once his tears started to dry up, Tyler blinked against the bright light of the headlights and looked over at Shani. "So who's Steven?"

Satisfied Tyler was comforted, Shani leaned back in her chair and smiled. "You remembered."

"Of . . . course." Tyler's second word was softer than the first as if he'd just remembered his power.

Shani crossed her arms again. "Steven is another man like you."

"He can release energy from his mouth?"

Shani chuckled. "No. He's invisible."

Tyler's mouth dropped open. "Really?"

Shani threw her head back, laughing, then nodded. "Really. Steven?" She called to the enormous warehouse. She heard him stop at the sound of her voice and head back toward them. In a few moments, he was right beside her. Shani presented the empty space where Steven stood with a flourish of her right hand. "Tyler, meet Steven."

Tyler blinked, searching the space Shani had indicated. Shani smiled, fighting back a laugh. "Steven, please introduce yourself to Tyler."

The empty space to Shani's right spoke. "Hello, Tyler. Glad you've joined the team."

Tyler jumped back, his chair scratching along the ground before it snapped shut as Tyler leapt to his feet.

"Tyler . . ." Shani cautioned, "please control your surprise."

The young man was staring wide-eyed at the void who'd just spoken, but he nodded without shifting his gaze. He swallowed once, blinked a few times, then reached down for his chair and set it up without moving his eyes from that same spot. "How . . ." he started as he sat back down. "Where did you come from?"

Steven chuckled, a deep, throaty laugh that seemed to come out of thin air. "I was a guard at the museum where the globe was on display. It turned me."

Shani was watching Tyler's reaction like a hawk. She could sense all of his emotions, but she couldn't quite get a read on what he'd do next. She'd need to be careful.

Tyler was nodding. "That's messed up."

Steven laughed again. "Yes. But it's not without perks."

Tyler's eyebrow went up. "Oh, yeah? Like what?"

Shani could sense Steven's bloodlust as he remembered his earlier kills. So she interrupted him; they didn't have time for Tyler to right the wrongs in his own life. "Okay, boys, that's enough. There will be plenty of time to explore your powers after we're done."

"Done with what?" Tyler was back to his reserved self.

Shani stood. "We have some work to do." She filled Tyler in on the Four, their dangerous powers, and how they had to be stopped. She left out a lot, but she told him just enough for him to want to join them.

And when she was done, as she predicted, he agreed to do so. He gave some excuse about being able to take his finals online . . .

Shani smiled at her newfound soldier in this war. She hoped he'd be a good one. Probably better than Steven, anyway.

But it was time to wrap this up, so she motioned for the boys to pile into the car. Shani wanted to head to the private airport where a plane sat ready for them to depart, but they had a stop to make first—an important, absolutely necessary one.

They'd just have to make it quick.

She knew that any more time spent in Orlando only delayed the inevitable and greatly increased the odds that the Four would discover *the* story, the story of the artifacts, likely detailed in the Codex. The story of the treasure the Elders collected over the centuries and hoarded from the most deserving. Like her.

She deserved those artifacts so much more than the Four did; she was of true Mayan descent, after all. Those Americans should never have been given the Power of the Codex, and they certainly didn't deserve her Clan's treasure.

She would stop them. She had to. She would find the artifacts and take them for herself. It was the only way she could protect herself from the Four, from the powers of these two men.

And if the globe was going to be giving more and more people powers—as she suspected it would—she would need to protect herself from powers that hadn't even been created yet.

Which made this brief stop even more important. Shani sighed as she pulled into a small, palm-tree-lined cul-de-sac, streetlights lighting up patches of the road in a predictable, orange-colored pattern. The globe wasn't done—she could sense it—but she could use that. She was nothing if not opportunistic.

She parked Tyler's coupe in the driveway of a cute home with only an upstairs light on. Shani ordered the boys to stay in the car, grabbed her black bag, then headed up the walkway to ring the doorbell.

This whole thing with the globe was going to be a huge mess. But maybe this would help, just a little. If it worked.

Shani smiled as a pretty young girl with long, blonde hair and brown eyes answered the door. "Yes?"

Shani's smile widened at the sight of the girl she'd come to see. "My name is Shani. I have something very important to discuss with you."

The girl blinked then shifted her gaze to the bag Shani was carrying. "Are you sure? Me?"

Shani smiled again at her innocence. That would change. "Yes. Mandy sent me; she needs your help."

Recognition flashed in the girl's eyes before the fear set in. "Oh, no! Is she okay?"

Shani nodded, the sweet smile still plastered on her face. "Yes, of course! She just couldn't come herself."

The girl's face relaxed. "Oh! Okay." She opened the door widely, and Shani stepped over the threshold.

Moments later, a light brighter than the sun glared out from the home's front picture window and shattered the darkness, but only for a moment. Then all was dark once again.

Main Anthropology Lab, University of Central Florida

Mandy waved them over as soon as they walked through the door. "Look! Holun found something!" She jabbed at the page more than once. Kayla could feel her friend's excitement from the second Mandy had called her to the lab.

Kayla walked over to examine it, reaching for the mobile camera and adjusting it until the text showed on the nearby monitor. She zoomed in carefully then leaned toward the screen.

For a few seconds, the room was silent. Then Kayla gasped. "Grady!" She turned to face him. His eyes were wide, and in that moment she just wanted to run to him. Instead, she let him take a few steps toward her.

"What is it?"

Kayla couldn't help the grin that spread across her face. "This text here"—now she was jabbing at it like Mandy had been—"means that we can save you. If this is true, we *will* get your memories back."

Grady froze. Kayla understood; denial came first, a natural response to unbelievable yet incredible news. "Are . . . are you sure?"

Kayla nodded vigorously, stepping toward him, reaching for his hand. She led him to the book. "Look! Read for your-self."

Kayla looked on as Grady perused the text. He took longer to translate it than she'd taken, but Kayla knew the minute he did.

"See?" Kayla felt like she would jump out of her skin.

For a moment, nobody moved. Then Grady whipped around and threw his arms around Kayla, sweeping her off her feet and into the most uninhibited hug she could've imag-ined. They stayed there for several long moments, and Kayla sunk into his embrace. Here, in his arms, she could almost believe this nightmare was nearly over.

Grady eventually set Kayla down and pulled away, but only far enough to see her face. "Does this really mean we can defeat Shani's mind control without needing to defeat her?"

Kayla nodded at him with a teary smile. "Yes. It says this artifact has the power to combat mind control."

"That's incredible! If it's true, this nightmare may soon be over." Kayla thought the way their thoughts were so similar sometimes was amazing. "So where do we find it?"

Mandy was already transcribing the text into English. "I'm not sure. There's a part here I can't quite decipher . . . Holun? I could use your expertise."

Holun came around the table and looked at the text. Then all the blood drained from his face.

"Holun," Mandy started, "what is it?" She placed a hand on his shoulder.

Holun was a concerning shade of white, especially considering his skin was usually several shades darker than Mandy's fair skin. She glanced over at Justin, who was sitting on a stool behind her. He shrugged then went back to watching Holun.

Mandy hoped Holun would speak soon. Though slightly illogical, she felt responsible for him. If anything happened to him, she wouldn't be able to forgive herself.

Then Holun spoke, his voice monotone and dull, his eyes still trained on the page. "I know where the artifact is."

Mandy knew there would be more, so she waited.

"Belize."

Mandy blinked. "Belize? Where in Belize?"

Holun's eyes finally left the book, and his gaze fell on Mandy. "Home. At least, my old home. The Clan has it."

Mandy gasped.

Kayla jumped in, and Holun felt her gaze on him. "How could that possibly be, Holun? Why would your family keep an object like that? How do they even know about it or what it can do?"

Holun sighed then reached for a stool, hoisting himself on top of it. This was going to be a long story.

He swallowed once then began. "My Clan was created shortly after the Old Ones destroyed the Mayan empire, separated the book into four pieces, and scattered them across the continents. The story goes that we fell from heaven in the form of lightning to guard the Secret of the Codex—after the Old Ones denounced their powers and abandoned the book— so it did not fall into the wrong hands. When we 'fell from heaven'"—Holun raised his hands to give air quotes—"several other pieces of the history of the Old Ones came with us. Our most important job, of course, was to keep the locations of the four parts of the Codex secret, watching over them to make sure they were not disturbed. Which worked for centuries—until you four came along, that is." He smiled, but he could tell that it didn't reach his eyes.

"But we were also given several artifacts to keep hidden, to protect until they needed to be used. I always thought they were for us to use in the battle to protect the Codex. But since my Clan lost that battle—and Na-um did not even use them—perhaps they were meant for the four of you all along." Holun paused to take a breath.

"Some of the artifacts may be worthless now or simply lost; no one really seems to know. There were so many, and the stories about them got so complicated that no one can say for sure what the artifacts look like or where they are hidden.

It is said that the Elders alone know where the most valuable are stored. I would imagine this artifact would be among those; if it is still around, they probably used it when they were working with Shani to protect themselves against her. I would think that this artifact, the one that protects whoever has it from mind control, is being held very close to the Elders."

As Holun finished talking, he realized suddenly that his mouth had gotten very dry. He tried to swallow, but his tongue felt like it was sticking to the roof of his mouth.

He would have to face his Clan again. He would have to account for the time he'd been missing, suffer the insults and agony of the Clan's reprisal for his betrayal, face rejection from everyone he'd ever known or loved.

He thought he was going to be sick.

Kayla, seated right next to Holun, just sat thinking about all he'd told them. It really made sense, didn't it?

Makes perfect sense to me, too. Justin chimed in.

Mandy nodded from where she sat.

"Oh, come on, guys. I can tell when you're reading each other's minds, remember?" Grady interjected. "You each need to work on your poker face."

Kayla reached for his hand. "We're sorry. I know this must be so frustrating. We were just thinking that what Holun said makes sense. And once we go retrieve the artifact, you'll be able to hear us, too, and only Holun will be left out."

"Hey!" Holun crossed his arms and scowled. Kayla laughed.

"So what do we do next?" Grady asked. "How do we get the artifact from the Elders?"

Kayla looked over at their young friend. "Holun? I think we need a plan."

CHAPTER 12

The Power of One Man

Just Outside the Lamanai Archaeological Project,
Northern Belize

IT'D BEEN HOURS SINCE he'd last seen another person, right? It had to have been hours; he sensed the sun had long since dropped below the mountains to the west.

He glanced down at the floor where he sat raking his fingers through the cool, loose dirt as a chain clinked beside him. He cursed to himself. He'd been here for several days, but he'd never get used to the shackles around his wrists and ankles. Considering he was behind bars—as unlikely they seemed in this primitive cave—the shackles seemed redundant anyway.

"You!"

Na-um cringed at his guard's command in their native tongue. What did Sochan want now? Sochan, the same man who'd followed him into battle against the Americans just a few months ago, now clearly relished treating his former leader like a dog.

Na-um jumped to his feet, head bowed, obliging the guard whose hand was already fingering the whip on his hip. His long, black hair fell in front of his face. He knew if he didn't stand right away, he'd feel the sting of that whip across his bare back. He'd already learned that lesson, several times. He had plenty of scars to prove it.

Na-um bowed deeper for the man glaring at him through the bars, keeping his mouth shut.

"Your dinner." The man threw a rotting apple, a moldy piece of bread, and a surprisingly delicious-looking piece of cooked meat through the bars and into the dirt beside his captor then sauntered off.

Na-um sighed as the guard left. Scraps. That's all they ever gave him. He missed his hut in the village, one of the largest, and the ample feasts that awaited all warriors upon their return home. Even in the woods, he would have fared better than this. Why hadn't he just run when he'd had the chance?

He leaned down to wipe the dirt off the bread, removed the moldy part, then took a bite of the stale piece as he returned to the ground.

The meat was cooked well but was long since cooked and had gotten quite cold. Na-um ate it eagerly, though, grateful for the courtesy of cooked meat—and meat that wasn't rotting. There'd been more than one day he'd gone hungry, opting to forgo sickness from rotten meat.

The apple was nearly a lost cause, but Na-um found a few edible pieces. After his small meal was over, he stared up at the rocky ceiling, wondering for the millionth time where he was. This was a cave of some sort, that much was obvious, but his Clan did not dwell in caves. And who knew how these bars got here?

He'd taken to counting the days by scratching in the dirt with his finger. He barely got a sense of daylight from the turn in the tunnel Sochan always used to come and go, but he could sense which meal was his last for the day and when the guard was first awoken or tired at the end of the day.

He glanced over at his count in the dirt, adding another notch to the unfortunate art piece. Yes, he'd been here nearly two weeks.

He leaned his head against the back wall, closing his eyes and recalling, again for the millionth time, how he'd come to be imprisoned here. The circumstances were really stupid— no, *he'd* been really stupid—and now he was paying for his perceived "sins" against the Clan. It had all started with that horrible battle, the one with the Americans . . .

Suddenly, something shattered the usual quiet in the cave, and Na-um's eyes shot open. He sat straight up, chains protesting loudly around him.

Then the men who'd disrupted his night rounded the corner in the tunnel and came into view. He froze as his stomach dropped.

The Elders, all five of them clothed in identical long, white robes, entered the small room and formed a straight line in front of Na-um's cell. He shifted his weight and looked away from their piercing gazes. He felt like an animal in a cage. Which, he supposed, was pretty much true.

Na-um continued to stare at the ground, knowing meeting their gaze would probably bring some unspeakable punishment, one much worse than Sochan could ever dole out. He didn't dare utter a word.

"Na-um." Even without looking up, Na-um knew the unmistakable command had come from Chac, the Elders' unofficial leader. But he also knew such a command must be heeded, and immediately. So he glanced up to meet Chac's gaze. The pit in his stomach grew larger.

"Na-um, we came to discuss your fate." Zotz, the oldest and most revered Elder began the conversation in their native K'iche. "On your feet."

Na-um jumped up without hesitation.

"We wanted to see if you have changed your mind." Chac didn't waste time getting to the point.

Na-um knew exactly what he was referring to. It was the reason he was in here in the first place. "I have considered all my options."

"That's not an answer!" This came from the hothead, Bacob.

Perceptive, Na-um thought. He had no idea how to get out of this one, so he was stalling, hoping against hope that something would come to him. He couldn't give them the answer they wanted, not really. For all he knew, they would know if he was lying.

Tohil, the most agreeable Elder, saved him. "Na-um, we just need you on our side. You show us you are, and you will be released from this godforsaken cave." He glanced around at the monotone walls, ceiling, and floor then back at Na-um.

Na-um cocked his head to one side. Was Tohil offering him a way out? "How could I do that?"

Kucumatz, the youngest but still wise Elder, jumped in. "We need you to do something for us."

Na-um nodded but stayed silent. Where were they going with this?

Chac took over. "We have received word that the Four are headed here."

Na-um swallowed hard. This was the first time he'd heard the Elders refer to the Americans as the "Four." This was the way the Clan's prophecies spoke about them, and the simple fact that the Elders were now calling them that meant the rules were changing. If the Elders had accepted them as the new keepers of the Codex and all its powers, they must have a new plan. And if Na-um could help them with it, get out of this cave . . .

"What can I do?"

Bacob now smiled. It may have been the first time Na-um had seen him smile; it looked out of place on his large features. "You must help us evade them—with the help of your sister."

Na-um balked. "Shani is *here*?"

By now, all of Bacob's teeth were showing, and Na-um shifted his weight.

Tohil cut in. "She is on her way."

No one said anything else, so Na-um sensed he should move past it quickly. He nodded once. "Of course. Anything I can do to help."

Evading the Americans—that should be easy enough, right? Of course, that's what he'd thought this summer, and they all knew how that had turned out . . .

His mind drifted back to their battle with the Americans—their shameful loss against four utterly unskilled, unprepared civilians who knew little about the Codex and the powers it held, but four civilians who had nevertheless defeated them and forced Na-um and the remainder of his army to retreat.

The sound of keys rattling drew his attention back to the present. Chac inserted the skeleton key into the door of the cage he was in, unlocked the door in one swift motion, then bent to remove the shackles from Na-um's wrists and ankles.

Na-um rubbed his wrists as Chac motioned to the exit. Na-um glanced his way then stepped outside of his cage for the first time in weeks. He followed the Elders through the cave and out into the warm darkness of the evening.

Orlando International Airport

Kayla set her book on the cushioned bench beside her and glanced around the packed waiting area, overrun despite the late hour. She never would've imagined she'd be preparing to board a flight for Belize once again, and this quickly. Since she wasn't sure when they'd be back—they needed to find the Clan, who Holun heard had moved, and obtain the artifact they needed to help Grady, after all—she'd made sure her TA could cover her classes on Tuesday. The class before Thanksgiving was always poorly attended anyway, especially since her students turned their papers in electronically.

Grady had done the same for his Monday and Wednesday classes, so hopefully they would have at least a full week to resolve this. She hoped it would be enough time.

She'd shot off a quick text to confirm with her TA before they'd left UCF then made two quick pit stops: first at her condo, where she packed quickly, then on to Grady's place. She'd kept Grady company as he packed, and they'd promised Mandy and Justin they would meet them at the airport to catch the red-eye to Belize City.

Kayla was not looking forward to meeting any members of the Clan again. The first time was definitely bad enough.

One does not easily forget a huge army trying to kill them.

Kayla glanced across the aisle to where Mandy and Justin were sitting, spied Justin's hand closed around Mandy's on the seat between them. Kayla felt a tugging at her heart and longed for the day Grady would remember touching her like that.

She glanced over at Grady, who was sitting beside her, and gave him a warm smile. He returned it, but somehow it was less than satisfying. She needed him to come back to her. She needed him close to her with no reservations.

She really just needed this to work.

If what the Codex said about the artifact was true—and Kayla suspected it was; the Codex had never led them wrong before—she would have Grady back soon. She couldn't wait.

Lamanai Archaeological Project, Northern Belize

Kayla stepped out of the vehicle they'd rented at the airport and surveyed the dig, lit up by spotlights in the early morning hours before sunrise. Had it really only been a few months since they'd been here? She glanced over at Grady, who was looking around as well.

So much had changed.

As she and the others gathered their bags from the back of the Jeep, something tugged at her heart, something she couldn't quite put a finger on. She missed being close to Grady, missed their relationship, but there was more to it; she could tell. Though missing Grady was a large part of it, something else still wasn't quite right.

He'd determined to start working on their relationship again, start getting to know her again, but she felt like it was falling short. Not that she wasn't grateful—she most certainly was—but Grady wouldn't be *her* Grady again until he remembered her, remembered them, remembered everything.

But what if he never did? What if, somehow, what Shani had done was permanent?

Could she live with that?

The question had been haunting her the whole plane ride here despite the nerves that showed up whenever she flew. Could she survive in a relationship with a man she loved if he didn't know the whole story? Didn't know her completely?

She could reason it away, say that their current relationship started when he started wooing her again, but she would always know this other story—their original story—that would forever hold a special place in her heart. The story that Grady might never remember.

She wanted to be okay with it, she really did. And she really did love Grady, with everything she had. But how did she reconcile this?

And there at the edge of the steamy rainforest, as they walked through the early morning darkness to the mess tent she remembered so well, Kayla felt a shift happen. A tiny fissure opened up, one that cracked the seemingly immutable bond between her and Grady inside her, and Kayla felt that something bad was coming. She loved him, yes, but something was now between them, something she didn't know how to fight.

She longed for this nightmare to be over. She longed for Grady, the way they were just days ago, where nothing was hidden between them. Where their love was pure and complete, and nothing could shake them.

Because now something had. And down in the depths of her soul, she wondered if they would ever be the same again.

There was really only one answer, only one thing that would make this all okay. She knew that no matter what happened, she had to fight. So she made up her mind, then and there: They would find the artifact, block Shani's mind control, and destroy her.

Mercenaries' Camp, Northern Belize

Shani, the boys, and her newest recruit had arrived in Belize early this morning. Shani had easily been able to persuade someone from the Clan to pick them up at the airport, even in the early morning hours.

She'd felt butterflies in her stomach the entire trip here. Chac had assured her that the help she'd offered the Clan this past summer had atoned for her past misdeeds—the reason she'd left in the first place, so many years ago—and that she was welcome anytime, but she still had misgivings. There were likely some who did not agree with the Elders' decision.

As the SUV neared the camp and the canvas tents came into view, Shani wiped a tear from her cheek and turned toward the window. She was grateful the Clan had been willing to take her back, but what of her beloved Alex? She hadn't spoken to him since last summer, since she'd run away in shame to hide from her brother, his army, and those insufferable Americans. She desperately missed him, and just knowing he was so close—being in the same country was rare for them lately—but she wouldn't be able to see him tore her heart into pieces.

This had all started because of her love for him, and now Fate had thrown a cruel wrench in her plans. She just wanted this done so she could go back to him without fear of reprisal —from the Clan, the Elders, Na-um, or the Four.

If that would ever be possible.

The four travelers and their driver reached the camp just as the sun was starting to appear over the mountains to the east. Shani jumped out of the passenger side, adjusting her khaki shorts and fitted black t-shirt as she did, then took a deep breath. She'd been away for so many years, yet the smell of campfires and damp earth still brought her back to her childhood here in Belize, her years spent growing into the woman she was now. She gritted her teeth at the thought.

But despite the less-than-happy memories in her past, she missed that simpler time, one before she knew about the Secret, the Elders, the Power of the Codex and its prophecies, any of it. Before she'd been banished from her Clan for loving someone outside of it. Before she'd been forced to make the impossible choice to leave everything she'd ever known to run into the arms of the only man she'd ever loved.

She blinked hard to keep another tear from running down her cheek.

"Shani!" Chac's thunderous welcome sounded from a good distance away. Shani quickly pasted on a smile—one that she was certain would pass as genuine—as he approached in a long, white robe cinched tight with a leather strap tied around his waist, the same garb all the Elders commonly wore. His long, white hair fluttered untamed in the light breeze.

She grabbed her bag out of the back of the vehicle and set it on the ground next to her as he neared. His impenetrable gaze caught hers as he reached the SUV.

He embraced her then pulled back to look her over. "My dear, how you have grown! You have become quite a beautiful young woman." Only then did he seem to notice she wasn't alone. "And who are your friends?"

Shani motioned to Tyler, who was helping unload their luggage. She put her arms on his shoulders after he set the last suitcase on the ground and stepped to her side. "Chac, this is Tyler. We met him in Florida. The globe affected him."

Chac raised a white eyebrow toward Shani as he shook Tyler's offered hand. "Affected? How?"

Shani was shocked he didn't know already. Or maybe he did, but he wasn't sharing for some reason. No one really knew exactly what the Elders could do—or how they knew so much. "The globe has started, um, *turning* people, or giving them powers. Tyler here has the ability to focus pure energy out of his lungs and through his mouth with the power of an explosion, as we've already witnessed." Shani smiled over at the young man, who was staring at Chac wide-eyed. Surely he was balking at the way he was dressed. She supposed she should have warned them. "Tyler?" She squeezed his shoulder.

Tyler blinked and closed his slightly open mouth. "Oh, sorry . . . nice to meet you, Chac." He stumbled over the pronunciation of their leader's name, but Shani thought he made a decent effort.

Though no one knew *all* of the Elders' powers, Shani knew that Chac's perceptions were among the sharpest in the Clan—he would feel Steven's presence, probably even stronger than she did, so she introduced her first recruit quickly. "The man you don't see is Steven. I believe it's quite apparent what power the globe gave him."

Chac smiled widely, nodding in Steven's direction. "Yes. Nice to meet you, Steven."

Shani walked over to the back door of the SUV, pulling on the handle carefully, slowly, so as not to spook her last passenger. Shani beckoned her latest recruit forward, who stepped out carefully, eyes wide and darting around at the surrounding rainforest. Shani guided her toward Chac without touching her. "And this is the newest globe transformation." She smiled down at the young woman, who looked up at her with unspeakably innocent eyes. Her fitted wrap dress covered in delicate flowers only amplified her naïveté. Ah, to be that young and trusting again . . .

Shani dropped an arm around her shoulders, pulling her into a side hug. "This, Chac, is Alexia. Her power is . . . complicated."

Chac eyed Shani for the briefest of seconds then extended his hand to the girl, his smile warm and friendly. "It is very nice to meet you, Alexia."

The girl nodded once then whispered a quiet "thank you" as she quickly shook Chac's hand then pulled it back, shoving it in her pocket.

Chac nodded toward their driver. "Sochan here will show you three to your tents." He nodded at them before they headed into the village. "Shani, may I speak with you alone?"

Shani nodded, knowing no other response was an option. Chac led them into the forest, away from the village and any prying eyes—or ears. "Did you bring the globe here?"

Right to the point, I see. Shani swallowed once. "I did, but I have it buried in my luggage." She looked back toward the village where she'd left her black bag on the ground.

Chac actually looked a little concerned. "Did you not think of the risk in bringing it here?"

Shani *had* thought about that, but she knew that they would need it. She was certain they wouldn't have any chance against the Four without it. "Yes, I thought about the risk. But if we are to ever gain an advantage over the four Americans, we must have it on our side."

Chac sighed, his hands on his waist as he paced in a short line. "Yes, I agree. But how can we prevent it from turning our people? Clearly, it has been activated, and it likely will not stop in its effort to give powers to everyone it comes in contact with."

Shani dared speak up; it was too important to overlook. "It seems to only be turning people with Mayan heritage."

"Which is our entire village!" Chac's voice uncharacteristically rose, and Shani blinked. He quickly recovered. "Please keep the globe away from the population as much as possible. Bury it here in the forest if you need to. Or . . ."

He paused, and Shani leaned in. "What?"

Chac was still pacing and now looked back toward the village, his brows furrowed. "We have somewhere to hide it, a place where it shouldn't be able to turn any others."

Shani raised an eyebrow but remained silent.

Chac sighed again then stopped his pacing to stand right in front of her. "Yes, I know just the place." Then he smiled, his nearly black eyes kind, as he placed his hand on Shani's shoulder and led her back toward the village. "So how have you been?"

Shani returned his smile as they walked. "I have been working for several years tracking the four Americans. Now that the time has come to implement our plans, it seems almost surreal."

Chac chuckled. "That it does, Shani. That it does."

Just then, right before the canvas tents came into view, an unbearable metallic screeching reached Shani's ears. She cringed, folding in two as she covered her ears, groaning.

Chac seemed to be hearing it as well, and Shani instantly knew what had happened. She sprinted back to where she'd left her bag and saw a young girl no more than thirteen years of age—and dressed in the Clan's unmistakable natural cloth, strips of leather, and animal fur—bent near it. Her arms were outstretched toward the SUV, which was currently being mangled in the most horrific and unnatural manner Shani had ever seen.

No, not again. Not so soon! Shani's stomach dropped, and she ran over to the girl, grabbing her and pulling her away from the globe and what was now a destroyed pile of scrap metal.

The girl was crying. "I'm . . . sorry. I, I didn't . . . know . . . I couldn't stop . . ." she gasped in their native K'iche between sobs.

Shani pulled her close and stroked her hair. She could play the compassionate mother when she needed to. "Shh, it's okay. I know," she repeated on a loop, trying to calm the girl down. As she did, the metallic screeching slowly subsided.

The girl's sobs finally quieted, and Shani looked up at Chac. "We need to get that out of here now."

Chac nodded, all humor gone from his features. "I will make the arrangements immediately."

From behind a tree at the edge of the forest, out of sight of Shani, Chac, and the girl, a young woman stared wide-eyed at the scene playing out before her. She turned and leaned against the back of the tree, hidden from the others, squeezing her eyes shut as if to block the images she'd just seen, the sounds she'd just heard.

Then she felt something, a tingling in her hands that moved up her arms, down her torso, out to her toes, up to the top of her head. She opened her eyes, hesitantly lifting her trembling hands to waist level and slowly lowering her gaze.

Her hands were glowing. The girl closed her eyes again to slow the breathing that had just become rapid, shoving her hands behind her as if being hidden would stop them from shining.

She stayed there several minutes, only opening her eyes and leaning around the tree after she hadn't heard any movement for a long while. After she was certain she was alone, she quickly darted into the clearing and headed back to her tent.

True to Chac's word, just over ten minutes later a small procession was headed outside of the camp, into the rainforest, toward the mountains. Shani wanted to ask where they were going, but it seemed a ridiculous question—and quite possibly an insubordinate one—so she kept quiet. She would find out soon enough.

They quickly reached the base of one of the mountains she'd seen from the camp and started up it in a haphazard line. Shani followed behind Chac, her black bag in hand, trying to emphasize her subservience by staying quiet and compliant. She knew that would be the best way to gain the Elder's trust.

She could tell the surface was evening out before they reached it, so she wasn't surprised to climb up on a flat plateau, one surrounded by rainforest and rocks on three sides and a steep drop off on the other. She eyed the drop off from a safe distance—she'd never been a big fan of dangerous heights.

Far away from the edge of the cliff, Shani set down the bag that contained the globe and surveyed their surroundings. This rocky plateau—larger than even the largest of the Elders' tents—seemed innocuous.

Why on earth had Chac brought them here?

She eyed the rest of their small procession as they arrived on the rocky plateau and formed a line off to the side, facing Chac. Shani recognized some of the handsome soldiers from her childhood—and by the looks some of them were giving her, they recognized her, too. She hid her eyes.

Chac and his helper—one of the oldest soldiers, Shani surmised—moved to the center of the plateau, a strong gust kicking up the long robe of the Elder. Then Chac turned his back to the dizzying drop off and faced Shani and the soldiers. His gaze caught hers, and she shifted her weight under his stare until she realized he was staring like he could see right through her. What did she know—maybe he actually could.

Shani turned and looked behind her. All she saw was a large boulder nestled up to the side of the mountain, not very wide but quite tall, looking completely unimportant.

"'Always look for more than meets the eye.'" Chac answered her unasked question in their native tongue with a common saying of the Clan.

How did he know what I was thinking?

Chac smiled at Shani and extended his hand toward her. She joined him hesitantly.

"I can sense your heart, my dear. I sense your fear of heights as well as your inability to see what's right in front of you." Chac pointed to where she was standing just moments ago. He was smiling so serenely that Shani couldn't even take offense. She just followed his pointed finger and stared.

Right before her eyes, that thin but tall boulder started to open up. She cast a sideways glance at Chac, whose arms were both outstretched toward the boulder, looking just like he was coaxing a set of doors apart from a distance.

She glanced back at the boulder, where a hole large enough for a person to walk through now gaped open.

Chac had been doing exactly what she'd thought.

Lamanai Archaeological Project, Belize

Kayla awoke with a start. Her eyes shot open, scanning the ceiling of her tent lit by the morning sun. *What was that?*

The sound came again, making Kayla certain she'd heard something that had wrenched her from her sleep. She had probably only been asleep a few hours—given their late night, they had all decided to get some rest before planning their next move.

She sat up straight, her cot creaking under the sudden movement. Her instinct was to call out, but she knew that was reserved for the young girls in horror movies who died horrible deaths. Instead, she reached for her flashlight, the closest thing nearby she could think to use as a weapon. She held it backward, readied it by lifting it in the air as she swung her bare legs around and brought her feet to the floor silently.

Again, the rustling sounded, this time just outside her tent's opening. She got to her feet, thankful for the height of the orange canvas tent.

The flap of her tent moved.

Kayla jumped out of the way in the tiny space as a figure entered her tent. She had moved where she knew the person wouldn't immediately see her, so she used her advantage to jab the flashlight into the person's side. The dark figure moaned, much more quietly than she would've imagined, and stumbled but quickly recovered, turning toward her.

She saw the figure's face and immediately froze, her eyes wide.

No.

Kayla wanted to fight, wanted to scream, but her body wouldn't let her do a thing. She was certain she had stopped breathing, her mind perhaps reacting as if she'd seen a snake, thinking that this intruder would not see her if she didn't move. Logically, it didn't make sense, but she was still frozen in place.

Her attacker took the opportunity to reach around her, grab her by the waist, and clamp a hand on her mouth.

She cursed her brain for abandoning her like this as the figure—she now knew it to be a man and a dangerous one at that—pulled her to the ground. Her eyes were wide, her breathing shallow and rapid as she stared into the eyes of death.

The man who had hunted them, the man she saw in her nightmares, the man who wanted her dead was in her tent and had her completely under his control.

Na-um was here.

CHAPTER 13

The Enemy

"SHHHH!" NA-UM GROWLED at her, his hand still clamped across her mouth. She was finding it hard to breathe. "If you will not talk, I will remove my hand."

Kayla nodded.

Na-um's hand moved slightly, giving her a little room to breathe. Once it seemed he was satisfied she wouldn't make a sound, Na-um sat back, directly across from her.

Kayla just stared at him, feeling self-conscious in her tank top and sleep shorts, certain that any sound from her would make this supremely dangerous man even more angry. Though he didn't seem exactly upset at the moment . . . what was he doing here?

"Why are you here?"

Kayla almost smirked at Na-um's question; he'd asked her the same thing the first time they'd met. But then she remembered that he could probably kill her with his bare hands so quietly that Grady in the next tent wouldn't even wake up, and she thought about what he might be expecting to hear. Somehow, much like last time, she didn't think he'd be satisfied with a lie.

"We are here to find you." Well, it wasn't really a lie. Just not quite the whole truth.

And it had the effect she'd wanted. Na-um blinked. "Me?"

Kayla shrugged with forced nonchalance. "Well, you and your Clan."

Na-um crossed his arms and looked her over. "And why would you be doing that?"

Kayla sighed. She supposed there was no use in lying. "We have come to claim what's rightfully ours."

One side of Na-um's mouth turned up. "Have you?"

Kayla nodded, her words—and his reaction to them—emboldening her. She straightened. "Yes."

Now Na-um was smiling, probably at her defiance. "What here in Belize is 'rightfully yours,' as you say?"

Kayla looked him right in the eye. "Some artifacts."

She thought she saw Na-um's eyes harden, just a little, before they softened again. He swallowed once. "And what artifacts are those?"

"The ones that are part of the Codex. The ones that belong to the keepers of the Codex and its powers." She knew her words would anger him, but she couldn't seem to help herself.

But he didn't seem angry. Instead, he placed his hands on the ground behind him, leaning back, and . . . was he fighting a smile? "There are some who would say those artifacts do not belong to you. That they belong to our Clan."

"The Codex says differently." As soon as the words were out of her mouth, she kicked herself. Now Na-um would know they had translated at least part of the Codex and were on their way to discovering the whole of its Power.

But maybe she could use that to her advantage. He'd never actually read it, right? No one, save the Old Ones, had, and they hadn't read anything added since they'd died. So she could conceivably tell him that the Codex said anything she wanted it to . . .

So she continued. "As the keepers of the Codex and its powers, we are entitled to all the artifacts that contain its Power. We are here to acquire them. The Codex told us where to find them; we just have to go get them." *Maintain eye contact, don't flinch,* Kayla told herself, using the bluffing strategy she'd put to good use in the past. *You've got this. He just needs to take the bait.*

Na-um looked her over, his features still soft. "And why did you not go obtain them as soon as you arrived?"

Kayla groaned internally. Did he know she was bluffing? She'd have to play this carefully . . . "It was a long flight, and we were tired. Plus, it was the middle of the night. We were headed out as soon as we'd gotten some rest." *Not too many details, only enough to be believable. Keep it together.*

Na-um hesitated then nodded. "Okay."

Kayla just stared. "Okay?"

Na-um nodded again, pushing to his feet. "Yes. I will help you."

Kayla's mouth dropped open—she couldn't help it. "You'll . . . *help* us?"

Na-um smiled. "Yes."

"Why?" She had to ask.

Na-um reached out a hand toward her. Against her better judgment, she took it. Soon, she was standing. "The Elders have abandoned the mission, the true purpose of the Clan. Once we realized the Codex was meant for you and your friends, the Clan should have moved to help you, assist you in your new mission. But instead, the Elders are plotting to kill you, to steal the Power of the Codex back for themselves. They believe it to be rightfully theirs."

Kayla blinked and stared at the ground, her mind trying to make sense of everything Na-um had just told her. Could it be true? Could he be on their side now? Could she even trust anything he was saying?

She looked up at him. "Why should I believe you?"

Na-um shrugged, an odd gesture on the man dressed in straps of leather and animal fur. "I no longer answer to the Elders."

Kayla eyed him, wishing she could believe him, wishing Grady was here to give her a second opinion. Thinking about Grady immediately shifted her thoughts, and she momentarily forgot the man in front of her, her eyes staring at the canvas wall that separated her and the outside wall of Grady's tent.

Na-um noticed. "Listen, um . . ." He stopped, clearly waiting for her to fill in the blank.

"Kayla."

"Listen, Kayla. I am truly here to help. You may ask Holun to read my intentions in the morning."

At the mention of Holun's name, Kayla jerked. It was nearly imperceptible, and she hoped Na-um didn't notice. How did he know Holun was here?

"Why would you say that?"

The corner of Na-um's mouth turned up. "Come now, Kayla. I know he came here with you. As do the Elders."

Kayla's eyes grew wide.

Na-um waved his hand. "No, I am not working with them, not how you think. You do not trust easily, do you? I learned what they knew then escaped when they fell asleep. I came to find you—to help you."

Kayla wanted to believe him, wanted to believe that this particular journey would be easier than the one that had preceded it in this very spot.

But what did she do? What were her choices? Let Na-um rest on the floor of her tent until the others woke up so she could ask them what to do? That was just foolish. She couldn't wait until they all woke up on their own. She couldn't go back to sleep knowing Na-um knew where they were. Whether he was telling the truth or not, he was still a very dangerous man—she couldn't forget he'd tried to kill them not even six months ago—and she couldn't let him be here without everyone knowing.

She'd have to go wake them up.

Just Outside the Mercenaries' Camp

Shani followed Chac into the side of the mountain, her black bag in tow. She couldn't quite believe her eyes. She'd heard the stories of her Clan, ones that told of mysterious caverns, magical powers, and divine prophecies, but she realized in this moment that she'd never really believed in most of them —not really—until now.

With the rest of the group still above ground, Chac led her down a stony staircase into the depths of the mountain. Shani couldn't see much in the near darkness, but she was thankful for the superhuman sight afforded to the warriors of the Clan. She was able to see much more easily in the dark than an average human could, and she could make out some of her surroundings.

The staircase was long but curiously even, and venturing down it took a great deal of time, but Shani eventually found herself at the bottom. They were so far away from the surface that any light that had initially guided their way was completely swallowed up, the opening a mere pinprick of light at the top of the stairs.

Chac reached around the corner for something as Shani just stared, letting her eyes adjust to the complete blackness. But just as they did, the entire room was suddenly ablaze.

Shani squeezed her eyes shut against the pain. Why was it so bright in here?

Once she'd gathered the courage to once again open her eyes, she did so slowly. What had Chac done to create such a bright light?

Then Shani's eyes finally adjusted.

Her mouth fell open.

Kayla took Na-um to the mess tent and tied his hands to a table leg with a thick yellow rope. Not the best restraint—he'd actually rolled his eyes as she'd done it—but it was the best she could come up with on only a few hours' sleep. Besides, if he wanted to leave, he would. It was merely a gesture of trust—if he was there when she came back, they might be able to trust him.

Maybe.

She came back a few minutes later with Grady, Mandy, and Justin in tow, and Na-um was still sitting there, staring off into the morning fog of the surrounding rainforest. As soon as he came into view, Justin started toward him, his eyes narrowing. Kayla could hear his teeth grinding from here.

She put a hand on his chest. "Justin, stop. Just hear what he has to say."

Justin's eyes bored holes into Kayla's, but he quietly followed the others to the table where Na-um sat. Kayla carefully watched their faces to try to see what they were thinking as they took their places around the table. At the moment, their telepathy seemed to be down. Maybe that in and of itself was a bad sign, one that they couldn't trust Na-um. What if he had an artifact on him to block their telepathy so they couldn't plan a surprise attack on him? She wouldn't put it past him.

Grady began, his hair adorably matted and voice groggy but his eyes sharp. "Na-um, why did you come here?"

Kayla hadn't said much when she woke them up, only that someone was here. She wanted their unbiased opinion, as unbiased as their opinions could be about the man who'd tried to kill them. She'd thought waking Holun was unwise until the Four could assess his former commander's authenticity.

"I am here only to help."

"Help with what?" Justin growled from across the table, his blond hair similarly tousled.

"I came to help you find the artifacts the Codex speaks about, the artifacts that rightfully belong to all of you."

"Why would you do that?" Mandy asked.

Na-um offered them the same explanation he'd given Kayla. From the looks on their faces, Kayla couldn't tell if they were buying it.

"Why come now?" Grady sighed.

"It was the only time I could get away. I had a little . . . problem . . . with the Elders and was locked away until yesterday when they offered me my freedom in exchange for my help. And you all were not here yet, anyway."

Grady's eyebrow shot up, and Kayla jumped in. "So how can we trust you're not actually here to sabotage our efforts? That you aren't truly working for them?"

Na-um sighed, glancing her way with all the patience of an exasperated parent. "I told you this; they have abandoned the truth, the Clan's purpose. I am here to fulfill that."

"By yourself?" Justin asked.

Na-um shrugged. "If I have to, yes."

Kayla looked over at Grady, who sat between her and Na-um on the picnic table's bench. What was he thinking? She couldn't read him. The longer his memory of her was gone, it seemed, the less she understood him. She desperately wished for the days she could hear his thoughts—even the intrusive ones—for the millionth time since she'd lost him.

The Four left Na-um at the picnic table and pulled away to discuss the situation. Holun had told them about the Clan's ability to hear things from far away, so they went to the other side of the dig to talk. Not that it would really help, but Kayla felt a little better putting some distance between them.

"So what do we do? Can we trust him?" This came from Mandy, right to the point.

"What choice do we have?" Justin shrugged. "He seems to know a lot of our secrets, and he may actually know where at least some of the artifacts are hidden. If he's telling the truth, that is."

"That's precisely the point, though," Grady interjected. "*Can* we trust him? What if he really was sent here by the Elders to spy on us, find out what we know, and lead us into a trap?"

The group fell silent. Then, hesitantly, Kayla spoke up. "I told him we knew where the artifacts were."

"You *what*?" Justin nearly yelled.

"I didn't know what to say!" Kayla shot back. "He assaulted me in my tent and interrogated me before he said he was here to help. I didn't want to give too much away."

Grady's eyes flew to hers, and he raised an eyebrow. "Assaulted?"

Kayla glared right back. "Yes. *Assaulted.*" She crossed her arms.

Grady stared at her for another moment before dropping his gaze. Then he nodded. "We can use that. We just all have to play the part."

Kayla looked over at Mandy and Justin, who both nodded as well.

"Okay," Grady started, "then we see how this plays out. But we give him very little latitude until we can get a better read on his motives."

They all nodded. Then Mandy spoke up. "Why can't we hear each other's thoughts anymore?"

Kayla glanced around. She'd hoped it was just her that was blocked. "You can't hear Justin?"

Mandy shook her head, and Kayla's stomach dropped before she spoke up. "There are two possibilities as I see it," she started. "One, Na-um is lying and has an artifact that is blocking our telepathy. Well, I guess he could still be telling *some* part of the truth, but he certainly isn't being forthcoming. In which case, we watch our backs."

"I had that thought as well. And we're watching our backs with him, anyway." Grady smiled at her.

"What was the second possibility?" Mandy asked.

Kayla sighed. "Shani followed us here."

CHAPTER 14

The Treasury

Just Outside the Mercenaries' Camp and Lamanai, Deep Underground

SHANI COULDN'T BELIEVE WHAT she was seeing. Nothing her eyes told her made sense. She turned wide eyes to Chac, who returned her gaze with a grin.

"Shani, welcome to our Treasury," Chac began in nearly perfect English, which Shani knew was to make her more comfortable. She hadn't spoken K'iche in a while.

Chac entered the room with a flourish, sweeping his arms wide in front of him as if to display the room to his guest.

But Shani could see for herself. She blinked several times, unmoving, before Chac turned back to her.

"Shani, my dear, are you coming?"

Shani swallowed hard, blinked again, then finally acknowledged Chac's question. "Um, y-yes . . ."

She took a step into the room, still not quite believing what she saw.

The walls of the gigantic room she now found herself in were perfectly straight and made of cement and what appeared to be porcelain tiles. She looked up, identifying the source of the blinding light as an infinite number of rows of fluorescent lighting. What had to be hundreds if not thousands of heavy, tall, metal shelves stood in perfect rows, housing artifacts from different eras and cultures, centuries of treasures displayed in an enormous underground warehouse. The rows continued past what her better-than-human eyes could see.

"H-how . . . why . . ." Shani stuttered, unable to form a complete sentence.

Chac turned and moved to stand at her side. "This, my dear, is the largest collection of artifacts of which the world never knew."

Shani blinked again, her mouth still hanging open. "But . . . how . . . where are we?"

Chac smiled gently. "This warehouse originally was created by the British as a bunker for troops and civilians alike back in the eighties. This was at the height of the territorial war with Guatemala, and Britain was worried about the people of Belize. So they created this place as a refuge.

"Unfortunately, it was sealed shut some time ago, and presumably lost to history. But when we discovered its location, our collective power opened it to us."

Shani finally found her voice. "How did you come to collect all these artifacts? How did you get them all here? Where were they before?"

Chac placed a hand on her shoulder and started leading her further into the room. "That is a story for another day. But look here." Chac walked over to the shelf closest to them and picked up a small object, one that looked like a scepter but was only the size of a large pen. As he turned it over in his hands, Shani admired the inlaid gems—jade, ruby, and sapphire—that almost seemed to glow against the flatness of the tan stone shaft. Chac held it up to the light. "This can increase our ability to hear across large distances." He placed the end of the shaft in one ear to demonstrate its use. "I've been told it can increase our range to at least a mile."

Shani's mouth fell open again. Despite her own abilities, which she assumed science could explain away, she'd never believed in this stuff, thought it was all fairy tales designed to keep children entertained and the less intelligent sated. "Really? The most I've ever been able to hear is about a hundred yards away."

Chac nodded with a smile, setting the object carefully back down on the cloth lining its shelf. "Yes, that's what Naum has reported as well." Chac led her down the aisle, clearly headed somewhere. "We've collected several millennia worth of artifacts from around the world and now store them here for safekeeping. Some of them we aren't even certain can give the bearer power, but we store and catalog them anyway. We never know when an artifact might activate."

Shani stared at the back of his head. "Like the globe . . ."

She could hear the smile in Chac's response. "Yes, exactly. We have had several become quite powerful."

Shani followed behind Chac down the seemingly endless aisle, craning her neck left and right then back again, trying to take in everything. It was proving an impossible task. "Who does the cataloging?"

Chac pointed to their left, and Shani noticed a large window on the left wall through a break in the shelves. A dark-skinned man looked up from a desk behind the glass and nodded at them as they passed. "We have someone here to do that day and night. He lives here, takes care of the collection. You could say he is our curator, in a manner of speaking."

Chac abruptly took a right turn through another break in the shelves, headed parallel to the aisle they'd just come from, then headed up another aisle. Shani was surprised he could move so fast with those long robes around his ankles and his advanced age. No one really knew how old the Elders were, but they had to be ancient—they wouldn't be called "Elders" otherwise, right?

Chac chuckled ahead of her, a twinkling, lilting laugh that sounded almost musical. He had to have heard what she was thinking. "Come, Shani, we are reaching the end of our journey."

Shani hurried to catch up with him as she adjusted the bag on her shoulder. This globe was really getting heavy. "Thank you. And sorry."

Chac slowed near a door that seemed to come out of nowhere and turned back to smile at her. "No worries, my dear. Nothing I haven't heard before."

Shani nodded once then eyed the suspicious door.

Chac reached in his robe and pulled out a key. *You need a special key for a closet in a hidden underground warehouse?* Things just seemed to keep getting stranger.

Chac opened the door then held his hand out to Shani. "The globe may be placed in here for now. We keep all confirmed supernatural artifacts in here until they can be cataloged."

Shani took a hesitant step forward, peering around the edge of the doorframe without stepping too close.

Chac's lilting laugh sounded once again. "We are safe, my dear. There are no artifacts in here right now. Paulo keeps on top of things around here." He nodded in the direction of the windowed office they'd passed.

Shani released the breath she'd been holding and stepped into the dark room.

It actually *was* a closet, which Shani found even more curious. She didn't know what she'd been expecting—another giant warehouse, perhaps?—but she was surprised to find a small, dark room with a single lightbulb swinging from a cord in the middle of the room. The tiny, brown, wooden closet held only a few cloth-covered wooden shelves. She set her bag down on the ground and lifted out the globe, which glowed slightly at her touch. After setting it on one of the many empty shelves, she collected her bag and headed back out into the main warehouse. This tiny little dark room was giving her the creeps.

Chac's melodic laugh sounded again as he locked up the room and pocketed the key. He turned and headed back the way they came.

Shani's head was spinning as they made their way up the impossibly long staircase and into the midday air. So many questions raced through her mind that she could barely put a coherent thought together, so she stayed silent all the way back to the village.

When they neared the tents, Chac stopped and turned to her. "You will need time to process all you've seen, and you will need rest. Please take the tent we've given you, and relax today, as much as you are able. I've seen to it that Tyler, Alexia, and Steven are well taken care of for the day as well. Are you hungry?"

Shani simply shook her head.

"Nonetheless, I will have some food delivered to you." Chac started walking once again, and soon they were walking through the village. He dropped her off next to a canvas tent that looked like plenty of room for one person to sleep, but not much else. At this point, though, the events of the past few days were catching up to her, and all she could think of was closing her eyes and resting. So she didn't really care.

She went inside and was asleep within minutes.

Holun awoke, rolling over in his cot and blinking at the bright sun shining through the canvas tent. What time was it? He reached for the small clock Kayla'd left him and pulled it close. It was already past eleven? He shot up, jumping off the cot and reaching for a nearby shirt before running out of the tent to find the others.

He didn't find them in their tents, which were right next to the one they'd let him sleep in. Where were they? What was going on? He couldn't think—he wasn't used to getting this much sleep.

He ventured further into the dig but then realized he was hearing whispered voices, ones that seemed far away. Other than his visions—which he'd only been using sparingly as of late—he hadn't tapped into his other powers recently, so the sudden sound of far away voices in his head startled him. Where were they coming from? He stopped to listen, and suddenly he could hear them clearly and knew immediately who they were. Kayla, Grady, Mandy, and Justin were talking about something they found . . . or discovered? And they—

Wait. Holun froze. Was that a fifth voice? He listened a moment longer. Yes. His stomach dropped as he placed the voice, the one he heard in his nightmares. Holun quickly identified the source of the sound—it was coming from the east—and he took off running.

When he arrived, the Four were huddled around a table in the mess tent, but it was clear someone else—no doubt the person he'd heard—was with them.

"What are you all doing with *him*?" His voice came out in a growl. He was pleased it sounded so authoritative and strong.

Kayla turned toward him, and he read something in her eyes that seemed almost like . . . was that pity? "Holun, we were going to wake you. We needed to get all the facts first."

Holun just stood a safe distance away. If anything could be considered safe with his former commander just yards away. "What facts would make the four of you sit down and speak with this man?" He still hadn't seen Na-um's face—it was blocked by the back of Mandy's head—but he knew when he was in the presence of that monster.

Then, in the next moment, Na-um stood, revealing his face. Holun involuntarily took a step backward.

"Holun, please," Grady began, "just hear him out."

Holun was staring at Na-um's face and didn't react to Grady's plea.

Kayla stood and crossed to his side. "Holun, please come and sit. You need to hear this." She lowered her voice, though she knew Na-um would be able to hear if he wanted to. "Besides, we need you to read his intentions."

"I don't read minds, Kayla! Why don't you ask Mandy to?" Holun shot back in a hoarse whisper.

Kayla glanced back at the others, knowing she shouldn't give too much away with Na-um listening but not seeing another option. "We can't."

Holun just stared at her as she turned back and met his gaze but didn't say anything. Perhaps he had figured out what was going on without her having to say it and give all their secrets away. Then he nodded. "Okay, I'll give it a shot."

Kayla smiled at him, placing a hand on his back and leading him to the table.

Once both Na-um and Holun were seated, Holun slid his eyes shut. Kayla always thought he looked so peaceful when he did that. After a moment, he opened them. His eyes shot daggers at Na-um. "I can't tell if he is telling the truth. The Elders are searching for us, however, and are trying to stop us. That much is true."

"You see? I *am* telling the truth!" Na-um nearly jumped off the bench.

Grady stretched out a hand toward him to keep him in his seat. "Hold on, this just means that *some* of what you've said is true."

"Why would I lie?"

Grady glanced over at Kayla, and her stomach tied in a knot, remembering all Shani had taken from her once again. Grady continued, turning back to Na-um. "You tried to kill us, and not too long ago."

Na-um let out what could only be considered a growl. "You are not listening! The Elders have decided that our prophecies about the Codex and our role in protecting its Power are no longer relevant. They have become hungry for the Power themselves and will stop at nothing to gain that Power. Including killing all of you." He glanced around the table.

"We understand that, Na-um," Kayla began. "But you expect us to believe that you'll go against the Elders—the men who rule your people—to help some Americans you tried to kill just a few months ago?"

Na-um's nostrils flared, and Kayla could see his chest heaving, but he stared at the table until he calmed down. She hadn't seen this side of him before—one where he held a semblance of control over his emotions. Perhaps he was evolving?

His voice was even when he spoke. "I need you to understand some things about our Clan." He glanced over at Holun, who still didn't seem too happy with him. "Holun could tell you this: The Clan is loyal to our cause and to the Codex. We always interpreted our texts to mean that we were to prevent the Power of the Codex from being unleashed. I tried to kill you last summer because I and my Clan believed you were close to obtaining that Power unnaturally, that you needed to be stopped. But when all my efforts failed, I realized you four were the true keepers of its Power. When you received that Power and discovered the Secret of the Codex, something changed. Though I tried to fight it—and you as well—I finally realized, much too late, that the Clan was actually created to help carry out the Power's true purpose on this earth, in *this* time. It's why the Elders captured me and were holding me. I started to tell others in the Clan about our true mission, and the Elders couldn't have that. They hid me away until last night, when they released me to help them find and capture you."

"Why would they believe you would help them, if you were speaking out against them before?" Justin crossed his arms, but Kayla was pleased to hear his voice was missing the hostility from before.

"The Elders have long believed in the loyalty of their subjects, and they are blinded by their long-held position in the Clan. They truly believe that I will fall in line and follow their orders, as I always have, despite my brief departure weeks ago. Perhaps they thought I would be so grateful they let me out that I would change my mind." Na-um grinned. "And I am their best warrior, so they need me on their side."

Kayla stared at Na-um, trying to figure out if what he was saying was the truth. Could they believe what he was claiming?

On one hand, she wanted to believe that someone—even Na-um—would see the truth and do what was right, help them in their cause. It would certainly help if someone could give them inside information on the Clan, too; Na-um knew much more than Holun, and his knowledge would be invaluable.

But on the other hand, he could just as easily be playing them, acting like he was on their side to learn their secrets and report back to the Elders.

Each scenario seemed equally likely. Kayla frowned. They would have to be careful around him, certainly, but she couldn't help but feel that he was on their side. Was it blind hope, wishful thinking? Or was something else there?

As she looked at Na-um, *really* looked at him, while he continued answering the others' questions and outlining the best strategies for getting to the Elders, she saw something beneath the surface—beneath the straps of leather clothing he wore and his long, black hair—that made her think there may be more to their former enemy than she'd originally thought.

She barely noticed she'd considered him a *former* enemy.

CHAPTER 15

Unsettling

IT HAD BEEN SEVERAL HOURS since she and the others had met with Na-um in this very spot, but Kayla found herself headed back to the mess tent yet again, this time for a late lunch. Na-um was the only one around, sitting at a far table in an incredibly common dark t-shirt and shorts. Where did he get those?

Na-um was free to go—like they would have a choice if he really wanted to leave—but for some reason, he was still here, eating a protein bar he'd clearly procured from the food table. The way he was sitting, eating a bar, and wearing such a normal outfit reminded Kayla a lot of the first time she'd met Grady here, one of the many moments she'd fallen in love with him, and her heart ached.

Na-um looked up as she approached. "Kayla, hello." He stood slightly as he extended a hand to the seat across from him.

Kayla didn't take her eyes off him as she grabbed a snack and a water bottle off the food table on her way to his table, and even eyed him as they both sat. She couldn't help but wonder what he was thinking. "Hello, Na-um. I see you're still here."

Na-um smiled, just a little. "Of course. Though I did have to go report to the Elders—to keep up appearances, of course." He smiled wider, glancing down at his bar before catching her gaze. "I really am here to help."

Kayla shrugged, looking away from his piercing gaze. She shifted in her seat then rested her arms on the table in front of her.

Na-um extended his hand part of the way across the table then pulled it back before he touched her. "I truly am sorry for this summer. I believed I was in the right, but clearly, I was wrong. I am trying to make up for that now."

"Seems like too little too late." She didn't know why she said that; she just couldn't stop herself. Her eyes involuntarily shot to his.

But she saw his eyes held no malice, no hint of ill intent. How could that be? "I know that what I did to you—to your friends—was unforgivable. I am not even asking for forgiveness; I am asking for a little trust."

Kayla was past holding back now. "That's the same thing, Na-um."

His nostrils flared as his voice raised. "It is not!" He paused, took a deep breath, then continued, his voice calmer. "Kayla, what I did was horrible, to be sure. I have *killed* in the name of my Clan. I tried to kill you all. Do you not think I feel that?"

"Do you?"

Na-um sighed. "My Clan is all I have ever known, but my beliefs are, too. And I knew killing others was wrong, even though I forced myself to believe otherwise. Now that I see the truth—that the Elders were only trying to steal the Power that belonged to you—I deeply regret my actions. All of them. But especially those against you."

Na-um had caught her gaze and now stared deeply into her eyes. Somehow, Kayla thought he wasn't talking about the group of them but about her, specifically. "Me?"

Na-um nodded slowly. "Kayla, you may have been hurt the most by my actions."

"How is that? Justin lost his parents because of you!" Kayla was getting louder, but she couldn't seem to help herself.

"I know." Na-um's words were barely a whisper. "And I deeply regret that as well. But you were always the leader of this group; you were the one leading the others to the Codex. I imagine you suffered the most along the journey."

Kayla blinked then looked down at the table. How could this man, this former enemy of theirs, be so insightful? How could he know of her guilt in leading the others into this largely unwanted destiny, the relentless pain from her visions, and the shattering grief over losing those she knew and loved? He was right; she felt responsible for all of it. If only she hadn't looked into the globe that day with Grady, none of this would've happened . . .

"Kayla?" Na-um's hand stretched across the table, but this time, he didn't stop until his hand reached her arm. She flinched when he touched her but didn't pull away.

Na-um cleared his throat then waited until she looked up, his hand still on her arm. "I know words will never give back what I took from you, but I am deeply, truly sorry."

Kayla's throat tightened, and she felt a tear well up in her eye. She swallowed hard, her voice coming out as a whisper. "Thank you, Na-um."

Na-um sat back, pulling his hand off Kayla's arm. Despite the afternoon heat, she could still feel the warmth from his hand on her skin. "So, Kayla, what's the plan?"

Kayla blinked. "Plan?"

Na-um smiled, crossing his arms. "Yes. You say you know where the artifacts are; what is your plan to go retrieve them?"

Kayla felt blood rush to her cheeks. "Well . . ."

Na-um leaned forward, resting his forearms on the table and folding his hands. "Well, what?"

Kayla swallowed again. "Well, I wasn't exactly honest with you before."

"Shocking."

Na-um's face was so deadpan, so emotionless, and his response so out of character, that Kayla burst out laughing.

"What?" Na-um was smiling again, looking her over. Kayla had the sneaking suspicion that he was enjoying watching her be happy. It was a little unsettling, but she still couldn't stop laughing.

"Nothing, nothing." She tried to wave it away between breaths.

"You are just trying not to tell me what you lied about earlier."

Kayla, still laughing, simply nodded.

Na-um just sat watching her until the joviality died down, a slight smirk on his face the entire time. "Are you okay?"

Kayla grabbed her water bottle and took a drink as she nodded. "Yes."

Na-um pulled his folded hands into his lap. "You were saying?"

Kayla nodded once, her features once again solemn. "I told you we knew where the artifacts are . . ."

". . . but you do not really know, do you?"

Kayla nodded slowly and shrugged.

Na-um's piercing brown eyes appraised her. "Well, that makes things more difficult, does it not?"

"Yes."

"Can I ask why you told me that before?"

Kayla jumped right in. "You came into my tent, woke me up, assaulted me, then started asking all these questions. I didn't know what to say!"

One corner of Na-um's mouth turned up. "You are cute when you are angry."

Kayla's eyes shot wide as her mouth dropped, convinced something had been lost in translation. "What did you say?"

Na-um's brow furrowed. "I was merely giving you a compliment; am I not supposed to do that?"

Kayla's stomach erupted in butterflies. She *had* heard him correctly—and his intent was now abundantly clear. "Um . . . no, but . . . thank you."

Na-um smiled. "You are the strong one. I see that clearly." He reached again for her arm, and Kayla didn't pull away this time, either.

"Na-um . . ." Kayla shifted in her seat, hating that she liked the feeling of his hand on her arm.

"You can trust me, Kayla."

She looked back over at him, her volume dropping. "How do I know that?" But she already had her answer. Gazing into his deep, boundless eyes, she knew that he was telling the truth.

"Kayla, I am not leaving. I am here to help you find what you need, whatever it takes."

His words sounded so impossibly sincere that Kayla's stomach lurched. She searched his eyes for any hint of deception, and he stared back at her, his hand sending a warm current through her body. For a moment, neither blinked, neither broke their gaze. Kayla just stared, knowing she should look away, but finding herself drawn to him.

When they'd met last summer, she'd been so distracted by the Codex, by Grady, that she'd barely given him a second glance. Now with Grady so far away—at least figuratively—and much of their lives up in the air, her brain considered Na-um without her permission. His muscular physique, his strong jaw, the way his tanned body moved under that dark t-shirt . . .

Kayla blinked and looked away. *Get a hold of yourself, Kayla,* she quickly admonished herself. *You love Grady. You are in love with Grady. What's wrong with you??*

Kayla glanced back over at Na-um, who was still staring at her, then quickly looked away again. Kayla kicked herself for allowing her mind to think about Na-um in any other way than just an informant. She *did* love Grady. Just because he wasn't as accessible to her now didn't change that.

But somewhere in the recesses of her mind, as Na-um pulled away and finished his protein bar, Kayla knew her thoughts about Na-um could not be forgotten. She'd opened the door, one she feared she wouldn't be able to easily close.

She prayed this whole thing would end soon, that Grady's mind would be whole once again, and that she could leave this godforsaken place and the inhabitants of it—one in particular—behind.

Mercenaries' Camp

Shani slept through most of the rest of the day and the entire night, having woken up only for a few hours to eat a late dinner before heading back to bed to catch up on some much-needed sleep. She woke the next morning feeling refreshed, dressed in a rainforest-appropriate ensemble—khaki shorts, t-shirt, and hiking boots—then grabbed some food someone had left for her next to the tent's sole entrance. As she ate, she sat staring at the tan canvas wall, her thoughts swirling in her head. The tent wasn't fancy—it certainly paled in comparison to her old hut—but she suspected even the Elders were living in tents since they'd just moved. She'd wondered why, but now she suspected the reason. They needed to be close to their treasure in case the Americans came looking for it.

She'd heard the stories growing up—and read even more after she'd left the Clan in the research she'd been able to dig up—about the treasure the Clan cared for. At one time, she'd assumed they were referring to the Power of the Codex, but now she was certain she'd been mistaken.

Because she'd seen it for herself.

Deep in a mountain to the east—dangerously close to Lamanai, she only now realized—lay a treasure trove of artifacts from days past. The Clan had watched over it carefully, which hadn't been hard since even a backpacker who happened upon the plateau wouldn't have noticed anything out of place, but Shani knew the Four could find it if they wanted to. The Codex and its keepers were too powerful.

Which was precisely the problem.

Chac had graciously introduced her to the artifacts and the Clan's—the Elders'—treasure, and Shani could sense the power inside. Power she'd like for herself, if possible. She'd come all this way for it, after all—she just hadn't thought it would have been this easy. Who knew it would be handed right to her?

Shani finished her meal and sat up straight on her cot, crossing her legs beneath her and quickly gathering her strength as she guarded her mind from any intruders. The Elders couldn't hear this part, didn't deserve to.

Because she needed to come up with a plan.

CHAPTER 16

A Brief Glimpse
of Hope

Lamanai Archaeological Project, Belize

THE NEXT MORNING DAWNED sunny and hot. Mandy was up first, and she hurried to grab her things to get a shower before Justin woke up. The five of them were meeting early with Na-um to figure out the best way to obtain the artifacts—and Mandy wanted to be ready. She glanced at her watch on the way out of the tent; she had an hour.

After a quick shower, she exited the bathing trailer, checking her bag to make sure she had everything. Hairbrush, towels, the clothes she'd slept in, toothpaste . . . and ran right into someone.

"Oh, sorry!" Mandy quickly apologized as she looked up then jumped back as if something had bitten her. "Oh—Na-um . . . I'm sorry, I . . . I didn't see you."

Na-um smiled at her, and for once, she didn't think it looked smug. "It is perfectly okay. I was in your way." He stepped aside and stretched out his arm for her to pass.

Mandy swallowed once, nodding at him as she passed by. "Thank you."

The brief encounter hadn't lasted ten seconds, but Mandy was shaken nonetheless. This was a vastly different man than they'd known this past summer, the man who'd tried to kill them. She almost had to remind herself of that—was he really the same man?

As she walked back to the tent she shared with Justin, she couldn't shake this new feeling. Something about Na-um was different; and if he truly was on their side now, perhaps that was a good thing.

Justin was up when she got back. "Hey, morning, babe," Justin grinned from where he was sitting on his cot, shirtless.

"Nice hair," Mandy grinned at his bedhead as she started to unpack her bag.

Justin reached his hand up to smooth it out. "You like it?" He stood and crossed to her cot, reaching an arm around her waist and spinning her against him. "We could do something about that before the others wake up."

"Justin!" Mandy's voice was a hoarse whisper as he pulled her closer to kiss her neck. Her eyes fell closed for a second. Then she reached her hands between them and pressed on his hard, bare chest. "The others will hear us!"

Justin shot her a devilish grin, the one she loved. "Then you'll have to be quiet." He eagerly pressed his lips to her mouth.

Mandy waited to respond to the kiss, feigning irritation despite the feelings coursing through her body at his touch. This was the game they frequently played, her acting like she wanted to keep quiet, him wanting to throw caution to the wind. She secretly loved it.

After waiting a few more moments, she leaned into him, kissing him back like she desperately wanted him—finally showing him the truth—and she felt his reaction immediately. She loved that, even after more than three years, she still had that effect on him.

She let him pull her to the ground, not an inch between them.

Several minutes later, they resurfaced to the sound of someone screaming. Mandy's eyes shot to Justin's, then a second later they were both reaching for their clothes.

When they got outside, it was clear that Holun was the one screaming. Mandy ran to his tent, throwing back the canvas flap, her eyes searching for him. She quickly spotted him thrashing on his cot, almost as if he was having a seizure. Mandy dropped to her knees next to him, grabbing his shoulders and shaking him gently. "Holun! Wake up!"

When Holun didn't respond, Mandy looked up at Justin, who still stood in the tent's opening. He shrugged, so Mandy just shook her head and tried again. Nothing.

Na-um appeared in the opening just behind Justin, and Mandy tensed, looking back at Holun. Would Justin start something with Na-um without Kayla here to mediate? Now was not the time.

I know that, Mandy.

Mandy gasped, her eyes flying to Justin's again.

Justin's eyes were wide. *I heard you. You can hear me, too?*

Mandy just nodded. *Does this mean that Shani has given up?*

I doubt it. Justin stepped into the small tent. *Maybe she's just focused on something else.*

At the thought, the two of them slowly turned back to Holun, who was still screaming and thrashing on the bed.

Mandy had the thought first. *Could she be doing this to Holun?*

Justin just stared at the young boy before him. Then: *I don't know. Maybe.*

"What's wrong with him?" Na-um asked from the doorway. Mandy had all but forgotten he was here.

"We don't know." Mandy glanced his way before looking back. She tried shaking Holun again and calling his name, even knowing it wouldn't work.

Na-um stepped inside, crowding the already small tent. "Let me try."

"Try what?" Mandy looked up.

Na-um stepped closer, kneeling next to Mandy. "Just let me try." He pushed toward the boy, nudging her out of the way. She reluctantly moved, straightening to stand next to Justin.

"What are you going to do to him?" Justin asked from behind him.

Na-um didn't answer but instead put his hand on the boy's forehead. Almost immediately, Holun calmed down— still asleep, but no longer screaming and thrashing on the cot.

Mandy was staring; she couldn't help it. "How did you do that?"

Na-um finally lifted his hand from the boy's head and sat back, looking over at her and Justin. "My people have always had a special bond between us. We can sense when others are hurting, and our touch can dull the pain."

Mandy blinked. *Is he serious? That's insane.*

Justin glanced over at her. *Um, that's what you're going to consider insane? We can communicate telepathically, and you can read people's thoughts. I can bring fire from my hands and control it. That's insane, too, right?*

The corner of Mandy's mouth turned up. *Okay, sure, you're probably right.*

Thank you! Justin grinned and put an arm around her. *I usually am.*

She hit his shoulder.

Holun still wasn't waking up, but he seemed to be more peaceful now. Perhaps Na-um's touch did in fact dull his pain. Mandy hoped so. Whatever she thought about Na-um, she knew Holun was on their side, and she was glad Na-um had helped him.

Mandy sighed. She felt for the kid. Someone so young shouldn't have to be dragged into all this mess. But, unfortunately, Holun was right at the center of all of it.

Mandy had stationed herself on the floor at his side while he slept. She idly wondered where Na-um had run off to, since Justin had gone to find Grady and Kayla and get them up to speed.

Holun stirred. "Mandy?" he choked out in a raspy voice.

"Holun?" Mandy sat up straight and grabbed his hand. "How do you feel?"

Holun blinked a few times then swallowed hard. "Could I please . . ." His voice cracked, and he cleared his throat. "Could I please have some water?"

Mandy nodded quickly then reached for a bottle she found sitting at the foot of his bed. She quickly uncapped it and handed it to him carefully.

He sat up slightly and took a drink then handed the bottle to Mandy and laid back down with a sigh. "Thanks." His voice was less raspy but still sounded tired.

Mandy ventured a question. "Holun, do you know what happened? Do you remember anything?" Then she called for Justin. *Babe, Holun's awake.*

No response. Crap.

Holun was still on his back, gaze trained on the orange canvas ceiling, his voice quiet as he spoke. "It was a vision." He coughed once. "But worse than I have had before. Even worse than when I saw Kayla's vision." Holun had shared one of Kayla's visions last summer; it had helped them find the Codex and receive their powers, but Holun had gotten a taste of how bad Kayla's visions had really been. Which Mandy knew had been extremely painful.

Mandy nodded. "What did you see?"

Holun glanced over at her before looking back at the ceiling. "I think . . ." His eyes grew wide. "The Elders aren't going to stop coming after us. Not until every one of us is dead."

Mandy gasped. "What? Why do you think that?"

Holun turned his head to look at her. "I saw a great battle, one larger and much more violent than your first, one where the Elders were tearing people apart."

Mandy swallowed hard, her eyes wide. A giant pit formed in her stomach. "Holun . . ." her voice sounded strangled. "Who were they tearing apart? Was it us?"

Holun moved to sit up then shook his head. "I didn't see who it was. But their power—I don't know how they got so much power."

"What did they do?"

"They were grabbing people by the arms, legs, even their heads—anything they could get their hands on—and literally ripping them in two. It was . . . horrible." Holun's face was a sickening shade of white.

Mandy leaned up on her knees and reached over to rub his arm. "I'm so sorry." She paused. "But you know your visions don't always come true. They're just a version of what could happen if we don't stop it." Mandy lifted off the ground to sit by him on the cot and draped her arm across his shoulders.

"I know, Mandy, and thanks." Holun looked over at her and attempted what turned out to be a weak smile. "But the way they were fighting . . . it was not fair, not right. And those people! No one deserves to die like that. Not even the Elders themselves."

Mandy nodded once then pulled his head to her shoulder, her arm around him. Holun let her hold him, and she was grateful. She had a feeling that this young man hadn't been shown much affection in his life.

Holun pulled away a few moments later and looked up at Mandy, his eyes glistening. "But, Mandy, I still do not trust Na-um. He seems different, but I am not convinced he has changed. I knew him well, and I watched him as he pursued all of you. I watched as evil came over him, and not many can return from that. We must be careful."

Mandy pursed her lips, gazing at the wall of the canvas tent while considering his words. After a few moments, she spoke. "Na-um certainly has a bad history with us."

Holun nodded.

"I agree, we need to be careful, and you know him best. But don't you think it's possible he's changed?"

Now Holun paused before responding. "I suppose it is possible, but I feel like something is wrong."

"Wrong?"

"Like he might not be telling all of the truth."

Mandy smiled then pulled him to her in another side hug. "You're probably right."

"Why are you smiling?" Holun asked as she pulled away.

Mandy's smile grew wider. "Nothing. Just the way you worded that."

"Was it wrong?" Holun leaned back slightly to see her face.

"Not really; we just usually say 'the whole truth' instead of 'all of the truth.' But I knew what you meant."

Now Holun was smiling. "Thank you! I need someone to tell me if I am speaking wrong."

"Incorrectly."

"Incorrectly?"

"Yes, not 'wrong,' the word is 'incorrectly.' Wrong is usually used differently."

Holun shook his head. "I will never master this language."

Mandy patted his leg. "Yes, you will. You are doing wonderfully! It's a difficult language to fully understand."

"That is true."

Mandy chuckled as she stood. "Let's go find the others, tell them about what you saw."

Holun nodded then followed her out of the tent.

Mercenaries' Camp

Shani'd had to use every ounce of her self-control not to scream. When the vision had finally left her, she'd been able to get back to her mind control over the Four, increasing it to block their telepathy completely—not too long after she'd formulated the plan to get the artifacts, at least some of them, for herself. But now she found she could barely breathe.

She'd never gotten visions before. She was able to alter the minds of others, sure, and she could communicate telepathically, but she'd never once seen the future. And after that, she didn't care to again.

A bloody battle had played out in her mind, one where the Elders were fighting an unidentifiable enemy. She couldn't tell who'd won, even who'd gained the upper hand, but it was gruesome, nonetheless.

And *painful.* Was this that little brat, Holun? He would pay for this.

Shani hurriedly dressed then went to find Chac and the other Elders. They needed to know about this new development. Maybe it would give them some insight into how they could defeat their enemies.

She still wasn't sure if the Elders were on her side, but, for now, they had a common enemy, and that made them her ally.

Shani found them quickly and explained the vision and her thoughts about it to the three Elders she could find. After assuring her they would report this to the others and collectively make a decision, they ushered her away.

Shani stood outside their tent for a long time before moving back to her own, unsure of what to do next. She had a plan, but she would need to wait a little while to begin.

She sighed, looking over the collection of tents. She supposed she should go talk to the three she'd brought here with her, perhaps find the young village girl who'd received powers just yesterday and explain to her what was going on.

She shoved her hands in her pockets and sauntered over to their tents. Tyler, Steven, and Alexia first, then the young girl.

Shani sighed. Being a parent was something she'd worked hard to avoid for a very long time.

CHAPTER 17

The Artifacts

Lamanai

GRADY COULDN'T FIGURE OUT what was wrong. For the briefest of moments, just before he'd heard Holun start screaming from a few tents down, he'd gotten a glimpse of his life with Kayla, their life in Orlando—even the briefest of glimpses into their love story, here at Lamanai and all throughout this summer—but now it was gone again. He knew he'd seen it, but he couldn't access the memories. Why was Shani messing with him? If they couldn't find her, they needed to find those artifacts so he would be whole again.

Where was Kayla? He'd barely seen her since they'd arrived at Lamanai, and something about her was troubling him. He felt like something had come between them, and he couldn't figure out what. Was it his memory loss? Being back here likely brought up a lot of memories for her. Was that why she had become so distant?

His stomach dropped. For the thousandth time in the past few days, he wished with everything inside him that he could fix this, that he could *remember*.

But no matter how hard he tried, his life with Kayla was gone. They could start again—and he would fight for that if it killed him—but unless they could fix this, reverse it, their relationship would never be the same. Maybe that's what he was feeling; maybe Kayla sensed that, too.

So he decided to focus on the only thing he could control: locating and obtaining the artifacts, specifically the one that would block Shani's powers of the mind. One that would make him remember again, and for good this time. One that would bring him back to Kayla.

He just hoped it wouldn't be too late.

Kayla and the rest of the Four, along with Na-um and Holun, met an hour later in the mess tent, early enough that the lunch crowd hadn't shown up yet. Though there wouldn't be much of a "crowd" anyway—staffing for the dig was light this late in the fall semester. Most had already gone home for Thanksgiving, which was only a few days away.

"So, Na-um, where do we start? Do you have any idea where the artifacts are?"

Na-um looked up at Kayla's question, his eyes probing. Kayla immediately averted her eyes, subconsciously rubbing the spot on her arm where he'd touched her before, keenly aware of Grady sitting right next to her. She hoped he hadn't seen their interaction. "Possibly. The Elders will not be far from them."

"But the Clan has moved, right?" Justin asked. "So the artifacts will be mobile?"

Na-um nodded. "Perhaps. The Elders wouldn't like to leave those behind. Unless . . ."

"Unless, what?" Mandy jumped in.

"Unless, they have them so well hidden that they do not fear them being discovered."

Justin chortled. "Like that worked out so well for them before."

Na-um actually smiled, and Kayla noticed a kindness there she hadn't seen before. *Stop it, Kayla,* she warned herself, adjusting in her seat, sliding slightly closer to Grady despite the midmorning heat. "Yes," Na-um continued. "I never got a look at many of the artifacts, but I have heard the stories. The Elders have to be keeping a large number of artifacts hidden, and they could be anywhere. But I can almost guarantee that they will have at least some of them with them, probably the ones they consider most valuable."

"Like the one to block mind control," Kayla interjected.

Na-um caught her gaze and smiled again. "Yes. I am certain that is one they keep very close. They would never have worked with my sister unless they could be certain of their immunity to her powers. The Elders must exert their control over everything and everyone—and they cannot accept that they might not have complete control over something." His eyes were still locked with Kayla's, but she found herself not wanting to look away. She sensed Mandy's eyes on her and glanced over. She didn't want to answer the questions she saw in Mandy's eyes; she hoped her friend wouldn't remember to ask them later.

No chance of that.

Grady jumped in. "Na-um, you know where the Elders are now, right?"

"Yes. They are not far, in the rainforest at my Clan's camp."

"Well, we can assume they at least have the one we need in their possession. So we go to the camp and find it."

Mandy nodded across the table. "Makes sense to me. But how do we get close to the Elders without them being suspicious?"

The group was silent, but Kayla was looking back at Na-um. "I believe he can."

Na-um nodded. "Yes, I will be the way in. They will be heavily guarded, but they think I am on their side." He paused, staring off into the rainforest. "Yes, I should be able to get in."

"And the artifact?" Justin asked.

Na-um's eyes shifted quickly across the tabletop, back and forth. "Chac, the leader, always keeps an amulet around his neck. I do not know where it came from, so there is a good chance it is the one we need."

"Makes sense that a protection artifact would need to be worn," Kayla surmised.

Na-um smiled at her. "Yes, that does make sense."

Kayla glanced away and noticed Mandy staring at her again. She winced internally, knowing Mandy was definitely going to ask her about it the first chance she got.

After the group dispersed to get some rest before planning for the mission, Kayla heard a quiet rustling at her door.

"Can I come in?"

Kayla knew it would be Mandy before she'd even spoken. She supposed this could not be avoided. And better to have the conversation now than when the others could listen in through their thoughts. This was not a conversation Grady needed to hear. "Sure, what's up?"

Mandy walked in and sat in a cloth chair opposite her cot. Kayla dropped to her cot, her stomach clenching.

"Are you okay, Kayla?"

Kayla took a breath then nodded. "Sure, of course! I'm just ready to get this done so I can have Grady back, and we can go home."

Mandy cocked her head a little to the side. "I know. But what's going on with you and Na-um?"

Kayla shifted on the cot, fidgeting with a blanket at her side. Mandy was always a little more perceptive than most. "What do you mean?"

Mandy sighed, leaning forward. "You know exactly what I mean. What is going on with you two?"

"Nothing!" Kayla didn't like where this was heading.

"Kayla, what I saw over there was not nothing. Did something happen between you two?"

Mandy's eyes were piercing. Kayla looked away, her voice quiet. "It's nothing."

Mandy sucked air in sharply, and her words came out in a harsh whisper. "Something *did* happen!"

Kayla hesitated then nodded slightly.

"Oh, Kayla . . ." Mandy groaned. "What happened?"

Kayla paused again, not even sure where to start.

Mandy crossed the tent and sat next to her on the cot. "Kayla, this will stay between us as long as I can help it."

Kayla nodded, and she felt tears welling up in her eyes as the story came tumbling out. "I don't know, Mandy. I just . . ." She was crying now, and she sniffed. "I went for a late lunch yesterday, and Na-um was there. He was apologizing for everything, and he seemed sincere—he really did. He was being all open and vulnerable . . ." Mandy gasped, but Kayla pressed on, her tears subsiding. "And he was being all insightful and everything. Then we were talking about the plan for getting the artifacts back, and I told him I'd lied to him about knowing where they were—"

"You told him that?" Mandy cut in. "I wondered how he knew!"

Kayla nodded. "I told him I'd lied, he asked me why, and when I got angry and explained, he said I was . . . cute when I was angry." Kayla caught Mandy's gaze as she finished.

Her friend's eyes shot wide. "What did you do?"

Kayla turned to stare at the ground. "I thanked him."

"You *thanked* him?"

Kayla nodded again. "Yes. Then he reached for my arm and held it. I stared into his eyes for much too long, and . . ."

"And what?" Kayla was watching Mandy nearly jumping up and down on the cot beside her.

Kayla put her hands over her face, her words coming out muffled. "I checked him out."

"You *what*?"

Kayla looked up at her abruptly. "He just looked so *normal* in that t-shirt and shorts, and so . . . attractive . . ." Kayla reached for her friend's arm as she groaned. "Mandy, what do I do?"

Mandy grabbed Kayla's other arm. "What do you mean?"

"How can I be attracted to Na-um if I still love Grady?" Kayla whispered the question, knowing these tent walls were very thin.

Mandy paused for a moment. "Do you love Na-um?"

Kayla snorted. "Of course not."

"Do you see a future with him?"

"No!"

"Then why are you worried? You and Grady are so in love that you will find a way to make your relationship work. You're just out of sync right now, and an undeniably gorgeous man expressed interest in you. Have you done anything wrong?"

Kayla stared at the side of the canvas tent. "Well . . ." She swallowed hard. "Mandy, you weren't there. You didn't feel what I felt. There was a definite attraction there, from both sides. I looked into his eyes, and I knew he wasn't lying. But more than that, I *knew* he was sincere, that we could trust him. And even worse, I found myself *wanting* him to keep his hand on my arm, keep talking to me, keep spending time with me, keep staring into my eyes as I stared into his deep-brown ones. How can a woman who loves another man do that? How could I love Grady as much as I say I do and still be attracted to Na-um?"

"Kayla," Mandy started, bringing her friend's attention back to the present. "Listen to me: You did nothing wrong. The heart—or in this case, probably more like hormones—wants what it wants. Attraction is shallow and fleeting. Love —the deep, true love you share with Grady—does not go away so easily. Even though he doesn't remember you, he senses how important you are to him and is choosing to fight for the two of you. He doesn't remember you, yet he still chooses you! Do you know how incredible that is?"

Kayla had started crying again during Mandy's speech, and she reached to wipe a tear that had fallen on her left cheek. "Yes, I know." She sniffled, trying to collect her composure. "But what do I do about Na-um?"

Mandy smiled gently. "We work with him to get the artifact we need, you avoid him as we do, then we take you and a healed Grady back to Florida."

Kayla smiled at her friend, nodding, but she couldn't help but think there was no way it would be that easy.

CHAPTER 18

Training

GRADY CAME TO KAYLA'S TENT a few hours later, after she had just woken up from a brief nap. "Kayla?"

Kayla was lying fully clothed on her cot, and she smiled at him when his face appeared in her doorway. She sat up. "Come in."

Grady smiled back at her then came and sat in the chair Mandy'd used only a few short hours ago. "I had an idea."

"Yes?" Kayla ran her fingers through her hair, hoping that her hair wasn't a mess. This may have been normal for them before Grady'd lost his memory, but she didn't want him to see her like this right now.

"I think we should train."

"Train?"

Grady nodded, leaning forward. "Yes. It feels like we haven't used our powers in forever, and my memory is already shaky. We need to remember how to use them, train ourselves to use them more easily."

Kayla thought about it for a second then nodded. "I think that's a great idea. You're right—we haven't used them much since this summer, except those few times recently, and we probably could all stand to brush up on how to use them. We can't expect to rely on something we don't know how to control."

"Exactly!" Grady was grinning now, and Kayla found herself smiling back.

The silence between them lasted a little longer than Kayla thought was comfortable, but she didn't know what to say next.

Grady broke the silence for her, his tone more reserved. "So how have you been? What's it like for you being back here?"

Kayla blinked but tried not to hesitate. "It brings back a lot of memories."

Grady nodded somberly. "I can imagine. It's so weird knowing my memory is gone, knowing that the gaps I have in my memory were of you, but not being able to access them."

Kayla was tearing up, so she simply nodded.

"Kayla," Grady began, crossing the tent and sitting beside her, much like Mandy had. He reached for her hand and held it. "I am so sorry for all of this. You, most of all, don't deserve what Shani is doing to us."

"She's doing it to you, Grady." Kayla sniffed quietly.

"But it's affecting you the most. I know that something's wrong, but I can't put my finger on it. You know exactly what's wrong, but you can't fix it."

A tear slid down Kayla's cheek, and she didn't reach up to wipe it away.

Grady reached over and wiped it off for her. She'd forgotten how good it felt just to feel him close to her, touching her skin. "Kayla . . ." Grady leaned in and brought his lips slowly to hers, pulling her into his embrace.

Kayla melted at the feel of his lips on hers, all other thoughts falling away. The kiss was much too short, but when they separated, Kayla could still feel the butterflies in her stomach. A gentle peace came over her so completely that she momentarily forgot where she was. "I love you, Grady."

As soon as she said it, she wished she hadn't. It wasn't fair to spring this on him so early in his relationship with her— early for him, anyway. He hadn't had time to fall in love with her yet, and with everything going on, she didn't know if he ever would. She kicked herself for saying it and opened her mouth to take it back.

But before she could, Grady spoke up, catching her gaze and holding it. "Kayla, I know I will love you forever. I can feel that I did before, and that I will again. And now . . . I can feel what was between us, and I know that it's real. I can sense our love, even though Shani is trying to take it away. But no matter what, I will always love you. Shani cannot take that away from us. We can't let her win."

Kayla nodded through her tears, reaching to pull him into a long-awaited hug. His embrace felt just as she remembered it, warm and comforting despite the heat, and she finally felt, for the first time since his memory loss, that they might actually have a fighting chance.

When they pulled away, Kayla stood. "Okay, let's go get the others. We have to get our powers ready to fight."

Grady grinned at her then grabbed her hand to lead her outside.

Mercenaries' Camp, Northern Belize

She couldn't stand these two. They kept prattling on like schoolgirls and just wouldn't shut up.

Shani had found Tyler and Steven after she'd eaten lunch —they didn't know where Alexia had run off to—chatting loudly around a fire, eating something that her people no doubt had to procure for them. These boys didn't seem capable of making their own meal, say nothing of catching it.

She'd joined them for several minutes, but now she'd reached her limit. Shani flipped her raven hair behind her shoulders and stood, stalking away from the fire. Those two seemed to be the best of friends and would clearly entertain each other. She had more important things to do anyway.

She went off in search of the newly powered girl from this morning, deciding to look for Alexia after she was done with the younger girl. That poor girl would be extremely confused, and she deserved an explanation. Shani sighed. How had it come to this? How did she get roped into having to explain everything about their powers to every new recruit? Didn't seem fair . . .

But then again, it was probably because she'd taken it upon herself to steal the globe and see what it could do. She supposed this was just an unwelcome side effect of creating her own superpowered army.

Superpowered army. Shani grinned. It certainly had a nice ring to it.

She reached the tent where the girl was living—Chac had pointed her in the right direction before she'd left him—and was promptly allowed inside by a short and mildly attractive woman with the long, dark hair common to the Clan. She introduced herself as Akna's mother, which Shani just now learned was the girl's name, then left so they could talk.

Akna, her knees pulled up to her chest and her arms wrapped tightly around them, eyed Shani from the ground where she sat on a makeshift bed at the back of the large tent. Shani approached carefully, trying to understand exactly how this young girl must be feeling and figuring out how to cater to that.

She crouched down as she reached the girl, her hands in the air to indicate that she didn't mean any harm. When she finally spoke, she spoke softly and in their native language. "Akna? That's a pretty name."

The girl just stared.

Shani moved to sit next to her on the ground, right next to the pile of leaves and underbrush that softened the hard ground under her blankets that made up her bed. She kept her posture open, her face kind, but kept her distance. "Akna," she purred, "I came to explain what happened to you."

The girl's eyes grew wide, and she pulled her knees closer. Shani wouldn't have thought that possible.

"Please, let me explain. Is that okay?" Shani stopped herself from reaching out toward the girl. No need to scare her any more than she already was.

Akna didn't seem like she was going to answer for a moment, then Shani saw her nod.

Shani smiled at her. "Excellent." She took a deep breath. How to explain this to someone who knew nothing of the power of their Clan? "The . . . power . . . you received was given to you by a globe, a mystical object that can grant powers to people of Mayan descent, people like you."

Akna's eyes widened even further. Shani sensed she had a question—probably many questions—so she stayed silent as the girl processed the information Shani had given her.

Finally, her soft voice broke the silence. "I . . . how?"

Shani widened her smile. "The globe has been activating powers in people destined to receive them, like you."

Akna swallowed hard. "Me?"

Shani nodded. "Yes. You seem to have been given the power to manipulate metal with your mind."

Akna just stared.

After a few moments, Shani filled the silence. "I'm sure you have many questions." She paused, judging Akna's response. She continued when the girl nodded once. "You may ask me at any time. And also . . ." Shani paused again, this time wondering about the wisdom in introducing this young girl to Tyler and Steven, but she supposed they would be best able to answer the questions she was sure to have. "There are others like you, others who have been given special powers."

Akna blinked. "There are?"

Shani nodded, smiling again. "Yes. Their names are Tyler, Steven, and Alexia. I can take you to them if you'd like."

Akna stared at the tan canvas tent walls for a few moments, then turned back to Shani and nodded. "Yes. I would like to meet them."

Shani stood then extended her hand to the young girl. After only a moment's hesitation, Akna took her offered hand and let Shani help her to her feet. Progress.

She led Akna out of the tent and over to where Tyler and Steven still sat in front of the fire. Once Akna fully understood what had happened to these men—Steven, in particular—she seemed to be a little more at ease. Shani breathed a sigh of relief as she began talking to Tyler in broken English—the two seemed as if they were quickly forming a fast friendship, almost as if Tyler was the long-lost older brother she never knew she'd had. Perhaps this would be easier than she thought.

Tyler pointed her in the direction Alexia had gone—he figured it was to her tent—so Shani left the girl in the care of the guys as she stole away, promising to return when she could.

She found Alexia's tent quickly and called out as she approached the closed tent flap. "Alexia, may I come in?"

She heard some rustling inside, a sniffle, then: "Sure."

Shani carefully lifted the tent flap, slowly stepping inside the tent and sitting on the ground opposite the cot where Alexia sat in a loose-fitting blouse covered in large, colorful flowers and jean shorts. Her eyes were red and puffy.

"Alexia, honey, are you okay?" Shani blinked a few times and furrowed her brow to emulate the concern she was supposed to be feeling.

The girl nodded once and rubbed her nose, sniffling again. "Sure," she repeated, but Shani knew there was more to the story.

"What's wrong?"

Alexia lifted her tearstained gaze to meet Shani's and sniffed. "I just . . . I just miss my family, my friends, my life in Florida."

Shani nodded sympathetically. "I understand."

Alexia's eyes grew just a little wider than normal. "Really?"

Shani smiled kindly, moving to sit next to her on the cot. She turned to Alexia. "Of course! I, too, was a student like you at UCF."

"You were?" Alexia blinked.

Shani's smile widened. "Yes! I even worked with Dr. Harrington and Dr. McGready." She'd had years of practice hiding her emotions, which helped her not snarl now when she said their names.

Alexia's face brightened. "They are so nice."

Shani placed a hand on the girl's shoulder, still smiling, and nodded. "They are." The two words left a bad taste in her mouth.

Silence fell between them for a brief moment before the girl looked up at her and spoke again. "So . . . what happens now?"

Shani met her gaze, her smile fading slowly. "Well, we have to stop some people who are out to hurt us."

Alexia gasped, and Shani simply nodded.

"Yes, they have enormous power, and they intend to use it to stop us." Shani almost believed her fabricated story. It was sort of true, really.

"Stop us from doing what?"

Shani took a breath. "Alexia, what do you know about what you were translating in the lab at UCF?"

Alexia's brow furrowed, and her head tilted to one side before she responded. "Hmmm . . . not much. Mandy usually had me help in bits and pieces—I did see a book at times, some sort of ancient text."

"Really?"

"Yes. At least, that's what I thought it was. Sometimes I'd help Mandy translate from an old book, but I never actually got a chance to read the full text of what we were translating. I assumed it was really old and fragile—it appeared to be— and that was why I didn't translate from it directly most of the time."

Shani hadn't quite expected this, but this development was better than she could've anticipated. She could definitely use this. "You were translating an ancient book, one that holds incredible power."

Alexia's eyes widened. "Are you sure?"

Shani nodded solemnly. "Yes. And that Power, in the wrong hands, could cause incomprehensible damage. Terror, even. And I mean to stop it." It wasn't all a lie.

Alexia thought for a moment then nodded back. "Okay. What can I do to help?"

Shani smiled again. "For starters, we need to know exactly what your power can do. Have you discovered any more about it yet?"

Alexia frowned, her eyes drooping. "Not really. I haven't even figured out how to activate it."

Shani wanted to scream, but instead, she took a deep breath before answering. "That's okay. We'll figure it out. We'll have it working reliably in no time. Sound good?"

Alexia smiled at her. "Yes! I just really want to help. But I'm still not sure how this helps Mandy."

Shani cringed internally at the deception she used to get this girl on the plane with her. She'd told her that Mandy needed her help, that she was special and could help the woman who'd given her a job translating an important text. She'd been eager to agree, but Shani sensed the story would come back to bite her someday.

That day apparently had come. "You don't need to worry about that now, honey. It will become clear very soon." Meaning that she needed some time to come up with a better lie.

Shani stood, effectively ending the conversation and the questions. Before leaving, she encouraged Alexia to find the others and get to know them. She didn't say it aloud, but Shani knew that was the only way they would work as a team when she needed them to.

The small matter of her newly superpowered cadets handled, Shani made her way back to her tent, where she was keeping the few things she'd brought with her to Belize. Most she wouldn't miss if for some reason she had to leave them here, but one thing in particular was too critical to leave behind.

Her black bag was lying on the ground at the foot of her cot as she entered her tent; she snatched it up and threw it on the bed, digging around in it. She knew it was in here somewhere . . .

Aha! Shani reached into the bag and pulled out something on a long chain. She held it up in front of her eyes, and the charm on the end of the chain glinted in the sunlight streaming through the canvas. The charm was a crude rendering of a lightning bolt, the Clan's symbol of their mission, their power.

The Clan had been around for centuries, and a lightning-bolt necklace had been passed to each new member since their inception. It stood for their power and strength, but Shani knew there was more to it than that.

The necklaces, to those chosen few who *really* knew all they could do, were precious commodities. Inside the charm, a small portion of the power of the Clan, of the Elders, was stored. They held within them enough magic to accomplish minor tasks, but it would be helpful, nonetheless. She was glad she'd thought to bring hers along.

Shani grinned then dropped the chain over her head. An anticipation started to build inside her as she did. She wasn't even sure how her plan would work; she just knew she had to try.

She headed outside and started walking through the camp, glancing up at the mountains directly in front of her. No one knew that a massive treasure was hidden beneath its rocky surface. How could they?

Shani strolled past the last of the canvas tents and into the rainforest. She had a plan, and though obtaining access to that vault of artifacts was high on the priority list, she had something more pressing to do first. Something that just may make obtaining that access possible, even probable.

Once she was out of sight of the camp, she started running. Soon, the trees, bushes, and undergrowth were blurs beside, above, and beneath her as she ran, the wind blowing her long hair like a midnight flag behind her. She loved the freedom of running through the forest, but she didn't have time to think about that now. Because she had to hurry. The longer she was gone, the more the Elders may suspect her.

And she couldn't have that.

Just Outside Lamanai Archaeological Dig

Mandy eagerly jumped at the chance to work on their powers when Kayla mentioned it to her—just like Justin had, as she knew he would. They'd all told Na-um and Holun where they were going—and turned down their requests to join; this was too personal for them—and headed out in search of a clearing just out of earshot of the dig. Out of earshot of their superhuman cohorts, anyway. At least, she hoped so.

They took their time finding the clearing. Mandy suspected they were faster now with the Power of the Codex flowing through their veins—perhaps even as fast as the superpowered members of the Clan—but she'd been hesitant to bring it up with the others, hesitant to even consider it herself. She didn't know why. Maybe because admitting it meant she had accepted their new shared destiny. And she wasn't sure she was ready for that.

Superpowers were cool and all, but how could she accept that her entire life had changed in an instant?

Mandy shivered despite the heat as they made their way through the thick, green foliage. Change wasn't always good

—she knew that better than anyone. Her parents had been happy, then her dad had left. Her mom had gotten remarried, but even that marriage had its ups and downs. And her long-time boyfriend—the one before Justin—had cheated on her, changing the trajectory of her life.

And that was just relationships.

Graduating with her bachelor's degree had signaled something new. Her impending graduation with her master's degree would just be another change. She'd have to find a real job, venture out into the real world, and try not to fail completely. And Justin . . .

Okay . . . admittedly, he'd been a good change.

But still, though getting superpowers seemed great on the surface—and feeling the power in her veins was thrilling, to say the least—Mandy was still cautious. She'd meant what she told Holun a few days ago—she loved her life, just as it was. Justin, school, their friendship with Kayla and Grady . . .

Okay, that had been a good change, too. And they never would've become such great friends if they hadn't gone on the quest for the Codex together. Mandy hadn't ever had good friends like them—especially Kayla, who she could talk to about anything—and she hadn't realized how much she'd needed them in her life.

So as they stepped out of the trees and into the wide clearing, Mandy drew in a deep breath, luxuriating in the feel of the warm, fresh air filling her lungs. She smiled, looking around at their close-knit group, people who had become an essential part of her life not in spite of but *because* of change.

Maybe this change wouldn't be so bad after all.

Kayla took the lead when they arrived. "Okay. With our telepathy down, we have to find another way to communicate in a fight."

Mandy put her hands on her hips. "The Elders have powers, too, Kayla, and we don't even know what they are. They probably know everything about what we can do, probably even more than we do! And we don't even know everything Shani can do."

"But they don't have the element of surprise," Grady jumped in. "Remember the Power of the Codex is stronger than the power of the Elders, even Shani. That's how it was designed, right? That's why they want it sò badly."

Kayla smiled at Grady and reached to squeeze his hand before she released it. "Grady's right. We shouldn't even need our powers if Na-um does what he says he's going to do. This is just in case." She smiled. "Plus, it feels good to stretch our powers. Trust us." She looked over at Grady, her smile widening. He grinned back, nodding.

"Justin, would you like to start?"

Justin nodded at Kayla then started jumping up and down, shaking out his arms and bobbing his head from side to side. Kayla always thought he looked like a boxer getting ready to fight in the ring or a basketball player setting up for a free-throw shot. Then he abruptly stopped jumping and stood calmly, legs separated and arms slightly extended off to his sides. His eyes slid shut, and Kayla thought he looked a little like Holun when he was getting his visions.

After several quiet moments, Justin suddenly straightened his arms, palms down, and froze. Nothing happened. Justin opened one eye. "Anything?"

Mandy shook her head at him. "Nope, babe. Nothing."

"Let me try it again." Justin started jumping up and down once more, cycling through his warm up. He calmed himself then again abruptly straightened his arms toward the ground. This time, a spark flew from his hands and sizzled a tiny hole in the grass before fizzling out.

"That's it?" Justin moaned.

Grady took a few steps toward him. "We suspected it would be difficult. We relied on our telepathy to make our powers work before, and we had just received the Power. Maybe the Power has dissipated over these past few months. We really have to start training regularly to keep our powers working well."

Mandy nodded. "Definitely."

Grady looked over at her as she spoke. "You wanna try next?"

Mandy shrugged. "I can, but my power tends to be more telepathic. It may be down with our common telepathy."

Kayla spoke up. "Worth a try." She stuffed her hands in her pockets and shrugged.

Mandy closed her eyes, stretched her arms out at her hips with her palms forward, and stood still for several moments. Then Kayla felt a wind at her back.

Mandy's eyes opened. "Did something happen? I felt something . . ."

Kayla had a sudden thought. Was that . . . ? "I felt a wind that I didn't feel before."

"Wind?" Mandy asked.

"Yes. I think it was from you."

"Really?" Mandy's eyes were wide.

"Sure, baby!" Justin came over to her and put his arm around her. "I know it hasn't worked this way before, but the symbol on your book *was* the symbol for air. Maybe this is your more active power." Justin was smiling.

Mandy grinned right back. "Awesome!" Kayla always thought she sounded like Justin when she said that. "Let me try again."

She closed her eyes a second time, and Kayla felt a strong wind come from behind her almost immediately. Soon it was so strong she had to brace herself against it.

Mandy opened her eyes and stared right at her friend, eyes wide. "Whoa."

Justin was grinning beside her. "Awesome, babe!"

Mandy had her arms out in front of her, controlling the wind coming from behind Kayla. Then Mandy swept her hands up, and Kayla felt the wind travel upward, along her back, and disappear into the sky. The Four watched as the trees above fluttered, then waved, then violently shook as the wind passed by. Mandy swept her arms around the canopy above them, the wind obeying her every silent command. Kayla hadn't seen their power work so smoothly since the cave, when they first received their powers. And this was Mandy's first time.

"Are you sure you haven't done this before, Mandy?" Grady asked from Kayla's left.

Mandy chuckled. "Nope, never. Promise." She somehow still held on, moving the invisible ball of wind up and down, over and back, around the clearing. All four sets of eyes kept following it.

Then Mandy brought the wind toward the ground. The grass shook violently as it settled into one place. Mandy drew in a deep breath then clapped her hands together. Instantly, the wind dispersed.

"Amazing," Grady breathed from beside Kayla. She smiled to herself. Despite the struggle she was having recently connecting with him, Kayla really did love Grady. And realizing just how much she loved him made her heart ache. She frowned, and a pit formed in her stomach. She desperately missed him.

So she decided to do something about it. She walked to his side and leaned in. "Grady?"

Grady was staring at Mandy and Justin, who had moved a ways away and were currently attempting to display their powers to each other. It looked like Mandy may have been giving Justin some pointers—and by the looks of it, he wasn't getting it.

At the sound of Kayla's voice, Grady jumped.

"Sorry! Didn't mean to scare you." Kayla leaned back slightly, trying to give him some space.

Grady smiled at her. "No, it's fine. I was just watching those two." He nodded across the clearing at their friends before turning back to Kayla. "What's up?"

Kayla paused. What was she going to say to him? That she wanted him, needed him close to her? That wouldn't work . . . "How are you feeling?"

Grady blinked but answered. "Okay, I think. It's still really hard missing all this information, but I'm learning to trust the three of you to fill in the gaps."

Kayla nodded, unsure of how to respond. She thought back to the many memories she'd made with Grady this summer, memories she knew he couldn't remember, and her shoulders slumped. This was so unfair. Grady didn't deserve any of this.

And neither did she! She'd gone through a really bad relationship and years of none before she finally fell in love with Grady. They'd gone through so much to find each other—they deserved a happy life together, one unaffected by tragedy or loss. But in a matter of seconds, it had been ripped away from her. She just wanted to scream.

"Are you okay?"

Grady's voice broke into her pity party, and the tone of his voice abruptly wrenched her thoughts to the present. Even when he wasn't fully there—with his memories gone— he somehow still knew how to reach her.

Immediately, her thoughts softened, and she actually smiled. "Grady, sorry. And thank you."

"Thank you?" Grady's brow furrowed.

Kayla smiled wider, reaching for his hand and squeezing it before she could stop herself. "Yes, thank you. Somehow you know just what to say and how to say it to bring me back to myself."

Grady smiled back at her, holding tightly to her hand as if refusing to release it. "Happy to help."

Kayla enjoyed the feel of his hand in hers for a few moments before a thought popped into her head. "You know, we haven't tried our powers out yet. Not since you lost your memory. At least, I haven't—have you tried yours?"

Grady shook his head. "I think I've almost been afraid to, worried it may hurt my memory more. Or maybe I'm just worried that those memories are gone, too."

Kayla nodded. "I get it. I've had the same thought since our telepathy went down." She sighed. "But I suppose we'll need to at least know if our powers are working before we face Shani and the Elders. You wanna give it a try with me?"

Grady's mouth turned up. "Of course, anything with you."

Kayla felt the blood rush to her cheeks before she turned away, dropping his hand. She cleared her throat. "Okay, mind if I go first?"

Grady shook his head again and took a step back, spreading his arms out with a flourish and a slight bow, giving her the floor. "By all means; ladies first."

Kayla smiled at him then let her eyelids fall closed. For what seemed like the first time since the lounge at UCF, Kayla allowed herself to focus on the present moment. She zeroed in on her breathing, in and out, in and out, until the only sensation she felt was the earth beneath her feet and a slight breeze ruffling her hair. She drew her arms away from her body slightly, allowing the warm breeze to calm her, soothe her.

When she felt like she was fully concentrating, she started to gather her power to her, like she'd done in the past. It was a little like stretching an internal muscle she hadn't used in a while, but it felt good. She gathered her power from deep inside her and felt it start to make its way to her arms, legs, and head.

But before she could release it, it suddenly fizzled out. What was going on? She opened her eyes to see Grady staring at her, his head cocked to the side, his brow furrowed.

She sighed. "Sorry, I couldn't get it to work. It's there, but I can't figure out how to release it."

Grady blinked and relaxed his features. "Let me try." He closed his eyes, took a deep breath, and looked a lot like what Kayla imagined she'd looked like just a few moments ago.

And the result seemed to be the same as well. After a few moments, Grady let out a loud sigh and opened his eyes. "Nothing with me, either."

Kayla felt herself frowning. "So how did Mandy make it work?" She glanced over at Mandy and Justin, who were still working on their powers together. Justin seemed to have made a little more progress than the last time she'd glanced their way. "And apparently Justin?" Kayla felt her pity party coming back on and chastised herself. *Stop it, Kayla. You're not a child.*

I don't think you're a child.

Kayla jumped, startled by the other voice in her head. What ... who ... *Grady?* Kayla found his wide-eyed gaze and held it.

Kayla? I can hear you?!

Kayla nodded at him, her eyes just as wide as his. *Yes, whatever we just did must've helped us break through Shani's powers. Can you hear them?* She nodded toward their friends.

Grady glanced over for a moment then shook his head. *No. Can you?*

Kayla shook her head as well. *No. I'm just grateful to have you back. Is anything else back?*

You can ask if my memories are back, Kayla.

She offered a slight sad smile.

But no, they're still a mystery to me. Perhaps our concentration helped us break through Shani's hold on our telepathy, but she's still very powerful. And something tells me the power and concentration it takes to steal someone's memories requires an awful lot of energy and focus. Maybe we just got lucky, and she's tiring?

Kayla shrugged. *I doubt it. Shani's much too powerful for that. You've seen how long she's been able to keep your memories from you—I wouldn't assume she's slowing down. I wouldn't want to underestimate her.*

Good idea. Grady paused then spoke again. *Should we try to use our powers now? Perhaps the telepathy will let us join our collective power and help it break through.*

Kayla smiled at him. *Why didn't I think of that?*

Grady grinned back. *Well, you know, sometimes I have a decent thought or two ...*

She chuckled softly. *Of course you do. Let's do it.*

Kayla started to close her eyes, but before she could, she felt Grady slip his hand into hers. She smiled at the warmth of his touch in the heat of the sun. As her eyes fell closed and she slipped into her meditative practice, she felt Grady do the same, and her heart warmed. They could definitely use some good news in all of this.

After a few moments, Kayla felt her power building. This time, instead of slowly building then fizzling out, her power rushed through her so quickly she barely had time to let go of Grady's hand before it shook her body. Kayla's arms straightened in front of her as the Power rushed through her arms, wrists, hands, fingertips, and finally released toward the ground. The ground ahead of her disintegrated, creating a large hole just in front of where they stood.

She heard Grady struggling to contain his power as well, and she looked over just as he released a torrent of water into the large hole she'd just made. Kayla's eyes were wide as a tiny lake formed right in front of them.

We did that, Grady.

Grady nodded beside her, reaching for her hand once again. *I can't believe it. How did we manage that?*

The water in front of them, originally undulating as if by a current, finally started to settle. Kayla just stared at it. *The Power. It was there all along. The telepathy, our powers—we've had them all along. We just didn't know how to access them.*

We let Shani get in the way.

Kayla froze at Grady's astute observation. *You're right.*

It happens.

Kayla laughed aloud.

Just Outside Lamanai

Despite being the middle of the afternoon, Shani moved unseen through the rainforest. Though not invisible, the powers afforded her by her Clan allowed her to anticipate where others were and avoid them. Not that there were many people in the rainforest, anyway.

She silently pulled to a stop just before she reached the clearing and listened. She'd heard the Four off in the distance, doing *something*—what it was she couldn't really tell, nor did she really care—but they were off-site for the time being and, more importantly, out of her way. She peered through the thick vegetation to the dig, the place she used to call her temporary home. It seemed like a lifetime ago.

Only a few people were around, and they'd be easy to avoid. She knew from her years at the university and on digs such as this one that most of the dig personnel had already headed back to the States for the upcoming holiday season. This would almost be too easy.

She started to head into the clearing, but then she sensed him. She froze.

She knew Holun was here—he'd most likely been the one to give her that vision, after all—but she hadn't realized the other one, the one she should've sensed from miles away, was here.

Things just got exponentially more complicated.

CHAPTER 19

The Strength of Four Superheroes

AT THE SOUND OF KAYLA'S laugh, Mandy turned to find her friend. She'd been working with Justin for who knew how long now, and he was just starting to get it. She loved teaching, but this was a lot of work.

Hey, I heard that!

Mandy blinked. *Justin? How are you hearing me? Did something happen to Shani?*

How would I know?

Mandy rolled her eyes at him then grabbed his hand to lead him toward Kayla and Grady. *We should see what . . . wait —what is that?*

What is wha—oh! Did they just create a lake?!

Mandy and Justin ran up beside Kayla and Grady, staring at the body of water that had just appeared out of nowhere. "How did you . . . did you . . . how . . ." Mandy stammered.

She knew she wasn't making sense, but words were failing her.

"Did you guys seriously just create a lake out of nothing?!" Justin's voice got a few decibels louder than it normally would have been, but Mandy completely understood.

Kayla laughed again. "Yes."

Mandy cocked her head to the side. "Is something else going on?" She looked from Kayla to Grady then back to Kayla. *Something is definitely different with them, Justin.*

Justin glanced over at her, crossing his arms, then looked at their friends. *I think you're right.*

Kayla shared a glance with Grady before answering. "Yes. We can hear each other again." She reached for Grady's hand, and he took it without hesitation.

Mandy's mouth fell open. "Us, too! I was wondering how, why, then I heard you . . ."

Justin continued for her. "What she means to say is that we can hear each other, too. But not you guys." He shrugged.

Grady took a step closer to Kayla. "We can't hear you, either. But the crazy thing was that as soon as we could hear each other, we were able to connect and make our powers work. Is that how it worked for you?"

Justin shook his head. "No, Mandy was just giving me some pointers. It took me awhile to get it." He turned to glare at Mandy, who stuck her tongue out at him.

"Maybe you should try again, now that you can hear each other," Kayla suggested. "We were able to really tap into our powers when we connected in that way."

Mandy looked over at Justin. *Worth a try?*

Sure, why not? Justin reached for her hand, and Mandy closed her eyes. Soon she could feel the heat building up in Justin—then suddenly he released a fireball into the air so hot that the four of them all jumped back. Mandy opened her eyes, releasing a gush of wind to put out the fire in midair.

"Wow! That was incredible, babe!" Mandy yelled.

Justin was grinning. "Yes! Should we try again?"

Mandy nodded, and the others nodded right along with her.

The next couple of hours were spent in the clearing, learning about and practicing their powers. All four of them practiced individually, but soon they started to join forces and use their powers together to create an even bigger impact.

And Kayla quickly noticed that bigger was right. She created what could only be considered a small mountain out of the ground, leaving only a small depression in the ground where she'd displaced some of the earth to create it. She honestly wasn't even sure where the rest of the dirt came from to make up the mountain—was she *creating* it?

Grady had summoned a waterfall out of thin air, and he and Kayla recreated their mudslide move from the first battle with Na-um this past summer, just to prove to themselves they could do it again. But they both soon got bored with the same moves and tried some new ones.

Kayla threw some dirt into the air, and Grady added water at just the right places to create little mud bombs, balls of thick and heavy wet earth that smashed into the ground and left large depressions in their wake. Kayla used the earth to create a wall of sorts, then Grady used a torrent to destroy it, splattering mud from the wall on anyone or anything who would dare to stand nearby.

Soon Kayla called over Mandy and Justin, who had been working on their own tricks. Kayla could see they had already mastered Justin creating a fireball and Mandy directing it around the clearing, but she wanted to see what more they all could do together.

"What if we try using all our powers together? I'm sure we'd be able to accomplish so much more—and be much more powerful, for that matter." Kayla felt a wide grin spread across her face.

Justin wrapped an arm around Mandy. "Sure! What did you have in mind?"

Kayla glanced over at Grady, who reached for her hand and smiled. "Here's what we were thinking: We're not actually sure where all these things come from, right? It seems I can create earth out of thin air, and Grady can bring water out even though there doesn't seem to be much around. We know you can create fire from your hands, too, Justin. So what if the things that we create have different properties than the natural things we can control?"

Mandy cocked her head to one side. "What do you mean?"

Kayla grinned. "I think that maybe Justin's fire may be waterproof. And perhaps my earth can serve as a conduit for it as well."

Justin was staring off into space. "Wouldn't that go against the laws of nature?"

Kayla shrugged. "I don't know, maybe? But it's certainly not natural for us to be able to control these things, right?"

Grady spoke up. "I say we try it. It can't hurt, right? And we may discover something that we can use, something no one would be able to anticipate."

Mandy shrugged. "Sure, why not? Is there any part I can play in this?"

Kayla looked over at her. "Maybe. Yours is a little harder to understand, because there is always natural air to use to create wind. But maybe . . ." Kayla stared off into the woods for a moment. "What if . . . Mandy, can you tell me what I'm thinking right now?"

Mandy frowned. "You know I can't, Kayla. I already told you we can't hear you and Grady."

"I know," Kayla started, "but I have an idea. I think the air you create unknowingly has the ability to pass through objects. And, more importantly, people."

"How does that help me hear you?"

The corner of Kayla's mouth turned up. "I think you can pass through the human body and into the brain to hear our thoughts. To hear the thoughts of anyone. You remember that happened before, in the cave?"

Mandy gasped. "I'd forgotten all about that! I heard Naum!" Mandy shuddered. "I didn't really care for that."

Justin pulled her close. "I know, babe, but it helped us defeat him. You may have the most important power of all, the one that may make the difference when we fight."

Mandy looked up at him, but Kayla didn't think she looked too sure about that. Mandy took a deep breath then stood up straight. "I can try."

Mandy closed her eyes, calling her power to her. This time, instead of focusing on calling air to her to create wind, she drew air from within her and released it. And it felt different, thinner, almost ethereal.

She let the wind from her fingertips go and sent it toward Kayla. And suddenly, she could hear Kayla's thoughts.

"Kayla! I hear you!"

Mandy? Can you try to talk back to me, see if it works both ways?

Kayla? Can you hear me?

Kayla nodded. "It's faint, but I can hear you. We can make it work." She smiled at her friend.

Mandy smiled back. "I'm so relieved. I was so worried we wouldn't be able to stay in touch with you guys during the battle!"

"Who knows, babe?" Justin jumped in. "Perhaps with the adrenaline of battle, we'll be able to connect to each other, after all. Then you will only have to use it on our enemies."

Mandy didn't like the sound of that at all.

Lamanai

What was she going to do? She couldn't face him, couldn't see that same hurt look on his face he'd directed at her this past summer. She couldn't stand the fact that she'd been forced to hurt him, even though he'd rejected her—but she couldn't let him get in her way now.

Shani entered the clearing, moving quickly to the work trailer and hiding behind it, avoiding the windows and the personnel inside. She already knew where Holun was—he'd been easy to sense—but the other one seemed to be away at the moment.

This was her chance. She'd have to move quickly, even more quickly than she had in the forest, but she knew she had the ability. She would have to grab what she came here for and get back into the rainforest before the other man even noticed.

Because Na-um could move just as quickly.

Shani looked down at the lightning-bolt charm hanging from her neck. Her mental reserves had been gradually dwindling, so she knew she wouldn't have the strength to accomplish her task and control Na-um's mind as well.

With the chain still around her neck, Shani reached down and pinched the charm between her thumb and forefinger. She pressed her fingers together, the dull, pointed, metal edges digging into her skin. As she did, a red glow began to emanate from behind the charm, lighting up the space behind it.

She hadn't done this in a while, but the action came naturally. Shani grinned then directed the glowing red light around her until it encased her as if in a bubble.

Once she was sure the shield was in place, she made her move, sprinting toward the tent where Holun was staying. She should be able to get in and out in a matter of seconds.

She reached the tent then threw aside the canvas flap. Holun startled from his position on the cot, but Shani knew it was only from the movement of the tent flap and not from her. Because her charm was currently shielding her from being seen.

Since Holun couldn't see her, she was able to get a hand clamped down on his mouth before he could scream. She wrenched him from the bed and was outside in no more than a second. He was struggling—and he'd certainly developed the muscles that were common among the young men in the Clan—but she was strong, and she managed to get him into the rainforest without a sound.

She was so preoccupied with getting Holun out quietly that she didn't notice the well-dressed man eyeing her from the window of the nearest work trailer, a handsome man whose eyes and mouth fell open at the sight of her.

CHAPTER 20

The Imprisonment

SHANI RAN, HOLUN on her back. Even with the extra weight, she was making good time.

She soon reached her destination, a dark cave on the side of the same mountain where the treasure was stored. Shani entered the cave, eyeing the shackles she'd already installed there, then tossed him in the dirt. He was bound to the back wall in a matter of seconds, but still he struggled, his eyes shooting daggers at her.

That pleased her very much.

She grinned back at him, crossing her arms and standing over him. "I hope you enjoy your new accommodations," she trilled in a singsong voice, "because they will be your last."

She grinned even wider as she watched all the blood drain from his face.

The Clearing Outside Lamanai

Kayla was pleased with the progress they were making, but she was starting to get tired. And a little hungry. Wasn't it dinnertime about now?

She looked up at the sun, which had sunken far lower to the west than Kayla had realized. She glanced over at Grady, who was currently practicing his powers with Mandy and Justin a few yards away.

Hey, Grady, you ready to go?

Grady glanced over at her, and she was grateful their telepathy was still intact. She didn't think she'd ever take that for granted again.

Grady nodded at her then jogged to her side. He reached for her, pulling her into a hug. She loved being close to him. She'd never take that for granted again, either.

Grady pulled away enough to lean down for a quick kiss then reached for her hand. She squeezed it with a smile in his direction, which he returned. Her heart melted. How had she ever survived without him?

We can go, sure.

Kayla led him back toward the edge of the rainforest. *Great, thanks. I'm starting to get tired—and hungry!* Her stomach growled as if on cue, and she chuckled.

"Mandy, Justin! You coming?" She yelled across the clearing to their two friends, who were still enthralled in practicing, by the looks of it.

Mandy glanced over her shoulder as she held a fiery ball several feet over Justin's head. "No, you both go ahead. We'll wrap up and head back soon; we're just not quite ready yet."

Kayla waved at her. "See you soon!" Then she glanced over at Grady with a smile as they stepped into the rainforest, hand in hand.

Just before they reached the dig, Grady stopped, her hand still in his. She turned around to look at him. "Grady? Is something wrong?"

He stared off into the trees. "I think . . ." He swallowed hard. "I just . . . I need to talk to you before we get back to the dig." He turned to catch Kayla's gaze. She nodded, and his next words came out as a whisper. "I'm worried."

Kayla reached her free hand up to cup his cheek. "What about?"

Grady leaned into her hand then turned and kissed it. "That I'll lose you. We got our telepathy back, but I still can't remember you from before. And I'm worried it's going to stay that way."

She felt tears burn the back of her eyes. "Oh, sweetie—I'm right here. You won't lose me. No matter what happens—even if you never remember—I'll be right here."

Grady nodded then brought his hand up to lay over her own. His eyes fell shut, and Kayla could feel his thoughts—his anxiety, his concerns—come to the surface and swirl around in his head.

She desperately wished she could take it away from him. She wished she could make his thoughts pleasant again, reassure him.

But she couldn't think of anything to say.

Just then, she heard a rustling behind her. Kayla jumped to Grady's side as they peered through the trees.

"Kayla, Grady!" Na-um shouted as he came into view. "I heard you approach. Come quickly! Something has happened."

Kayla's stomach dropped. This couldn't be good.

Grady spoke as they followed Na-um back to the dig. "What's wrong?"

Na-um barely glanced back. Kayla could tell he was getting frustrated, probably with how slow they were moving through the forest. "Holun is gone."

"Gone?" Kayla asked, carefully stepping over a fallen log.

Na-um nodded, still ahead of them and not looking back. "Yes. I left him for a minute to get something from the mess tent, and when I came back, he was gone."

Kayla's head launched into blame mode, but she bit her tongue. This could've happened to anyone—no need to unleash on Na-um. Besides, they needed him. She heard Grady agree.

"What do you think happened?"

Na-um glanced back at Grady's question just as he stepped into Lamanai's clearing. "I cannot be sure, but I think it may have been Shani."

"Shani?" Kayla kicked herself for her second one-word, inane question, but she couldn't seem to help herself.

Grady was smiling at her internal dialogue. She gave him a sideways glance, and he wiped the smile from his face.

Na-um led them to Holun's tent. "Yes. The Elders told me she was here in Belize. They did not say, but I got the sense they thought she was up to something. Maybe this was it." Na-um held aside the canvas flap. "This is just how I found it."

Grady stepped inside to examine the interior. Except for an unmade bed, nothing seemed out of place. And for a teenaged boy, the bed didn't really seem out of place, either. "How long ago did you discover him missing?"

"About ten minutes. I heard you in the forest just after I found this and immediately ran to get you."

Grady nodded then looked over at Kayla who stood just outside the tent's door. "How do we find him?"

Kayla frowned. "I'm not sure. But we sensed Shani was here in Belize; maybe this is her way of making her presence known."

Grady stepped outside to join Kayla and Na-um, nodding. "Makes sense. But why? Why would she need . . ."

Kayla saw the blood drain from his face as he realized just why someone as powerful as Shani would need Holun.

His visions.

Kayla nodded. *She's planning something.*

But what? Does she know about the artifacts, too? Is she trying to get to them before we can? I wouldn't put it past her.

Me neither. "Na-um," Kayla started, "does everyone in your Clan know about the artifacts?"

Na-um stared past her into the rainforest then shifted his gaze back to the two of them. "Not everyone, but some of the warriors do."

"And your sister?" Kayla pressed.

Na-um sighed. "She would probably have devoted her life to learning all the secrets and prophecies of our Clan. She was tracking you all for *years*, after all—she had to be doing something to keep herself busy."

Kayla felt sick. Shani knew a lot of their secrets and just how to get to them. Now, in all likelihood, she knew about the artifacts they were after and probably where they were located. She always seemed to be one step ahead of them.

Grady looked over at her then spoke up. "Any ideas?"

Na-um eyed him. "Yes, actually. We need to translate more of the Codex."

At his last word, Kayla's stomach dropped. Was this his end game after all? Would he betray them once he found out what was in the Codex—or worse, would he try to steal it once he knew where it was?

Kayla, we have to see this through. And he's right about this, you know. We need to know everything the Codex says.

That doesn't mean I have to like it.

Grady grinned at her.

Mandy and Justin got back half an hour later, and Kayla, Grady, and Na-um met them in the mess tent for a light dinner. The dig was still well-stocked, especially considering the skeleton crew that was here this semester, but Kayla thought it would be wise to keep some meals in reserve. Just in case they were here awhile.

While they ate, Kayla reluctantly told Mandy and Justin about Holun's kidnapping. They were both livid, but it took a good twenty minutes to talk Mandy out of running into the forest after Holun. They had no clue where Shani had taken him, after all—they'd be wandering around aimlessly, which would just waste a bunch of time.

Eventually Mandy understood, but it still took another ten minutes to convince her that their next best step was translating the rest of the Codex.

So once they finished dinner, Mandy pulled the Codex from her luggage and brought it to the work trailer. She set the book down on the large, stainless steel table in the middle of the trailer and spread it out in front of the four of them—they all thought it best not to involve Na-um right away, see if they could make some headway on their own. Kayla nodded a quick hello to the Central American Institute of Archaeology's liaison—one of the few personnel still left on the dig—as he packed up and headed outside.

But after several minutes had passed, Kayla sighed. She sensed they may be here for a long while. They still needed to find the artifacts, and she didn't have the first clue where to look. And they needed to find Holun, but they didn't have a clue where to find him either. Besides all that, the globe, the only thing that had helped them in the past, was in the hands of their enemy. She was beginning to lose hope that anything would go their way.

You okay? Grady's voice broke into her thoughts, and she reached for his hand under the table, squeezing it.

Sure, she replied, *just thinking.*

Holun will be okay.

Kayla shrugged. *I hope so. But who knows what Shani will do to him?*

She needs him. She won't kill him.

Kayla looked over at him and caught his gaze. *That's what I'm afraid of. She could hurt him and still get what she wants.* The thought chilled her blood, and Kayla shivered. They all felt a strong protection instinct when it came to Holun, and she was no different. She just wished she knew where he was so they could go rescue him.

She desperately needed a distraction. "Mandy? You find anything?"

Mandy had been poring over the Codex for the last half hour. Surely she would've found something by now.

Mandy sighed. "Ugh. Not much." She stood and flipped her hair behind her shoulders. "Holun was the one really helping us make headway."

"Well, he's not here!" Kayla yelled.

Grady grabbed her by the elbow and pulled her toward the door.

"Kayla," Grady started once they were outside in the waning light. "You know you can't treat Mandy that way. She's doing the best she can."

"It's not good enough, Grady! She has to step up her game before something happens to Holun."

"Kayla, stop." Grady needed to get her under control. He could sense the rage inside her and knew it would consume her if he didn't help her stop it.

"No! Holun could be out there right now, scared and alone and hurting, all because we wanted to go play in the woods! This is our fault! This is *my* . . . fault." She'd stopped shouting by that last sentence, and now she quieted. "It's my fault, Grady. I should've been here to stop her."

"Kayla, no." Grady reached for her hand and pulled her to him. "Even if you had been here, who knows if we could've stopped her? This isn't your fault. It's Shani's."

Grady pulled Kayla to his chest as she started crying. She sobbed into his soft, black t-shirt, and Grady just held her. He knew they didn't need words, knew that just holding her while she cried would be enough.

Eventually, her tears subsided, and she blinked up at him. "Thank you, Grady."

Grady smiled at her, running a hand through her hair. "It's okay, Kayla. I've got you."

Kayla smiled back at him, but it quickly faded. "What are we going to do, Grady? It feels like everything is falling apart."

Grady looked off into the darkness, nearly complete on this side of the dig save the lone spotlight on the work trailer. "I've heard it said that sometimes things need to fall apart for other things to come together."

"But it's Holun!"

"I know," Grady rubbed her hair again then leaned down for a quick kiss. "But Holun is stronger than we think. He can take care of himself."

Kayla blinked up at him then shook her head. "I hope you're right."

A Cave Somewhere Outside the Mercenaries' Camp

Holun couldn't see any sunlight from here, so he wasn't really sure how much time had passed since he'd come here. He supposed it was nearly dark—even with his extrasensory eyesight, he was starting to have trouble seeing his surroundings clearly. Earlier today—or possibly yesterday, since he'd fallen asleep of few times out of boredom more than anything else—he'd been able to see a little sun shining through the cave's person-sized entrance. But now, only diffused light lit the small space.

Shani had brought in a few meals since he'd been here, spaced out in what felt like normal intervals, but he couldn't really be sure. Maybe a day's worth? Had it really been a full day? Longer?

Holun heard a rustling at the entrance of the cave that was becoming commonplace. It could only mean one thing: Shani was returning.

She stepped into view, her sneer ghoulish in the lengthening shadows, and Holun scowled at her. She just laughed, throwing her head back. "You are a fighter, aren't you?" Shani walked over to him and crouched down beside him. Suddenly, she grabbed the hair at the back of his head and yanked his head back, exposing his neck. Holun sucked in a sharp breath, wincing. His eyes squeezed shut against the pain.

"I will tear you down until you don't have the *will* to fight." Shani whispered inches from his ear. "You *will* help me, Holun."

"I will never help you, Shani," Holun growled through clenched teeth.

His hair was yanked tighter for his trouble, and he called out.

Shani laughed again then finally let go of his hair and stood. Holun stretched his neck, trying to work out all the kinks. "You will help me. You will not have a choice."

Holun just glared at her.

"Fine, think what you'd like. You will find I am telling the truth. And that's a promise, Holun." Shani spun and exited the cave. A moment later, a metal tray was tossed into the room, the cup on it spilling as the tray hit the ground. On it were scraps of food.

Holun supposed this would be all he would be getting in the way of meals from now on. He must've really hit a nerve.

CHAPTER 21

Yatzil

HOLUN WOKE WITH A START, blinking. He couldn't see any light in here—the subtle glow from earlier was now gone, and pitch-black darkness had invaded. He thought he'd been sleeping awhile, but he couldn't really be sure. He couldn't really be sure of anything at this point.

He heard a rustling in the darkness, much too close. He sat up abruptly, eyes straining to see the source of the sound, which was probably what had woken him up.

There it was again. Holun scooted up against the wall he knew was behind him, the one that his shackles were bolted to. The iron bonds dug into his wrists as he strained against them, his eyes still searching the darkness.

He heard a scratching noise; then, in the next second, he squeezed his eyes shut against a bright light.

When he opened them again, his eyes saw the face of an angel.

"Hello," the girl, probably about sixteen, sang in the Clan's native tongue. Holun could only see the edges of her long, dark hair framing her perfectly symmetrical, tanned face and a little bit of her rustic clothing, but all the clues pointed to her being from the Clan. Plus, she did seem a little familiar . . .

"Hi." Holun wasn't sure what else to say, but he didn't want this beautiful woman—the most wonderful thing he'd seen all day—to leave.

She smiled in the light. "I am Yatzil." The young woman sat down across from Holun. The light from the match she'd lit danced in her warm, brown eyes as it burned dangerously close to her hand. She blew it out and lit another. "And you are Holun, correct?"

How does she know who I am? She does look familiar . . . Holun didn't want to keep her waiting. "Y-yes. I am. Holun."

The girl laughed. "You are wondering how I know who you are, right?"

Holun just nodded.

The girl laughed again. "The whole Clan knows of you, Holun. They say you betrayed us."

Holun stared at the ground, lowering his head.

But the girl reached under his chin and raised it until her gaze locked on to his. "Do not be ashamed of your choices, Holun. I am sure you only did what you thought was right."

Holun cocked his head to the side as she discarded and lit yet another match. Something she'd said . . . oh, yes! "I remember you . . ." Holun ventured, hoping he was right and he wouldn't look foolish in front of this entrancing creature.

Yatzil smiled at him. "We trained together. At least, the training the children in the Clan were allowed to do."

Yes, now he was sure he remembered her. His mind took him back to that place, several years ago, when a young girl stole his heart as she prattled on about anything and everything while they ate their midday meal side by side. She'd been captivating then, even at nine years old, but now her beauty clutched his heart in its grasp and wouldn't let go.

Holun felt his chest tighten, an overwhelmingly pleasant sensation. He had the thought that this woman could ask him to do anything in this moment, and he would.

Yatzil was still smiling, even as she lit another match. She stayed silent as she looked Holun over in the light. He shifted in his seat in the sand.

"So how are you here?" Holun wanted not only to continue hearing that lilting voice but also to keep her from leaving as quickly as she'd come.

Yatzil drew in a deep breath before speaking. "It is a long story."

"I am not going anywhere." Holun grinned.

Yatzil giggled. "No, I suppose you are not." She paused. "Are you sure you do not want to go back to sleep?"

Holun nodded vigorously.

Yatzil threw down her match but scooted over to sit next to Holun against the wall before lighting another one. "We have all heard of you in the village, like I said. Everyone made you out to be the villain, but I suspected you were not. After all, we knew each other when we were kids, right?" Holun nodded at her before she continued. "The boy I knew then would never have betrayed his people without a very good reason."

Holun wanted to open his mouth to explain but thought he should let her continue before he interrupted with his own story.

Yatzil kept going. "So recently Na-um disappeared, and the Elders started to act oddly again, like they did this summer. Then we heard that Shani was back." Holun stiffened beside her as she threw down yet another match. "I do not know Shani, but I have heard stories of her. I heard stories of her this summer, too, stories that . . ." Her voice trailed off. "I just know she should be taken seriously."

Holun nodded at her in the darkness, momentarily forgetting that she couldn't see it.

"Shani left camp—my mother works near the tent of Bacob and hears many things—earlier this evening. The Elders somehow found out she had kidnapped someone from the First Site." Holun knew she was referring to him and Lamanai, but he hadn't heard Lamanai called the "First Site" before. Perhaps this was a new development among his—um, formerly his—people? "They were discussing how to handle the situation, according to my mother."

Holun was staring off into black nothingness as she relit another match. When he realized she wasn't going to continue, he prodded. "How did you know she had taken that someone here? What made you come to this cave?"

Yatzil, for the first time, averted her eyes. Holun noticed a slight crinkle in her forehead as she looked away.

"Yatzil?" he encouraged.

The beautiful young woman finally turned back toward him. "This may sound crazy."

If she only knew . . . "I am . . . comfortable . . . with crazy."

"Are you sure?"

Holun grinned at her, and he noticed her features soften just a little. "Okay." She drew in another deep breath. "I saw it."

Holun immediately understood and froze. Then, when he found his voice: "You *saw* it?"

Yatzil looked down and away again. Holun jumped right in, giving her previous words back to her. "Do not be ashamed of your gifts, Yatzil."

She swallowed hard, eyes flashing to his. "*Gifts?*"

Holun was smiling again. "Yes, gifts."

Yatzil just stared at him.

Holun jumped back in. "What did you see?"

The teenaged girl blinked rapidly then swept her eyes around the room as if someone might be listening. "I saw the woman, Shani—how she had violently torn you from your bed at the First Site—and somehow my mind followed her here. I played up here as a child when my mother and I would go into the woods for several weeks. I recognized it immediately."

"Wow," Holun breathed. "Was this your first vision?"

Yatzil blinked once, then her eyes stretched wide. "Vision?"

Holun chuckled. "Yes." He drew in a breath. "I get them, too."

Yatzil gasped, simultaneously discarding the match. She didn't reach for another one, and Holun idly wondered why. She swallowed hard before answering his question in the pitch black. "This was my first." Holun could tell by the sound of her voice that she was staring at the floor.

"Do not worry, Yatzil. Our visions are given to us to help."

"Help with what?"

Holun sighed. That would be a long story. "Maybe that's a story for another time."

Yatzil struck another match, and the light blinded Holun again momentarily. "I will be here all night."

"Is there not someone waiting for you?"

Yatzil's face fell, and Holun desperately wanted to fix whatever was bothering her. She continued. "I came to find you, Holun, though I didn't know why. I cannot explain the vision I had, but I must have been shown it for a reason. I think it was to save you."

Holun lifted his shackled wrists into the light and clanked the iron chains together. They made a harsh metallic sound in the otherwise-silent cave. "That may be difficult."

Yatzil was smiling that gorgeous smile again, the one that lit up her entire face and made her eyes dance in the light. "Yes. So right now I will stay with you and . . . oh! I almost forgot!" The match went out again, and he could hear her rummaging around in a bag or something like it.

A moment later, once she lit another match, Holun saw the second most wonderful sight he'd seen all day. Food.

Yatzil handed him the food she'd brought with her, and Holun was devouring it before he could stop himself. He felt like he hadn't eaten in ages, since Shani's latest "meal" was nothing but scraps.

"Easy . . ." Yatzil cautioned. "This will have to last you until tomorrow night."

Holun blinked as he finished up an apple. "Tomorrow night?"

Yatzil smiled at him in the flickering light, and Holun's heart skipped a beat. "Yes. I will be back each night with food."

Holun just stared. "Why are you helping me? Besides the vision, I mean. I am not exactly the most popular man in the Clan."

"No, you are not, Holun." He loved the way his name sounded on her lips. "But my new mission is to help you in any way I can. Then, eventually, I will find a way to save you."

Holun couldn't believe that this beautiful girl would have any interest in him at all—even if romantic interest wasn't on the table, even a passing interest was astounding—but he chose to be grateful for the company.

He started to ask her questions about life in the Clan after the battle—after he'd left—and soon they were talking about anything and everything as if they'd been best friends since the beginning of time.

When Yatzil started to sense daylight coming—at least that was the excuse she gave—she gathered her spent matches and snuck off into the darkness of the rainforest before Shani came back. Holun immediately felt a profound sense of loss at her exit, but he found himself grateful even to have met her.

Shani would be back soon. Holun wasn't sure what to expect from her—yesterday was mostly just sitting and waiting for her to return in periodic spurts—but who knew what she really wanted?

She was determined to have him help her, she'd said as much. But help her with what? He couldn't offer much to a woman who had him tied up and helpless in a cave, except . . . wait.

No.

He couldn't use his visions to help Shani. They were an intensely personal thing for him—and he'd vowed to only use them to do good in the world. His brief foray into danger with Na-um had resolved that in his mind for him. He would only ever use his visions to further the right causes in the world, not the selfish ones.

And no doubt Shani's intentions were selfish. Holun couldn't be sure, but he sensed that what Shani was after was only to further her own cause.

And then she was back, her arms loaded with supplies.

"Hello, Holun," she singsonged to him in English as she entered the cave with little more than a scrap of food for breakfast among the other items she now sat down near the cave's entrance. Not that Holun really cared about the food, but it gave him another reason to glare at her. She seemed to enjoy it, but he still couldn't help himself.

"Shani," he growled.

"My, my, we are testy this morning!" Shani tossed the small piece of what had to be stale bread down in front of him, which landed face down in the dirt. Appetizing. "But we have a big day ahead of us, so eat up."

Holun glanced down at the bread lying in the dirt. "I am not hungry."

Shani rolled her eyes. "A hunger strike? Now that's not very original, Holun."

He just shrugged at her. He loved how nonchalant it made him feel.

Shani crossed her arms as her eyes narrowed. "Fine, don't eat. We'll just get to our agenda for the day that much sooner."

"And what agenda is that? I told you I would never help you."

Shani laughed then lunged forward, inches away from his face. "And I told you that you would." She grabbed the front of his sky-blue t-shirt, pulling him to his feet, his shackles clanking around him and hanging heavy on his wrists. "And you *will*, Holun."

"What do you want, Shani?" Holun was proud again for keeping his fear from his voice.

"You will help me."

"With what?"

"Whatever I ask."

Holun stared her down. "That is very vague."

Shani tossed him against the back wall, letting go of his shirt. "I will soon be going after something, and you will use your visions to help me get around anyone who might possibly get in my way. Including your new friends."

Holun looked past Shani to the other side of the cave. So that was her plan. He suspected as much. But there was still more to find out . . .

"What are you searching for?"

Shani rolled her eyes again. "None of your concern. Your job is to see visions of my journey to make sure I am successful."

"You have to know it does not work like that."

Shani grinned, and Holun felt nauseous. "I can be very persuasive."

Holun just stared off to the other side of the cave.

Shani laughed again then backed up. "So let's begin." Shani reached for a camping chair she'd brought with her and set it up in the middle of the cave, a few feet from where Holun was standing. He bent his knees and sunk to the ground, using the back wall for support.

The entire day was spent verbally sparring with Shani, and it was exhausting. She hadn't laid a hand on him—not yet —but she kept promising more severe punishments if he kept refusing her. And the implication was clear: She would do whatever it took to get Holun to help her.

As Shani left for the night, Holun breathed a sigh of relief. He'd nearly forgotten about Yatzil—as if he could ever have really forgotten about such an enchanting woman—but as Holun laid back to rest from the mentally grueling day, he found himself praying to the gods he wasn't even sure he believed in that she would come back tonight.

The Mercenaries' Camp

Yatzil spent her days gathering food, washing clothes, caring for the needs of others as she'd done for the past few years, once she'd been old enough to work. Her "mother"—who was actually just the woman who had cared for her from childhood until she'd been able to take care of herself—was not her biological mother, but Yatzil had still spent her childhood feeling well cared for. Loved, perhaps. Her caretaker was a kind woman, a practical one, and took good care of Yatzil. But the young girl still wished for a family she could call her own.

At the end of the day, Yatzil would gather the few commodities she'd earned for that day and take it to the "market"—a daily exchange where fruits, vegetables, breads, meats, weapons, clothing, and anything else that met the daily needs of the members of the Clan could be traded for whatever form their wages came in. Today, she'd received a few sharp arrowheads. Her employer had been kind; she knew they would fetch a good price at the market. Both she and Holun would eat well tonight. Some days, she barely did.

Thinking about Holun started her mind off in a different direction as she headed to the market. She was amazed by how their relationship had started—if she hadn't had the visions herself, she wouldn't have believed they'd actually happened. And she was probably crazy for seeking him out, but she couldn't seem to help herself. She'd followed her heart—for probably the first time in her life—and desperately hoped she wouldn't regret it.

She'd spent only one night with the man, but something told her this was different. *He* was different. She'd known all about the gossip, heard all the rumors going around camp about him, but that hadn't been her experience last night. He'd been caring, funny, kind, insightful, and, above all, moral, which confused her greatly. How could someone so hated in their Clan be so . . . good?

Yatzil reached the market and exchanged her goods quickly for some food and other necessities. She even had enough to hold back an arrowhead to trade at a later date, saving it for a lighter day. Yes, today was a good day.

With the sounds of the evening jovialities of the Clan surrounding her and her bag full, she started the trip back to her modest tent. She'd been given one as soon as she was able to work for herself—the Clan took good care of its orphans—and she was grateful for her own place. Besides, she didn't need much space at all. Just a shelter to sleep in, really.

Then she heard a crash nearby, and she jumped as a large cast iron pot flew across her path, right in front of her. Her bag fell to the ground as she backed away, peering around the side of a canvas tent at what made the commotion.

She saw a man—definitely not of the Clan—laughing oddly, like he should be loud but was instead almost silent. Yatzil blinked at him as he ran past her to retrieve the pot. What was going on?

She watched as the man brought the pot back to a particular spot, placed it on the ground, then drew in a deep breath. What was he doing?

Then the man yelled.

Yatzil gasped as the pot and the earth surrounding it flew through the air in the same trajectory as before. She put her hand over her mouth to stifle a scream.

The man retrieved the pot again, but this time Yatzil ran for her tent while his back was turned.

What on earth was that? How could he do that? Her mind was spinning as she entered her tent and sat down, considering all the possibilities.

There was really only one. She'd heard of members of the Clan having special powers—she and Holun shared one of visions, after all, and there were definitely more out there—but she'd never seen them in person until a few days ago. Though her hands had glowed in the woods when Shani and her group had arrived—and she still couldn't figure out what that had meant—she hadn't even really believed any of it was real until she'd had her vision yesterday.

She couldn't really deny it now.

But that brought up another question: How did that man, one who wasn't a part of her Clan, come to have powers, too? Yatzil could accept the Clan having powers—it was part of what they were created for if the stories were true, and she suspected now that they were—but how did an outsider come to have them?

Yatzil pondered the possibilities then remembered the stories she'd heard about Holun and his betrayal. How four Americans came to uncover the Secret of the Codex—the Secret she knew her Clan was here to protect, though she didn't know what the Secret actually was—and received powers as a result. Was that what had happened here? Was this man one of them?

She hoped not. Knowing Holun now, though only for one night, she sensed he would only align himself with people who were good, and just, and kind. Not irresponsible children, like that man seemed to be. She resolved to ask Holun about it some time.

So as darkness began to chase away the sun, Yatzil began her preparations, packing the sole bag she owned with a lantern she'd just purchased—using all those matches could get very expensive—and the provisions she'd bought earlier that evening.

She felt butterflies in her stomach as she thought of going back up the mountain. She'd made a promise, one she fully intended to keep, but it was more than that. She felt drawn to Holun, as if something stronger than her visions was pulling them together. She needed to find out more about him, how he'd gotten himself in so much trouble.

As soon as night had fallen on the camp, Yatzil stole out of her tent with her bag on her back and silently entered the comforting darkness of the rainforest.

Tyler trudged back to the tent that Chac guy had given him to share with Steven, his head hanging. Sure, testing out his power today had been fun—and it seemed like Steven, Akna, and even that quiet but pretty girl, Alexia, had enjoyed watching—but he was starting to get a little depressed. Back at school, he was able to throw himself into his fraternity, hang with the guys until the feeling passed, or binge on drinking, TV, or one of the many more-than-willing girls in the sorority house next door until he couldn't feel anything else anymore.

But here, deep in the Belize rainforest where he was alone with his thoughts, the sorrow seemed to grab hold of him and not let go.

He was glad that Shani woman had introduced him to that girl, Akna—she reminded him of his little sister, Kara, back in Minnesota. A single tear trailed down his face at the thought, and he quickly wiped it away. She often called and texted him for advice, sometimes about boys, sometimes about friends, sometimes about school. He was always the one that fixed her problems, even from several states away. But he hadn't heard from her in weeks, hadn't seen her in months, and he missed her. He missed them all, his whole family. Even his mother, who he hadn't had the best of relationships with over the years.

But still, family was family.

Then again, he wondered as his mood fell another several degrees, would he ever be able to go back to them? He cursed under his breath. He could not believe this had happened to him. He'd just been living his normal life—he'd been headed to meet a girl at his fraternity's beach house a couple of hours away—when this bomb had gone off and completely wrecked any semblance of normalcy he'd previously enjoyed. He just wanted to play football, finish school, sleep around, make a lot of money. What were his prospects now?

He stepped into his tent. He couldn't be sure, but he thought Steven was gone. He called his name just in case but received no response. Just as well.

He dropped to his bed—really just a pile of blankets—and lay on his back, clothes still on. He stared up at the canvas ceiling. He wished he could fix this, make it go away.

He'd been a jock in high school—the captain of his hometown football team—and continued his career in college, on a football scholarship at the University of Central Florida. His parents had money, so he'd never wanted for anything. Anything he did want, the money usually bought. Including the women, who gravitated toward the expensive things he owned like magnets. That part he didn't mind at all.

But he'd never really wanted much past the superficial, content to live his charmed existence without questioning it.

He cursed again, louder this time—almost too loud; the canvas covering above him shook a little—his face contorting into a scowl. There was no fixing this, was there? That woman, Shani, had been helpful, but wasn't this really her fault? Wasn't she responsible for this, for his new powers? She should pay.

Tyler clenched his teeth together, his mind starting to form a plan with little effort. But before he could, he heard a gentle voice at the door.

"Tyler?"

He sat up, turning toward the door and spotting Akna standing just outside the canvas flap that covered the door. Instantly, his mood changed. "Come in." When she didn't move, he motioned her inside.

Akna entered the tent, her steps hesitant. She stopped only a few steps in. "I talk you?"

Tyler smiled at her phrasing, nodding as he scooted over and patted the blanket beside him. "Sure, you may talk to me. What do you want to talk about?"

She walked forward and took his offered seat. "You teach."

Tyler blinked once, then he thought he understood. "I teach you?" He pointed to himself then to her to underline his words.

Akna nodded. "Yes."

Tyler smiled again. "Of course I will teach you! Although my power is different from yours, so I may not be much help."

"You not help?"

"No! I meant that I *will* help you—at least, I will try." Tyler patted her on the head.

The young girl smiled up at him then said something in her language that Tyler didn't understand. But her meaning, her intent, came through loud and clear.

"You are welcome, Akna," he replied, carefully enunciating his words in an attempt to help the young girl understand. It seemed like most of the kids around here were taught some English, but he could always help her learn more.

She got up and left the tent, and Tyler followed, smiling. He liked helping her. In a way, in some small way, he felt like he was helping Kara.

And the homesickness suddenly wasn't quite as bad.

CHAPTER 22

Feelings Are Confusing

The Mercenaries' Camp

SHANI FELL ON HER COT as soon as she entered her tent, fully clothed. Holun was being difficult, and she couldn't figure out why. She'd hoped with just one thinly veiled threat he'd give in, give her what she needed, and she could let him go, be done with this messy business. But it seemed his resolve was much stronger than she'd anticipated.

She sighed then reached to pull off her shoes. She needed another tactic, a way to make Holun do what she needed him to. Something that would ensure his compliance.

But as she laid there for what could've been hours, nothing came to her. She stared at the canvas ceiling, wondering what to do next. She *needed* Holun to help her. Her mind control capabilities were limited and being stretched thinner with each passing day. The Elders could not figure out her plans. That little brat *had* to help!

So as the darkness began to set in and sleep was still hours away, Shani finally came up with a plan: She would do whatever it took to get Holun to help her. She would have to steel herself against the uncomfortable, the distasteful, and remember why she was doing this in the first place.

As sleep finally came, Shani smiled at the thought. Her vision would finally be realized; no little sixteen-year-old bastard would get in her way.

Lamanai Archaeological Project

After apologizing to Mandy, Kayla had dug into the translation right beside her. With the two of them—and a lot of Naum's help, to be honest—working on it exclusively, the translation was coming along even more quickly than it had at UCF.

Kayla felt helpless—it had been days since Shani had kidnapped Holun, but they didn't have any leads. She wished they could send out a search party, but they all decided it would be better to stay and translate the Codex. Grady thought perhaps the Codex would hold some clues as to where the artifacts were, and possibly even another way for them to track Shani. Kayla supposed it was just wishful thinking, but maybe that's all they had at this point.

Grady had contacted the school for them and found TAs to cover their classes and administer their finals, so they were off the hook for the rest of the semester. They also arranged for Mandy and Justin to take their finals when they got back to Florida—benefits of being best friends with the professors—so they wouldn't have to worry about it now. Kayla was even able to play off their translating as a work study to the dean of the department, who agreed to give Mandy and Justin extra credit for their trouble.

Kayla was glad those two were here with her and Grady. With everything that had happened this summer—to all of them—she wouldn't have blamed them for digging in their heels and staying home, despite their newfound powers. But she supposed they were in just as deep as she and Grady were, and Kayla was grateful for their common bond, even if it meant they were constantly being thrown into danger.

Na-um was being a big help; Kayla had to admit that he was the reason the translation was going so well. Their Clan made a big deal out of teaching their people other languages, especially English, so he made quick work of the Codex translation—even with him leaving periodically to go "check in" with the Elders before returning no more than an hour later. It had seemed a little suspect to Kayla at first, but if he truly was working against the Elders and with them, he would still have to do it to keep up appearances with the Elders, keep reporting back about his progress with the Americans. Either way, it was impossible to tell whose side he was really on.

After about a week, Kayla realized they didn't have much left to translate. They'd found mostly backstory, interesting but not particularly helpful. At least not in helping them find Holun.

But they'd learned a lot more about the artifacts, things even Na-um seemed to be surprised to read. According to the prophecies outlined in the Codex—ones Kayla had no reason to question—the Elders and those who'd preceded them had been stashing artifacts away since the inception of the Clan. Kayla couldn't even fathom how many artifacts they could have accumulated over the centuries.

But that just begged another question: Where would they hide all those artifacts? A stash like that couldn't just be transported around with the nomadic Clan. There had to be a single place, one accessible within a few hours of the Clan's many locations over the centuries.

When Grady and Justin left to go to the mess tent for a midday snack, Kayla stayed behind with Mandy and Na-um to continue the translation. Kayla really wanted to discuss things with Grady, alone. They still had their shared telepathy—for which she was extremely grateful—but he still couldn't remember any of their life together before Shani had stolen his memory of her. It was killing her, but she was trying to be thankful for what they did have. Kayla stepped over to the door of the trailer to have a private conversation with him.

Grady?

Nothing.

Kayla frowned. She hadn't tried their telepathy when they weren't right next to each other yet, so maybe this was just a side effect of Shani's mind games. The rules just kept changing, and Kayla was getting sick of this. She certainly hoped their telepathy was only temporarily down because of their proximity—she didn't think she could stand losing him again.

"Kayla?" Na-um called to her from the work table. "We think we may have found something."

Kayla moved back to the table. "What did you find?"

Mandy pointed at the book. "It sounds like there may be some clues here about where the artifacts might be."

Kayla craned her neck to see where Mandy was pointing. "Like what?"

Mandy picked up the handwritten translation lying near the book and read it silently before summarizing. "In addition to what we found earlier, the Codex details another prophecy about the artifacts. It mentions a location, but, of course, this is prophecy, so it's not super clear." Mandy frowned at the page.

"What does it say?" Kayla leaned in closer.

Na-um read the jumbled, nondescript, obnoxiously vague prophecy. Kayla recognized the words, but they made absolutely no sense together.

She blinked. "Was that even English?"

Mandy smirked but shrugged. "Yeah." One corner of her mouth turned up. "At least it's something to go on."

Na-um nodded beside them, clearly in thought. "Yes . . . this . . . I think I can decipher . . ." he mumbled to himself, grabbing a nearby pad of paper and making notations on it. After a few long minutes, Kayla finally saw him let out a breath. "Yes. I know right where this is."

Kayla caught his gaze and furrowed her brow at him. "Are you sure?"

Na-um looked over his notes again. "Well . . . yes, about eighty percent certain."

She rolled her eyes.

But Na-um was grinning. "I say we do some reconnaissance."

Kayla glanced over at him. "Of this imaginary place you're twenty percent *not* sure you know?"

He crossed his arms and shrugged. "Yes. And of the village, too. We should do that first. We may even find where Shani is hiding Holun."

"How would we ever be able to find that out?" Mandy asked, frowning as she looked him over.

Na-um paused before answering. "Shani has to be back working with the Elders, right? So we try to get close, see what the Elders know, and maybe we will get lucky."

Mandy cocked her head to one side, frowning. "Hmm, maybe."

But Na-um headed for the door. "Come! Let us go find your friends. We can leave tonight."

The Mercenaries' Camp

Shani spent most of her time each day between that hidden cave in the mountains and here at the camp training Alexia. Tyler and Steven seemed to be doing just fine on their own, but Alexia's power was different, special. Difficult to control, even more difficult to understand.

But undoubtedly powerful. Shani hated when it was turned on her, but she needed to know exactly what that girl could do. And she was certain, if she could get Alexia to learn to control it well, that it just may be what would bring the Four down.

Alexia was doing well, learning a lot. Shani was convinced that she was close to mastering it. She remembered all too well the times Alexia successfully used it on her.

But as the girl was growing in confidence of her powers, her confidence in general was growing as well. During one of their many training sessions this week, in their usual secluded clearing a few miles from the camp, Alexia had asked about why they were training, what Shani had planned.

Shani hesitated, hiding her face from the girl as she decided what she would say, what the girl should hear, what the girl needed to hear to still help her. She'd served as Mandy's assistant, Kayla's assistant, on the Codex translation project, and Shani sensed her loyalty to them even now. She didn't have any reason to question them, after all.

So Shani supposed she'd have to give her one. Shani knew they would eventually come face-to-face with the Four, and she didn't want this girl to have any doubts about their mission, give the girl any reason to leave her side and fight with the Four against her.

Shani called her over. "Alexia, come sit with me." She walked over to a fallen log and patted the seat beside her.

Alexia obliged, her brow furrowed, but her expression open. *Good.* "Do you remember what I said to you when I first stopped by your house in Florida?"

Alexia's brow furrowed, and she tilted her head to one side before answering. "Yes, you said Mandy sent you, that she needed my help?"

Shani nodded, catching her gaze. "Yes, but that was only partly true."

"Huh?"

Shani pasted a soft frown on her face, knowing the girl would buy her imagined remorse. "Mandy *does* need your help . . . but she didn't exactly send me to you." She paused for effect. "I came to you on my own, sensing that you would be able to help them."

"Them?"

Shani almost smiled, realizing again that this girl was much more perceptive than Tyler and Steven. Probably more so than the two of them put together. "Yes. Her boyfriend, Justin, and their professors, Harrington and McGready."

"Dr. Harrington and Dr. McGready? What do they have to do with this?"

Shani took a breath and let it out slowly, trying to figure out how to explain this so the girl would believe her. "Well . . . let's just say something happened to them this summer."

"Something like what?"

Shani paused again. "Hmm . . ." How did she put it? "Well, you know how you now have a superpower?"

Alexia grinned. "Yes."

Shani smiled back at her. "They were given superpowers this summer, too."

The young girl gasped.

Shani nodded. "They are very powerful. So powerful, in fact, that their power has gotten out of hand. And it can no longer go unchecked."

Alexia's eyes were wide. "What happened?"

Shani hesitated again, wondering how far she could stretch the truth, how little she could lie so it was still believable. Then it came to her—and it wasn't even a lie. "They . . . they have killed many people."

Alexia gasped again. "They've *killed* people? Mandy, too?"

Shani nodded solemnly. "Yes, this past summer. Hundreds of my people." She glanced toward the camp for effect.

The girl's eyes started to fill. "I . . ." She sniffed, and her next words were barely a whisper. "I didn't know that."

Shani simply nodded, her brow still furrowed as she caught Alexia's gaze again. "Yes. They are too powerful, and they must be stopped. That's why we're here, why I'm working you so hard, so that, when the time comes, we can stop them."

Alexia's tears had mostly dried, but now she stared wide-eyed into the surrounding forest. She paused before responding, one word finally passing through her lips. "Okay."

Shani blinked, surprised though she'd gotten the response she'd hoped for. "Okay?"

Alexia nodded, wiping her nose then standing. "I will help you."

Shani smiled mildly, tamping her enthusiasm. "Great. Let's keep going then." She stood and reached for Alexia's hand.

Alexia took it with her own smile, letting Shani lead her to the middle of the clearing once again.

As they began to practice, Shani noticed a new determination on the girl's face, a new passion. She realized with a smile that she should have told this girl about all of this much sooner.

Outside the Mercenaries' Camp in the Mountains

Yatzil, true to her word, had come back every single night. Some nights they talked through the night, some nights they fell asleep—Shani's unrelenting yet unsuccessful attempts to get Holun to help her had gone from exhausting to downright painful, and Holun had the cuts and bruises to prove it—but she always brought food. And Holun was grateful—not only for the food, but even more so for the company.

Tonight would be the seventh night she'd come. Until now, they'd talked about their lives, their friends in the Clan, her life back at the camp, even her childhood, but never once had she asked him how he came to be here, why he was working with the Americans, how he became the Clan's enemy number one. Tonight was the night. Tonight he would tell Yatzil everything about himself, all the things most in the Clan wouldn't understand.

But he sensed that she would. When you spend hours on end every single day with a person, you start to know things about them, things you can intuit about their personality. Things that you don't have any knowledge of but still somehow just *know*.

As Holun watched Shani leave for the night, he started to feel a little nervous. He knew Yatzil well, of course, but he hadn't known her long enough to erase *all* doubt. He hoped, prayed even, that she would accept him for who he was, not who she'd imagined him to be.

Holun laid his head back against the wall, careful to avoid aggravating the long, deep cut across his lower back as his thoughts swirled in his head. In just six short days, he'd completely fallen for Yatzil. She was an incredibly brave woman, impulsive but thoughtful, independent and strong. The kind of woman he'd always imagined he'd meet. The kind of woman he'd always imagined he'd fall in love with.

Now he was even more nervous. Holun shifted in the sand and raised his head to eye the entrance. She would be here any moment.

Then he heard the familiar rustling near the cave's entrance and a wave of calm settled over him. Holun smiled widely as Yatzil, the woman of his dreams, entered his life yet again.

Lamanai

The Four met with Na-um in the mess tent just after dark to plan their strategy. Kayla hated to let Na-um take the lead, but she couldn't come up with any other way it would work.

"Okay, so here's where we'll enter the camp." Na-um was pointing at a crude, handwritten map he'd drawn of the Clan's camp. "I will find one of the Elders—hopefully Chac or Tohil, the easiest ones to work with—and give them my report."

Grady crossed his arms, widening his stance. "And how will this be any different from your other check-ins?"

Mandy jumped in. "Yeah, why do we even need to come?"

Na-um paused then looked over at Kayla. "Because Kayla needs to be there with me."

Kayla's stomach dropped, and her eyes found Mandy's before she could stop them. Mandy was staring holes into hers. She looked away, finding Na-um's piercing gaze.

"*What*?!" Justin yelled from beside her.

Na-um nodded, still looking at Kayla. "Yes, she must accompany me. The Elders may already be on to me. If she goes, she can stay in the shadows and listen in then come back for you if I am caught."

"Why can't someone else go?" Grady reasoned. "Why does it have to be her?"

Kayla just stared at Na-um. Her mouth suddenly felt very dry.

Na-um finally tore his gaze away from Kayla long enough to glance over at Grady's questions. "Because she knows the language best, and she can talk her way out of a situation if anyone sees her. Not many in the Clan know what you all look like, after all, mostly just the Elders and the few survivors from the battle." Na-um grew quiet.

Kayla's mind was reeling. Was she really ready to go into camp—go on a mission with—the man who'd tried to kill them? With the man whose history with her was getting more complicated by the minute? She glanced at Mandy again, whose eyes were still shooting daggers at her, but her thoughts were quiet.

But what else could she do?

"Okay, we'll do it your way, Na-um." Kayla sighed. "But I'll pull the plug immediately if I sense anything—and I mean *anything*—amiss. Understood?"

One side of Na-um's mouth turned up. How could he possibly be amused at her right now? "Understood."

Grady's thoughts broke into hers. *Kayla, are you sure? You don't know what you could be walking into.*

Kayla glanced over at Na-um standing just a few feet away. *I don't think I have any other choice, Grady.*

He paused, following Kayla's gaze and staring down Na-um. *I hate this.*

Kayla didn't think that was meant for her to hear.

The Hidden Cave in the Rainforest Near the Mercenaries' Camp

"Hi." Holun greeted Yatzil when she came in. She lit her lantern before sliding up next to him, as had become her custom. He didn't mind that at all.

"Hello." Yatzil smiled at him, responding to him in English. Holun had learned she knew a lot of English, like all the young ones in the Clan had learned, but she hadn't had much opportunity to practice. So Holun had, of course, volunteered. Not that he was the best teacher, but he just couldn't help himself.

Holun grinned back at her, pleased that she scooted in a little closer to him until the entire side of her body was up against his. He could get used to this. Who was he kidding—he already was.

Yatzil reached into her bag and pulled out the food she'd brought for Holun. But instead of snatching it up like he always did, he set it to the side.

"Is everything okay?" Yatzil asked, eyeing the food.

Holun nodded then turned to look at her directly. Her wide eyes, so innocent and beautiful, found his and held his gaze. Holun determined right then and there that he would do anything to protect this young woman, to make sure no harm came to her. She'd become too vital to his very survival.

"Yes. I just . . ." He drew in a deep breath, wincing at the pain in his back, then exhaled before continuing. "I wanted to talk to you about something. About . . . me."

Holun looked away, too worried about her response to look her in the eye. But, as he knew she would, Yatzil leaned into his line of sight, placing a long finger under his chin and bringing his gaze back to hers. "I would love to know everything about you, Holun."

Holun was convinced his heart had melted at her words. How could this enchanting creature have so completely changed his life in one short week?

Holun took another deep breath then launched into his personal story. He honestly wasn't sure why he hadn't told her before. To her credit, she listened silently but with wide eyes until he was finished. Until he had told her everything.

She blinked when he was finished, frozen in the same cross-legged position in the dirt she'd been in when he started. *Please, say something. Anything. I am dying here.*

"Holun . . ." Her voice cracked, and he didn't quite understand why. "I am so sorry."

"Sorry? For what?" He couldn't imagine what she could have done to be sorry for. Holun's brow furrowed as he reached for her hand. She let him take it.

"For everything you have been through. That must have been very . . ."—she searched for the right word in English —"painful for you."

Holun's face softened. This girl just kept getting more amazing. "Thank you, Yatzil. It was painful, but I got through it."

Yatzil reached for his other hand and held both of his hands in hers. Holun loved the warmth of her hands between his. "But you are still not through it, as you said. You are still unwelcome in our Clan! Your . . . *family.*" Holun saw a lone tear escape her eye and trail down her cheek. He reached up to wipe it away, and Yatzil smiled through her tears. "Thank you for sharing that with me, Holun."

Holun reached for her hands again. "No, thank *you*, Yatzil. Aside from the Americans, you are the first real friend I have found. And you are the only one from the Clan who would dare speak to me, spend time with me."

Yatzil started smiling. "Because I am that nice."

Holun laughed, loving the release he felt here with her. "Yes, you definitely are." He slid back into place against the wall, leaning up against it. He patted the ground next to him, and she scooted back beside him, laying her head on his shoulder.

Holun winced again, but this time, Yatzil noticed. "Holun, is something wrong?"

He'd hoped she wouldn't see his pain; he'd hoped she'd only see his brave side. But no secrets. "Just some cuts and bruises—I will be fine."

Yatzil pulled away and looked him over. She ran her hands along his arms, his chest, his back, and Holun had to focus on something other than the trail of sparks Yatzil's fingertips left in their wake.

Then he cringed. She lifted up his shirt and gasped. "Holun! What did she do to you?"

Holun pulled his shirt back down, adjusting carefully back into what passed as a comfortable position these days. "It's nothing."

She looked him in the eye. "That was not nothing. Shani did this to you?"

Holun laid his head back against the wall and nodded.

Then she got quiet, so Holun looked up at her. "It's okay, Yatzil. I will be okay."

"Holun . . . I'm so sorry. I wish I knew how to get you out of here."

Holun smiled at her then patted the ground next to him again. "Just you being here is enough. Please, come sit with me."

Yatzil hesitated then slid in next to him, more carefully this time but just as close. Holun smiled and laid his head back, thinking he could be perfectly content just sitting like this, close to this beautiful woman in this hidden cave.

Then suddenly, Holun wasn't in the cave anymore. He was outside, on the side of a mountain somewhere, a plateau lit by the light of the moon and stars. Then he was somewhere dark, walking down a staircase. When he reached the bottom, he saw an enormous warehouse stuffed full of old books, papers, gold, silver, bowls, gemstones—and all kinds of things he didn't recognize. What was this place?

Then the vision was gone as soon as it had come.

CHAPTER 23

Reconnaissance

Just Outside Lamanai, in the Darkness of the Belize Rainforest

KAYLA WAS ON THE GROUND, her mind reeling. She hadn't been getting regular visions since they'd placed that globe in the museum, but this one had come unrelentingly, stealing her consciousness and forcing her to see what was going to happen.

She'd hoped she'd gotten past all this.

Grady held her as she recovered from the vision, his arms around her as she sat on the ground, trying to catch her breath. When she finally did, she looked up at him and smiled. It didn't help the strain in his features.

"I'm okay, Grady, I promise."

She watched Grady swallow hard before nodding. "I assume that was a vision? What did you see?"

Kayla blinked then eyed the others who had stopped at the sound of her collapse to the ground. "I saw a wide plateau in a mountain, a dark staircase leading underground, and an enormous warehouse with all manner of artifacts."

Na-um drew closer at this news. "The artifacts! That must be where they are storing them. An underground warehouse?"

Kayla nodded, swallowing hard. "It didn't exactly look like something your people would have."

Na-um was staring off into the darkness. "No, I suppose not." He paused. "But then . . ."

"What?" Mandy asked.

"Even when I was working for them, the Elders seemed to have another agenda. Like they were working with someone else. Sometimes, they even commanded others to do things against my instructions. Plus," Na-um continued, "they seem to know everything that goes on, even in the States and at the other Codex sites. There must be something more going on, something bigger than them." Na-um paused again, then his eyes shot wide. "The Elders are powerful, but they cannot be everywhere at once. What if they have people all over the world that report back to them? The Power of the Codex is a great power, probably the greatest Power the world has ever seen. What if they enlisted more than just the Clan to protect it?"

Kayla thought about it. His theory made a lot of sense. "So what do we do? How do we find it?"

Na-um walked over to her and sat down on the ground beside her. "Describe it to me with all the detail you can remember."

Kayla did, and when she was finished, Na-um grinned. "I know just the place. First, we find out what the Elders are planning, then we go find those artifacts."

"And Holun?" Mandy jumped in.

Kayla frowned. "We still don't know where he is. Maybe we'll get lucky, but this is all I know to do right now."

Mandy shrugged. "I suppose. I just hate that he's all alone with Shani."

Kayla felt tears well in her eyes. "Me, too."

The Cave Outside the Mercenaries' Camp

"Holun?" Yatzil leaned up to look at his face. She immediately sat up straight, her eyes wide and piercing. "Holun! Are you okay?"

Holun blinked the rest of the vision away. His visions weren't like this—they didn't just come without him looking for them. Which probably meant that this vision was from Kayla, one of hers.

Yatzil was still staring at him, waiting for an answer. "Yes, sorry . . . I am fine."

She reached up to push some hair out of his face. Only then did he realize he was sweating. "You do not look fine. Are you sure you are okay?"

Holun nodded, swallowing hard. "Yes." He forced a smile for her benefit. "It was a vision."

"A vision? I thought you had to look for them to see them?"

She didn't miss anything. "Yes, normally that is what happens. But this time . . . it was different. But it has happened before." Holun furrowed his brow. Did this mean that Kayla got that vision, too, that perhaps they were headed to that underground warehouse, or, even better, headed here to rescue him? That last part was too much to hope for.

Yatzil pulled her knees up and hugged them to her chest. "When?"

He'd already told her everything else—no sense holding back now. Besides, he didn't want to. He wanted her to know everything. "Kayla, one of the Americans I was with, she would get visions. But hers were given to her by a globe, and since they were not hers since birth, they would come to her at any time, and they became very painful for her."

Yatzil's eyes were wide, but she stayed quiet.

"She actually sent me a vision before she even knew who I was—I don't even think she meant to. Somehow, the vision came to me, just as she saw it. It was what made me leave the Clan and join the Americans." Holun leaned his head back against the stone wall, his eyes falling shut. The vision had exhausted him.

Yatzil, who was staring off into the distance, nodded slowly. Then she looked back at him. "And what was this vision about?"

Holun's eyes fluttered open, finding hers, then he smiled at her. "I saw an underground warehouse, hidden up in the mountains somewhere."

Yatzil was looking toward the entrance with an odd look on her face.

"What? Does that mean something to you?"

She turned back toward him. "Maybe . . . where was this underground warehouse located? Do you know what mountain?"

Holun closed his eyes, trying to see the vision again. It made his head hurt. "All I saw was a plateau overlooking a vast valley. And . . . oh! You could see Lamanai in the distance. But that was all I saw." Holun shrugged.

"That is okay, Holun," Yatzil offered, smiling. "I think I may know where it is."

Holun's mouth dropped open. "How?"

Yatzil's smile grew bigger. "I saw it."

"You saw what?"

"The warehouse." She was grinning ear to ear now, and she moved to sit on her knees, leaning toward Holun. "I had a dream, a vision like you call it. I saw the plateau, the staircase, the warehouse."

Holun's mouth still hung open. "When was this?"

"A few hours ago, just before I came here."

"And you did not tell me?" Holun couldn't stop himself from raising his voice.

"You did not ask." Yatzil stared directly into his eyes, all levity gone; Holun shifted his weight under her harsh gaze.

After an uncomfortable silence—for Holun, anyway—Yatzil continued. "So before I came here, I went looking for it. And I think I found it. It is not far from here."

Holun sat straight up, leaning forward. "Where?"

Just then, a noise sounded at the entrance of the tent. In all the nights he'd spent with Yatzil, he'd never even entertained the possibility of Shani coming back while she was here.

But it was much too late for that now. The small cave had no hiding places, no tunnels for her to run to. The woman he loved was just as trapped as he was.

So Yatzil and Holun just stared, wide-eyed, as Shani entered the cave first with frozen wide eyes then with an evil grin spreading across her face.

The Mercenaries' Camp

Kayla stayed close behind Na-um as they approached the dig under the cover of darkness. He'd told her that the Elders' tents would be near the middle of the camp but off to the west side, so they would have to circle the camp to come at it from there.

The firelight of the camp had quickly come into view, but the trek around it seemed to be taking much longer than it did to get here, and Kayla was getting a little tired of being scraped up by every branch, twig, weed, and everything else that seemed to be lurking around her ankles. She was trying to be a good sport, trying to keep up, but Na-um was much more at home in these woods than she was.

Grady and the others had stayed behind at the edge of the camp nearest Lamanai. Once Kayla and Na-um had gone into the woods, Grady's thoughts had faded from her mind. She hated being apart from him, but maybe the lack of distraction was good at this point. She needed to stay focused, and all the complications with Na-um were just making things, well, complicated. More complicated than she'd ever care to admit.

Na-um raised his hand to her, indicating he was slowing down. She kept forgetting his background was in hunting; if she lost him, she would never be able to find him again.

Na-um leaned back to whisper to her. "You see those five tents there?" He pointed to a cluster of what had to be the largest tents in the camp, all lit up but appearing to be unoccupied at the moment.

Kayla nodded, coming up alongside Na-um to get a better view.

"That is where they will be." He was still whispering.

Kayla whispered back. "They look deserted."

Na-um, still staring into the camp, nodded once. "Yes, but trust me, they are not."

She just looked over at him.

He straightened. "Stay back, but move with me. I will be trying the tent of Tohil first, the farthest tent to the left." He indicated it with a sweep of his hand, and Kayla nodded again. "If Tohil is not there, I will go to the next one, which is the tent of Chac. I am confident at least one of those two Elders are present."

"Okay."

Na-um nodded at her, placed a hand quickly on her shoulder and squeezed, then stepped into the light of the camp.

Kayla waited until he'd gone several yards before she ventured a step out of the woods. She was careful to remain unseen by the inhabitants of the camp—she knew she wouldn't exactly get a warm welcome if any of them figured out who she was.

Kayla approached the leftmost tent with caution and hid behind some bushes near it. She could hear Na-um already talking, so she listened more carefully.

". . . could not come. I came here as soon as I could get away." Na-um's voice reached her ears.

"And the Four?" came from another, unfamiliar voice. *The Four? They call us the Four, too?*

"They are still at Lamanai. I have been waiting for a chance to bring them to you."

Kayla scowled. Would she find out Na-um had been lying to them all along? Surely he knew she was listening—it was his idea, after all.

"And?"

There was a pause. Then: "They will not come willingly. I hope you all understand that."

"We know that, Na-um." She heard the other voice sigh loudly. "Perhaps, you can simply take us to them."

"That may work better."

"Good. You will contact us when you know more." *Contact them? Surely these men don't have cell phones—do they have a shared telepathy as well? Or just their superhuman hearing, maybe?*

"Yes, of course."

"Good. Anything else to report?"

Na-um again paused. "Well . . . yes."

"And? What is your report?"

A branch snapped nearby, much too close to Kayla, and she jumped. A boy of about seven was staring at her with wide eyes from about five feet away, a large ball under his arm. Wasn't it too late for this kid to be awake?

"Hello, what's your name?" Kayla asked in their native K'iche.

The boy just stared at her, so she tried again, still in K'iche. "Where do you live?"

The boy was still staring, but Kayla quickly realized he wasn't staring at her. He was staring at the large man behind her, the one who suddenly and violently ripped her off her feet and dragged her into the tent.

CHAPTER 24

The Kiss

The Cave Outside the Mercenaries' Camp

"HOLUN, I SEE YOU have made a friend." Shani grinned at the two of them, who were just sitting staring up at her.

Holun wasn't going to say a word. He wasn't sure what that would accomplish, but he wasn't going to give Shani any more ammunition against him.

"And who are you?"

Holun stayed staring at Shani even as he reached for the hand Yatzil had hidden in the dirt between them and squeezed. Yatzil squeezed his back without Shani ever seeing the exchange.

"Answer me!"

"I am Yatzil."

"Yatzil . . ." Shani played with the name on her tongue. "And what are you doing here, Yatzil?"

Holun didn't know how he would protect the woman he loved. He just knew he had to. "She has nothing to do with this, Shani. This is between you and me. Let her go."

Shani just stared at Holun, and Holun thought, for a second, she might oblige his request. Then she laughed. "Oh, but you have made it between the three of us now, Holun."

Holun cringed internally but kept any expression from his face. He wouldn't give Shani any satisfaction in this.

"Let her go."

Shani crossed her arms and looked off into space then shook her head, turning back to him. "No, I don't think I will."

Yatzil stood. "Do what you want with me, but let Holun go."

Yatzil, no!

Shani laughed again, this time presumably at her hubris. "I can't do that, honey. Holun here has something that I need."

"His visions?"

Shani blinked, and Holun thought she may have actually been surprised. But she recovered quickly. "I see you and Holun have had a lot of time to talk. How long have you been coming here, child?"

Yatzil didn't reply.

So Holun spoke up, a last ditch effort to avoid any pain coming to this young woman he loved more than anything. Because if she stayed, she most certainly would experience pain, and probably a lot of it. "Shani, please let her go. She was merely keeping me company."

Shani eyed him like a curious specimen. "Oh, really? Then why are you trying so hard to protect her? You feel something for her, that's very obvious."

Holun's eyes flickered to Yatzil, whose wide eyes were trained on him.

"It's true, isn't it? We have ourselves a budding romance." Shani was grinning, and Holun couldn't tell if it was genuine. "I wouldn't dream of breaking that apart." At once, Shani lunged at Yatzil, grabbing her by the wrist.

"No!" Holun yelled, fighting his restraints.

Shani glared at him as she wrestled Yatzil down next to him and reached for a rope to tie her down. She tied Yatzil's hands in front of her then connected them with a longer rope to the iron brackets that held Holun's shackles. "*You* did this, Holun. She is here because of you. Always remember that." Then her face spread into that sickening grin again, and she chuckled. "Anything that happens to her from here on out is *your* fault."

Once she was satisfied Yatzil was secure and wouldn't be going anywhere, Shani glanced at the food Holun had discarded on the ground in front of him. "Go ahead, eat, you two. One less thing for me to worry about tomorrow."

And at that, she left.

Shani couldn't breathe. She stumbled out into the early morning air, gasping for her next breath, tripping over herself in her urgency to get away from that cave.

If anyone who knew all the facts had been watching, they would've been impressed by her performance. She'd maintained the perfectly insane captor persona that she'd upheld while holding and torturing Holun this week.

But inside, she'd been screaming.

Holun was one thing—a useful but inconsequential pawn in her game—but the *girl*.

Shani felt like someone was squeezing her chest. *Yatzil* . . . That girl's voice saying her own name echoed constantly in

Shani's head. *Yatzil . . . Yatzil . . . Yatzil . . .* sang as a constant refrain in her mind, driving her crazy.

It couldn't be her. Not her. Not now.

But Shani couldn't deny it; she'd felt it the moment she'd laid eyes on the girl, the moment she looked into her eyes.

The eyes were unmistakable.

Tears started streaming down her face as she began gasping for air between sobs. Not this girl, not here. Shani could've handled anything, anyone . . . just *not her.*

With the tears still streaking down her cheeks, Shani managed a shaky, deep breath and began running. She needed to think, needed to clear her head. Running always seemed to work.

As her long, black hair trailed behind her in a blur, Shani pushed herself harder and faster, running from the one thing she regretted, the one thing that reminded her of all she'd lost, the one thing she just simply couldn't forget.

Yatzil.

She pushed herself to the breaking point as she sped through the forest.

Mercenaries' Camp, Tohil's Tent

"Na-um, you brought us one of them?" The disembodied voice Kayla had heard from a distance now had a body attached, one covered in a long, white robe.

"Yes, Tohil, I brought Kayla here with me."

"I thought you said they would not come?"

Na-um nodded. "Only she would. She came under . . . *other* circumstances."

"And what circumstances were those?" Another man entered the tent, asking the question Kayla was asking herself.

Na-um addressed the new Elder. "Chac, hello."

"Please answer the question, Na-um."

Na-um nodded at the new arrival. "She . . . she thought I might not be safe. She wanted to make sure I came back to her in one piece."

The man called Chac raised an eyebrow, and Kayla knew how he felt. What in the world was Na-um talking about? "Back to her?"

Na-um smiled then reached for Kayla's hand and pulled her to his side. Kayla couldn't keep the surprise from her face as his muscular, strong hand gripped hers. "Yes. We have . . . something . . . between us."

Kayla wanted to scream, but she kept any emotions from her face and her mouth shut. How dare he pull this? What game was he playing?

Kayla wasn't sure either Elder was buying it. The first one, Tohil, spoke up. "It's only been a few weeks, Na-um. You expect us to believe that she's fallen for you in that time?"

Na-um looked over at her and grinned. "I can be persuasive."

Kayla wanted to smack that grin right off his face, but instead she managed a smile back. Funny how she now seemed to trust that he knew what he was doing.

Chac drew in a deep breath, and it seemed that everyone else was waiting for him to issue his judgment. "You tell an interesting story, Na-um. But this woman looks a little unsure." He turned to Kayla. "Tell us; is what Na-um is saying true?"

Kayla blinked. How could she betray herself—betray Grady—like this? But this seemed the only way to avoid capture and possibly death at this point. "Yes." Kayla stretched her arm around Na-um's waist and pulled him closer. The well-defined muscles in his back flexed against her arm. She looked up at him in what she thought was a fairly impressive performance. "He can be quite convincing."

Tohil and Chac exchanged glances for a few excruciatingly long moments, then they both turned and smiled at the "couple." "Well, then congratulations are in order!" Chac smacked Na-um on the shoulder with a wide grin, and Kayla felt it radiate throughout her body. "Welcome to our Clan, Kayla. Any friend of Na-um's is a friend of the Clan."

The mood turned downright celebratory at that point, and Kayla felt as if she was meeting her boyfriend's parents for the first time. More members of the Clan were invited in, and Kayla had to meet each and every one of them.

As Kayla graciously accepted the three-hundred-and-fifteenth congratulations of the night, she eyed Na-um from across the large, brightly lit tent. If he had been telling the truth about his time out of their good graces, there was no trace of it now—he seemed to have found his way back to the Clan. The Clan that had tried to kill her. The Clan who believed she was in love with the man who'd led the charge in trying to kill her.

Was this even real?

After some time, the festivities died down, and Na-um was able to pull them away. He excused them to go for a walk outside, promising they wouldn't leave just yet, that they would be back.

When they were a sufficient distance away from the others, they found an abandoned log to sit on, and Kayla groaned. "Can't we head back yet?" She knew, to keep up their ruse, she would have to keep her questions in line with the lie they'd told. Any number of Clan members could be listening in.

Na-um just smiled at her. "Not yet. Almost."

She lowered her voice, considering how to word the question she wanted to ask before opening her mouth. "I was worried the Clan would not accept . . . us." Her voice broke on the last word, and it tasted bitter on her tongue. She still couldn't believe she was doing this.

Na-um seemed to understand what she was asking. "Like I mentioned before"—he hadn't—"the Clan has loosened their rules against mating outside the Clan."

Kayla, her skin prickling at the word "mating," looked over at him, the questions she wanted to ask certainly obvious in her gaze. His eyes caught hers and held them tightly.

But Kayla found she didn't want to look away. Somehow, though she couldn't explain it—and despite the many reservations her logical brain was throwing at her—she felt safe with him. Comfortable, certain, like she could count on him to be a certain person, act a certain way. With all the uncertainty in her life right now—with Grady, their telepathy, their powers, the artifacts—her mind sought out the only sure thing it felt she could find.

That was just crazy. She must be insane. But yet . . . despite her muddled logic, the truth was obvious, right in front of her.

He was right in front of her.

And she could no longer deny the attraction she felt for him. Without even thinking about what would come next, she reached for his hand. She told herself it was just to keep up the ruse in case someone walked by and saw them, but she was lying to herself. She *wanted* to touch him, be close to him. The wild attraction she felt for him was animalistic, primal, and overwhelming.

"Why did you come to us, Na-um?"

Na-um just stared down at their hands between them for several long moments. Then he gave the answer that caused butterflies to erupt in Kayla's stomach until she felt she couldn't contain them. "I came to *you*, Kayla. I couldn't stay away."

Na-um looked up at her, catching her gaze again and holding it with the strength of ten thousand chains, binding her to him until she knew of nothing else but her attraction to him. Kayla's breath caught. She knew she should look away, knew she should get up and leave this place, but she found herself frozen in this moment.

The man she hated to love leaned forward, his eyes beckoning her closer. Kayla was screaming at herself for allowing this to happen while still going through with it. Yet she felt drawn, pulled closer to him as he drew closer to her, and Kayla suddenly couldn't breathe.

As Na-um's lips touched hers, she felt a flame spark through her, like a blaze starting a reckless forest fire. She let him kiss her, let his mouth explore hers even as her mind screamed for her to stop.

But she couldn't stop. Every second that passed bound her more strongly to him, to his fierceness, to his inescapable magnetism. She simultaneously wanted him to stop and begged him to continue. The thoughts scrambled in her brain as she found her lips exploring his, tasting the forbidden fruit.

He moaned slightly, and her attraction leapt into dangerous territory. She found herself moaning back, her lips answering his every unasked question, coaxing, pleading with him to stop, imploring him to keep going.

Na-um's lips parted slightly, and Kayla parted hers even as alarms went off in her head. His tongue ventured inside, and Kayla gasped as hers connected with his, as she tasted his sweet essence. Her head was swimming as she begged herself to end this. But she just couldn't seem to, no matter how hard she willed it, as his mouth opened wider and stole her breath.

Mercifully, he pulled away first. Kayla found herself breathing hard, trying to catch her breath. She couldn't understand how that had happened. She'd done exactly what Mandy had warned her against—she'd found herself alone with Na-um, and somehow had managed to become known as his lover. Then that kiss . . .

She jumped to her feet, taking a few steps back. Na-um's brow furrowed as he stared up at her. Then his expression changed, and Kayla felt as though he may have actually understood.

"Not here," he muttered, standing up and grabbing her hand then pulling her toward the rainforest.

"But the others . . ."

Na-um glanced back as they reached the edge of the clearing and headed into the rainforest. "They will merely think we could not contain our passion for each other." Na-um stopped abruptly to look directly at her, and Kayla blushed. Then he pulled her onto his back in one motion and started running.

"Where are we going?" Kayla whispered in his ear.

"Far away, where no one can hear us."

Kayla held on, fighting with herself the whole way. How could she let this happen? What on earth was she thinking? She had no future with Na-um, no life with him, but everything to lose with Grady. And in one disastrous moment, she'd jeopardized all of it. She thought she was going to be sick.

Na-um stopped several miles from the camp, from Lamanai, from civilization, and set her down on a nearby rock. He was barely breathing hard, which made him somehow more attractive.

"Okay, get it out."

Kayla blinked up at him, choking out a single word. "What?"

Na-um's arms were crossed, accentuating his muscular chest. "Everything you want to say to me. About that . . . kiss."

Kayla blushed in the moonlight, hoping Na-um didn't notice. She didn't even know where to begin. She hadn't even sorted out her own feelings yet. She shook her head to try to clear it.

So he filled the silence. "Kayla, I . . . it was the moment and the situation, and it seemed to fit the story . . ."

Kayla just nodded.

Na-um was pacing, one hand on his trim waist and one now waving in the air as he thought through everything out loud. "Not that I did not want to—I did. I have been waiting to kiss you since that day in your tent . . ." Na-um stopped pacing and glanced over at her from a few feet away. "You knew that, didn't you? That I felt an attraction to you even then?"

Kayla shook her head in response, still feeling as though her voice got lost somewhere between here and the camp.

"I did. It did not make sense, and I do not even know if it was right, but I could not help but want to be near you. Your passion, your curiosity—I and my people have taken so much from you. I just wanted to give it all back."

Kayla swallowed hard. She definitely did not think this was where this conversation would go.

"Kayla, please say something."

Now he was begging? This didn't seem like the Na-um she'd built up in her head. The one who was only here to get between her and Grady, mess her life up, then head back out of it as soon as he'd come. No; this was a man who seemed to genuinely care for her.

That made this so much harder.

"Na-um . . ." Kayla started, still not sure where she was headed. She sighed, supposing the truth was the best place to go. "I . . . I'm in love with Grady."

"Grady?"

Kayla nodded.

Na-um squatted down in the dirt, played with a stick he found there, then looked over at her, his eyes now at her level. "You kissed me."

Kayla's heart broke. "Yes, I did."

"Why?"

Kayla had been asking herself the same question a million different ways. "I . . . I'm not sure. I felt—I was attracted to you in a very primal way, but . . . I don't know. Na-um, things were not supposed to get this complicated."

Na-um stood and walked over to her, sitting down next to her. "This should not be complicated. Attraction is not complicated."

"It is for me," Kayla whispered as she stared at her hands. She'd begun playing with the zipper on her jacket. "I am attracted to two men."

Na-um sighed beside her, and Kayla sensed him staring off into the darkness of the rainforest. Silence stretched between them for several long moments before he spoke. "And you are in love with him." It wasn't a question.

Kayla's heart broke again at the pain she heard in his voice. She hated this. How could she have been so stupid to lead him on like this? "I am. I was just . . . confused. Shani—"

Na-um perked up at the name. "What does Shani have to do with this?"

Kayla just stared. He didn't know? She'd assumed he did. "Shani stole Grady's memory. His memory of me. He can't remember anything about me or our relationship before a few weeks ago."

"When was this?"

"Like I said, a few weeks ago. When we were still in Florida."

Na-um jumped to his feet and started pacing again. "I did not know she was so powerful."

Kayla just watched him pace, trying to figure out what had gotten him so agitated. "What's going on?"

Na-um stopped. "Shani is much too powerful for us to fight alone. If we want to get Holun back—and find those artifacts—the only way is to destroy her."

Kayla's mouth fell open. "You mean *kill* her?"

Na-um face fell. "I am afraid we may have to."

"But why? How does her stealing Grady's memories make her more powerful than you thought? Couldn't she already control minds? Doesn't that make her pretty powerful?"

Na-um crossed his arms again. He nodded. "Yes, but stealing someone's memories is so much more difficult than just controlling what they are thinking. That goes back into months, years, of thoughts and actions. She is having to keep all of that from his mind."

"We have noticed her slip a few times, and he's gotten his memory back for a few seconds before it leaves again."

"Right." Na-um placed a hand underneath his chin. "Yes. This must require an extraordinary amount of effort on her part."

Kayla stood. "But that's a good thing, right? Because she will eventually become unable to keep it up?"

Na-um was staring into the rainforest. "Maybe, maybe not. If she gets her hands on an artifact that could increase her power, Grady's memory loss may become permanent. At that point, she may be too powerful to stop."

"Then we have to stop her first."

"Agreed." Na-um nodded again. "We cannot let her get her hands on those artifacts. And since she has taken Holun—and you said she already has the globe—we have to assume that is her next step."

Kayla nodded once. "Makes sense to me."

Na-um offered his hand. "We need to tell the others. You up for another ride?"

She hesitated—she had something left to say. "Na-um . . . I'm sorry for leading you on. You don't deserve that."

She watched in the moonlight as a cloud fell over his features then lifted as quickly as it had come. "I understand, Kayla. You chose him. And that is okay; you two deserve to be together after everything you have gone through. I will just keep my eyes open for my own love to come my way." He smiled at her, and as he lifted Kayla onto his back and ran back through the rainforest, she hoped someday he would.

CHAPTER 25

One More Time

The Hidden Cave in the Mountains Outside the Mercenaries' Camp

HOLUN TURNED TO YATZIL not long after Shani left. "Are you okay?"

Yatzil struggled a bit against the ropes around her wrists then sighed. "Yes, I am okay."

Holun frowned, his heart breaking. "I am so sorry, Yatzil. I am sorry I got you into this."

"Holun, stop." She turned to him awkwardly, her hands still tied in her lap. "Do not listen to Shani. This is *not* your fault. I chose to come here. To save you." She made a face, and Holun laughed.

She laughed with him, and Holun thought even the sound of her strained laugh was still the best sound on earth.

"So now what do we do?" Holun glanced at the cave's only exit and sighed.

"Well, at least we are together." Yatzil grinned over at him.

Holun grinned back. "Very true."

"And she left the lantern and the food."

Holun glanced over at the light sitting several feet away, the food beside it. "Thankfully."

Then she paused, and Holun wondered why. "Um, Holun?"

"Yes?"

She took a deep breath. "Can I ask you something?"

Holun's mind was reeling. "Of course."

"Was what Shani said true?"

Holun drew in a quick breath. He suspected he knew what she was referring to but decided to play dumb. "Which part?"

Yatzil shot him a sideways glance. "I think you know."

He was discovering he could never get anything past her. He nodded slowly. "Yes."

"All of it?"

She was relentless, wasn't she? It was one of the things he loved about her, just not so much when it was directed at him. "Yes, Yatzil, Shani was right. I . . . feel something for you."

Holun heard her inhale sharply, and he suddenly felt his stomach drop. Had he read her incorrectly? Did she not feel the same way?

Then she spoke, but it wasn't at all what he expected to hear. "Okay."

"Okay?" He couldn't help himself.

Yatzil nodded, adjusting her position in the sand. "Yes. What else should I say?"

Holun turned his body fully toward her, ignoring the slicing pain in his back as he twisted. "What else should you say?

How about telling me how you feel? I just laid my heart out there, bared my soul, and you—"

Suddenly, Yatzil's lips pressed into his, and his breath left his body, effectively cutting off his words. In an instant, everything he'd felt for her over the past week flew to the surface, and the rush of feelings made his head swim. He kissed her back as gently as he could figure out how to do— he'd never kissed someone before—and he hoped he was doing it right.

Though he sensed she'd never kissed someone before, either, they both seemed to instinctively know what to do. His lips softly brushed hers before she pressed tighter to his mouth, deepening the kiss. He let his body lead as he savored the feel of her soft lips massaging his.

He couldn't think of what he'd ever done to deserve this amazing woman. He couldn't have deserved her if he'd lived a thousand lifetimes. At the first touch of her lips, he was lost. Gone. Yatzil had him forever.

Finally, she pulled away. "Does that answer your questions?"

Holun was just staring at her, his eyes wide. He couldn't seem to manage anything else.

Yatzil laughed, a twinkling symphony of wind chimes and butterflies, at least that's the closest thing Holun could think of to compare it to. And in that moment, Holun didn't care what happened to him as long as Yatzil was okay, as long as she cared about him. He would take a thousand more cuts and bruises for her, if that's what it took to keep her safe. Her kiss made him feel like he could conquer the world.

"That was fun." Yatzil grinned at him.

He was still staring at her, frozen like an idiot. He finally managed to find his voice. "Yes."

"Oh, good, you are back!" Yatzil teased.

Holun scowled at her, but a smile broke through. There was no way he could actually be mad at her. Especially not after *that*. "Of course." He chuckled. "That *was* fun. I was not . . . I was not even sure how to tell you how I felt."

Yatzil smiled at him, reaching for his hand with both of hers and holding it as she scooted up close to him and leaned against the wall, just as they'd done every night for the past week. Holun fell right back into the familiar position and smiled at her as she spoke. "I was not sure, either. I guess we can thank Shani for that."

Her statement made him think. Shani really did bring them together, didn't she? She was a horrible woman, evil even, but what she meant to hurt him had actually saved him. And Yatzil made him realize that.

As he gazed at the young woman he now knew he loved without question, he was eternally grateful that she had come into his life. She made him a better man, a kinder one, and helped him see the world in a wonderful and beautiful new way.

She'd changed him into a much better version of himself, in ways he never imagined he needed to change.

He'd always love her for that.

Somewhere in the Northern Belize Rainforest

Shani didn't know how long she'd been running, but she sensed it might have been quite awhile. The moon and stars lit up the sky and her path through the forest where the light shone through the canopy overhead. Shani slowed.

Her tears had long ago dried on her face, but she reached up to wipe her eyes anyway, finding a fallen tree and sitting on it. She wished her run through the forest had given her a clear course of action, but she still felt lost. What did she do next? She couldn't bring herself to hurt that girl or even hurt Holun in front of her.

But why not?

Yatzil didn't know her from anyone else, had no clue who she really was. The girl knew her as ruthless, probably a little insane, and as someone who'd tortured the boy she'd come to visit. How that had ever happened, Shani didn't have a clue.

But now the girl named Yatzil was with Holun, tied up in the cave, the cave Shani had tied her up in. How did everything get so out of hand?

She sighed. She needed a distraction, and she missed him. She hadn't heard his voice in forever, say nothing of actually wrapping her arms around him, holding him close. As she gazed up into the starlit sky, she wondered where he was at this moment. He was probably sleeping, but where? What assignment did they have him on now? She'd been away from him so long that she didn't even have a clue. And that made the whole situation even worse.

Outside the Mercenaries' Camp

Na-um got Kayla back to the camp then back to the others in no time. Na-um returned to Tohil's tent to say his goodbyes—to save face, keep up the ruse—while Kayla filled the others in on what Na-um suspected about Shani.

"So now we *do* have to kill her?" Mandy asked. Kayla knew she would like the prospect least of all.

"Na-um seems to think so. He thinks that she is more powerful than any of us realize, that if she gets her hands on any artifacts that increase her power, she may become unstoppable, and Grady's memory loss may become irreversible." Kayla shuddered, realizing how devastating this would be not only for Grady but also for her as well.

"So what do we do next?" Justin asked. "How do we even find her? And let's not forget about Holun!"

"My vision can give us a clue. Na-um seems to know where it is. When he gets back, we can head that way."

Kayla noticed Grady hadn't chimed in yet. *Grady, are you okay?*

He glanced over at her at her thought in his head. *Sure, I'm okay. I just didn't like that you were gone so long. With him.*

Kayla sat still for a moment then nodded toward the rainforest. She stood and walked into the trees, letting Mandy and Justin know she and Grady would be back shortly. Grady followed her.

They continued their conversation telepathically, wary of being this close to the Clan and having someone overhear them.

Grady, is something going on?

It's nothing, Kayla. I'm just glad you're safe.

Are you sure? Kayla didn't want to push him, but she sensed something was amiss.

Kayla . . . She could hear the strain even in his thoughts. *What happened?*

Kayla paused, and she struggled to keep the events of the night from her thoughts. She brought to mind the time she was hiding behind the bushes and got captured.

Grady heard it all in her head. *Anything else?*

Grady . . . please, don't do this. I can't . . .

You can't, what? Something went on there, Kayla, something happened. I can feel it. I may not have all my memories of you, but I know you enough to know you are hiding something from me.

Just then, Kayla heard a rustling beside them, and Na-um burst through the foliage just ahead of Mandy and Justin.

And Kayla couldn't stop the memory from boiling to the surface. She replayed the whole horrific scene and her conversation with Na-um afterward in her head with Grady listening in. The kiss, her attraction to Na-um—everything came out. Nothing was hidden anymore.

When it was done, she couldn't look at Grady. She fell to a nearby log, tears streaming down her cheeks, the agony of what she'd done to Grady tearing her heart into pieces.

She finally got the courage to look at him and immediately wished she hadn't. All the love she felt coming from him since they first fell for each other was sliding down in razor-sharp shards around him, dripping from his body and shattering to the mossy ground. And all she saw beneath his clenched jaw and fiery glare was a deep, gut-wrenching pain that reached into his very soul and tore his heart from his chest. Unspeakable pain that she had caused.

Grady, please, she sobbed. *I'm so sorry.*

I understand now why you wouldn't tell me, Kayla. Was it worth it? Was he worth it?

Kayla's heart just kept breaking as the sobs wracked her body. *No, Grady, I am so sorry. You heard me tell him—I'm in love with you. Nothing can change that. Not a stupid, incredibly idiotic kiss. Not a ridiculous attraction to the man who tried to kill us. Nothing!*

Grady sighed and turned his back to her. *I can't think with you in my head right now. I'm going back to Lamanai alone.*

Grady! Please . . . I really am so very sorry.

I know, Kayla—I just can't right now. Please.

Then he just walked away.

CHAPTER 26

When Your Heart Breaks into Pieces

KAYLA COULDN'T BREATHE. She sat on the log gasping for air, not caring that Mandy and Justin were staring at her, asking her to explain, or that Na-um was looking on in pity. The most important person in her life had just walked out of it because of something stupid she'd done. Grady was gone, *really* gone this time—and it was all her fault.

Mandy knew immediately that something was very wrong. She hadn't heard a thing—she'd not even thought to try her telepathy until it was too late—but as Grady ran off into the forest and Mandy watched her friend fall apart, she knew something very bad had happened.

Kayla wasn't saying anything; she was crying so hard Mandy thought she probably wouldn't be able to form any coherent words. So she called her telepathy now to speak to her friend who couldn't speak to her.

And as she started to hear her panicked, scrambled, pleading thoughts, everything fell into place. The thing she'd warned Kayla about—getting close to Na-um—had happened, and Grady had found out.

Now everything made complete sense, and Mandy's heart broke.

Justin, what do we do? She'd heard him listening in—their telepathy had worked since the clearing, though only in close proximity, so he quickly got up to speed. She felt him ache for them, and she fell a little more in love with him in that moment, even through the pain she was feeling for their friends.

Babe, we can't fix this. Grady and Kayla have to work this out themselves.

Mandy frowned. She knew he was right, but was it even possible? Could their relationship—on already fragile ground, if she was being honest—survive this?

As she went to sit by her friend and draped an arm around her shoulders, pulling her close as she sobbed, Mandy imagined if this had happened with Justin. Could she forgive him? Could they start over, start again? Given her history, she didn't think they could.

For Grady, this would be starting for the third time. She hadn't fully understood Grady's predicament—she suspected no one could unless they were in the middle of it—but she knew he loved Kayla. She just didn't know if this was enough to break that fragile love, that trust, into pieces.

Grady started running. He knew the others needed him to help find Holun, retrieve the artifacts, destroy Shani, but he couldn't seem to care. The only thing he could feel right now was his heart breaking into a million pieces. So he ran to forget.

He couldn't remember his life before with Kayla, but she had still altered him in such an irrevocable way that this betrayal felt utterly devastating. In a cruel twist of fate, the one thing he *could* remember of the woman that was supposed to be in love with him was her reaching into his chest and ripping his heart out.

He picked up the pace and headed for Lamanai. He was finding it difficult to breathe even as he ran faster than he'd ever thought possible, but it wasn't from the exertion. He ran for miles, crossing them in mere minutes, letting the foliage and the trees fly past him as he wished they would just wipe it all away.

The man who couldn't remember just desperately wanted to forget.

Grady slowed to a walk before he reached the dig, wanting to avoid as many people as possible, the tears finally making their way to the surface. He knew that though the personnel on the dig was light, there were still a few people who would ask questions, questions that would claw at a much-too-fresh wound. Even at this late—he pulled out his phone—early hour.

He checked the perimeter of the dig before entering the clearing. The night was lightening into morning as he arrived, but he knew there would still be people around, people just waking up. He found a circuitous route and silently took it, sensing it would get him to his tent with the least amount of human interaction.

Finally, much later than he'd hoped, Grady spied his tent. The one next to Kayla's. The open wound in his chest shot a sharp pain through his heart at the thought. As tears threatened to spill over, he ran for his tent and threw himself inside.

He fell to the cot, and the tears finally came. Gut-wrenching, heartrending sobs shook his body as he silently languished in his solitary prison.

How could she do this to him? Hadn't he given everything to her? He couldn't remember their life before a few weeks ago, but he'd committed to her anyway, even without the memories, because he trusted that they were in love, trusted her with his heart.

Only to have it handed back to him in pieces.

As the tears ran down his face, his mind involuntarily took him back to the time when this had happened before. When the woman he'd loved had shredded his heart and walked out of his life.

Her name was Trisha. He'd been in his second bachelor's degree, and she'd been a TA in one of the classes he was taking. At first, he was enthralled by her. A couple of years his senior, the redheaded goddess was sophisticated, intelligent, and experienced, and Grady found that hopelessly attractive.

Their tryst had started like any other: stealing away for secret moments of passion, catching each other between classes and their part-time jobs, spending nights at his apartment and weekends at hers.

For awhile, their affair had been exciting, new, provocative. He'd had girlfriends before, sure, but none had captured his heart—and honestly, the rest of him—like Trisha. He quickly fell for her—hard—and planned a life for them together in his head.

Then, one autumn day, it came crashing down. Trisha had been growing distant, though at the time, he'd missed it. Only looking back did he see her pulling away. He found her one day behind the library—among the fiery reds and vibrant oranges of the multitude of fall leaves covering the ground—with another man. He'd never taken that specific route, but a sick twist of fate—they were replacing the sidewalk on his normal route—had changed his course. And he saw another student like him, no doubt enthralled with her affections.

Grady ran then, too. It seemed his pattern. When things got too difficult, he ran. It was a great exercise plan, but one that always seemed to leave his emotions tattered for much too long.

His tears finally started to subside, leaving in their absence a stark emptiness that he wasn't sure he'd ever fill. Kayla—it even hurt to think her name—and the others needed him, but he was so destroyed in this moment that he couldn't even conceive of getting off this cot, leaving this tent.

The sun was finally peeking over the edge of the surrounding mountains, and Grady couldn't help but notice the irony. The world was waking up to a fresh, new day, but all he felt was despair, loneliness, a pervading darkness that captured his soul and wouldn't let go.

He sat up on his cot, unsure of what to do next. He would sit here all day if he could, but he knew the others would come looking for him eventually. Though he wanted to sprint into the rainforest and never look back, they needed him. Mandy and Justin, Holun—*they* needed him. They needed his powers, sure, but more than that, he knew they needed his leadership, his support.

He just wished he could offer it without having to see her again, hear her apologies, listen to her innermost thoughts.

Even though his mind told him he'd only known her for a few weeks, Grady now realized, much too late, just how much Kayla had changed him, stolen his heart, reached into his soul and altered his consciousness. Even as his mind, his body ached for her, his heart pleaded with him to walk away, never speak to her again, protect himself from further harm.

If only it were possible.

Grady ran his hands over his face to wipe the last of the drying tears away then stood. He had a job to do, and Kayla, though he hated it, was a big part of that.

He wanted to hate this place, this place that had given them powers, a destiny, each other, but he couldn't seem to do it. He knew his heart would heal, and he would move on, but he also knew that no matter how hard he tried, he would never really get over this, would never really get over her.

Grady sauntered to the bathing trailer to clean up, splash some water on his face, somehow refresh himself. The others would be back soon, and they'd come looking for him. As he stared into the glassless mirror, his warped reflection a fitting summation of his current state, he knew he would have to face this head on. He would have to face her, though he didn't know how at the moment. He supposed he'd learn as he went along.

That proposition seemed utterly exhausting.

When Grady left the bathroom, the sun was shining brightly in the sky, and the day was warming up fast. Grady headed back toward his tent to shed the sweatshirt he'd donned for their overnight excursion. As he did, he tried to push the thought of last night from his mind.

Then he heard some rustling behind him, and a voice interrupted his thoughts. "Um, Dr. McGready?"

Grady whipped around at the sound. "Mr. Barring?" He blinked over at the well-dressed man. "And please, it's Grady. What can I do for you?"

Alexander Barring, their dark-haired, olive-skinned liaison from the Central American Institute of Archaeology, was back at the dig assessing its viability for conversion to a tourist site. They'd met him here this past summer, but now he was back with a different mission. The discoveries this summer were groundbreaking, but all the processing of the site had been done earlier in the fall semester. Now the Institute needed to assess the dig to make sure all the proper protocols had been followed in its processing then put the proper protocols in place to convert it. Grady admired the man— though he dressed in suits in one-hundred-degree weather— because he consistently performed a rather thankless job. Someone had to do it.

"Please, call me Alex."

"What's going on, Alex?" Grady tried again.

Alex paused then cleared his throat. "You know that student you had with you this summer—what was her name?"

"Jackie." Grady gritted his teeth, giving the name he knew Alex would remember.

"Yes. Did I see her here the other day?"

Grady blinked. When would Shani have been here?

Then he remembered. Holun.

"Did you? I was off-site."

"Yes, I believe so. She was only here for a short time, to my knowledge."

Grady wasn't sure where this was going, but then he had a thought. "Did you see which direction she went?"

Alex crossed his arms and nodded. "Yes. She was heading northwest, I believe. It looked like she was headed toward those mountains." He pointed toward the peak just north of them. "That one would be my guess."

Grady nodded, his first smile in what felt like days spreading across his lips. At least now they had somewhere to start.

"Alex, thank you." Grady patted him on the back and started to walk away.

"Uh, Grady?"

He turned back around. "Yes?"

"Jackie . . . is she okay? I didn't see her much after the, uh, *event* this summer—I was worried something had happened to her." Alex's brow furrowed when he referenced the poisoning at the dig; he looked genuinely concerned.

Maybe Alex had no clue what had transpired between them. Or maybe he knew everything and was just trying to figure out what Grady knew. He could even be working with her!

Grady sighed. This stuff with Kayla had really messed up his head. He didn't know who to trust, where to find the truth.

But he knew Alex was waiting for an answer. "She is alive and well, Alex. Though I'm not certain of her current whereabouts. If you see her again, could you please let me know?"

Alex, worry lines still creasing his face, nodded. "Yes, of course." Then he turned and headed back toward the main part of the dig, presumably the way he'd come.

Nice talking to you, Grady thought, wishing in that moment that he actually did have a real, live person to talk to.

Your wish is my command.

Grady's heart wrenched in his chest as Kayla's voice sounded in his head.

Kayla, please . . . I don't know that I can right now.

He heard Kayla agreeing. *I understand that. I just wanted to say my piece, then I'll do my best to leave you alone.*

Grady thought about it. *Okay, I suppose that's fine. Can we meet?*

Grady nodded, knowing she would understand.

Thank you, Grady. Let's meet at our first discovery site. The deep tunnel in the ground.

Grady nodded again. *I remember that, vaguely.* He cursed Shani again for ripping his memories away from him. They wouldn't be in this situation now if she hadn't. Alex must not have known who she really was—he wouldn't be so concerned for her if he did.

Grady found the hole in less than a minute, just a short walk from his tent. Kayla was walking up as he arrived. The moment he saw her, he felt his heart tearing in two.

I don't know how much more I can take. Grady already felt like his chest was ripped open; he didn't know how long he could just stand here, breathing. Like a human.

"I'm sorry." Kayla spoke aloud, her voice carrying on the wind and resting on his ears like a soft blanket. Though he wanted to hate her and everything about her, his mind, body, and heart still belonged to her, and probably always would. No matter how much he tried to convince himself otherwise.

Kayla pointed to some nearby camping chairs and offered one to Grady. He took it, trying to remember how to keep functioning.

"I know I don't have the right to ask you to forgive me. What I did was completely wrong, unforgivable. But I wanted to try to explain. Not to make excuses, but hopefully so you will understand how much you still mean to me."

"You have a terrible way of showing that, Kayla."

Her head hung, and Grady almost regretted speaking.

"I know." Her voice cracked; she took a breath before continuing. "Please, let me explain. I felt our relationship straining, felt us being pulled away from each other. The way Shani messed with your mind—it really threw me off. I didn't know who to turn to for comfort, consistency, reliability. I had those things with you before Shani stole them from you, from us.

"So my brain stupidly presented Na-um as a reliable choice. One I could understand, somewhat steady and consistent in a world that had been turned upside down."

Kayla paused; Grady let her continue. He sensed there was more coming. He was right.

"Grady, please understand: I love you. I'm *in* love with you. I know it doesn't feel like I'm telling the truth right now, but I've loved you since I've known you."

Grady eyed her. "Kayla, that doesn't make any sense."

Kayla shook her head. "But it does. I knew you at UCF, even before we really even talked, but looking back on it now, I could sense I was drawn to you. I know now my love for you was a part of me even then."

Grady wasn't sure he believed her, but he almost wanted to.

"My heart will always be yours. No matter what happens, you've stolen it from me, and I'll never fully get it back." Kayla ran her fingers through her hair. "And I wouldn't want to. Your love changed me, Grady. Permanently. It's why I was so devastated when you couldn't remember me anymore, why I'm so heartbroken now though I have no right to be. Like I said, what I did was horrible, but I'm begging you to consider forgiving the unforgivable."

Grady swallowed once, analyzing her words. Could she possibly mean everything she was saying?

"Na-um means nothing to me, Grady. I've told him that, and now I'm telling you. The kiss meant nothing. Attraction is fleeting, shallow, and can be utterly misleading. I had a weak moment, one where I was longing to be close to you again, and I made the worst decision anyone could make: I made the decision to break your heart." Kayla's voice cracked, and she sniffed. "And if you ever trust me with it again, I will spend the rest of my probably very long life doing everything I can to put it back together."

Kayla had tears streaming down both cheeks. "I'm so sorry, really." She whispered through her sobs. "I know I don't even have the right to ask this, Grady. But what we had—and what we could have again—is astonishing. It's the kind of love they write stories about. Love that transcends time and anything Shani or Na-um or anyone else could throw our way. Even me."

Kayla sniffed again then wiped her eyes with her hands. "I promise to make this up to you forever, Grady. If someday you think you could ever have me again, could ever love me again, I will be yours alone, forever. Because I already am."

At that, Kayla fell quiet, and Grady mulled over her words. What could he honestly say or do? His heart wasn't ready to forgive, but his mind was trying to talk him into it. His heart cautioned him to stay safe, guard against any pain, but what would that get him, anyway? A lifetime full of regrets and missed opportunities.

Kayla, I understand all of this, I promise. I know you believe what you're saying, that you're telling me your truth. I just have to work through it. I just need time.

Kayla nodded back at him, and for the first time since last night, Grady started to feel something a little like hope.

CHAPTER 27

Going Home

The Rainforest Outside the Mercenaries' Camp

SHANI HAD BEEN WANDERING through the trees for what had to have been hours but was no closer to figuring out her next move.

It had been a week since she'd brought that brat kid here, and, despite her best efforts and what she'd thought were surprisingly sophisticated torture techniques, Holun hadn't given her anything. She had formulated her plan, but without Holun anticipating the Elders' every move, she was in great danger of being discovered.

Even now, as she struggled to keep them out of her head and keep Kayla out of Grady's at the same time, she worried they may still find her out. She'd been out of the Elders' good graces for so many years—and only was given a pass after she'd inserted herself in the lives of the Four, thus proving invaluable to the cause—that she didn't want to mess up their newly reacquired acceptance of her.

She'd never thought a teenaged, sensitive kid would be able to withstand even the slightest amount of discomfort, but he'd outlasted her countless cuts, bruises, punches, and slaps like a pro. Shani found it distasteful, but she hadn't seen another option.

So she'd done it, but what did she have to show for it? Another captive, and the girl named Yatzil, at that? Shani growled loudly, knowing only the foliage would be able to hear her. What did she do now?

She just missed him so much. He was the only person in the world that made her feel safe, loved. Taken care of. He was always there, a safe haven in her tumultuous life.

Just to hold him again would make this all worth it. But did she dare? She hadn't seen him in so many months, but she'd done all of this so she could be with him. To amass great power and authority so they could live like royalty. The power and authority that she and Na-um deserved from birth but was awarded to the Elders, old men who knew little of what true power meant.

She glanced up at the morning sun peeking out over the mountains. Those two weren't going anywhere, and they probably needed sleep given the night they had. She could afford a few hours to find him and make sure he was okay.

She started running, reaching Belize City in mere minutes. She easily found the Central American Institute of Archaeology headquarters, but his office was empty. Where could he be?

She politely fed the receptionist a lie about being his fiancée—which she supposed was true at one point, anyway—who told her that Alex was at the Lamanai assessment and would be for a few more days. As Shani walked out of the office, a wide grin reached her lips. Alex was right in her backyard. It would complicate things a little, but she couldn't bring herself to care.

Shani reached the edge of the forest and started running, faster than she ever had before. She felt lighter than she'd felt in months, since she'd last heard his voice.

She was going home.

"Mandy, Justin, we know the direction that Shani was headed." Grady met the others and Na-um—despite his better judgment on that last one—in the mess tent for breakfast to fill them in about what he'd discovered. He struggled to keep Kayla's thoughts out of his head—and it sounded like she was trying, too. He loved her for it, though he really didn't want to admit that to himself.

"How?" Justin asked through a mouthful of his protein bar.

Mandy rolled her eyes at him. "How did you find out?"

Grady nodded back toward the dig's main work trailer. "Alex Barring, from the Institute, said he saw Shani leave the dig and head north, presumably when she took Holun."

Na-um chimed in. "He saw her?"

Grady nodded, struggling to keep his expression blank. "Apparently."

"So what's our next move?" Kayla asked, sitting down next to Mandy and—quite obviously to everyone—*not* next to Grady.

Grady addressed the group in answer to her question, careful not to look over at her too closely. It hurt too much. "We go today. It will be easier to search in the light, and Shani probably won't be expecting us."

"Sounds good." Kayla affirmed as the others nodded.

"Okay, then." Grady stood. "We leave in fifteen."

Mercenaries' Camp

Steven was done with all this waiting. Only Tyler, Alexia, and that little native girl knew he was even here, and even they seemed to forget sometimes. Who knew being invisible would be so lonely?

He missed Hannah, though he would never admit it. After all, she'd deserved what she got . . .

But he couldn't shake the image of her last few seconds, her last few breaths—the breaths he had stolen from her—from his head. Her bloody corpse juxtaposed against the carpet tiles and cubicle walls of the museum's office, slumped up against the wall. Her eyes inexplicably holding his until they went blank—he'd watched the life drain out of them, out of her. He'd hated her for what she'd done to him. Hated that man, Simón, that she'd run to. Hated everything about her, except . . .

Steven stared at the ground, the deepest sorrow he'd ever felt sinking down on him like a wool blanket on a hot day.

What had he done?

As he sat alone in the tent he shared with a frat boy he barely knew, he dropped his face into his hands and wept.

Just Outside the Lamanai Archaeological Dig

Shani slowed as she approached the dig, the dig where she knew her love would be. She walked slowly into the clearing, careful to stick close to buildings, tents, and the larger equipment so she could hide behind them if the need arose.

She made her way toward the work trailer, the same one where she'd seen Alex here last summer, the one time in the near past that she'd actually been able to see him, touch him, feel him close to her. She hoped he'd be there now.

Once the dig's main work trailer came into view, Shani checked her surroundings, looking for any wandering eyes who could spot her and report back to Kayla, Grady, Mandy, or Justin. Or even Na-um. She supposed he was probably still here.

Shani went around the back side of the trailer, the side that faced the rainforest, and leaned up on her toes to peek through the window. At first, the trailer appeared to be empty.

Then she saw him. Her heart swelled, and she ran around the front of the trailer and threw open the door.

Alex jumped as the door opened. But when his dark-brown eyes found hers, Shani thought the grin that spread across his face was as wonderful as it was abrupt. Shani ran up the few steps, threw the door shut, and leapt into his arms.

She held him for a long time, let him hold her. She couldn't imagine a better feeling in the world; the man she loved so fiercely was back in her arms once again.

Shani reluctantly pulled away and went to each window, checking outside to make sure no one had seen them before twisting each set of blinds shut.

Alex pulled her close once again when she was done. "My Shani . . . how . . ." Then he blinked. "What are you doing here? Aren't you in danger?"

Shani nodded. "Of course. But I had to see you." Alex frowned, and Shani's heart dropped. "What? What's wrong?"

Alex glanced toward the door. "They are still here. They asked me to tell them if I saw you again."

"Again?" Shani's eyes narrowed. She didn't want to get mad at him, not when their time together was so short, but she couldn't seem to help it. She frowned.

Alex's piercing gaze went right through her. "Yes. I had to find out if you were okay. I haven't heard from you in months!"

Shani looked away, unwilling to meet his eyes. She hadn't called, hadn't even sent a text to let him know she was okay. And in this moment, she didn't know why. Perhaps she'd had a litany of excuses, but none of them came to her right now. "I'm sorry," she mumbled, still looking away.

Alex let go of her, taking half a step back, then reached for her chin and turned her head toward him, staring at her until she looked back at him.

"Shani . . ." He leaned down and gently pressed his lips to hers. Though they'd been together for several years—and married for most of that time, though Shani knew no court would officially recognize it; they'd made certain to keep everything under wraps for his safety—his kiss still caused butterflies to erupt in her stomach and her knees to get weak.

She leaned into him, kissing him back with all the enthusiasm she'd built up in the past few months they'd been apart. She'd hated to do it, but she'd left to protect him. She couldn't have those American bastards—the "Four" she thought with a sudden terrible taste in her mouth—discovering they were working together and taking it out on him.

The thought brought her back to reality, and she reluctantly pulled away. She needed to get back soon, but not quite yet—she had something she needed to say first. "Alex, I just wanted you to know . . . I love you."

Alex smiled down at her, pulling her close once again until his face was inches from hers. "I love you, too, my Shani."

Then Shani sighed and unwillingly changed the subject. "I met someone today."

Alex blinked at her. "Already this morning?"

Shani smirked; she couldn't help it. "Yes." She couldn't fault him for not understanding who she really was and the life she really lived; she wasn't exactly forthcoming with the details.

"Who?"

Shani reached for his hands, holding them in hers. "A young woman named Yatzil."

Alex froze, and his eyes went blank. His voice came out a strangled whisper. "A young woman?"

Shani nodded slowly, her eyes holding his.

Alex swallowed hard, then Shani watched as the life gradually came back into his eyes. He returned her gaze, eyes tightening. "Is she . . . ?"

Shani nodded again, even more slowly than before.

Alex looked like he was about to fall over. Shani led him to a nearby chair and helped him sit. She pulled up her own and sat across from him, reaching for his hands once again. "She . . . how . . ." he sputtered, eyes casting erratic glances around the trailer.

Shani shook her head then spoke, her voice gentle. "I'm not sure. I don't know how she even came to be involved with this."

Alex cocked his head to the side. "Involved with what?"

Shani sighed again then stood. That was the wrong question, and he didn't need to know the answer. With the expertise that comes with years of practice, she deftly avoided his question. "I must go."

Alex frowned back, standing with her. "You're sure?"

Shani nodded slowly, hating that she always had to be the strong one. "Yes. I must get back." She leaned up to steal one last kiss then turned for the door.

But Alex grabbed her hand before she could get far. "Um, Shani?"

She turned back around to look at him. "Yes?"

"What did you do to that boy?"

Shani blinked. "What boy?"

Alex's face relaxed, then his eyes narrowed, an expression Shani recognized well.

She'd never been good at playing dumb, not with him. "He is part of my plan to get what we need."

"And what is that?"

Shani paused, thinking. So far, she'd only told Alex what she felt he needed to know, and she'd like to keep it that way. Getting him more involved would just be too dangerous. "I have a plan to get away from my Clan for good; I'm not certain of all the details yet, but that boy will help me execute it."

Alex's brows furrowed, but he seemed to buy it. He usually did. "Okay. Just be safe." He leaned forward to kiss her forehead, and Shani smiled.

"Of course, my love." Then she did the hardest thing she'd done since she'd left this past summer: She turned and walked out on the man she loved.

CHAPTER 28

Vision and Pleasure

"HOLUN, ARE YOU AWAKE?"

Yatzil had spent a restless morning with Holun, both of them drifting in and out of sleep for fear Shani would come back and unspeakable evils would await them.

A groggy Holun stirred from where he lay in the dirt. "Sure," he mumbled, "I am now."

Yatzil placed a hand on his shoulder and turned him to face her. "Good morning."

As soon as he saw her, Holun smiled, the sweetest thing Yatzil felt she had probably ever seen. "Hi." Holun moved carefully to sit up, accommodating the still-fresh cuts on his back, sides, and stomach.

Yatzil winced as he moved. "Are you sure you are okay? Those wounds looked really bad."

Holun, finally in a seated position but breathing a little too hard, nodded. He reached for her hand, and she gladly let him take it. "I am okay, Yatzil, I promise. They will heal."

An errant tear slid down her cheek before she could stop it, and Holun reached over to wipe it away. "Yatzil, I will be fine." He reached an arm out for her, and she slid into place next to him, her head on his chest. "I promise."

Yatzil nodded against him feeling a little unsettled. She wasn't quite sure what she wanted to say, but she didn't know when that horrible woman would be back and what she'd do to them when she got here, so she thought she'd better say something while she had the opportunity. "Holun?" She leaned back to look up at him.

He looked over at her with an intense look she didn't quite understand. "Yes?"

She sat up. "I wanted to talk to you."

Holun straightened as well, carefully. "Okay."

Yatzil swallowed once. Still not knowing what she would say, she opened her mouth to see what would come out. "I am scared." Well. She certainly didn't expect that. She was supposed to be the brave one, the rescuer. Rescuers didn't admit when they were afraid.

"I know; I am, too."

Yatzil blinked. "You are?"

Holun nodded somberly. "Yes. I have seen—and felt—what Shani is capable of. She could really hurt you, Yatzil. I would never be able to forgive myself if anything happened to you."

Yatzil felt her heart start to race. She wasn't very familiar with the feeling, but she suddenly knew what she wanted. And it didn't involve any words.

"Holun?"

"Yes?"

Yatzil blinked then spoke the words that she only now realized had been on her mind all morning. "Kiss me."

She watched Holun's face go blank then seem to come back to life in the span of about a second. Holun leaned in, and their lips met again—but it was so much better than the first time. That time, she'd been too afraid to let him consider whether he wanted to kiss her or not that she rushed it, kissed him before he could stop her.

This time was different. Holun's kiss was still a little hesitant but warm and comforting, with an underlying hunger that Yatzil didn't quite know how to explain. She didn't want to admit it, but this morning's kiss was her first, and the thought of kissing Holun again had consumed her thoughts since—though she only realized that just now—so as their lips met, her heart finally felt content, settled once again.

Holun pulled away after a few long, incredible moments and searched her eyes. "Was that okay?"

Yatzil laughed. "Okay? That was amazing."

Holun shrugged, a half grin on his face. "Not that I am proud to admit this, but this morning, with you—that was my first time." Holun looked at the ground.

Yatzil's heart soared. She knew there was a reason she was drawn to this young man. She felt she understood him in ways that a stranger shouldn't understand, felt they were both equals while being perfectly complementary. She whispered her response. "Mine, too."

Holun stared at her with wide eyes. "You were perfect. I could not tell."

Yatzil smiled at him, and his returning smile melted her heart. She reached for his hand once again. "Even here, in this dark cave, with an evil woman headed our way any minute—I am glad I am here with you. I would not choose to be anywhere else."

Holun chuckled, and she loved the sound of it. "Pretty much what I was thinking."

Yatzil nodded, then, after a moment, she scooted up close to Holun again.

She let her mind wander. Had it only been a week since she'd known him? She tried to remember her life before Holun, just a short seven days ago, but it felt like a distant memory. She did remember that first vision vividly, however, the vision that brought her to him, gave her purpose, drew her to the man she was now certain she'd fallen for.

And she wondered what the future held. If they ever got out of this cave—which they would, despite the fact that she had no idea how—would they still be this close? She wanted to believe they would, but the outside world was a different place. She hadn't lived a long life, but she'd been through a lot, and she knew enough to know that when circumstances change, sometimes a relationship changes, too. She knew that all too well; it was what had caused her father to leave and her mother to run off into the rainforest after him, leaving a baby Yatzil to fend for herself. If the Elders hadn't found her, hadn't given her a home, she didn't know where she would be right now . . .

Holun broke into her thoughts. "So I was thinking . . ." Holun let the sentence trail off.

Yatzil decided to bite. "About what?"

Holun shrugged. "Well, we will not get any better at it unless we practice."

She was confused for a split second before the lightbulb went off in her head. *Oh!* Though she wanted to kiss him again with every fiber of her being, she decided to play coy. "Oh, really?"

Holun nodded with a shameless grin. "Yes."

Yatzil pulled her bound hands to her face, tapping her finger to her chin. "I think . . . well . . ." Then she grinned. "It could not hurt to try." Yatzil leaned into him so he wouldn't have to move and aggravate his injuries.

As their lips touched, she felt a pure, innocent warmth radiating from him that was unmistakably passionate, and she felt a fluttering in her stomach. She leaned in closer, lingering on his lips a little longer than before. She felt like she wanted to explore them further, so she tried it, her mouth moving more purposefully against his. A groan rumbled low in Holun's throat, and Yatzil felt the warmth from before build in intensity until it flared into a flame. Butterflies erupted at his reaction, so she leaned in closer, her lips moving in concert with his, undulating as if by the ocean tide.

Holun reached for her, placing his hands on her back and pulling her closer to him. Yatzil pulled back, staring into Holun's chocolate-brown eyes as she moved to sit in his lap, lifting her hands over his head, encircling his neck. For a split second, she was worried it would hurt him, but as their lips connected once more, Holun groaned again, and Yatzil knew it wasn't from the pain. Her mouth explored his as their lips parted slightly, and Yatzil's heart raced as his ragged breath rushed into her.

When they finally pulled away, Yatzil was still sitting in his lap, their foreheads touching. She should have been self-conscious, but it was Holun, and she felt completely comfortable with him. She slid off his lap and back into the dirt after a few moments, pulling her arms over his head as she did, her chest rising and falling as she tried to catch her breath. She heard Holun's heavy breath beside her as they waited for their breathing to return to normal.

Yatzil felt a wide smile spread across her face as her breathing slowed. This young man was amazing, and she sensed she'd only seen—felt—a glimpse of what he could do.

"That was incredible, Holun."

Holun laid his head back against the rock wall then looked over at her without moving his head. "Yes." His breath was still ragged, but he smiled over at her. "It was."

After a few long minutes of just sitting and mentally processing everything that had happened, Yatzil had a thought. "Um, Holun? I have an idea. One that may help us get out of here."

"I will take whatever ideas you have, my Yatzil."

Her heart leapt as he called her his. "Remember how you said Kayla could send you visions?"

Holun nodded.

"What if you tried sending her one? Maybe of where we are? You said they would be looking for you, right?"

Holun's eyes widened, and he leaned over to steal a quick kiss. She blinked, startled. "Yatzil, you are a genius!" Holun reached over and pulled her into a stifling hug that she didn't mind at all.

Then, after a few moments, he released her and leaned back, his eyes sliding shut. Yatzil stayed quiet, letting him concentrate, but kept her eyes on him the whole time. She didn't even know if this would work, but she figured it was worth a try.

What felt like several minutes later, Holun's eyes opened.

"Did it work?" Yatzil dared to hope.

Holun frowned. "I am not certain. Maybe?"

"So if it worked, we may be out of here soon?"

Holun nodded at her, smiling. "Yes, I hope so. If Kayla got my message, they should be headed here soon. We just have to outlast Shani."

The sound of her name caused Yatzil to shiver. "I sure hope they come soon." She turned to eye the entrance. *Please come before Shani comes back,* she thought to nothing but the wind.

Lamanai

Kayla was still kicking herself as she went back to her tent to collect her things. She'd promised Grady she'd leave him alone, but she knew it would be the hardest thing she'd ever have to do. They were a part of each other—she couldn't believe she'd let Na-um cloud her realization of that—and being away from him made her feel like part of herself was missing. Part of her soul.

How could she have been so selfish?

She struggled to keep her thoughts from entering his. It was the first time she'd wished their telepathy would go away. Funny. One of the main things she'd wished for in the past few weeks was now the source of a great deal of her stress.

She sensed he was close—she figured he was at his tent gathering his things like she was. She hurried, trying to get what she needed and head back out before they met up outside. She wanted to see him more than anything, but she would try her hardest to respect his request for time and stay out of his way as much as possible.

She threw everything she thought she might need into her bag and headed outside. As soon as she stood squinting in the sun, she spotted him coming out of his tent as well. Their eyes locked for a split second, then Kayla felt a sharp pain in the back of her head, and everything went black.

Grady watched her fall as if in slow motion. Immediately, he dropped his bag and ran for her. Though he still couldn't remember this past summer, he figured out what was happening from what Kayla had told him. And a vision strong enough to steal her consciousness couldn't be a good thing.

He fell to his knees beside her then lifted her head and cradled it in his lap. She was bound to have scrapes and bruises from her fall, but Grady could help prevent any further damage if she started to seize. He prayed she wouldn't.

Mandy and Justin ran up as if called by an unseen force. Mandy fell to Kayla's side as Justin squatted down beside them, and Grady was grateful for their company, but he couldn't honestly think of anything they could do to help. He couldn't think of anything *he* could do to help.

At least Na-um was keeping his distance—Grady couldn't deal with him right now.

Kayla stirred for a brief moment, but she didn't wake up. Grady gazed down at her, his heart aching for her. It was more than just concern over the vision—he longed for her. Even though his memory of her was incomplete, he felt drawn to her, even now, even after last night. He felt as though his heart would break into pieces—yet again—if anything happened to her.

And in that moment, he knew he loved her. Him now, not him from before his memory was stolen from him. Him with just the few weeks of memories of her. He had fallen for her —deeply—and, despite her kiss with another man, he was in love with her.

He just had to figure out how to forgive her for acting on her attraction to another man, sharing an intimate kiss with that man, and trying to hide it from him. Somewhere deep inside he wanted to, but he just couldn't find a way to let himself do it right now. He realized that her betrayal had hurt him as much as it had *because* he loved her, and the realization made him sad, confused, satisfied, angry, happy, bewildered, and unsettled all at the same time.

Kayla blinked then looked up into his eyes. For a split second, Grady saw all the unencumbered love in them that he knew they'd shared, just a short time ago, when things had been simple and severely less complicated. But then her expression changed, when she'd had time to realize where she was, and Grady saw just how much it was hurting her to keep her distance from him.

"Are you okay?" Grady wiped a stray hair from her forehead.

Kayla blinked again and slowly moved to sit up. Grady helped her up then pulled away. "Yes, thank you." Kayla kept it formal, and Grady's heart broke just a little again. Kayla's eyes widened, and he suddenly remembered that she could hear his thoughts.

So he swallowed hard, quickly changing the subject. "What did you see?"

Kayla flinched then jumped to her feet as if she'd just figured out what her vision meant. "I know where Holun is." She reached a hand out to Grady to help him up. Mandy and Justin leapt up as well, anxious to hear more.

Kayla grabbed her bag from the ground and headed toward the mess tent, where they had planned to meet Na-um. "Come on. We have to save him. We don't have much time."

The Cave Outside the Mercenaries' Camp

Holun was too wired to sleep. His feelings for Yatzil were causing him to imagine all sorts of nightmarish scenarios where Shani tortured her just to get to him. He determined that if she threatened Yatzil, Shani would get whatever she wanted.

Then he heard rustling at the entrance, and his stomach tightened. He gritted his teeth and reached for Yatzil's hand, holding it tightly, out of sight.

Shani entered the room with her characteristically sickening grin. Holun did his best not to narrow his eyes and stare at her—he knew it just bated her—but he couldn't help it.

"Good afternoon, children," Shani trilled, her voice condescending and cloyingly sweet. "I hope you both got a lot of rest. I sense today's going to be a big day!" She smiled at Holun, who was still glaring at her. "Oh, I know, Holun. You have been stronger than I thought you'd be, but I sense today things will go a little bit differently." She slowly, deliberately slid her gaze to Yatzil, and Holun struggled against his chains. The iron bindings clanked against each other.

"No! Shani, stop. I will give you whatever you want." Holun pleaded, his eyes trained on Shani, trying to anticipate her next move.

"Well! So nice of you to cooperate, Holun! We will work very well together." Shani walked over to him and abruptly bent down next to him. Holun jumped, and Shani laughed.

Then all joviality disappeared from her features, and her eyes narrowed, her face just inches from Holun's. He stared directly into her dark, flashing eyes, feeling defiance bolster his courage and give him strength he didn't know he had. "You will do *exactly* as I say. Everything. Or . . ." She whipped out a switchblade from her pocket, the same one still stained with his blood. Holun's eyes grew wide—he couldn't help that either. Shani pointed the blade at Yatzil, much too close to her beautiful face. "I shall have to motivate you."

Holun struggled against his shackles again, leaping toward Shani. "No! I will do everything you ask."

Shani stood then looked down her nose at them, grinning again. "Good." She snapped the blade shut, dropped it in her pocket, then reached for a nearby chair and unfolded it, sitting down. She crossed her arms, leaning back in the chair, a satisfied and wholly diabolical grin on her face. "Let's get started."

CHAPTER 29

Together but Apart

KAYLA RAN, HER LUNGS bursting, but her body loved the feeling. She hadn't really run in a while—and was doing so only now at Mandy's suggestion to the group—and she was surprised how fast she'd become. If only she'd known this *before* riding through the forest on Na-um's back . . .

The others were keeping up with her. She heard them beside and behind her, effortlessly gliding over fallen logs, gracefully dodging trees, sprinting through the foliage. Even Na-um, who she knew could run unbelievably fast, was right there beside them. Was he just being kind, or were they running as fast as he could? No, that wasn't possible—was it?

She glanced over at Na-um and noticed he was staring at her for a split second before he turned back to watch where he was going. She could've sworn he looked surprised.

She didn't hate that. She pushed herself harder, sped up as they crossed several miles a minute. The others sped up as well, echoing her movements. She loved this feeling—the freedom, the endorphins—and wished they could run all day.

But they were getting close to where she knew Holun would be. Even if Shani wasn't there, it would still be a feat to free him—he'd shown her his shackles. Though she'd come prepared—she hoped—it could still take some time to get him out.

Kayla slowed, and the others followed her lead. She hadn't had time to explain things—she needed to get Holun out of there before Shani did something horrible to him, and Kayla could sense that his time was running out.

Grady was by her side, and she was having an easier time keeping her thoughts from his than before. It helped to be so focused on something else—she suspected that once things died down, keeping her thoughts from him might prove nearly impossible.

But despite how much she hated it, she was determined to honor his wishes. He knew she was truly sorry—she'd felt he could sense her sincerity—but he'd asked for time. And she was going to give it to him if it killed her. She owed him that and much more.

Kayla came to a stop at the base of the mountain she'd seen in her vision, the one that Holun had somehow sent to her. Well, the one she assumed Holun had sent her—how else would it have been so specific?

She motioned for the others to follow her then started hiking up the mountain. They could run extremely fast, but hiking was slower—though she suspected that before their powers they would have been moving much more slowly. She had an entire lifetime's worth of experience to prove that to her, after all.

The entrance of the cave appeared quickly, and Kayla was pleased. The others gathered silently around her as they approached, Kayla in the lead. She glanced over at Mandy, who soundlessly gathered her power to her and forced it through the air into the cave. They couldn't hear much—Kayla wasn't about to ask Na-um to scope out the situation with his super-powered hearing; she didn't trust him that much—but before they'd left Lamanai, Kayla'd asked Mandy to read the situation when they got here. She'd sold it as good practice, and Mandy, though reluctant, seemed willing to try.

After a few moments, Mandy glanced over at Kayla. She mouthed "Shani's here" before visibly letting her power dissipate. Kayla nodded at her.

She heard Mandy's thoughts in hers. *What's the plan?*

Kayla glanced at the group. She heard Grady listening in as well—she could only hope Mandy would relay the messages to Justin.

She heard Mandy confirm. If they couldn't all hear each other soon, the impending battle would be exhausting.

We should figure out the best plan of attack, Kayla started. *Perhaps a distraction?*

Though she knew Na-um couldn't hear their thoughts, she had the uncanny feeling that he somehow still knew what they were thinking. He motioned toward them silently—it seemed he knew, like the rest of them, that taking Shani by surprise would be the best option.

He pointed at himself, indicating he would enter the cave first, then motioned that they should follow just after while Shani was still getting over the shock of seeing him.

Kayla nodded once at him, confirming the plan with the others, who nodded their assent. She led them closer to the cave's entrance, careful and silent, to execute the rescue of Holun.

Then they saw her. Kayla and the others froze as Shani gracefully ducked out of the cave and into the sunlight under the bright blue sky, her long, black hair blowing in the wind.

Then she turned their direction, and her lips curled at the sight of them. Na-um sprung into action, lunging for her.

He hit Shani with the force of a tornado, tackling her and spinning her toward the ground. They grappled in the dirt for several seconds, appearing evenly matched although Shani was considerably smaller than he was.

Kayla nodded at the others as Na-um subdued his sister, pinning her in the dirt face down. Kayla entered the cave first.

And her heart stopped.

Holun, the young boy who had helped them last summer and stolen their hearts, was shackled to the back wall of the small cave, his wrists bound with ancient iron handcuffs. His clothes were dirty and torn, especially his shirt. Kayla saw blood staining the fabric in telltale, sickeningly straight lines, and suddenly a wild rage rushed through her body. Her fists balled at her sides, and she immediately wanted to go outside and strangle Shani.

She felt a hand on her shoulder before she could make a move. She turned to see Grady blocking her way to the exit, and she nodded at him, unclenching her fists. *Thank you.*

Anytime was Grady's cryptic response, but Kayla had no time to analyze that now. They had to get Holun—and some-one else, she only now realized—out of here before Shani could get free and come back. Four against one was great odds in their favor, but she'd hoped to avoid a fight if at all possible.

Mandy was already at Holun's side, trying in vain to re-move his bindings. Justin appeared to be searching the cave for something—a key, perhaps? They could hope.

"Holun! Are you okay?" Kayla dropped to his side opposite Mandy, desperate to get this kid out of here.

Holun nodded, but then he winced as he adjusted, belying his response. "I will be fine. Please—get her out of here." He nodded over at the girl next to him.

"Who is she, Holun?" Mandy asked, moving to the girl beside him and quickly removing the ropes binding her to his chains.

"This is Yatzil. Yatzil, this is Mandy and Kayla, and Grady and Justin."

The girl named Yatzil smiled at them, moving to help unbind Holun as soon as Mandy removed her ropes. "It is nice to meet all of you. Holun has told me much of you."

Kayla smiled at her phrasing then glanced back at Justin. "Anything?"

Justin was still searching, then suddenly he stopped. He bent down and reached in the dirt. "Yes! I . . . oh." His face fell, and he threw whatever it was back in the dirt. "Sorry, nothing. I guess it wouldn't be that easy."

At his words, Grady headed for the exit. "I will get them." Then he was gone.

Kayla, trusting Grady's words, moved to check out Holun's wounds. They hadn't thought Shani would injure him so badly—they hadn't brought any first aid supplies. Oh, well—with how fast they could run, they would get him back to Lamanai in no time.

Grady came back in with the keys just a moment later, and Kayla idly wondered what he'd had to do to obtain them. Grady smiled over at her at the thought as he brought them to her. *It was easy,* Kayla heard, and she was suddenly abruptly aware of his proximity. She really did love him—if she hadn't been sure before, she was now.

Grady was frowning, so Kayla pushed the thoughts from her mind as she unlocked the first shackle. Holun sighed visibly as the chain clinked to the ground. As the second one fell away, he abruptly stood and stretched. He winced as he strained against the wounds on his back, but he seemed to quickly recover. He offered a hand to Yatzil first, then to Mandy and Kayla to help them to their feet.

"Can we go now?" Holun asked, eyes scanning the group.

Justin actually laughed then leaned in to pat the young boy gently on his back. Holun offered a forced grin in response. "Of course!"

The six of them headed outside. Kayla scanned the surroundings for Na-um and Shani, but they were nowhere to be seen.

Great. Who knew where they went, or what had even happened? She should've known they couldn't trust Na-um. Especially not when it came to his sister.

But that didn't matter now, not really. The more pressing matter was getting Holun back to Lamanai so they could dress his wounds. The group moved slowly down the mountain, but when the terrain evened out, Grady offered to put Holun on his back. Holun obliged gladly with a relieved sigh. After Yatzil assured them she was okay, the five of them ran back to the dig.

Kayla shouldn't have been surprised that Yatzil kept up.

Mercenaries' Camp

Alexia awoke suddenly, glancing around her small tent. Where was she? She sat up straight on her cot, blinking at the bright light streaming through the canvas walls. What . . . ? Oh.

The events of the past few weeks came rushing back, and she sighed. Not that she didn't love traveling—she'd always hoped she'd get a chance to fly out of the country, though she'd hoped it would've been to assist on a dig somewhere—but so many things had changed in such a short time that her head was still spinning, her mind still trying to catch up.

She was grateful that the woman who'd brought her here, Shani, had taken the time to train her to use her powers—she'd almost gotten the hang of them—but using them always tired her out. Her naps were becoming more frequent, which worried her.

She hadn't had a chance to bring it up to Shani, but she suspected that once this mess was over, she wouldn't need to use her powers as much, and she could get back to a semblance of her normal life. She couldn't wait for that.

She grabbed her sunglasses and some shoes then stepped outside. She blinked against the sun, hand shielding her eyes, just as she heard her name. She glanced to her left to see the boy named Tyler approaching.

Alexia smiled and waved in his direction. His returning smile caused butterflies to erupt in her stomach. She hadn't known Tyler at school—though it seemed more than a coincidence that they attended the same school—but he was definitely cute. She certainly didn't mind that he now knew her name.

"Hey, Alexia," he started as he walked up, and she offered a shy smile.

"Hey," she returned, kicking herself for not coming up with a more intelligent response.

Tyler nodded toward the nearby forest. "We're headed to the clearing to do some training—you up for it?"

Alexia followed his gaze then turned back to him. "Sure! I'm all rested up." She smiled again.

Tyler grinned. "Awesome!" He grabbed her hand, and she felt her heart leap into her throat. "Let's go." He led her toward the forest, and Alexia had to remind herself how to walk.

Lamanai Archaeological Dig, Northern Belize

With Holun recovering in his tent—and Yatzil with him after the dig's medic, Dr. Larson, looked her over to ensure she wasn't hurt—Kayla and the others met in the mess tent to discuss the next step of their plan. They still hadn't heard from Na-um, and Kayla's mind was going crazy considering all the possibilities.

First, he could've joined Shani. She was his sister, after all, and he clearly still loved her. Though he had told Kayla just last night that they needed to kill her . . .

Which brought her to the second option: Na-um could've killed her. But Grady's memory was still missing, so that told Kayla that Shani was probably still alive.

Third, Shani could've overpowered him and captured him. She supposed it would have been fitting, considering the time she'd spent in captivity under Na-um's control. She almost hoped that was what had actually happened—he completely deserved it—until she considered that it would put a huge wrench in their plans.

Kayla reached for a premade sandwich—she'd forgotten to eat earlier—and sat down with the rest of the Four. Since they all couldn't hear each other telepathically, they spoke aloud. Kayla just hoped that no one loyal to the Clan was nearby, listening in.

"So what do we do now?" Mandy asked the group, eyes searching each of their faces. Kayla could see how tired she was from the night's excursion and the emotional aftermath. She knew everything, after all.

Grady sighed from across the table. "The only thing we *can* do—we go after the artifacts."

"But how do we do that without Na-um?" Justin spoke up, his eyes flickering to Kayla almost imperceptibly before moving to Mandy. Justin knew, too. Kayla felt an overwhelming shame settle in the pit of her stomach.

A new voice chimed in. "I think I can help with that."

Yatzil and Holun walked up, Holun leaning heavily on Yatzil's small frame, but she seemed to be holding her own as she led him to their table and helped him sit down. As she slid in next to him, Kayla noticed an inner strength in Yatzil that she'd missed before. She suspected the girl was stronger than even she realized.

Kayla turned to her. "How is that?"

Yatzil shared a knowing glance with Holun, who offered her a pained smile. Whatever the medic had done to cleanse and dress his wounds had clearly aggravated them. "I saw it. We both did."

Mandy gasped. "You saw the artifacts?"

Yatzil smiled, nodding. "Yes. We both see . . . visions . . . as Holun calls them." She reached for his hand quite obviously and squeezed it gently. Kayla smiled at the sweet gesture, and a pang of jealousy pricked at her chest. "I went to where I thought it was, and I think I found the spot."

Kayla couldn't believe it. "Really? How do you know?"

Yatzil just blinked then whispered her response. "I just know." She looked over at Holun, presumably wondering if she was missing something, something that didn't quite translate well.

Grady spoke up. "That's great, Yatzil. Thank you."

Yatzil was smiling again. "You are welcome, Grady."

"When should we leave?" came from Justin.

Grady looked over at him then glanced back at the young girl. "How far away is this place?"

Yatzil frowned, and Kayla thought it looked out of place on her young, angelic face. "I would have thought it would take about half a day, but the way you run, I think we could be there in less time than that." She glanced at Holun, her eyes pleading.

So Holun translated for her. "Maybe an hour, then we have to hike up the mountain." He shifted on the seat, wincing again, but kept a tight hold on Yatzil's hand. Kayla wondered how they could have become so close in such a short time, but as she gazed over at Grady, it didn't seem so far-fetched. *When you know, you just know.* Her stomach knotted up.

Justin jumped to his feet. "Then I say we go now! Who knows what's going on with Shani and Na-um? We need to get to those artifacts as soon as possible."

Grady nodded beside him and stood as well. "I think you're right. We don't have any time to waste." He glanced down at the young man still on the bench beside him. "Holun, are you up for this?"

Holun grimaced as he placed his hands on the picnic table and lifted himself to his feet with apparent effort. "Yes," he murmured, breathless.

Yatzil was on her feet in no time, her lithe movements captivating Kayla. "Holun, are you sure? You can stay here— no one will care." She glanced at the others, eyes pleading again.

Mandy walked around the table to his side. "Yes, Holun, please stay here if you're not up for it. You need to heal."

Holun nodded once, but he still objected. "I must protect Yatzil." He shifted his weight a second time, and Kayla could tell he was trying very hard not to wince again. "And I must go with you. You need me."

Kayla looked him over, trying to figure out if he was really up for the journey. He probably wasn't, but he didn't look like he could be talked into staying, either.

He needs to go, Kayla. Can't you see he loves her?

Yes. Kayla sighed at Grady's question. *That much is obvious.*

Then we need to let him come.

Kayla stood with the others. "Okay, Holun, you can come with us. But you must let us know if you need to rest, okay?" She stared him down as she said this, hoping he'd see how serious she was.

Holun nodded gravely, and Kayla hoped he truly understood. In all likelihood, they would encounter all manner of horrible things in their journey to retrieve the artifacts— mostly since Shani would be involved—and that young man had already been through a lot. Too much. Certainly more than a boy that age should ever have to go through.

"Then it's settled," Grady broke into her thoughts as he stood. "Let's go."

CHAPTER 30

Can't Get Her Out of My Head

NA-UM SPED THROUGH THE FOREST, following the blur he knew was Shani miles ahead of him. He pushed himself further, faster, but he still couldn't seem to catch her. He knew he could run for a while, but he hadn't actually tested his limits. Who knew how long he could really last out here?

He felt so stupid. They'd been grappling in the dirt before they tumbled down a hill and she slipped out of his grasp and took off. She was *fast*. He hadn't realized just how fast she was.

He supposed it should have occurred to him before now— especially knowing everything she could do—but her powers still surprised him. How did she receive these powers? Didn't the powers only go to the warriors in the Clan? He'd never thought of Shani as a warrior.

But perhaps if she'd stayed, if she hadn't run off, she would have become one. It wasn't unheard of in the Clan for women to receive powers, it just wasn't as common.

He wasn't getting tired, which surprised him somewhat, but he was getting frustrated. He wasn't sure he'd ever catch her.

He followed as she turned in a wide circle to the left. Where was she going? Na-um pondered it as he pushed himself harder, begging his body to close the distance. He couldn't tell if it was working.

Shani veered left again, and Na-um thought he might be figuring out her plan. She wanted the artifacts, didn't she? Wasn't that why she'd been here this whole time? So it only made sense she'd make her way back to them.

Na-um slowed, sliding to a graceful stop and sending a spray of dirt several feet in the air. Then he turned and headed back the way they'd come. He knew where Shani was going—Kayla had explained the location in her vision, after all, and Na-um was fairly certain he could find it, though it might take some time—so instead of wasting effort chasing down his sister, he'd just meet her where he knew she was going.

Na-um walked back at a normal pace, sick of running. His thoughts were swirling around in his head. Thoughts of Shani, of what she'd done to Holun—Na-um had always liked the kid, even if they'd been on different sides at one time— pricked at his conscience, confused him. Shani was his sister, but she was unrecognizable from the lovestruck young woman he'd known long ago. And after today, this week, he realized she'd crossed the line. She must be stopped. If the Four couldn't do it, he determined that he would.

Thoughts of the Four brought Kayla unwillingly to his mind. A lump settled in his stomach, and his brow furrowed as he walked. That woman was incredible. He couldn't get her kiss off his mind. The way she smelled—so unique but yet so familiar, comforting even—and the way she felt was indelibly etched in his memory.

He'd only really known her for a little over a week, but the attraction had been almost immediate. Her strength, her grace, her very presence was intoxicating, captivating. He'd felt drawn to her from the beginning, even this past summer, though he only now realized it. Perhaps that was the real reason he couldn't kill her and her friends.

Na-um shook his head at his ignorance. How could one woman cause so many problems?

Then he thought of last night, of the kiss that had changed him completely. He hadn't let Kayla know, but he'd never felt that way in his life. He'd had his share of women—the leader of the Clan's warriors always enjoyed a great deal of popularity—but no one had even come close to making him feel like Kayla had. He felt like she'd invaded his life, his body, his soul then ripped herself out of all of it in the next second.

He'd played it off, convinced her that the kiss meant nothing to him, that he was over it . . . but he'd been lying, and in a big way. He could still remember the way she tasted, the softness of her lips, how they caressed his as they sampled each other. The touch of her skin, the scent of her hair—he was convinced Kayla would haunt his dreams until the day he died.

He couldn't remember when he'd started, but now he was running, sprinting back to the mountainside where he knew Shani would eventually be. He had to do something—anything—to get Kayla out of his head.

Na-um sensed it would be much more difficult to do than he hoped.

Northern Belize Rainforest

She needed a new plan.

Shani, sensing Na-um had given up the chase, circled back toward the mountain where the artifacts were being held. But she kept a careful distance—no need to be foolhardy, especially since she now had at least seven people gunning for her head. She found a thick, low-hanging branch that looked like it would hold her and sat down.

She hadn't been able to get much out of Holun since the Four had shown up so quickly—how on earth did they manage that?

Her eyes widened, and she cursed aloud, smacking her hand on the thick tree branch she was sitting on. Holun. He'd somehow told Kayla where he was. Of course. It was the only thing that made sense. Holun had invaded her mind once before—though it had been so painful and invasive that she swore she'd never allow it again—and she remembered how powerful the seemingly innocent boy really was.

This was going to be much harder than she thought.

Shani stood and began pacing. She hadn't realized how much trouble the Four and that boy would cause for her. And the girl! She drew a deep breath, trying to control the shaking spreading throughout her body.

She needed help. There was no other way around it. Fortunately, she had four ready-made, superpowered minions back at the camp. She was nearly certain that the Elders hadn't even figured out she had a plan to steal the artifacts, so she had to assume going back to the camp was safe.

Either way, it was probably worth the risk. She needed their help, if only to surprise the Four and hope to gain the upper hand. She grinned evilly as she realized the Four had never met Tyler or Akna—or the new and improved version of Alexia—and would not be expecting their powers. Especially Alexia's.

Dealing with Yatzil and Holun would be another matter entirely. A frown clouded her features at the thought. How did she deal with those two devious teenagers? She couldn't tell if Yatzil had any powers yet, but Shani could guarantee those powers were there, even if they were hidden or hadn't shown up before now.

Shani knew, better than anyone, that Yatzil's powers would show up when she most needed them—probably at the exact moment that Shani was attacking. And they would certainly be even more devastating than Alexia's. Being on the receiving end of such powers was something she always tried to avoid, albeit unsuccessfully at times.

Shani started walking through the forest, heading toward the camp. She'd collect Tyler and the girls—and Steven, if she could find him; she snorted at the irony of the thought—and head back to the mountain. All while avoiding the Elders, she hoped. Though if they wanted to find her, they most certainly would.

As the smoke from the campfires came into view and the smell of their midday meal reached her nose, Shani smiled sadly. These had been her people once, and she should be rejoicing in her homecoming. But it'd never felt like that to her. She'd only ever felt like an outsider, even before Na-um had found her and Alex together. The blowup with Na-um had just been the final straw; she had already been planning to leave.

Then something unexpected had happened, after she'd run off with her Alex. And several months later, Shani stole into the camp under the cover of darkness to drop off an infinitely valuable treasure at the door of one of the Elders' tents.

Then she'd left for good, and until only recently, she'd never looked back.

Northern Belize Rainforest, Near Lamanai

With Holun's injuries, their trek through the rainforest was excruciatingly slow. Kayla'd been arguing off and on with Grady about it for the past half hour, but his chastising looks had kept her from saying anything aloud.

He was right, after all; they needed to be patient. But she'd taken what Na-um had warned her about to heart—Grady's memory loss could become permanent if Shani gained any artifacts that increased her power. Despite everything, she needed Grady to remember her. What she'd done since was reprehensible, but he would not be whole again until he remembered everything. Her heart ached just thinking about it.

Kayla, stop. We'll get there in time.

You don't know that, Grady. She sighed as she stepped carefully over a fallen log.

I have to trust that we will. He shot a glance her way, pushing a large palm leaf out of his path. *Otherwise, Shani already wins.*

That doesn't make any sense.

Kayla.

Grady's one-word response calmed her, made her forget her argument. *I'm sorry.* She caught his gaze. *Everything with Holun, Shani . . .*

And Na-um . . .

Kayla's eyes narrowed.

Couldn't help myself. But he's a big part of this, and you know it.

As much as I hate it, Kayla thought, mostly to herself.

Grady nodded beside her. *Yes, but it's still true. This whole mess started with him, back this summer.*

Kayla bit her lip as they trudged through the undergrowth in relative silence. *Will we ever get past this?* she mused, momentarily forgetting that Grady could hear her thoughts.

But he gave a response anyway. *I don't know.*

Sorry, just popped into my head.

One corner of Grady's mouth turned up. *We're still not quite used to this telepathy thing.*

Kayla smiled back. *Nope, not really. Admittedly, we've been out of practice.*

Grady's smile widened in response. For a moment, their thoughts grew quiet again. Then Grady's voice sounded in her head. *So what do we do now?*

Kayla's brow furrowed as her eyes searched the ground in front of her to make sure she didn't trip. *What do you mean?*

With this—with Holun, with Shani, with Na-um, with . . . everything. With us.

She frowned without meaning to. *I really don't know.*

We probably should take one thing at a time.

Kayla nodded at him and offered a slight smile as she stepped over a small fallen tree.

Okay, so first things first—Holun. Grady moved another giant leaf out of his way. *He's in bad shape. He'll heal, but only if he rests.*

I agree. Maybe one of us can carry him?

I don't think we have superhuman strength.

Kayla smirked. *How did you do it before?*

Grady's lips pursed, and Kayla couldn't help but think it was cute before she could stop herself. *Thank you,* Grady replied, grinning, and Kayla felt the blood rush to her cheeks. *I think it was probably just an adrenaline thing. Or something.*

Or maybe we are stronger than we think?

Grady cocked his head to one side. *Possibly. Worth a try.* Grady looked over at the boy he was helping through the forest. Though with his injuries and the growth spurt he'd had after this summer, he could hardly be considered a boy. "Holun?"

Holun was watching the ground, carefully avoiding anything that might brush up against him or trip him up and aggravate his injuries. He only looked up for a second at Grady's question. "Yes?"

"Would you be willing to let me carry you?"

Holun opened his mouth, clearly about to protest. Grady spoke up again before he could. "You look like you're in pain —I think you could use the rest."

Mandy jumped in. "Please, Holun, let Grady carry you. It could mean a lot less pain for you."

The group had stopped in the middle of the forest, and now Holun caught the gaze of each one of them. His eyes finally landed on Yatzil, questions sparking through them.

She seemed to understand. "I think you should do it, Holun. Grady carried you before, and we need to get to the artifacts before Shani can take them for herself."

Holun's brow furrowed before he spoke up. "Okay, we can try it."

Grady bent down, allowing Holun to carefully climb onto his back. He stood, and Kayla noticed it barely took any effort. *Perhaps you are stronger than you thought.*

Grady grinned at her. *Perhaps.*

The six of them picked up the pace, and soon Yatzil sensed that the mountain was close. She held up a hand for the others to stop when they reached the mountain's base. Yatzil motioned for the others to be still, then she just listened.

She didn't sense anything amiss so she turned to the group. "We are not far. I can lead us."

The woman named Kayla nodded. "Of course. Lead the way, Yatzil." Kayla smiled at her, and Yatzil felt a warming sensation flow through her body. Holun's new friends were sweet and kind, just like him—why did she expect any less? She smiled back at Kayla.

Then Yatzil glanced over at Holun, who was climbing off Grady's back. Smart. This terrain was going to get a little rough, and Holun would need to be careful.

She turned to head up the mountain, grabbing Holun's hand in the process. She smiled at the feel of his hand in hers as she led the group toward the artifacts that were rightfully theirs, the artifacts that would save them all.

Mercenaries' Camp

Shani couldn't find them. Where did those kids run off to? She searched their tents, the campfire where she'd last seen them—nothing.

Then she heard the explosion. She rolled her eyes before taking off at lightning speed toward the sound.

Shani sprinted into a clearing right outside the camp just as Tyler was drawing in a deep breath, clearly preparing to launch something into the woods with the sound of his voice. Something large was sitting in a pile at the other side of the clearing, something Tyler was facing. As she approached, she tried to get a clearer look at it. What was . . . her stomach dropped.

The mangled, unrecognizable SUV lay in a pile on the other side of the clearing. She noticed the shape had changed, recognized Akna's handiwork just as she came out of the woods near Tyler and moved toward him. Alexia was sitting a short distance away, staring wide-eyed at Tyler's flashy display of his powers. Teenaged boys and their egos . . .

She had to stop this craziness. "Tyler!" she yelled abruptly. Tyler jumped, calling out, which sent a blast her way. Shani stepped to the side to let the energy pass by—his unfocused power was easy to deflect when it wasn't intentionally directed at her.

Shani approached the two girls staring at her as she walked up and the now-silent Tyler, who was wisely keeping his mouth shut. Shani was glad she had been right about him —he definitely had more smarts than Steven.

Who, she could sense, was nearby. "Steven?" she called, much more quietly.

An invisible void several feet away spoke. "Yes?"

Shani motioned the four recruits closer. "We have a problem. That group of very dangerous people, the ones I told you all about—they are coming to steal from us, from my people."

They all nodded at her slowly, eyes wide, then Tyler spoke in a whisper, eyes darting across the clearing and into the surrounding rainforest. "They're coming here?"

Shani shook her head. "No. There's a warehouse up in the mountains. They are probably already on their way there."

The void that was Steven spoke up. "What do you need from us?"

Shani blinked, a little shocked that Steven would jump on board so quickly. Maybe he was learning, overcoming his stupidity. She could hope. "Um, right now, we just need to get there. We can talk about a strategy on the way."

Tyler grinned at her, and she could tell Steven was pleased, though she didn't know how. The girls were still staring, but Alexia looked willing enough to do as she asked.

Shani knew that Akna would fall in line when she gave her the same speech in K'iche.

"Okay, then," Shani started, heading back the way she'd come, knowing they all would follow. "Let's get going."

Mercenaries' Camp, Chac's Tent

"Tohil, what are you saying?"

The Elders had gathered together to assess the situation at hand. Tohil had recently had one of his "episodes"—he could see things happening as they happened, even if far away—and was now relaying the news to the others. He really wished he hadn't seen this; he'd known the Elders, especially Chac, would not be happy.

Four sets of nervous eyes turned to Tohil as he clarified what he'd seen. "The Four are on their way to our warehouse in the mountains right now, Shani just collected her subjects and they are headed into the rainforest as well, and Na-um is out in the rainforest wandering aimlessly. Chances are he is headed to the same mountain." He nodded toward the forest in the direction of the mountain he'd mentioned.

A low murmur echoed around the room, and Tohil winced internally.

"What can be done about this?" Bacob growled.

Zotz spoke up from where he sat on a cushion on the ground, his long, white hair falling around his shoulders. "What is happening is foretold."

"No!" Bacob shouted back. "We must stop this. We cannot let them win."

Zotz actually smirked in response, an odd expression on his wrinkled and wind-hardened face. "And we will not. But they must try so we can stop them."

Kucumatz jumped in now, his head cocking to one side as he stared at his fellow Elder. "What do you mean?"

Zotz looked up at him. "We cannot approach them on their own playing ground, where they are strongest. So we will meet them at ours and stop them."

Bacob had started grinning. "How?"

Kucumatz spoke up. "Perhaps we use Shani? She may just have enough power to subdue the Four, then we can stop her before she amasses the power in the warehouse."

The Elders collectively fell silent, and Tohil heard them all considering the viability of the plan. Collective consciousness—similar to telepathy, but not quite the same thing—was another gift of theirs as the leaders of their small Clan. Then Zotz cleared his throat. "It may work. We shall have to wait and see how it plays out."

Bacob jumped in. "So when do we start?"

Tohil took a deep breath, calling his power to him, letting his eyes slide closed. After a few seconds, he saw the Four and the rest of their group closing in on the location. He opened his eyes and spoke quickly. "They are close. Extremely close. Might I suggest now?"

He scanned the group, gauging their reactions. They appeared to agree, but Tohil still held his breath anyway as Chac finally responded. "Yes. We must leave very soon for our plan to work."

Tohil exhaled as Zotz spoke up. As the eldest among them, his words carried a certain weight that caused his ideas to somehow be taken more seriously. "We will mobilize the men here at the camp and leave in fifteen minutes."

All five Elders nodded, silently agreeing to the plan.

Then, by some imperceptible signal that even Tohil didn't fully understand, the Elders immediately flew into action, each knowing what part they were to play in the plan.

Bacob, the obvious warrior, hurried out of the tent to gather the soldiers. After the catastrophe this summer with Na-um, the remaining men were understandably wary of facing the Four in battle again. Tohil knew that Bacob would lie to them to get their support—he might not agree with his methods, but he couldn't argue with their effectiveness.

Chac was assembling the Commanders they had remaining—he recognized the look on the leader's face as he spoke to them through his thoughts—and calling them to the gathering place at the southern edge of the camp, where Bacob would meet them with the soldiers. As soon as his expression cleared, he caught Tohil's gaze, nodded once, and exited the tent, headed out on a special mission Tohil knew would help tip the odds in their favor considerably.

Kucumatz had left the tent as soon as Zotz had finished speaking. Though the Elders couldn't hear each other's thoughts unless they deliberately intended for the others to hear them, their collective consciousness did give them a basic understanding of what the others were doing when they needed to know most. Tohil knew that Kucumatz was headed to gather the supplies they needed—and the men and women to collect them.

Zotz caught Tohil's gaze and held it for a few moments. And, as he often did, Zotz seemed to understand his hesitance.

"He is with them, isn't he?" Zotz asked.

Tohil simply nodded.

"He has made his choice, Tohil."

Tohil swallowed hard. "I know. That doesn't make it any easier."

Zotz nodded slowly, knowingly.

Tohil just kept staring.

"You know what you must do, Tohil."

The corners of Tohil's mouth turned down, and he felt the skin between his black-and-gray eyebrows crease into well-worn lines. "Yes."

That didn't mean he had to like it.

CHAPTER 31

The Mountainside Plateau

YATZIL BOUNDED UP THE FINAL incline and flitted onto the plateau. Kayla smiled. To have that energy and grace . . .

Grady's thoughts broke into hers. *You remember being that young?*

Kayla smiled to herself. *Barely. I was never that graceful, though.*

She heard Grady smile as they reached the plateau behind the others. Yatzil was already scrambling around the place, searching every nook and cranny for . . . what, Kayla wasn't sure. Something.

"Yatzil?" she ventured, hoping to get some clarity. This looked just like the fifteen other plateaus they'd passed on the way here. "Are you sure this is it?"

Yatzil spun around, a frown marring her adorable face. "Yes. I just cannot find . . ." She looked to Holun, who was resting on a boulder near where they'd first climbed up onto this rocky surface.

Holun shifted in his seat and winced. "What is it, my Yatzil?"

Yatzil ran to his side. "Holun, are you okay?" Her words came in a rush as she reached out a hand to touch his arm then pulled it back, seeming afraid to touch him.

Holun simply nodded, out of breath. "Please, Yatzil. What are you looking for?"

Holun's question seemed to make her remember why they were here. Yatzil resumed her frenzied searching, and Kayla smiled in spite of herself at the sight.

"A doorway, an opening, something. The warehouse is here, below us—I know it." Yatzil was frowning again.

Kayla walked over to her and placed a hand on her shoulder. The younger girl spun at the touch. "Can we help?"

Good idea. Grady was in her head again.

Yatzil just turned back around to continue her search, her frown deepening, so Kayla answered Grady. *Maybe . . . wait.*

Grady read her thoughts and grinned. *It's definitely worth a try.*

"Yatzil? I have an idea."

The young girl spun around again at the sound of her voice. *That girl's got to be getting dizzy.* She heard Grady chuckle under his breath. She smiled.

"What is your idea, Kayla?" Yatzil's eyes were wide.

Kayla motioned to the rest of them, Mandy and Justin included. "We may be able to collectively help. With the Power of the Codex, we may just be able to uncover the entrance to the warehouse."

Yatzil's eyes grew even wider as Kayla spoke. She looked over at Holun as soon as Kayla was done.

Holun's eyes were wide, too. He nodded. "They should try it. What do we have to lose?" He shrugged carefully, slowly, deliberately. "Maybe it is exactly what we need."

Kayla nodded at them then waved Mandy, Justin, and Grady over. *Okay,* she began, *I'm not really sure how this should work, but I thought we could tap into each other's powers. I think we can find this entrance with our combined Power.*

She heard Mandy and Grady agree with her and saw Justin nodding. She still couldn't hear Justin, but she knew that Mandy could and had relayed her message.

Grady spoke up. *So how do we do this?*

Kayla waited then frowned when she realized that Mandy hadn't heard him. *We've got to get this telepathy thing fixed, and soon. If Shani's coming here, we need to be on top of our game.*

Again, Mandy and Grady agreed, and Justin nodded a second later.

So Kayla proposed a plan. *First . . .* Kayla reached for both Mandy's and Grady's hand. The others followed suit, forming a small circle in the middle of the rocky plateau.

Kayla let her eyes fall closed, knowing the others would follow. *Now, we call our powers. We call on the collective Power of the Codex.*

How do we do that? Mandy asked.

Kayla wasn't quite sure how to answer that. *Maybe . . . I really don't know. Let's just try whatever comes to us, see if it works.* She hated that she didn't have the exact answer, but, after all the amazing things that had happened to them this summer, she was used to it by now. Almost.

The Four concentrated collectively, and Kayla soon felt something building in her chest. Their individual powers—she figured they didn't know how to call anything else—soon coalesced into a swirling chaos of pure energy. Pure power.

At once, the Power of the Codex showed up and took her breath away, and she could abruptly hear the other three in her head. Their telepathy was back—at least for the moment.

She felt the Power coursing through her veins once again, just like it had this summer, near this very spot. She struggled to maintain control, fought so it wouldn't take her over. And, like last time, Grady was there to ground her, talk her down.

Kayla, you've got this. Don't let it control you.

His words were so similar to those he'd told her before, and tears welled in her eyes. She could hear the others in her head—all of them—but she didn't care. She missed Grady— her Grady—more than any of them could know. Even Grady himself.

I miss you, too, Kayla. More than you realize. That's why this is so hard.

Kayla now wished Mandy and Justin weren't in their heads. Why did she always wish for the things she didn't have?

And suddenly, she was angry. More angry than she would've thought possible. At Shani, at Grady's loss of memory, at her own stupidity. The anger was too abrupt, too sudden, and a boulder nearby exploded, spraying a shower of dirt over the entire group.

Mandy yelped and jumped back, dropping Kayla and Justin's hands and severing their connection. "What was that?!" she screamed.

Kayla stared wide-eyed at the place where the boulder once stood. "I'm sorry." She couldn't figure out anything else to say.

Kayla. Grady's voice sounded in her head. She'd been wishing she could talk to him, but, right now, the anger held her tight. She was having trouble thinking clearly, having trouble catching her breath.

So Grady tried another approach. "We need to talk. Now." He clutched the hand he still held and pulled her back off the plateau. Before they stepped away, he looked back at the others. "Give us a few moments." Then they disappeared into the rainforest.

What was that?! Justin asked Mandy when Kayla and Grady left, echoing her own words. He'd heard them both for a short time until Mandy had broken their connection. Now only Mandy's thoughts swirled in his head.

I don't know, Justin. Mandy's brow furrowed, and the corners of her mouth turned down as she stared after their friends.

Did you feel that?

Mandy nodded, knowing exactly what Justin was referring to. The Power of the Codex was so much stronger than she'd remembered. Even in the clearing yesterday, the Power hadn't been this strong, probably because they weren't concentrating on focusing it for a common goal. With that Power coursing through her veins, throughout her entire body, she'd felt invincible. Unstoppable. Like they could—and would—defeat anyone who got in their way.

Whoa, Mandy! Slow down! We are not invincible.

How do you know that, babe? We could be! How else did the Old Ones never age?

Maybe, Justin conceded. *I just don't think we should assume that until we can test the theory.*

Oh, why not? Mandy shot back. Justin's eyes narrowed, and Mandy held up her hands. *Okay, I give. I'm sorry.*

I'm just worried about you, babe. You can't let anything happen to you.

Mandy nodded at him then pulled him into a hug, barely remembering they still had company. *I love you, Justin.*

I love you, Mandy. More than you know. He still would've liked to hear it aloud sometime, but he suppressed the thought before Mandy could hear it. Again.

Grady waited until they were a good distance away before he turned to her. "Kayla, what's going on with you?"

Kayla sighed, finding a fallen tree and sitting down on the trunk. She dropped her head in her hands. "I don't know, Grady."

Grady sat down beside her, his heart breaking. "Please, tell me. Let me help."

Kayla slowly turned to look at him. "Grady, I . . . I'm not sure. The Power was incredible, overwhelming, but you helped me keep that under control. Helped keep me sane, strong. But then . . . then I remembered everything that's been going wrong, and I was suddenly just angry."

"Angry?"

Kayla nodded, and Grady didn't miss her frown. "Extremely. Like I could tear someone apart if I wanted to."

Grady drew in a sharp breath—he couldn't help it. He reached for her hand to make up for it; despite everything, he loved the way her hand felt in his. He waited a minute before he spoke. "Did you want to?" His voice was almost a whisper.

Kayla stared off into the rainforest, her eyes sad. She whispered back, "Yes."

Grady stroked her hand absentmindedly. What could he say to make it better?

"You could tell me how crazy I am, how I'm a killer just waiting for my next victim." Kayla looked down at her lap.

Grady stared at where their hands met, his heart going out to the woman he knew he would always love. "I don't think you're a killer, and I don't think you're crazy. You've got this. You'll master these powers in no time."

Grady sighed then released her hand to pull her into a hug. He breathed her name into her hair as he drew her close.

Despite the rainforest's high humidity, Grady just held her. He couldn't figure out what was going on even though he could hear her thoughts, the thoughts that now ran scattered, jumbled through her mind.

Something was wrong. Kayla was stiff beneath his arms, not fully reciprocating his embrace. Why was she fighting him? He pulled away to catch her gaze.

"Kayla?"

She caught his eyes, and at once Grady's eyes widened. He struggled to gain his composure, fought to control his expression. Because the Kayla he knew and loved had changed. It would have been barely noticeable to anyone else, but he knew her better than anyone, even with his memories of her stolen from him. Kayla's thoughts were consumed with thoughts of Shani, of Na-um, of how badly she needed them to pay.

But just as Kayla couldn't keep her thoughts from his, Grady couldn't hide what he was thinking, either. She could hear his thoughts, the thoughts that told her she was scaring him.

"Grady, I just . . . I'm sorry. I just can't right now." Kayla moved to stand up. "We need to get back; the others need us to open the entrance."

He nodded then followed Kayla through the rainforest back the way they'd come. Her thoughts were still jumbled, but Grady could sense the underlying theme: revenge.

Shani knew they were only minutes from the warehouse; she could almost feel her skin tingling in anticipation. She hated that she was stuck with this motley crew—a much-too-young girl, an invisible killer, a frat boy, and a shy college student—but they were all she had right now.

What a depressing thought.

She turned to Tyler, who was unceremoniously picking his way through the dense foliage. Shani smirked but quickly hid it before catching his attention. "Tyler?"

The young man just nodded, his eyes trained on the ground.

"I saw you were practicing."

That brought his head up, and he stumbled as he nodded. "Yes," he whispered. "I think I've gotten the hang of it."

Shani smiled at him, her practiced smile that was anything but genuine; it just looked that way. She looked over at the girls, who were helping each other through the foliage. She nodded at Akna, who was not bothering to watch her step. She was as comfortable in the forest as in her own home. "And it's clear you have been practicing as well. Good! You all will be a big help at the mountain warehouse."

"Yeah." Steven spoke up from just behind her. "But you never really did tell us what the warehouse was like. Or what it held."

Shani glanced back in his direction, a subconscious habit that made no sense. "The warehouse holds many precious objects that belong to me and my Clan. The Four have no right to it and should not be able to take control of it." She was nearly growling by the end.

Alexia spoke up for the first time since Shani'd joined them. "And you said they were dangerous?"

Shani nodded solemnly. "Yes, very. And they will stop at nothing—they will kill each and every one of us to obtain control of that warehouse."

Tyler nodded beside her, whispering his response. "Okay. What should we do?"

Shani ducked around a low-hanging branch. "We'll have to play things by ear. We don't know if the Four will be there or not. I'm not even sure how to get inside."

Steven spoke up again, surprising Shani yet another time. "We're here to help. Whatever you need."

Shani couldn't help herself; she had to ask. "Where is all this coming from? How are you all suddenly on board with everything?"

Tyler grinned at her, and Shani somehow knew Steven was also smiling. "You gave us these powers. They're something to get used to, but they *are* pretty awesome." Tyler glanced back to where Steven was. "The least we can do is help you out." Alexia grinned beside her, nodding as well. Akna looked around at their faces then smiled, too.

Shani was almost moved to tears. She wasn't used to others helping her for no reason at all. She was used to people who would only do something for her if she'd do something for them. Not Alex, of course, but how often did she really even get to see him lately?

Their separation was her fault, though she didn't really have a choice. She had to protect him, had to keep him away from the danger in her world. She had invited trouble into her life several years ago, and though he'd been a part of her life even then, she'd sworn he'd never encounter the people who constantly put her life in danger. That she would keep him safe. No matter what it took.

But she hadn't counted on how much it actually would take. How much she would miss him, how badly she would ache for his arms around her, how desperately she needed the strength he always seemed to have for her though he didn't seem to ever have any for himself.

Shani sighed. She'd continue to protect him, no matter what it cost her. She'd already made that decision, long ago. As she trudged through the forest with her newly committed squad, she was beginning to think it had cost her too much.

The Mountain Plateau, Outside the Mercenaries' Camp

The Four were once again standing in a circle, hand in hand, arms stretched between them, eyes closed. Yatzil watched with Holun from the sidelines, hoping that this time they'd make it work. Their last three attempts had gotten them close —she could sense it—but the door still had not appeared. Yatzil knew just where it should be—she'd seen it in her vision—but no amount of staring at it had opened it. She'd definitely tried.

As the Four continued concentrating, Yatzil turned her attention to the man she loved who sat quietly beside her. She held his hand in hers and squeezed it gently as she caught his gaze. She smiled widely, but she could feel her brow furrow as he winced.

"Holun . . ." Her voice caught, sounding strangled. "Is there anything I can do for you?" She released his hand to wipe a stray hair from his forehead.

Holun drew in a sharp breath, placing his hands on the rock beneath him as he adjusted slowly. "My Yatzil, I will be fine. I will heal."

She could feel her eyes filling. "I hate to see you in pain."

Holun caught her gaze and smiled softly. He reached up and rubbed the skin between her eyebrows as if trying to smooth it out. "Please, I will be fine."

Yatzil nodded slowly, but she felt a single tear finally release and roll down her cheek. Holun brushed it away and kept his hand cupped around her cheek for a moment before releasing her.

Then she felt it. What, she didn't know. But *something* was happening.

She glanced over at the circle the Four made, wondering if what she felt was coming from them. No, it didn't seem likely. They were in the same position they'd been, trying to materialize the door in the side of the mountain.

Yatzil rose from her seat, but her feet weren't touching the ground. She hadn't even meant to do it, hadn't instructed her muscles to pick her up. She was just suddenly off the ground, off the rock—with nothing beneath her.

She gasped. The sound apparently broke whatever spell had her floating in the air, and she fell back to the rock with a harsh thump.

Yatzil caught Holun's gaze with wide eyes she knew mirrored his. "What . . . was . . . *that*?" Holun choked out. "Are . . . you . . . okay?"

Yatzil just stared. She wanted to nod, wanted to reassure him that everything was okay, but she'd just *floated in the air* like, like . . . a . . . a bird? A butterfly? How was that okay?!

What is happening to me? Her brain searched for a logical explanation, but none came to mind. She glanced at her body, checking her arms, her legs, her head, her torso, making sure everything was intact. Nothing looked off. The whole floating thing was really odd, but she suspected the only weird thing she was feeling right now was an aftershock of that.

She glanced over at the Four again, but none of them seemed to have noticed her. Only she and Holun had seen what had happened. And if he hadn't been staring at her like she'd just lifted a vehicle over her head, she may not have even believed it had happened.

But it most certainly had. What did it mean?

"Yatzil, my love, please talk to me! What happened?" Holun's voice was a whisper, presumably not wanting to disturb the Four's concentration.

Yatzil swallowed hard then found her voice. For a second, she thought she'd left it in the air where she'd just floated. *Floated.* "I . . . I am okay, my Holun. I . . . do not know what that was."

Holun was still staring but managed to blink for the first time in what felt like several minutes. "How . . . ?" he managed.

Yatzil shook her head. "I have no idea."

They fell silent, and Yatzil's mind started going a mile a minute. What *had* happened, really? She thought back. What was going on before she'd . . . she didn't even want to think it.

She'd felt something deep inside her, something pricking inside her chest, something sharp but not painful. Yes, but before that. What had been going on?

She'd been staring into Holun's eyes. He'd had his hand on her cheek . . .

But what had she been thinking, feeling? What had been going through her mind just then?

She thought for a brief moment, then it came to her. Her mouth dropped open. She'd felt as though she wanted to do anything she could for him. She wanted to heal him herself, impossible as that request might be. She wanted to take away his pain, wanted to make it float away . . .

No, that's crazy, she thought. She couldn't just *think* something and have it come true. That was not how these things worked.

Or did they?

Holun's hand was on her cheek again. "Yatzil? Yatzil, come back to me." His voice was soft but insistent.

She blinked, turning her gaze back to him. Then she smiled. "Yes, my love. I am here."

"What were you thinking about so intently?"

Yatzil's smile echoed the serenity she felt throughout her body. "I think I know how it happened, but it is impossible."

Holun leaned forward, for once not wincing at the movement. "I am not sure impossible is a good word to use with us."

Yatzil chuckled lightly. "No, I suppose it is not." She sighed. "I think I was floating because . . ." She paused, convinced she was crazy. "I wanted to fix you, heal you. I wanted your pain to *float away.* That was my exact thought." Her voice cracked at the end, and her last sentence was a whisper.

Holun's eyes flashed, then his face broke into a large grin.

Yatzil pursed her lips and scrunched her eyebrows together. "What?"

"That's amazing!" Holun had started laughing, more loudly than she would've thought he should. Wouldn't the noise cause the Four to have to start over? Her wide eyes shot over to them.

But she shouldn't have worried. Because a lot had changed since the last time she'd seen the Four. They now all stood with hands in the air, looking as though they were caressing the air in front of them into a ball of energy. How on earth did they do *that*?

The Four sent the ball of energy into the side of the mountain, where Yatzil had shown them the door should be.

Suddenly, a burst of light shot out of the mountain where the opening should have been.

Then it was gone, as quickly as it had come.

And a gaping hole now interrupted the surface of the mountain.

CHAPTER 32

The Door in the Side
of the Mountain

YATZIL ROSE FROM HER SEAT—on purpose this time, feet firmly planted on the ground—and moved toward the dark opening. She was closer to it than the Four, so she made it there first.

Just before she stepped through the opening, she felt it again. *Oh no.*

Holun came up beside her, and she grabbed his hand, squeezing it tightly, anchoring her to the earth. Who knew what would happen now?

She waited, holding her breath. But nothing seemed to happen. Really? As scary as it had been, at least she'd thought it'd be predictable.

No such luck.

Yatzil slowly, ever so slowly, took the first step into the darkness.

Her feet found an expected rocky staircase—she'd seen it in her vision. Once she'd taken the first few steps carefully, she sped up, nearly jogging down the stairs by the time she'd reached the bottom. She couldn't see much in this dark staircase, but her eyes were adjusting quickly—more quickly than she would've thought possible. Was that another power manifesting? She would never be able to keep all this straight.

Holun was noisily descending the steps behind her, and Yatzil heard the others following, albeit a little less obviously. Poor Holun. She wanted to cry at his pain.

She reached the bottom of the steps and turned left. But why? Her vision had only taken her to the stairs—she had no conscious idea of what came next, but somehow she seemed to subconsciously know.

As soon as she'd taken a few steps, she reached to her right. Her hand met the wall she knew was there, the wall she knew held the light switches for this place. She flipped them on.

She heard six identical gasps once the lights flickered on. She was surprised to hear herself included, but not even her vision could have prepared her for the sight before them.

Endless rows stretched as far as her eyes could see, rows of metal shelving that held the most curious objects. Yatzil moved to the first shelf and scrutinized the objects she saw there. She reached out her hand toward the smallest one . . .

Kayla's fingers grazed her wrist, stopping her before she touched the golden object. "Perhaps we should not touch anything until we know what it is." She quickly dropped Yatzil's arm, and Yatzil nodded but took half a step backward, away from the shelf. Her heart was racing; the artifact she had nearly touched had started glowing when she'd gotten close.

Yatzil blinked once then composed herself, straightening up, satisfied to leave these artifacts alone for now. She looked at Kayla. "So what do we do next?"

Kayla looked at Grady. *What should we do?*

Grady's brow furrowed. *Maybe we just need to check out this place? Split off in pairs, see what we find?*

Kayla nodded at him. *Good idea.* "Let's explore a little. We can keep in touch in here." Kayla tapped the side of her head. "Holun, are you okay to send me a vision if you run into trouble?"

Holun smiled slightly from where he leaned up against Yatzil. "Of course."

Kayla looked over at Mandy and Justin. *Can you still hear me?*

Mandy nodded at her, but Justin only seemed to hear her through Mandy's thoughts. This was exhausting. "We'll take this row." She pointed down an aisle to their left, then she and Justin disappeared behind the shelves.

Kayla nodded down the aisle they stood in. "Yatzil, Holun, why don't you head this way? Grady and I will check over here." She nodded off to their right.

Yatzil nodded once, her face grave. Kayla hoped this extended foray into danger did not scar that gentle girl for life. She watched as Yatzil helped Holun down the row, him limping at her side. Kayla bit her lip then turned and headed down an aisle to their right, Grady with her.

They'll be okay.

Kayla smiled at Grady's answer to her unasked question. *I know, I just worry about them.* Then her smile froze, and she felt her lips hardening into a straight line. *I can't believe that Shani . . .*

Kayla, you have to get that anger in check.

Kayla nodded once, but she didn't feel any less angry. Shani had to pay. And Na-um and the Elders, for that matter. They all had to pay for what she'd lost.

Kayla, I am not lost! Grady shouted in her head.

She stared at him with wide eyes. She couldn't form a coherent thought yet. Grady never yelled.

You have to get over this. And I know you think you've lost me, but I am right here, beside you.

But it—we—may never be the same. And it's her fault.

Grady sighed, his shoulders drooping. *The problems with us are not her fault, Kayla.* The thought was quiet but impactful, and it shot daggers through Kayla's heart. She knew exactly what he was implying.

I'm sorry, Kayla. I didn't mean . . .

It's okay. And you did mean it. Because you are right. This is . . . this is my *fault.*

Grady's eyes were sad as they passed their fifteenth identical shelving unit filled with a variety of artifacts from all different eras and locales, if what she had surmised was correct. Her heart felt heavy. How could she do this to him, to them? How could she ever forgive herself?

Grady's thoughts fell silent for a moment, so Kayla took the opportunity to start inspecting the artifacts more closely, falling back into her usual tendency to rely on work as a distraction from her feelings. This one appeared to be from the sixth or seventh century, perhaps from Central America, and this one was probably from ancient Egypt . . . How did all of these diverse artifacts get into this one warehouse?

Then Grady's voice interrupted her thoughts. *Kayla, I . . . I miss you.*

She frowned, stopping with her back to him, not even sure what to say. *Grady,* she began, *I really am sorry. I miss you so much. I miss how we were, sure, but I realize only now that it's you I miss. Just you. And your memory loss doesn't change that. Not in the slightest.*

Grady smiled at Kayla as he realized the truth of her words which echoed his own thoughts. They missed each other in the most vital, the most important way: They just missed being together. They missed being around each other. Missed sharing in the everyday, simple things, the seemingly inconsequential moments that made up a fulfilling, incredible life.

No matter what Shani had done to him, to *them*, he knew he had to get past this. Because he couldn't imagine his life without Kayla in it. He couldn't live without her, and he only now fully realized the consequences of that truth.

As they continued down the seemingly unending aisle, he realized that no matter what Kayla had done, he would forgive her. No matter how badly she'd hurt him, he'd give her his heart anyway. No matter what she did, no matter who she became, she was his, and he was hers. Nothing on earth could change that. Not Shani, not Na-um, not stupid mistakes or catastrophic disasters—he'd lived life too long without her. He wasn't about to give her up now.

He glanced over at Kayla, realizing abruptly that she hadn't heard the direction his thoughts had taken. Probably just as well—he'd find the time to tell her very soon. It would sound better after he'd had time to form his thoughts into words, anyway.

But he would tell her nonetheless. Tell her how much she meant to him, how he didn't care if she'd kissed Na-um, how he would always love her, forgive her, for the rest of their lives.

He was shocked it didn't scare him, the intensity of his feelings toward her. He knew they'd been in love before, but he couldn't imagine it had felt like this. He couldn't—

His head started spinning, and he stumbled toward a nearby metal shelf. He struggled against the vertigo and fought to stay upright, his hand nearly knocking a full row of artifacts to the ground.

He noticed the floor coming up much too quickly as he felt Kayla's hands on his arms—then everything went dark.

Grady blinked, his eyes struggling to focus before landing on the most beautiful creature he'd ever seen. *Kayla.* He smiled up at her—she was leaning over him, her face just inches from his.

The lines creasing her forehead smoothed, and she let out a breath. "Grady," she breathed, reaching toward him and brushing her hand across his forehead. "Are you okay?"

Grady blinked again, taking stock of his body. Everything seemed to be okay, but then again, he hadn't tried to move yet. "I . . . think so." He leaned up on his elbow slowly, testing the waters. Everything seemed okay. "What happened?"

Kayla sat down beside him and helped him to a seated position. "You fell."

Grady's heart warmed as he remembered saying the exact same thing to Kayla last summer . . . wait.

Kayla's eyes grew wide as he felt his own doing the same. *Kayla . . .*

Grady, you remember?! He heard the thoughts racing through Kayla's head and could barely keep up.

Yes. Kayla, sweetie . . . Grady felt tears start to fill his eyes. *I remember everything.* He could feel the awe in his words and knew Kayla heard it, too.

Grady pushed himself to his feet then reached down for Kayla's hand and helped her up. "Kayla . . ." He stretched a trembling hand out toward her, reaching under her hair and around the back of her neck, pulling her toward him. "My love," he breathed, leaning in and pressing his lips to hers.

He couldn't believe it, couldn't believe his memory was back, but that wasn't going to stop him. He pressed closer to Kayla, pulling her against him, his lips more urgent, more insistent on hers. He didn't know how long he had before his memory was gone again, but he was taking full advantage.

Kayla didn't seem to mind. She kissed him back, her lips desperate on his, her hands tangled in his hair. He pulled her even closer, not an inch between them as they explored each other.

Oh, how he'd missed this. Knowing everything now, their kisses before had seemed so empty, so hollow. *This* was what he'd been longing for, what his soul had been crying out for. Just her.

He pulled away to breathe, bringing his forehead to hers as he tried to catch his breath. Her chest was heaving as well, her breathing labored.

Kayla spoke first. "Grady . . . how . . . ?"

Grady smiled at her, pulling away slightly to look into her eyes. "I just . . . I remember everything. And Kayla, I'm sorry."

Kayla blinked at him. "What could you possibly have to be sorry for?"

Grady's smile widened as his breathing returned to normal. "For not forgiving you sooner. For holding your mistakes against you. I should never have done that."

Kayla was shaking her head before he was done talking. "No, Grady, this was my fault. It was all my fault. I'm the one who needs your forgiveness."

Grady grasped both of her hands in his. "And you have it, forever."

Kayla just stared. The man she loved had finally come back to her—had forgiven her completely—and she was still reeling from the suddenness of it.

But she knew it was true. She could sense the change in his thoughts, in his mind, and somehow she knew that this would stick, that this was real. He could finally *remember*, and Kayla thought that word was perhaps the most beautiful in the English language.

He was hers once again.

Yatzil was helping a limping Holun down the middle of the room. They'd passed a small opening to their left, one that showed a large glass window with only a beige wall behind it. The room had an odd bluish glow to it, but no one appeared to be present. She wondered what it was . . .

Holun groaned quietly beside her. She knew he was trying to hide it, but she'd heard him. Come to think of it, she wasn't sure how she'd heard him—she shouldn't have been able to hear it, even being this close. Maybe the superhearing powers of the Clan—like Holun had—were starting to manifest themselves in her?

Yatzil eyed a break in the shelves up ahead. "Just a few moments, my Holun. There may be a place to sit up here," she whispered as she bore more of his weight and nodded ahead. "Just a little bit longer."

She wanted to cry. She felt like crying. Holun was in so much pain, pain inflicted by that horrible woman, pain Yatzil desperately wished she could take away. She would take the pain herself if it meant Holun would be released from his misery.

Then suddenly—with a swiftness that took her breath away—she felt something slice across her lower back. She lurched forward from the impact, involuntarily releasing Holun and falling to her knees.

Holun, amazingly, was still standing. How was he doing that with the pain he was in? He was barely standing just a second ago!

Another slice across her stomach, and Yatzil fell on her hands, the air whooshing out of her lungs. She slowly moved to sit down on the cement then pulled up her shirt to examine her stomach. A bright-red cut slashed the surface of her flat stomach in half. She cringed at the sight of it, of her blood dripping from the wound.

Holun was at her side in an instant. "Yatzil? Yatzil! What happened? What . . . are you okay?!" His eyes tightened, narrowing as he winced at the slash on her stomach.

Yatzil could barely breathe. She gasped, trying to get a word out, trying to reassure him she was okay.

But was she? Really? It seemed an invisible sword had cut her deeply, twice.

Another slice, this time from the top of her back across to the opposite side of her waist. She cried out this time, unable to stifle the sound. What was happening?

Then she blinked and looked at Holun, the young man beside her, the one whose anxious brown eyes scanned her inexplicable wounds furiously, whose lips pursed at her every gasp, whose hands trembled with every movement Yatzil made. The young man who was leaning over her, reaching for her, caressing her skin.

The man who seemed to be in no pain at all.

"Holun," Yatzil gasped, reaching weakly toward his arm, "you . . . are you . . . your"—she coughed then winced—"your wounds."

Holun blinked, then his eyes grew wide. He slowly reached for the hem of his shirt and pulled it up. He stretched to find the edge of the bandage coiled around his waist then carefully unraveled it, letting the gauze fall to the ground around him until it was completely removed. Yatzil gasped.

His wounds were completely gone.

And suddenly, she could breathe again. The pain—the excruciating, agonizing pain—was gone. Completely. She lifted her shirt, and the deep cut across her stomach was gone, just like that. Like it had never been there in the first place. She couldn't feel the cuts on her back, either. Had she been imagining things?

But the way Holun was staring at her told her the cuts had been real, just as real as Holun sitting next to her. She just couldn't figure out why they were no longer there.

"My Yatzil." Holun reached his hand out and touched her face. "Are you okay? Are you in pain?"

Yatzil closed her eyes at the touch of his hand. She reached up to place her hand on his as she smiled over at him, her eyes opening and finding his. "Not anymore."

"What happened?" Holun kept his voice quiet.

Yatzil blinked. She barely believed it herself, but she knew in her heart it was true.

She had *healed* him. Call it her superpower, call it *whatever*, but Yatzil realized that she could manifest a power just by thinking it.

She sat back, pulling her knees up and wrapping her arms around them, her eyes wide and staring at the stacks of artifacts farther down the aisle.

Holun moved closer to her, all of his bandages now surrounding them on the gray cement floor, gloriously unneeded. He reached an arm around Yatzil's shoulders, pulling her closer. He seemed to know that she wasn't quite ready to talk about it, and Yatzil was grateful. She was trying to process it herself.

Then a shot rang out, the sound reverberating on the myriad of hard surfaces in this massive room. Yatzil gasped when Holun yanked her to her feet as he stood, grabbing her and his bandages and running further down the aisle, further into the warehouse.

Holun spotted an odd wooden structure up ahead to their right and sped toward it. It looked like a small shack—almost like someone had dropped an ancient, tiny cabin in the middle of this fairly modern warehouse.

They reached the door quickly, and Holun yanked on the knob.

It didn't move.

Yatzil glanced over her shoulder before turning back to the matter at hand. She reached for the handle, closed her eyes for a split second, then opened the door.

Holun stared, his eyes wide, as Yatzil entered the tiny room. He was certain that door had been locked.

"Holun!" Yatzil hissed through the opening, her voice a harsh whisper. "Get in here!" Holun felt her grab his arm and pull him inside.

Yatzil shut the door behind them, and the room went completely black. Holun couldn't even see his hand in front of his face, say nothing of knowing where Yatzil was.

Then, slowly, he started to see her to his left. Was someone turning up the lights?

He glanced around at their surroundings, trying to locate the source of the light. It didn't take long. The room continued to light up, and Holun could finally make out the contents of the room.

It wasn't much.

On three sides of the tiny cabin, open wooden shelves—the same color as the walls surrounding them, though covered with white cloths—sat largely empty. But the one thing they held, the thing that was now lighting up the room with an increasingly blinding light, was a globe.

CHAPTER 33

We Are Not Invincible

GRADY HEARD THE SHOT ring out and instinctively grabbed Kayla's hand, yanking her behind one of the many identical metal shelves in here.

What was that? Kayla's frantic question sounded in his head.

He glanced quickly around the side of the bookcase, seeing nothing abnormal, then looked back at her. *I'm not sure, but I'm guessing Shani has arrived.* He took a breath, uncertain of what their next move should be. *Can you reach the others?*

Kayla closed her eyes, and Grady recognized the expression from the UCF lounge—she was trying to concentrate. He tried to clear his mind so she didn't hear anything in his thoughts.

Then: *Grady* . . . His stomach dropped at her tone. *I can't hear them. Mandy and Justin . . . what if they're in trouble? We need to get to them. Now.*

Kayla pulled him out from behind the bookcases, and they sprinted back toward the entrance.

Justin was on the ground, pain shooting through him. Shani's gunshot had grazed his left arm. He held it tightly, trying to stem the blood flow. It hurt like nothing else he'd ever experienced, but he'd live.

On to more pressing matters. "Mandy, we need to go now."

Mandy was staring wide-eyed at his arm. "But Justin . . ."

"Mandy, we need to get out of here. Shani was close enough to hit me that time—she's probably only closer now, and getting even closer. We have to go." He gritted his teeth at the pain, underlining his words.

But Mandy still wasn't moving. "Justin . . ." Her voice was strangled, her words whispered. "We . . . we're not supposed to be able to get hurt, not seriously anyway. The bullet didn't even touch Kayla!"

Justin remembered this past summer all too clearly, when the woman he loved had stopped a bullet shot inches away from Kayla's chest.

But this was different. They hadn't had time to gather their power, for one. Hadn't even had time to react.

Justin flashed back to Mandy's earlier thoughts, when she theorized that they were invincible. Clearly, this proved they were not. "Mandy, baby . . ." He reached for her, pulling her close with his good arm. "I am *okay*. But we will not be for long if we stay here."

Mandy paused for a second before nodding. "Okay." She finally unfroze, snatching up both their backpacks as they headed further into the warehouse.

Shani ran back toward the entrance, back to her superpowered misfits. That warning shot seemed to have hit something, but she didn't think it wise to continue forward, take the direct approach. Not with her former professors and classmates. Not with the *Four*.

She wanted to eradicate the thought from her head. She still could not believe, even after all these years, that *they*—nobodies from America—had been chosen to carry out the Codex's work on this earth. They didn't deserve it. They couldn't.

Because she did.

She swallowed hard as she neared the entrance where her four sidekicks waited for her instruction. They really weren't all that bad. Though she'd only given them bits and pieces of the story, they'd been willing to follow her, accompany her here. She'd like to say it was her infectious leadership, but, deep down, she knew she was just lucky. And if—when—she made it out of here alive, she'd never forget them.

Because *they* probably wouldn't make it out alive.

Just before she reached them, avoiding their wide-eyed gazes at the still-smoking gun in her hand, she heard a noise off to her left. She held up a hand in front of them as she passed and headed off toward the sound. "Just a moment."

Shani slid the hammer of her gun into place and sped up, running now. Kayla and Grady were down this aisle; she was sure of it. She knew them well—better than most—and she knew they'd all split up to investigate. Predictable.

It would be their end.

She spotted a flash of blue and took a shot. She cringed at the sound as it reverberated off the probably thousands of metal shelves in here, but she kept moving forward, getting another shot off. Then she stood still, listening.

Nothing.

Just as well. Coming at them head on was always a bad idea with these four; she'd have to be satisfied with forcing them deeper into the warehouse.

Which gave her an idea. There had to be a large, empty space in this gigantic warehouse, right? This place was too big not to have one. She could direct them there, back them into a corner, and have her group unleash their worst. Her lips curled up at the thought.

She slid the gun into the waistband of her pants at the small of her back and pulled her shirt over it, heading back the way she'd come. These young kids—three of them were young, anyway—had already seen her with a gun, had heard it go off. No need to freak them out more.

Kayla and Grady were running up the aisle, but they quickly ducked behind a set of shelves as a second shot rang out, ricocheting off the shelves across the aisle. Kayla noticed how the sound was different from the first. *Grady, that shot . . .*

Grady nodded from beside her. *That first shot hit something, didn't it?*

Kayla nodded, a tear escaping her eye. She reached for Grady's hand. *Grady . . . who . . .* She couldn't finish the question. She reached out to Mandy, but she still couldn't hear anyone's thoughts but Grady's and her own. Which really had her worried.

Grady just squeezed her hand as he stuck his head around the shelf, but he quickly pulled it back when another bullet whizzed by.

We're pinned down, Grady began. *Shani's not going to let us out of here the way we came in. And we can't leave, anyway—if everything we've heard about these artifacts is true, this treasure trove is too powerful to let the Elders control it any longer. What should we do?*

Kayla blinked, taking her first good look at their surroundings. *Well . . .* She glanced behind them and spied a potential exit, at least from this aisle. She nodded over her shoulder. *I think we can squeeze through there.*

Grady saw where she'd indicated. *Worth a try.* He followed her through a set of shelves behind them and down another aisle as they ran further into the warehouse.

Shani smiled sweetly as she approached. "Okay, everyone. They've all split up, so we'll need to do so as well. Tyler, take Akna with you, go find Holun. He'll be the younger man and will probably be staggering from his wounds." She didn't tell them she'd inflicted them. "Steven, you're on Mandy and Justin. They headed that way." She nodded toward her right. "Alexia and I will go after Grady and Kayla. Her power should be reserved for the worst of them." She hid an evil grin from her face. Grady and Kayla would go up against this sweet girl's power and crumble beneath it. She couldn't wait to see it.

"Wait, my dear," a voice sounded from the entrance. Shani's head whipped up at the sound.

Zotz stepped into the light, three of the other Elders behind him. Shani's stomach knotted. The Elders *never* came into the field. The Elders *never* got their hands dirty. What were they doing here?

"Yes, Zotz?" Shani answered sweetly, thankful for years of practice.

Tohil stepped toward her and put a hand on her shoulder. "We have only come to help, Shani."

Shani smiled at him, though she suspected she wasn't getting the whole story. They had to have another agenda—nothing else made sense.

Bacob stepped out of the shadows and ushered the group to the side. "Please, everyone, make room."

Shani's eyes widened as she stepped aside and the entrance to the warehouse began to fill with an army of her fellow Clan members, armed and ready for battle. How . . . ?

Bacob laughed. "Shani, we can take it from here."

Shani blinked, searching her brain for a response that would satisfy both parties. "Tohil, what is happening here?"

The kindest Elder squeezed her shoulder with the perfectly appropriate amount of force, so perfect that Shani's teeth clenched silently. "Well, Shani, we knew you were going up against the Four, so we thought we'd bring our best to help you."

"But Bacob said . . ."

Zotz spoke again. "We will work together to stop them. Now, my dear, where have they gone?"

Shani stared at the group of Elders, at the now-crowded entrance to the warehouse. She swallowed once before speaking. "Kayla and Grady went that way, further into the warehouse." She pointed to her left, behind where she stood facing the entrance. "Mandy and Justin are that way." She pointed to her right, down the aisle farthest away. "I have not found Holun and Yatzil, but I suspect they are not far." She noticed Bacob's eyebrow raise at the mention of Yatzil, and the Elders exchanged a few glances, but no one said anything about it. Shani wondered if they really didn't know who she was.

Perhaps she could use that. As she watched everyone disperse according to Bacob's instructions—her crew as well as the army the Elders had brought—she started forming a new plan. A new plan that would not fail.

"Um, Tohil?" she ventured.

The Elder, one of only a few people staying to guard the entrance, looked up at the sound of his name. "Yes?"

Shani widened her eyes just a little, her best attempt at looking compliant, helpful. "I have an idea about how to stop them. But I will need Alexia for it to be successful."

Tohil glanced over at the young girl who stood hovering off to the side, eyes wide, shaking just a little. Shani explained a portion of her plan—the part she wanted Tohil to know about—and he nodded. "Yes, I think that will work just fine." He told her how to get to the large space critical to her plan, then he grinned at Shani as she took the girl's hand and stalked off.

As she hurried down the aisle, her hand now on Alexia's back to urge her forward, her eye caught something on a shelf nearby. With a quick glance behind her to make sure Tohil was otherwise occupied—and thanking her good fortune when she saw he was turned away—she snatched the object and pocketed it without breaking a stride.

Yatzil was staring at the globe like she had for the past ten minutes, mesmerized at the swirling light dancing in front of her eyes. Then something occurred to her. "Uh, Holun?"

"Yes?" Holun came up to her side slowly, as if he was scared of the globe. What on earth was there to be scared of?

"Did you say something about a globe that gave Kayla visions?" She swallowed hard, still staring into its center.

She felt Holun nod beside her.

Abruptly, without really knowing why, Yatzil reached for it.

"Yatzil, no!" Holun called out, but her hands were already on it.

Suddenly, the light in the room exploded, expanding to every inch of the small, dark space. Yatzil's eyes stretched wide as the brilliantly incandescent globe shone brighter than the sun between her hands.

She felt her back arch, felt a lightning bolt shoot through her. She thought Holun was screaming beside her, but she couldn't hear any sound except an odd rushing that had erupted in the room.

Then it was silent, and Holun was staring.

Holun reached for Yatzil the moment she'd picked up the globe, but she couldn't seem to hear him. He yelled, screamed her name, but she wasn't listening—or couldn't hear him.

And suddenly, with a swiftness that took Holun's breath away, a pair of wings shot out from Yatzil's shoulders, spreading wide and filling the room, the sound of rushing wind echoing in the small space. The wings swirled and undulated, wisping around the small room as though not quite corporealized. They were a beautiful midnight black with a subtle spectrum of color that Holun thought only his extrasensory eyesight could detect.

Then it was silent, and they were gone. Just like that.

Shani ran at human speed down the far aisle with Alexia, but she was still surprised the girl was keeping up. They switched aisles again to try to circumvent Kayla and Grady. They ran until the bookcases abruptly ended, and Shani found herself exposed in an extremely large, open space. She jerked to a stop and felt Alexia pull up beside her.

"What is this?" the girl whispered.

But Shani ignored her, because she didn't know herself, though she had suspected a place like this existed. Several rows of bookcases ended here, looking like rays of the setting sun radiating out from its center, behind where they now stood. In front of them, far in the distance, was a wall created by the stone this warehouse had been dug out of, still natural in shape. Part of the wall held a line of windows, but the room behind them was dark. She spied a heavy metal door complete with a hand wheel—straight out of a submarine, no doubt—presumably leading to that room, in the leftmost part of the wall, next to the windows. Several short shelves lined the space under the windows, filled with all manner of curious objects.

Further along the wall, to the right of the row of windows, a vast array of all manner of weaponry was affixed to the wall, covering its wide expanse. Shani grinned at all the tools that were now at her fingertips, ranging from samurai swords and modern throwing stars to a medieval mace and an impressive collection of Japanese *nunchaku*. But of course, if everything went according to plan, she wouldn't need any of them.

Back on the main floor, standing at the end of every bookshelf set, were wooden shelving units, their contents hidden behind thick wooden doors. Shani went to the nearest one and yanked open the door. The door slammed open, revealing a curious array of clothing. As Shani rummaged through the hanging clothes, she realized most of these articles were for protection—hazmat suits, lead aprons, bulletproof vests. She could only guess what sorts of things were in the rest of the closed units. If there were ever a nuclear holocaust, she knew where she'd come.

Shani took it all in, examining the site carefully, analyzing every inch of it. Noting the placement of everything surrounding her. Because this arena—about the size of a football field—was the perfect space to execute her plan.

"Alexia, honey?"

The girl moved to her side, tearing her eyes away from the curiosities surrounding them. "Yes, Shani?"

Shani looked over at her and smiled. "I now know how to best put your power to use."

Alexia blinked. "How?"

Shani's smile grew wider as she told the girl the relevant-to-her part of her plan, outlining its details, describing how the girl should carry it out.

When she was done, Alexia took a breath, looking around her for a moment before responding.

Then she nodded.

CHAPTER 34

Seeing Is Not Believing

KAYLA HELD GRADY'S HAND as they made their way into the depths of the warehouse. As far as she could see, these shelves were infinite, never-ending. She didn't know what they'd find, but she knew if they faced Shani now, separated as they were from Mandy and Justin both physically and tele- pathically, they would probably lose. So they ran away with- out a thought to where they were going.

Then Kayla wasn't in the warehouse. Suddenly, she was transported underground to a wet, soggy, pitch-black place, one that echoed with sounds of rats scurrying by and some- thing unknown slithering in the darkness. She couldn't see Grady any more, couldn't feel him beside her.

She fell to the ground, and she felt something prick her hand as she caught herself. She lifted her hand up to examine it before she realized she couldn't see anything in the sudden, inexplicable darkness.

This was the tunnel underground where Steven had taken her. She knew it in her soul and fought the panic rising in her throat. Fought the feeling that just as soon as she'd gotten Grady back, Shani would once again steal him away from her. Suddenly, she was having trouble breathing. She reached up slowly, found the same stalactites she'd encountered before, just above her head. Only Grady was just beside her, and she was just in Belize, in a curious warehouse under the rainforest.

She tried to move but ran into another hard rock, and the panic threatened to take her over. *No . . .*

Then she saw a small white light, similar to the one she'd seen on Grady's phone the first time she'd been down here. It was her only saving grace in this darkness, the only thing she could see.

So she started crawling.

Grady was no longer in the warehouse, either, though he was nowhere near that underground prison. Grady was back at his old school, back behind that library, back on that fateful autumn day when the love of his life up to that point had torn his heart out of his chest.

He rounded the side of the library without wanting to, knowing instinctively what he would see next. And he did. There, in front of him, was Trisha.

Except . . . it wasn't Trisha.

Kayla Harrington, the woman he loved more than anything, was there among the fallen leaves in bright reds and burnt oranges with her arms around another man. Her eyes were closed, her lips on his, her body clearly responding to him.

Then she seemed to notice they weren't alone. She pulled away, opening her eyes to stare at Grady. The man turned, too, and Grady's heart broke again as Na-um stared back at him, a smile spreading across his face.

"Justin?" Mandy called out, confused. She blinked, taking in her surroundings.

She was back in Montana, back in the Stanfords' home. Justin's parents' home. The home where she'd met his parents for the first time, the home where she'd seen them wheeled out on stretchers.

Her breathing was ragged as she moved through the front entrance, down the hallway, back to the kitchen. The kitchen was just as she remembered it, just like the last time she saw it. Blood streaked down the cabinets, splattered against the bright and sunny curtains, pooled on the linoleum floor. Nausea threatened as she slowly entered the room, averting her eyes until the last possible moment, much as she had the first time, expecting that when she did, she'd see Justin's parents side by side on the floor, hand in hand, throats cut and bodies lifeless.

But she didn't. What she saw was so much worse.

The love of her life, Justin Stanford, was there on the ground where his parents should have been—his throat cut, lips blue, eyes glazed and lifeless, staring right at her, right through her.

Mandy started screaming.

Justin was back at school, sitting outside at a wooden picnic table, waiting for Mandy to get out of class. He blinked against the sun, feeling out of place. Hadn't he just been . . .

Mandy Carlson walked up, the smile he loved on her face as soon as she saw him. She came to sit beside him, promptly pulling out her phone and typing on it. As soon as she was done, she pulled the Codex out of her bag and started poring over it, pulling out a notepad and working on the translation. Then Na-um was there, sitting at the table, and Kayla, too. Then Alexia, Grady, even Holun showed up.

"Uh, Mandy . . ."

She looked over at him, gave a quick, halfhearted smile, then went back to her work.

Justin's shoulders slumped. He knew what was going on: Mandy didn't have time for him. She had important things going on, so many things to do and accomplish, but he didn't seem to rate on that list.

Then suddenly everyone else was gone, and Mandy was just sitting there, still working. Justin decided to try again. "Mandy, I . . . I need you. I love you."

Mandy just shook her head. "Not now, Justin. I'm busy."

Justin's throat was burning as he held back tears. "But my parents . . . I need . . ."

She turned to him, her eyes on fire. "Your parents are dead! Get over it! I have more important things to do than baby you as you cry over them. Seriously, Justin, you're really being needy."

Justin's eyes filled up.

"And now you're going to cry again, is that it? Can't you see I'm busy? I'm too busy! I'm too busy to deal with *you*!"

Justin turned away and stood up, but Mandy caught his arm before he could get far. He whipped around, and they were suddenly at a beach house, *the* beach house, the one where they'd spent their first anniversary and their third, the beach house where he planned to propose to her before graduation.

And he was on one knee on the wood floor, dressed all in white and holding a tiny, white, cloth box up to her. A gentle breeze blew in the open panoramic windows overlooking the ocean, rustling the gauzy white curtains and flowing white dress Mandy stood in front of him wearing.

She looked down at him, her brow furrowed, her head shaking, her lips turned down. "Justin, do you seriously think I actually want to marry you?"

Justin stared down at the box, at the ring he'd already purchased, the ring that was hidden in his sock drawer back in Florida. He snapped the box shut, fell to his hands, and wept.

Kayla was still crawling toward the light, but it never seemed to get any closer. Still she kept crawling, fighting to get to it, fighting to get out of this darkness.

Then she heard movement beside her, much too close, and she froze.

"What, sweetie?" Grady's voice—but somehow not Grady's voice—materialized out of the black. "You think you'll find me once you catch the light? You think I'll take you back after what you've done?"

Kayla's throat constricted, and she stopped crawling. The voice was right. She didn't deserve Grady's forgiveness, didn't deserve for him to take her back. She only deserved darkness, blackness, utter loneliness.

So she sat there, letting the tears come. And the voice kept going. "Yes, you are very alone here, aren't you? Good.

After what you've done to me, you deserve to be alone for the rest of your life."

Kayla was sobbing now, tears streaming down her cheeks. The voice was right . . . Grady, but not Grady . . . wait.

Her tears quieted, and she sat up straighter. *This isn't real.*

She moved to her hands and knees, felt around in the dark that seemed to want to consume her, felt the rocks, the hard, wet ground beneath her. She reached up, touched the unmovable rock deposits threatening to stab her.

Then she stood.

At once, the underground cave disappeared, and she was back in the warehouse. But she didn't recognize where she was; the first thing she saw was that she was standing in a large, open space, a rock wall on one side and rows of bookshelves surrounding her on the other three. Then she saw Shani, who first blinked then started grinning evilly. Her hand concealed something at her side.

"Well, Kayla, I see you've joined us. How kind of you. The others will be here shortly." That sickening smile was still stretched across Shani's face as she spoke, and Kayla's stomach dropped.

And she was suddenly frozen in place. She couldn't move as she stared at Shani, her eyes widening. Somehow, though she didn't know how, Shani had found a way to overpower her before she knew she even had to defend herself.

She felt a sharp pain at the back of her neck, then everything went black.

Tohil ran to the bookshelf to his right, scrounging around in the objects, looking for something. It wasn't here.

He scurried to the next one, searching each shelf as well. Still nothing.

Then he saw one empty spot, the spot where a very particular object was always stored, the spot where that object should have been. He felt the blood drain from his face.

Kucumatz, Tohil called through his mind, using the telepathy they shared with only each other and could call as needed. *Gather the others. We may have a serious problem.*

Kayla didn't think she'd been out long, just long enough for Shani to tie her to this metal chair with—she tried to move her hands, but they were trapped behind her, probably attached to the chair—great, chains. She'd heard them quietly clink.

But she'd had a little experience in subterfuge of late. She kept her head down, eyeing Shani from across the arena with as little movement as possible. Shani's back was turned to her as she watched Alexia, who was standing with her arms out to her sides, her eyes closed, clearly deep in concentration.

Kayla closed her eyes quickly, faking sleep. Maybe Shani wouldn't notice she was awake and ignore her. Because Kayla needed to come up with a plan—and fast.

Grady couldn't breathe. He sunk to the cold sidewalk, feeling as though his heart had been permanently removed from his chest. He couldn't think, couldn't reason his way out of this. His mind told him this was happening now, that this was his life.

But it wasn't, was it?

Then he heard her: *Grady, sweetie, come back to me.*

Kayla? He reached out to her in his head, hoping against hope that the Kayla he was seeing right now, the Kayla sneering in front of him, was just a figment of his imagination.

But she felt so real.

Yes, sweetie, I'm here. Fight it.

Grady was confused. *Fight what?*

Shani—or maybe Alexia?—has taken over our minds. But as soon as I acknowledged that it wasn't real, I came out of it. You can, too.

Grady blinked at the Kayla in front of him, the one still holding Na-um. He watched as she faded into a wisp of smoke, and Kayla—his Kayla—was in front of him once again.

He was only relieved for a split second before he saw Kayla tied up in the middle of the arena, head slumped over as if she was asleep. Then Shani turned to him, and suddenly he couldn't move. And everything went black.

The Elders met up halfway down the leftmost aisle. Tohil came running up as the rest of them arrived.

Kucumatz spoke first, his brow furrowed and eyes wild. "What is it, Tohil? What is so important that it halted our army's advance?"

Tohil was out of breath. "Shani . . . she . . ."

Zotz put a hand on his shoulder. "Tohil, please, what is it?"

Tohil took a deep breath, tried to calm his racing heart. "Shani . . . she has the artifact."

Everyone instinctively looked at the chain around Zotz' neck. The amulet Chac always wore—the one that protected them from Shani's mind control powers—hung around his neck while Chac was away, attending to an important matter.

Tohil shook his head slowly. "Not that. I doubt even it will protect us now. She has the other one. The one she could never have. The one she now possesses."

Tohil watched the others as the news sunk in. They'd been afraid of this, but no one had dreamed that she'd have known which artifact would help her most, the most dangerous one for her to have in this entire place.

Bacob spoke first. "What do we do?"

Zotz was staring off into the distance, eyes unseeing. "We have to stop her. Now."

The other Elders murmured their assent.

Kucumatz ventured, "But how?"

Tohil glanced at him then closed his eyes, searching for what was happening right now, what he could see. Then . . . there.

He smiled, opening his eyes. "My brothers, there is another way. And he's just about here."

Zotz just smiled back at him as the others exchanged glances, brows furrowed. Bacob finally asked the question. "Who?"

Kayla had given up feigning sleep when Shani had brought Grady over. He awoke less than a minute later, a moan reverberating in his head as he did.

You okay, sweetie? Kayla asked, eyeing him as Shani secured his chains and walked back to where Alexia stood against the back wall, her eyes still closed.

Sure. Grady glanced over at her and forced a pained smile. *Just feeling a little déjà vu here,* he quipped, and Kayla almost laughed.

Me, too. Then she switched gears. *So what do we do now?*

I'm not sure, Grady sent back, *but I'm glad we can figure it out together.*

Kayla smiled at him, making sure Shani couldn't see it.

Kayla . . .

Yes?

What did you see?

Kayla hesitated then decided she didn't want to keep anything from him any longer. No secrets. *I was back underground, where Steven and Shani kept us. It was dark, and I thought I saw your light . . . but I couldn't find you.*

I'm sorry, sweetie. He paused. *Was there more?*

Kayla nodded. *Yes.* She swallowed once. *Your voice was in my head. It told me you'd never take me back.*

Oh, sweetie. I'm so sorry. You know that's not true, right?

Of course, I do now. Kayla smiled. *What did you see?*

Grady paused then said just one word. *Trisha.*

Kayla nodded, swallowing hard as her face fell. This past summer, their minds had opened to each other so completely that she'd seen all the events of his life in an instant. So she knew what he meant, and she quickly realized what he must have seen, what the vision must have meant to him. Her stomach dropped, guilt gutting her. *Oh, Grady. I am so sorry. Did you see me there instead?*

He nodded slightly, his hair blocking her view of his sapphire-blue eyes.

Kayla thought she might be sick. *Grady, I . . .*

He shook his head slightly. *It was just a bad dream, nothing more.* He looked over at her and smiled, and it warmed her heart. The pain in her stomach eased just a little. *I told you I forgave you, and I meant it. Let's just focus on getting out of here, okay?*

Sure, of course! Kayla looked around. She didn't see anything out of place. *I guess we need to try to reach Mandy and Justin. Have you been able to hear them at all since your memory came back?*

No, sorry. Only you.

Me neither. Kayla sighed; she couldn't help it. *Okay, I'm going to try.*

Maybe we need to try together again. It worked before, right?

Yes, let's do it. She couldn't help the grin spreading across her face as she moved as close as she could to him without Shani noticing. Soon their legs were touching.

It wasn't much, but it was enough. As soon as she started to call her power—and felt Grady beside her doing the same thing—they could hear Mandy and Justin.

Guys! Where are you?

But they didn't seem to be listening. *Grady, I think they're seeing something like we were.*

Grady simply offered a subtle nod.

We have to get them out.

Agreed. How?

You take Justin, I'll take Mandy. Talk them out of it. Bring them back.

Grady nodded, and she heard him reach out to Justin. Kayla turned her attention to Mandy. *Mandy, please, listen to my voice. You need to fight this. What you're seeing isn't real.*

Kayla, where . . . where are you? Kayla could tell she'd been crying.

Don't worry about that now. What are you seeing?

Justin . . . Her words were strangled, even in her mind.

Fight it, Mandy, she pleaded. *It's not real.*

But Justin, he's . . .

He's here, Mandy, Grady's talking to him.

Justin . . . he's alive?

Kayla's heart broke as she wondered what on earth her friend was seeing. *Yes, Mandy, you just need to believe that. Once you do, you'll come out of it.*

She heard Mandy crying. *Justin . . .*

Then Kayla heard the sound of footsteps coming up the aisle to the right, and Mandy walked into view. She started toward Kayla and Grady just as Justin walked up. She turned and ran to him as soon as she saw him, hugged him tightly.

Kayla didn't even have time to warn them before they both froze then fell to the ground.

Shani had already pulled over two more metal chairs and set them up against the back of Kayla and Grady's chairs, and, in the next instant, Kayla heard her chaining their friends' arms behind their backs and interlocking their chains with Kayla and Grady's.

Unfortunately for them, she made quick work of it, and Mandy and Justin's hands were bound before they woke up. She stepped back toward Alexia, away from the group.

Justin was characteristically the first to speak up when they did, and Kayla could almost hear the eye roll in his voice as he clinked the chains that bound him in place against his chair. *Oh, geez, she knows she's dealing with the Four, right?* Justin almost snorted.

Justin, stop it. No need to get cocky, Grady shot back.

Sure, whatever. But we can get out of this whenever we want to, right? She has to know that.

Then Mandy stopped their thoughts in their tracks. *But can we?*

What? Justin blinked at her.

Can we really get out of this? Has anyone tried?

Kayla looked at Grady, her eyes wide. *We were trying to get you both out of your . . . whatever that was. We didn't try to escape. Grady . . . can we even escape?*

That's when Shani broke into their thoughts. "Hello, everyone. It seems we have a nice little reunion here." She grinned. "I think this will really help us get to know each other even better." She held up an object in her hands, one that reflected the bright fluorescent lights above.

It was slightly larger than her palm, about the size of a small music box by Kayla's estimation, and made of what looked like a hard obsidian. There were indentations in the surface, but Kayla couldn't tell what they were at this distance—markings, perhaps, or maybe just the way the stone was etched? Shani held it up in her palm, a smile spreading on her face.

Kayla struggled against the chains, but they held fast and somehow seemed to be getting tighter as she struggled. She closed her eyes, her heart racing faster in her chest with every passing second, and tried to call her power. Tried to see if she could conjure up some dirt in this place to, um, she didn't even know. Somehow break these chains that were binding them to each other? Anything.

Nothing.

Grady . . . can you call your power?

She heard Grady try to conjure some water, but nothing came to him. He caught her gaze, his eyes wide, and Kayla's stomach dropped.

Mandy, Justin, anything?

But she knew before she asked what they would say. They were stuck down here with a killer, one who'd already shot Justin, one who'd been after them from the very beginning—and they had no power.

They were trapped.

CHAPTER 35

The Gathering

HOLUN DIDN'T KNOW WHAT to do. He'd heard the shots ring out before Yatzil had even touched the globe—probably Shani, he'd figured—and had decided to try to venture out after Yatzil's powers had emerged. But then he'd heard an army of men marching past their tiny cabin, and they both decided to stay put for a while, at least until they could figure out what was going on outside their private hideaway.

Yatzil now had her ear up to the door, listening to hear if anything was out there waiting to snatch them once they exited.

But Holun hadn't heard a sound in several minutes, so he pulled Yatzil to him, whispering in her ear. "I think we're safe to go out. Besides, they probably need us."

Yatzil turned to catch his gaze then nodded once. "Yes." She leaned over and kissed him on the cheek.

Holun grinned as she opened the door. "And if you need to get away, you can always use your wings."

Yatzil grinned back as they carefully checked the aisle then headed right, further into the warehouse.

Shani knew she'd have to act fast—she suspected the Elders were already on to her plan. Something about the way Tohil had acted when she left . . .

The army would undoubtedly be here soon, and she needed to gain the upper hand, now. In a more permanent way—those chains wouldn't hold the Four for long.

The box she held in her hand was increasing her power; she could feel it. She'd only happened upon it, saw that it was labeled only as "power enhancing" and snatched it up. She knew if she had a chance of getting out of here alive—without the Four or the Elders or the Clan's army killing her first—it was with this artifact.

So she'd taken a shot, and it was paying off big time. She could sense that Grady had gotten his memories back, but that honestly was a blessing. Though stealing Grady's memories had been a key part of her plan to devastate Kayla and destroy the Power of the Four, keeping so much from Grady's mind—especially as he continually fought it—had been wearing on her.

And it hadn't even worked.

But now she felt stronger than ever. Her power coursing through her veins, stronger than she'd ever experienced, was intoxicating.

Steven was nearby; she could sense him. *Steven?* She reached out to him like she did back at the museum, hoping to keep the Four in the dark. Keeping Alexia in the dark didn't hurt, either.

She could sense Steven's confusion.

It's okay, Steven. Come to the area at the end of the book-shelves. Bring Tyler, Akna, and the men. Bring everyone. I have captured the Four.

She heard him pause but then spring into action, finding everyone he could and herding them toward her.

Perfect. They all needed to witness the end of the Four, the end of their short reign as the protectors of the Codex.

Because soon it would be hers alone to protect.

The Elders collectively heard Shani calling Steven, heard her ask him to bring everyone to the middle of the warehouse.

She's in the practice arena, Tohil thought to the others.

Yes, Zotz answered. *It sounds as though she has captured the Four there.*

And what of the boy—and the girl? Kucumatz asked.

No one had an immediate answer.

They have still not been found, Bacob offered.

Zotz spoke up. *We must go to the practice arena. If she has that artifact—and she probably does if she was able to contain the Four—we will need to find a way to stop her.*

Agreed, Tohil answered for all of them, then he heard movement at the entrance. Chac had arrived—he could sense it—but Tohil knew someone else was near as well. *You all go. Kucumatz, will you please handle the other matter?*

Of course, Kucumatz responded, and he soon came into view and jogged toward the entrance, nodding to Tohil on his way back up the staircase. Tohil heard the rest of them start making their way to the middle of the warehouse, the area where they tested all their newly acquired objects. He greet-ed Chac with a single nod as they followed the other Elders, then he sent his thanks telepathically to Kucumatz for attending to this other matter, one they all knew about, one they all signed off on.

Because it just might be the only thing that would save them all.

Shani sauntered toward the Four, balancing the artifact on her palm as she did. A wide smile was spreading across her face; she couldn't help it. Soon this would be over, and the Power of the Codex would be hers alone.

"You know," she began as she approached their collection of metal chairs, unable to help herself, "I've been waiting for this day for a very long time. Since I found out you all were the ones from 'the North'"—she gave one-handed air quotes for effect as she rolled her eyes—"that our prophecies spoke about, I have been planning to stop you. And now I have." Her grin widened.

She stopped just in front of Mandy. "I found you to be the most insufferable. You just couldn't stop being perfect all the time, could you?"

Mandy just glared up at her, and Shani let out a laugh. "No matter. You will get what you deserve. Every single one of you will."

"And what is that, Shani?" Justin spat from Mandy's side.

Shani leaned down quickly, getting right in Justin's face. He blinked, but he didn't flinch. She didn't like that very much. "Death."

Shani stood up straight, planning her next move, figuring out the most satisfying way to end their lives. She was so involved in her plotting that she barely noticed the girl, Alexia, standing off to the side, watching every exchange, hearing every word. She barely noticed the girl's eyes get wide, barely noticed her catching Mandy's glance . . .

Then she was no longer in the warehouse. She was back at Lamanai, back in the work trailer with Alex. Only this time, Alex stepped outside, pulling her by the hand. And the Elders, the Clan, Na-um, Holun and Yatzil, the Four—everyone was there.

Immediately, Shani was hit with the realization that Alex knew everything. Everything about her, all the horrible things she'd done, all the things she'd done for *him*.

He turned to her, sadness first in his eyes which morphed into disgust then revulsion. "You are a horrible woman, Shani. Despicable. I don't know how I could have ever loved you." He tried to pull away.

Shani gripped his hand, pleading. "Alex, no. Whatever you've heard, it's not true. Please!"

"So you didn't torture a young boy? You didn't create killers, didn't give innocent young people powers and distort their beliefs so they'd help you? You didn't lie, cheat, and steal to get what you wanted?" Alex spat, his words biting.

Shani was crying now, begging. "Alex, please . . ." She could barely breathe between sobs. "I . . . I did this all for us. So we could be free of them!" She glanced at the crowd and met the eyes of every venomous face glaring back at her.

Alex finally freed his hand from her grasp. "No, Shani. You did this all for you. All of it. It was only ever for you."

Shani fell to the ground and wrapped her arms around her, sobs wracking her body.

Mandy nodded her thanks to Alexia, smiling. The girl ran over to her, stepping around the incapacitated Shani, and immediately went to her wrists. "I'm so sorry, Mandy. Justin, Kayla, Grady—I'm just so sorry." She was crying as she tried to loosen the chains that bound them.

Then she went flying across the open space, sliding across the cement floor and into one of the wooden bookshelves. She hit her head hard on the corner of the shelf and immediately fell still. Mandy screamed before she could stop herself. *What was that?!* she asked the others.

She heard Grady's disgust even in his thoughts. *Steven is here.*

Yatzil and Holun weren't making very good time. Holun couldn't hear much of what was going on elsewhere in the warehouse—everyone had gotten eerily quiet—but he could still hear the army moving up the aisles ahead of them. They deliberately took their time so they didn't catch up—no need to draw unnecessary attention to themselves.

Then Holun felt a burning in his veins. It just kept growing, searing him from the inside out, getting so painful he couldn't help but cry out, fall to his knees. Yatzil fell down beside him. "Holun! What's wrong?"

Then she started writhing on the floor next to him, her face contorted, matching his own. Though he felt that this pain would kill him swiftly, he would gladly take on her pain, too, to never see that look on her face again.

A figure appeared from between two bookshelves, and Holun blinked. The pain must've altered his vision somehow, right?

He blinked again then noticed Yatzil look up as well before she screamed and fell backward, somehow scrambling away despite her pain.

And he realized the pain wasn't making him see things that weren't there—he wasn't hallucinating. The man—if he could be called a man—looked as though his entire body was covered in third-degree burns. His skin was bubbled and blistered on every visible surface, the sight made worse because the man wore no shirt.

Then the horrific apparition spoke, his voice strangled. "Help . . . me . . ." He reached his charred arms toward them.

Yatzil screamed again, crawling away from the figure, and Holun helped her to her feet. Then, despite the acid ripping through their veins, they stumbled around the man and further down the aisle, the burning inside them clearing up with every step.

Grady, can you hear me? Are your powers working?

Grady looked over at Kayla's questions. He tried to call his power, but it was still down. *No, you?*

Nothing. She frowned.

Grady sighed. *We're right back where we started. How do we get out of this?*

I don't know, Grady. Kayla was still frowning, and it broke Grady's heart. *Shani . . .* She looked up just as Shani was standing up, her hand once again holding the ancient stone artifact.

She must've figured out a way to beat the vision, too, Grady surmised. *Or maybe it stopped when Alexia got knocked out.*

Kayla nodded, her eyes wide, trained on Alexia. He could hear her trying to will the girl awake. It wasn't working.

We need a plan.

Kayla nodded at him. *Yes. Mandy, Justin? Can you still hear us?*

Loud and clear, ma'am, Justin answered.

Grady scowled at him. *Does anyone have any ideas?*

Why aren't our powers working? Mandy asked in response.

Grady looked over at Kayla. *We think it's because of that stone Shani is holding. We think it increases her power, and she's somehow blocking us.* Kayla was nodding beside him.

They could all hear Mandy didn't like that answer.

Grady, how is your memory? Justin asked.

Back and as good as ever, Grady replied, throwing a smile Kayla's direction.

Well, that's good at least. Mandy shrugged where she sat, frowning.

No, Kayla interjected at the defeat in Mandy's voice. *We are stronger than this. We can't give in to despair. If we do, Shani's won already.*

Grady smiled to himself, falling in love with her all over again.

Oh, geez, Grady. Get a room already.

Leave it to Justin to lighten the mood.

Kayla smiled over at Grady, and his answering smile warmed her heart.

But then it faded as he spoke. *Okay, it doesn't seem like any of us have a clue how to get out of this. If Steven's here, and Shani's awake, the others can't be far behind.*

Kayla nodded. *Has anyone heard from Holun or Yatzil?*

No one had.

I'll try them then, she offered. She closed her eyes, blocked the others from her mind. It was getting easier to do so; she was grateful for that, at least.

She couldn't reach either of them through her mind—perhaps a side effect of Shani's sudden power boost—but then she remembered that she usually shared visions with Holun to get his attention. So she called the power she didn't know how to call to send him a vision, praying it would slip past Shani's defenses.

At first, she couldn't come up with anything. Then, with a force that took her breath away, she knew she'd done it—she'd told Holun where they were. And she somehow knew, though she didn't know how, that they were on their way.

Mandy watched the vision that rushed through her friend's mind and smiled. *Maybe they can surprise Shani, get us out of here?*

Justin shrugged beside her. *Maybe.*

Guys, stop! Kayla yelled. *We are better than this. We have to fight.*

But how? Mandy asked, biting her lip. *Our powers aren't working, Shani's only getting stronger, and . . .*

And nothing! We are the Four—*we can beat her. We have the Power of the Codex.*

They fell silent, and Mandy could feel them all processing Kayla's words. Then: *Kayla's right,* Grady said. *We can do this.*

I'm open to suggestions, man. Justin looked over at Grady.

Mandy glanced over her shoulder at him, too.

Grady nodded at them. *Let's call our power. Now. Together. Our power can beat hers if we all tap into it at the same time.*

Before Mandy could respond, Shani grabbed her chin and spun her head to the front, forcing Mandy to look directly into her eyes. Mandy was staring into the eyes of Death Herself, but she felt an unfamiliar defiance in her own eyes, felt a smile spreading across her face as she worked to call her power as Grady had suggested. She felt the others doing the same thing, and Shani must've sensed it. Because her glare faltered, just a bit.

Shani let go of Mandy's chin, standing up slowly, eyes widening.

Because something was happening. Mandy felt it building from the bottom of her feet, up through her body, filling her being. And she knew the others were feeling it, too.

At once, the Power of the Codex erupted between them, and a geyser of earth, water, fire, and air burst from the ground and into the warehouse, breaking the chains that held them, sending Shani flying across the room and into the wall of weapons, a waterfall of knives raining down around her as the artifact she held tumbled to the cement floor, just out of reach. She cried out, but Mandy didn't look over to see what happened.

Because she was somehow on her feet in the middle of the warehouse, facing the others, standing where their chairs had just been, the chairs that seemed to have just disappeared along with their chains. The Four formed a rough circle, just like they had in that first cavern, when they'd first received the Power.

She could feel it in her veins once again. The Power had been there since this summer, but she hadn't been able to fully access it until now. The Power coursing through her was overwhelming, thrilling. She felt unstoppable.

You're not invincible, babe, Justin called to her, hearing her thoughts. *None of us are.* He looked pointedly at his arm, the drying blood on his torn sleeve accenting his words.

Mandy nodded at him, reaching for his hand and smiling. *Okay, so that was easier than I expected. What next?*

We need to get the box. Grady's voice echoed in her head.

Mandy searched the arena and finally spied it near where Shani lay on the ground, still but moaning. *Guys, look.* She nodded toward the box.

Justin? Can you get it? Grady asked. He was closest.

Justin nodded, but before he could sprint off, the noise of shuffling feet entered the arena, and the Four turned as one toward the bookshelves, the artifact temporarily forgotten.

Because an army of men began filing into the open space. As each one entered the arena and began to assemble in orderly lines, they smirked at them, the four small, inexperienced Americans. A college-aged man and a young girl, looking out of place among the Clan's scantily clad, adult army, came out from behind them and moved around the Four to stand near where Shani lay on the ground. Mandy only now noticed she was bleeding.

Grady looked over at Kayla, grabbing her hand and pulling her close to his side. Mandy and Justin moved closer, too. *We really need a plan.*

"Holun, wait." Yatzil slowed to a stop as she noticed the aisle start to open up a little ways in front of them. She could hear the army of men just out of sight, moving into formation. Something big was about to happen; she could feel it.

Holun stopped, but his eyes shifted back and forth, unfocused. Yatzil knew he wanted to get to Kayla and Grady, to Mandy and Justin as soon as possible—it had been the only thing he'd talked about since Kayla had sent him that vision telling him they needed their help. "What is it, my Yatzil?"

Yatzil bit her lip, her eyebrows creasing a line between her eyes. "If we just walk out there, any one of those people could kill us. We need a way to help our friends without being seen."

Holun nodded, but he was staring off toward the end of the row. "Okay. Do you have an idea?"

Yatzil glanced around then pulled them off to the side behind a bookshelf full of artifacts, her mind racing. What could they do? Her eyes scanned the shelves, hoping an idea would materialize out of thin air.

Then something occurred to her. "Holun . . ." she whispered, not sure what to do next, not sure if her idea would work.

But she knew when it did.

Holun gasped. "Yatzil!" he whispered. "I can't see you!"

She grinned then reached out a hand to him. As soon as she grabbed his hand, her shield passed to him, and she saw his eyes find her once again. "I think as long as we don't touch anything and we stay quiet, no one will know we're here."

Holun nodded silently, his eyes still wide, as they made their way up the row of shelves to find and rescue their friends.

CHAPTER 36

Taken Over

GRADY HEARD A GROAN from behind them.

"Shani," he growled through his teeth, ignoring the growing army in front of them, and turned to look at her. If they were ever going to get a chance to deal with Shani, the time was now.

The Four effortlessly fell into formation—Kayla and Justin faced the army, keeping their eyes on them, while Grady and Mandy stood at their backs, facing Shani—and started inching their way closer as a group to where Shani still sat on the ground, her arms cut and bleeding in several places.

Shani held up a long, exposed arm, palm out. "No, wait . . ." She sucked in a breath then staggered to her hands and knees.

Is she okay? Is she really hurt? Mandy asked.

Grady answered her. *Probably not. Keep your guard up, everyone. Mandy, if you want to try to read her thoughts . . .*

Mandy shook her head slightly. *No, not with that.* Her eyes indicated the black box Shani held in her left hand against the ground. Grady followed her gaze. *I think the only reason we were able to use our powers before was because we caught her off guard. As long as she has that box, she can stop me from reading her mind, stop all of us from using any of our powers again. Plus,* she continued, *she might retaliate if we try.*

Kayla nodded once. *We need another tactic. Grady? Any ideas?*

Grady just stared at Shani, at the artifact clutched in her hand. *Unfortunately, no.*

Mandy's eyes widened. *What do we do now?*

Uh, guys? Justin chimed in. *Whatever you're doing, do it fast. We're literally surrounded.*

Just then, as if to underline his words, Grady heard movement behind them. He and Mandy whipped around in unison, moving to stand beside Kayla and Justin, Shani momentarily forgotten. Grady's eyes widened, seeing for the first time just how large the Clan's army really was as they moved even further into the large space, spreading out. The Clan had been holding out on them.

We should have killed them all when we got the chance. Grady heard Kayla's thoughts in his head, and he winced internally at her cutting words.

Kayla, stop. I told you: You've got to get that anger under control. Grady glanced her way quickly, making sure she heard him and fully understood.

But she didn't answer him.

Kayla . . .

Kayla was staring straight ahead, refusing to meet his eyes. He walked over to her, forcing himself in front of her, forcing her eyes to his. As he did, he noticed a coldness there, a hardness he'd never seen before. And it terrified him.

"Kayla," he began, reaching for her hand. But she yanked her hand away, staring past him at the approaching army, and Grady saw something in her eyes that scared him more than the anger.

Her eyes were the color of sand, just like in the cavern this summer, when they'd first used their powers. But this time, they were different, darker almost, like the sand on a beach after a rainstorm.

But somehow what Grady *felt* concerned him so much more than what he *saw*—he felt Kayla pull away from him, away from them. She pulled away from the good part of their power, the part that allowed their human side to coexist with the supernatural one.

She'd let the Power of the Codex win.

"Kayla, no!" Grady screamed, leaping toward her.

Kayla, but somehow not Kayla any more, stepped away from him, pushing him out of the way more harshly than Grady would've ever thought she'd be with him. He stumbled and fell at the force of her shove. Kayla took a step forward, toward the army, reaching out her hands in front of her. Then she jerked her arms once, straightening them suddenly, and a massive stream of earth exploded toward the men, destructive and unrelenting.

What do we do? Mandy was wide-eyed as she helped Grady to his feet. He knew she could sense Kayla's power, had seen their exchange. She was on the verge of crying.

Justin came up beside her and put an arm around her shoulders. *Grady, seriously. How do we stop her?*

Grady didn't have a clue. The three of them just stared as Kayla single-handedly took down hundreds of men in seconds, burying them in a mountain of her own making.

The room started shaking. The lights above—steel housings on long chains hanging from the impossibly high ceil-

ing—started swinging in the haze created by Kayla's ava-
lanche of dirt and mud. Everyone not being relentlessly attacked by her power was staring, mouths open, eyes wide,
seemingly unable to move.

Brown, nearly black veins crawled across Kayla's skin,
snaked up her neck and along her cheeks as sweat broke out
over her forehead. The crazed, wild look etched in her face
made Grady's heart stop. Because he suddenly realized that
the woman he loved—the woman he'd just gotten back—had
left him. Again.

Shani, the trembling earth jarring her to full awareness, started screaming at her crew. "Stop her! By any means necessary!" She repeated it in K'iche for Akna so she would fully
understand.

With only a moment's hesitation, they sprang into action.
Akna stepped a few feet away then called her power and collected all the metal objects hanging on the wall above her
head. They gathered in the air surrounding her, parallel to
the ground, preparing to be launched through the air.

Shani screamed again in K'iche. "Do it! She's killing them
all!"

Akna raised her hands then shot them forward. As she
did, an army of various sharp instruments sliced through the
air, directly toward Kayla.

Shani grinned wickedly.

Grady saw the knives coming, saw them heading for the
woman he loved. No matter what was happening now, he had

to save her. He couldn't lose her again, especially not like this.

"Noooo!" he yelled as he ran, calling his power as he went, stumbling around the newly formed cracks in the cement from the earthquake Kayla was creating. "Mandy!"

Mandy looked over at him, clearly understanding. She froze as best she could despite the bucking floor, and her eyes closed for a brief second, then she opened them, forcing a shield from her body and toward Kayla, much like she'd done before, in the cavern this summer. Her eyes—the irises, pupils, sclera, everything—were a light blue, her entire body taken over by the Power.

The weapons hit her shield and fell to the ground with a clatter. Mandy pulled down the shield, her breathing labored.

Then she fell.

"NO! Mandy!" Justin screamed, running to her side. When he reached her, he noticed tiny cuts all over her, as if the knives had somehow punctured her skin when they'd hit her shield. Her eyes were closed as if she was merely sleeping—Justin hoped against hope that was the case.

Grady, if she's really hurt . . .

Grady just nodded at him but didn't look his way. He was carefully constructing a wall of water between Kayla's attacks and the men, clearly trying to save those he could. Soon Kayla would realize what he was doing, and Justin wasn't entirely sure what she'd do to stop him.

Get her out of here, Justin, Grady's voice came to him. *I will handle Kayla.*

But—

Holun and Yatzil are on their way. I can hold her off until then. Grady was struggling, sweat beading on his forehead, but he was holding. For now.

Grady, you can't expect me to leave you now.

Mandy needs you, Justin. You need to go and take care of the woman you love. Let me do the same.

Justin didn't like it at all, but there was no sense arguing with Grady further, distracting him more. He picked Mandy up in his arms and sped down an aisle to the left, moving too quickly for Shani to even try to stop him.

Holun and Yatzil ran up the aisle hand in hand. Yatzil was confident that her invisibility shield—or whatever it was—would hold, and they could move undetected.

But as soon as they got close to where they knew the others were, she saw a mountain of dirt, sand, and mud blocking their path, reaching nearly to the stories-high ceiling.

"How do we get around this?" Holun whispered in her ear.

Yatzil frowned, trying to figure that out herself. Then it came to her. "Come on. I have an idea."

Holun shrugged then let her lead him to the left, around the inexplicable mountain that shouldn't have been there at all.

The men were dying. A lot of them, all at once. And they weren't even fighting back. Why weren't they fighting back?

Shani had to do something, anything to stop Kayla from killing off every last member of her Clan. Though she didn't really care about them, their presence still gave her an awfully good chance of getting out of here.

She sensed her artifact would no longer be effective against the vicious power Kayla was now wielding so indiscriminately. And Alexia probably wouldn't help her, either—so she called Tyler over.

"Tyler, use your power on Kayla. Stop her."

Tyler stared at her, eyes wide.

"Now, Tyler!" she growled.

He turned toward the crazy woman in the middle of the wide opening, the one surrounded by mountains of her own making, and screamed.

Grady felt it coming before he saw the effects. The hairs on the back of his neck stood up straight just before he saw Kayla go flying through the air, toward the large mountain to her right.

"NO!" he screamed as he ran toward her.

He reached her as she fell to the ground, the loosely packed dirt of the mountain she'd conjured thankfully breaking the worst of her fall. She hit the ground and went limp, her body spent, her eyes closed.

Grady fell to his knees beside her. Why did this happen? What on earth would make her abandon herself like this, abandon *him* like this?

Ignoring the remaining army surrounding them, Shani and her crew closing in on them, and the Elders entering the space at his back, Grady just knelt beside her and wept.

Kayla felt herself waking up, felt Grady beside her, holding her hand. Felt the sobs wracking his body. Why?

"Grady?" she ventured, but her voice cracked like she hadn't had water in days. She swallowed with a little difficulty. "What's . . ." She moved to sit up, but her body wasn't responding. She blinked, staring up at Grady. "What's going on?"

Grady looked down at her with the most curious expression on his face. Kayla stared at him, at the face of the man she loved, and . . .

Suddenly he was gone, ripped from her side in an instant. Kayla scrambled to her feet, ignoring the stabbing, slicing pain well, everywhere, and using the giant dirt pile next to her to gain leverage. How . . . ? She glanced at it. How did *that* get there?

She stood up straight and took stock of the arena she was in.

And it hit her, all at once. Everything she'd just done. Giving in to the Power. Killing all those men . . .

She thought she would be sick, and she leaned a hand against the dirt to steady herself. Then she bent over and started crying, her breaths shallow and desperate. What had she done?

Justin ran, Mandy in his arms. He hadn't gone far before she stirred, but he stopped anyway, hoping they were safe to rest for a moment.

"Mandy, baby, are you okay?"

She blinked, swallowed once, then nodded, looking around. He set her down on the ground. "Yes, I . . . I think so."

Justin's shoulders relaxed. "It's so good to hear your voice, babe."

Still lying on the ground, Mandy blinked up at him then smiled. "You, too. I guess I scared you pretty good, didn't I?"

Justin just nodded.

"So what do we do now?" Mandy stood carefully, Justin's hand steadying her.

Justin looked at the multitude of bookshelves surrounding them as he helped her to her feet. "I'm not sure. But I think they need our help." He nodded back the way they came.

Mandy bit her lip. "Yes, but . . ."

"But what?"

Mandy sighed. "Justin, that tiny young girl there almost killed me. There's an army of men—not to mention the Elders, probably history's most powerful group of men—and a crew of superpowered freaks waiting to kill us! Kayla's gone crazy, Holun and Yatzil are who-knows-where, and Na-um probably took off and is never coming back! When do we catch a break?" Then she looked down at the ground, whispering her next words. "How do we even fight this?"

Justin put an arm around her and pulled her close, kissing the top of her head. "First of all, baby, the Elders are not history's most powerful group of men—the Old Ones were. And we have their power. Second, Grady will stop Kayla; I'm sure of it, or I wouldn't have left him there, right? Third, Holun and Yatzil are here, somewhere, and fourth, Na-um's probably already on his way." He grinned. "So we fight. We go back and help Kayla and Grady, we use the Power of the Codex to stop Shani, stop Steven, stop those kids, stop the Elders, stop the army before any of them can kill us. Okay?"

Mandy looked up at him for a brief moment then leaned in for a kiss. "You always know just what to say, don't you?"

Justin grinned at her, glad she was back to her normal self. "Of course."

Mandy smiled back. "Okay, babe, let's do it." She took his hand and pulled him back the way they came.

Where is she taking us? Holun wondered as he followed Yatzil between bookcases, down aisles, weaving in and out of an endless array of ancient artifacts. Holun idly thought it would be fun to spend a good deal of time down here, exploring this place, seeing what all these objects could do—when their friends weren't in danger, of course.

Then she stopped at the edge of a shelf, abruptly, and Holun ran into her. "Oh! Sorry . . ." he muttered.

Yatzil just smiled back at him then peered around the shelf. Something had caught her attention.

For a moment, Yatzil was perfectly still. After Holun waited for what seemed like an eternity, he opened his mouth to ask what she saw just as she whispered "there" and pointed.

Holun followed her outstretched hand and saw an odd, blue-lit room through the clear windows. A man was in there, looking down at something—a desk, perhaps—and muttering to himself. Holun couldn't tell from this angle as his face was completely in shadow, but he thought he looked oddly familiar . . .

Yatzil pulled Holun back and continued whispering, this time in K'iche. "That man that stopped us earlier, the one who looked like he'd been burned with acid . . ."

Holun nodded, realizing then why that man looked so familiar.

Yatzil continued. "I've been thinking a lot about him, where he came from. I realized that since the globe is turning people, whoever was working here when it was brought in was probably susceptible to its powers. It just made sense to me that he was the one, since we didn't recognize him. I thought I'd take a shot and come back here, see if he'd returned to his office." She glanced over her shoulder at the man, who was now looking over the warehouse through the large glass windows. Yatzil pulled Holun farther behind the bookshelf, fully out of sight. She must've let down her shield for now.

Abruptly, Holun leaned over and kissed Yatzil right on the lips. She blinked up at him.

He smiled. "You're adorable. I love the way your mind works."

Yatzil kissed him back then pulled away, smiling. "Well, my brilliant mind found him. Any ideas about how to get him to help us without getting burned?"

Justin, Mandy . . . Kayla's words sounded strangled in Mandy's head. She seemed to be back to her normal self, but something was clearly wrong. *What happened?*

Kayla? What is it? Justin responded first.

We . . . Kayla paused. *Grady needs your help.* Mandy could hear her fighting off tears.

Mandy glanced over at Justin, their eyes wide before they both started running.

Grady was on the floor to the far right at the Elders' feet. Steven's punches—always unexpected and unseen—were getting tiresome.

But he could deal with that. It was so much easier than dealing with the Elders, Shani's nearly unstoppable powers, even Alexia's cruel power. And he was right here in the middle of all of it. Alone.

But he wasn't alone, right?

As if on cue, he heard Kayla call out for him, heard her voice in his thoughts. He waited for the sound of her voice to calm him down, but her thoughts were scattered and fractured, which just scared him more.

Grady lifted to his hands and knees, staring at the bottom hem of the white robe of the Elder nearest him. He raised his head slowly, looking up at the man who was staring down at him with his black eyes narrowed, his muscled arms crossed. Grady certainly wouldn't be getting any sympathy from this guy.

He crawled away from the Elder on his hands and knees then scrambled to his feet just in time to see Shani, looking completely sane and wholly satisfied with herself, limping toward Kayla, black box in one hand, her other hand clutching at her chest. He caught Kayla's gaze just before Shani reached her, and Kayla's eyes were frenzied and wide. Grady drew in a sharp breath as Shani touched her.

And Kayla disappeared.

CHAPTER 37

Wrong Must Be Made Right

JUSTIN AND MANDY ENTERED the large space at full, superhuman speed then skidded to a stop at the same time. Mandy spotted Grady first on the far side of the space. Even at this distance, she could see something was very wrong. *Grady! Are you okay?* Mandy shouted through her mind. When he didn't answer, she scanned the room. *Where's Kayla?*

She could tell Grady heard her, but he wasn't answering. Instead, she saw his shoulders slump, his gaze dropping to the floor.

Without a thought, she sped toward him, Justin on her heels.

Justin reached Grady just behind Mandy, and they flanked him as they jerked to a stop. Grady was staring at an empty spot in the large expanse, which made no sense to him.

Until it did.

Where did Kayla go, Grady? Where is she?

Grady just kept staring.

Grady? Snap out of it! We need your help to find her! Justin felt as though he'd lost both of them at this point, so he reached out to Grady, grabbing him by the shoulders and shaking him.

Grady finally looked over at him, but his eyes were devoid of life. *Justin, she's . . . Shani took her.*

Mandy chimed in, putting her hand on his shoulder. *Grady, we will find her. You won't lose her again. Not after all you've been through.*

Grady nodded, but something told Justin he wasn't buying it.

Justin pursed his lips together, thinking. They needed a plan of attack; they needed to go on the offensive. Everything they'd done until now had been in response to Shani's attacks, Alexia's attacks, Steven's, Tyler's, Akna's, even the army's. They'd gone on the defensive, gotten distracted. But Justin realized that if they were to pool their power, really gather it to them and use it, they would be unstoppable. That's how the Power of the Codex worked, right?

Mandy was staring at him, listening to his train of thought. She was nodding.

Grady? Justin asked. *Will you help us? This is the only way we can get Kayla back.*

Grady blinked at him then nodded slowly.

Justin smiled, just a little. *Okay, I know what to do.*

I'm listening, Grady sent back.

Grady, work on a waterfall, get it really flowing around us.
Grady nodded. *Mandy, when I give you the signal, put up a shield around us. Do you think you're up for that?*

Mandy nodded. *What are you going to do?*

Justin just grinned.

Kayla was in a cold, dark place, sitting on the ground, but she wasn't back in the underground cave where Alexia had dropped her. This was very real—she could feel Shani next to her.

"Shani, where are we?" She couldn't help herself.

Shani's grip tightened on her arm. "Shh!" she whispered loudly. "We wouldn't want them to discover where we are, would we?"

Kayla had the thought that she really *would* like that and smiled to herself.

Then it occurred to Kayla that she hadn't felt them actually go anywhere, hadn't felt them move. She realized abruptly that they were in the exact same spot she was when Shani grabbed her. She tested out her theory, reached her hand blindly in front of her, felt a large crack in the cement she knew she'd put there only a few minutes ago. So why couldn't she see anything? Where had everyone gone?

Where had *they* gone?

Yatzil approached the wall next to the windows in a circuitous route, shield down. She didn't want them to just suddenly appear and scare him. For all she knew, that's what activated his power.

She reached the door next to the windows, guessing that was how to get into that glassed-in room. She motioned for Holun to stay outside the door and keep watch then twisted the handle slowly, as quietly as she could, and stepped inside.

She wasn't sure what she expected—maybe a small hallway that led to another door into the room—but the door had opened into that bluish room, and the man startled. Yatzil felt the now-familiar, horrific burning start searing through her veins.

Yatzil called out to the man as she hunched over from the now-debilitating pain, her hands out in front of her in surrender. "Please!" she cried in her native tongue, hoping he'd understand. "Stop!"

The man stared, then Yatzil felt the burning drain from her insides. She took a deep breath, stood up straight, and held her hands up. The burning wasn't gone, but it was manageable. "I just wanted to talk to you."

The man's eyes grew wide, and he answered her in K'iche. "Me?" His voice was raspy, but she could understand him clearly.

Yatzil nodded as the burning faded away. "Me and the other man you saw me with. He is just outside, waiting for us." Yatzil swallowed, lowering her hands slowly. "I am Yatzil; he is Holun." She motioned toward the door with her head and smiled to underline her words. "What is your name?"

"P-Paulo . . ." the man stuttered, blinking at her.

Yatzil dropped her hands to her sides. "Nice to meet you, Paulo. We need your help."

Grady had started building the waterfall, his arms leading the flow of water into what was turning out to be a large stream in the middle of the room. The makeshift torrent cut the army off from them, blocking any attempts the remaining soldiers—who were only now starting to recover from Kayla's onslaught—may try to get back at them.

Grady was trying to remain hopeful, optimistic even, and knew that working with Justin and Mandy on this was their best shot. But he couldn't help but miss Kayla, couldn't help but think that they'd be so much stronger if she was just here to help them.

He could feel Justin watching him from a few feet away, waiting to implement whatever the next phase was of his plan. He'd gotten bits and pieces in his thoughts, but he didn't think the plan was fully formed yet, so he wasn't entirely sure what Justin was going to do.

Yeah, me neither came from Justin, and he smirked. Grady just looked over at him and shook his head as he controlled the water, coaxing it toward the ceiling.

If you boys are ready for me . . . Mandy stepped forward.

No, babe, not quite yet, Grady heard Justin tell her.

What was he planning?

Tohil leaned back, arms crossed, watching everything take place with the rest of the Elders who'd come here with him. Shani had disappeared with Kayla, the army was holding back and looking more and more unsure of themselves with every passing moment, and the young kids Shani'd brought with her were cowering against the wall of weapons. They would need to do something to turn this around, and quickly. The Four would soon gain the upper hand, and all would be lost.

He looked over at Bacob, who was scowling, almost growling in anticipation. Tohil knew he'd be the one itching for a fight.

Can I get involved now? Bacob asked him. Tohil had told the others to stand down and see how this played out before interfering.

Tohil shook his head once. *No,* he answered Bacob. *Not until . . .*

Until what?

A noise sounded beside them, and suddenly three new figures entered the arena. Tohil felt Bacob grin beside him, felt the army begin stirring, felt the other Elders' surprise.

His mouth went dry.

Yatzil and Holun, Paulo in tow, entered the vast arena with wide eyes. Holun surveyed the area quickly, seeing Grady's river—though it looked like he was creating a wall of water, getting higher by the second—and Justin and Mandy standing near him, but no Kayla. He saw the kids Shani'd collected and brought here—but no Shani. He saw the Elders, much too close for comfort, saw the army that was being held at bay by Grady's wall.

He grabbed Yatzil's hand at once. If they were going to help, they needed to know the plan, which meant they needed to get to the middle of the arena, and fast. She nodded at him, seeming to understand as she reached for Paulo's hand. Then they took off, sprinting toward the center of the room, pulling Paulo along with them. They reached their friends so quickly that the Elders and the army didn't even have time to react.

"Holun! Thank God!" Mandy yelled and reached to pull him into a hug. She released him quickly, hugging Yatzil before releasing her. Then she eyed their strange guest. "And who's this?"

Yatzil looked over at the man she'd brought with them. "This is Paulo. He's here to help." She grinned.

Justin smiled at their newest recruit. "Welcome. We need all the help we can get. What is your power?"

Paulo looked over at Yatzil, who answered for him. "He can burn someone from the inside out. Though I think it is all in their heads . . ."

Mandy gasped, and Holun glanced over at her. Her eyes were wide but determined. "Okay, we can definitely use that. Does he understand English, Yatzil?"

Yatzil eyed him again, then she shook her head. "I do not think so."

Mandy nodded once. "Then just tell him to be ready when we give him the signal." She looked over at the scared group of kids behind them, the army in front of them, the Elders to their side. "And be sure to tell him who the bad guys are."

Yatzil and Holun both grinned.

"Shani, come on. This is getting ridiculous." Kayla kept her voice low, but she was desperate to get out of this stalemate. Nothing seemed to be happening any time soon, and Kayla was getting tired of waiting.

"Kayla, my dear," Shani crooned, her voice low as well. "Patience is a virtue."

Kayla gritted her teeth then spoke through them. "Shani, we need to get out of here. Are you scared of us all getting back together?" She smirked in the darkness.

Shani paused, and Kayla wondered what she was thinking. "No, I believe you are scary enough all on your own. Tell me: Did you enjoy killing all those men single-handedly? Men who'd done nothing to you?"

Kayla slumped over, the arms that were around her legs dropping to the floor. Shani was right. Those men hadn't deserved to die. She could almost feel Shani sneering beside her. "Okay, then, Shani—what's your plan? Are you just going to hide here in the dark, wait for everyone else to kill each other before running away?"

Shani let out a low chuckle. "Oh no, of course not. Our time has almost come."

Kayla's stomach knotted.

Tohil was eyeing the boy, the boy he raised from such a young age, the boy he loved. The boy who was now a young man, a young man who'd betrayed his family, their Clan. A young man who'd betrayed *him*.

Holun has made his choice, Zotz's voice came to him.

Yes, I know. Tohil didn't have any other response to give him.

You must protect us, protect our secrets, Tohil. This came from Bacob, suddenly insightful.

Tohil just nodded.

What are you going to do? Bacob asked, and Tohil could feel his piercing gaze burning his skin.

Tohil sighed, staring at the scene playing out before him. Time was running out; soon they'd all have to act.

He'd just hoped it wouldn't have had to come to that.

Justin watched as Grady's wall of water expanded to nearly the ceiling, towering over the mountains Kayla'd created in her rage, the sound of its rushing water like a massive waterfall. He'd gathered the wall around them, encircling them in an impenetrable silo, protecting them from their enemies on all sides.

Now he turned to the others, holding one hand up to maintain the wall. "What now?" He looked over at Justin.

Justin's eyes fell closed in response, trying to sense what was coming next. It wasn't his power, wasn't any of their powers, but it couldn't hurt to try, right? An attack was coming any moment, and he needed to be able to anticipate it.

Then he felt it, though what "it" was exactly, he didn't know. His eyes shot open. "We have to act now."

Five pairs of wide eyes just stared at him. He started barking out orders. "The Elders will attack soon, probably give orders for the army to attack the wall, force it down. We will have to retreat toward the wall of weapons." He nodded behind him, looked over to where the group of Shani's minions still stood. He suspected Steven was with them, but he couldn't be sure. "We will have to fight them when we get there."

His face fell at the thought. They were mostly innocent in all of this; they couldn't have truly known Shani's evil intent.

"Paulo, we may have to use your power. Use it on anyone not in the circle, unless it's Kayla."

He looked at Yatzil, who set to translating.

"Mandy, if we need protection, give it. You sure you're up for it?"

She nodded.

Justin took a deep breath. "Grady, hold the wall for as long as you are able. If Kayla and Shani show up, try to get Kayla inside if you can."

He looked at Holun. "Holun, you're our eyes and ears. Try to anticipate the Elders' next moves. Try to anticipate what's coming next."

Holun nodded then slid his eyes closed.

Then he turned to the last member of their group. "Yatzil, have you figured out your powers yet?"

Yatzil nodded at him with wide eyes. "I think so."

"Okay, good. I'm not sure I understand all of it, but I think you'll know what to do when the time comes."

She smiled at him, nodding again.

"Okay, team, we've got this. Hold everyone off the best you can, and no killing unless it's necessary." He glanced over at Grady; he couldn't help it. Grady was frowning.

We'll get her back. Again, Justin sent to his friend, knowing he and Mandy could hear as well, but no one else could.

Grady nodded, but Justin wasn't convinced he believed it.

Alexia was just watching the scene playing out in front of her and her new acquaintances. She'd watched Shani disappear, watched Grady create that wall of water. Who knew he could do *that*? Though she could create someone's reality around their greatest fear, so she supposed anything was possible.

The girl, Akna, reached for her hand, and Alexia squeezed it. She supposed this was scary for a girl of her young age. No girl should have to be exposed to any of this—they'd just watched Kayla kill hundreds of her tribe, after all—and she wished she could hide her away until this was all over. But

Shani had brought them all here for a reason, and Alexia was beginning to suspect that reason wasn't good.

What did she do now? Her entire reality felt as though it were upside down. She'd trusted Shani, but Shani had disappeared at the first sign of trouble, and Alexia wasn't sure she believed in her cause anymore. She'd asked Alexia to betray her friends, her professors, the people who'd taught her everything she knew about archaeology, the people who'd given her a chance and let her help translate an ancient book. Alexia had been hesitant but had agreed when Shani told her how dangerous they all were.

Her stomach dropped, and she realized in that instant that Shani had been lying. Not about the Four being dangerous— that truth was readily apparent—but about everything else. Shani had used her and her power to torture her friends. She didn't understand much about how her power worked, but if she was able to make people live through their greatest fear, wasn't she just as bad as Shani?

She looked over at Tyler, at the boy from her school that she'd gotten to know thousands of miles away from where they both lived not even a mile apart, and wondered what he believed. His power was much more direct, more neutral. He could use his power to hurt people who wanted to hurt him.

But neither Kayla nor Grady—and certainly not Mandy or Justin—had ever wanted to hurt her. She now knew that, in the depths of her soul. Yet she'd still hurt them, attacked them because an insane, evil person had asked her to.

Though she'd tried to deny it, she felt how her subjects felt as they experienced their greatest fear. She'd tried to push it down, ignore it, but the lingering fear, their private pain, echoed in her being, reverberated in her mind, her heart, her soul.

Her power couldn't be a gift, couldn't be good. Not if it made them feel—made *her* feel—like this. She was a monster, and her power *made* her one.

She wished she'd never come here, wished she'd never let Shani into her parents' home. Wished she'd never learned about the Codex, wished she'd never seen that infernal globe.

Because if she hadn't, perhaps she'd still be back in Florida, back with her friends who only cared about which boy they liked, what clothes they'd wear to the coffee shop, the best angle for their social media selfie. Easy, simple problems.

She longed for it, pleaded with the Universe to go back. But that wasn't her power, was it?

So as she knew it wouldn't, nothing happened. She was still here with that cute guy, Tyler, the little girl, Akna, and that invisible, creepy guy, Steven.

She'd have to figure out a way out of this mess. She'd have to figure out how to get rid of this power or suppress it somehow. Or, she hoped against hope, she'd have to figure out how to use it for good. But how? It just seemed impossible.

Her mind swirled in circles, warring with the truth she only now realized—with a jolt and a lump in her throat—that she already knew: Her power was evil, and that made her evil, too.

Tohil realized, his stomach knotting, that the time had come. Shani wasn't here, but he sensed she would be soon, and she would probably be bringing Kayla back with her. Despite her enhanced powers, Shani wouldn't be able to keep Kayla away forever. The Four would be reunited, and soon they would be unstoppable.

The Four already had the Power of the Codex—that had been Fate's first mistake. Shani going after it had been an unfortunate development but not wholly surprising. The Elders had worked for years, as those who'd gone before them had, to amass the power in this warehouse not only to keep the Power in check, but also to obtain it for themselves.

The prophecies had indicated that something would happen with the Power in their lifetimes, and they'd prepared for it for decades, waited for it, prayed for the time to come. Now that it was finally here, he sensed the others couldn't wait to see their plans fulfilled.

But Tohil wasn't as sure. He'd been prepared to do whatever it took to stop the Four, stop Shani, obtain the Power for themselves. But Holun . . . that boy had gotten in the way. He'd chosen the wrong side. All the years of raising him to be a good soldier, compliant and respectful but mentally strong, he'd imagined Holun by his side when this time came.

But now . . . he'd sided with their enemies, with the keepers of the Codex's Power. The wrong choice, the wrong side. Tohil felt sick, wishing Holun had just made the right choice, chosen him, chosen their Clan.

But he hadn't. And now he must pay for it.

CHAPTER 38

The Monarch

HOLUN'S EYES FLASHED OPEN, and he saw that all eyes in their circle were on him, as if waiting for the report of what he'd seen before they'd spring into action.

It wasn't good.

"We have to go now!" he shouted then started running toward the back wall.

He felt—though he wasn't sure how—Grady struggle to keep the protective wall around him, around them as they ran, but he somehow managed. The wall of water undulated, changed, but still managed to stay up. Holun was grateful. He'd seen what would happen if it came down.

They managed to get to the back wall, Grady's wall of water now adjusting to cover them on three sides. He included Shani's crew inside, and Holun looked over at them just as his jaw connected with something very hard, something like . . . Steven's fist.

Holun went flying across their safety zone, almost into the wall of water. He sensed Steven coming for him, and he scrambled out of the way. Yatzil was screaming, running toward him.

The boy, Tyler, opened his mouth and screamed toward the water. Holun looked up in time to see Grady fighting to keep it up, teeth clenched, hands in the air, veins standing out on his forehead. He started growling with the effort.

Holun rolled out of the way of Steven's fist. He didn't know how he'd anticipated it—maybe his power was growing?

Yatzil was at his side now and fell down next to him. "Yatzil, don't . . ." he eked out before rolling the opposite direction to miss Steven's fist again. Steven connected with Yatzil's shoulder—Holun almost felt the punch as he watched her shoulder shoot backward—and she yelped and skidded across the cement floor.

Holun screamed and leapt to his feet, flying into a run as Yatzil crashed into the hard rock wall. He closed his eyes for a brief second, anticipating Steven's next move, before forcing his eyes open and his fist into Steven's face. A growl emanated from the empty space in front of him, and Holun ran over to Yatzil before Steven could recoup.

"Yatzil, are you okay?" He bent down beside her, reaching for her arm.

She nodded, out of breath, just as he felt the air preceding Steven's fist reach the back of his neck. He tried to jerk out of the way, but Steven caught the side of his head, and Holun's vision blurred as he fell at Yatzil's side.

"Holun, get up!" Yatzil screamed at him, the panic evident in her voice. "Get up, my Holun!" Holun could feel her hands on him, pulling on his shirt, but they felt far away.

Then Steven's fist connected with his chest, and his world went dark.

Tohil called to Bacob, not bothering to use their telepathy. That didn't matter now. "Bacob, activate the men. Now."

Tohil watched an utterly sinister grin spread across Bacob's face as he moved to stand in front of the rest of the army, barking out an order of attack. The men, loyal to the end, cheered in unison, a mind-numbing war cry. Collectively, they raised their swords, their bows, their shields, as they charged toward their prey.

Paulo and Justin were working on Tyler and Akna, trying to keep them from hurting their friends further. Justin didn't see Alexia as a wave of fire blazed from his fingertips; he supposed she was in a corner somewhere, staying out of the way. Just as well.

Tyler yelled but cut off abruptly as Paulo glared at him. Justin looked over at his new friend and smiled. Paulo grinned back then lifted his attack, stepping away from the boy and turning toward Akna, who promptly started screaming.

Tyler was still writhing on the ground.

Shani's grip tightened on Kayla's arm, and Kayla sensed something was coming. She'd have to act fast; the others would need her. She couldn't contact them here—undoubtedly Shani's doing—but hopefully when she returned she could hear them, find them quickly, and move to help them.

"Okay, my dear, brace yourself." Shani's words came just before Kayla blinked and the world returned to normal.

The effect was dizzying—had she felt that when she'd gone in? Kayla stumbled to her feet, blinking at the sudden light, trying to make sense of what she was seeing. Where were the others?

Then she spotted the wall of water at the back of the room, spied Grady's dark-blue shirt through the water. She cried out his name, but he didn't even turn and look her way.

So she started running for him, calling out for him in her mind, trying to reach his thoughts.

She didn't know why Shani just let her go, but she couldn't think about that now. All that mattered was that Grady needed her. She knew how hard it was for him to keep something up like that, and given what little she could see through the wall—bodies flying around, running, jumping, crashing—he would need her help.

She reached the wall of water, put her hand up to it, but she couldn't get through. She yelled again at the top of her lungs. "Grady!"

Nothing.

What was going on?

She glanced back at Shani, who was sneering at her, and at the army of men that was circling around her as they sprinted toward Grady's wall.

Kayla's heart thudded in her chest as she backed up, stopped by the wall of water at her back, frozen by the wall of men coming directly for her.

"Grady!" Mandy yelled, jumping again out of the way of Tyler's attack. She'd already been thrown across the space twice by his power—she didn't care to go through that again. "I think . . ." She jumped in the air to avoid the metal shards Akna had just hurled her way. The shards struck the wall of water then fell to the ground. Grady flinched, but the wall held. "I think Kayla's back!"

At her words, Grady flipped around, gazed outside the wall.

Just beyond it, Kayla stood, her back to them. He screamed her name, but she didn't turn around.

Mandy ran toward Akna, not wanting to hurt the girl but realizing that she had to be stopped—she'd nearly decapitated Justin in her last attack, and that would not stand. She barreled into her, forcing her into the wall of water to their right, holding her up against its impenetrable shield. Grady clenched his teeth. "Mandy! I can't hold this much longer, and you're making it more difficult!" He was breathing hard, sweat dripping from his forehead.

Mandy pulled the girl away from the water and threw her against the rock wall, not quite as hard as she probably could have. She didn't want to kill her. She glanced over at where Kayla stood then finally saw beyond her, and her heart leapt into her throat. "Grady, get Kayla in here. NOW!"

He looked over at her tone then followed her gaze. She watched all the blood drain from his face.

Grady didn't know how to let down just one portion of the wall. He'd been holding it up for so long, he was losing strength. It would have to be all or nothing.

Taking down the wall with an army of hundreds of men barreling toward them would almost certainly be suicide for all of them. But not taking the wall down would mean Kayla would get the full force of the army on her alone. The army who'd just watched her kill hundreds of their fellow soldiers.

He couldn't lose her like that. He couldn't lose her again.

"The wall is coming down now!" Grady yelled, hoping Justin, Mandy, Holun, Yatzil, and Paulo could hold their own. He took a deep breath, forcing the last reserves of his power to him, then released the water toward the men, arcing it around Kayla's body, hoping to at least slow the army down so his friends would have time to regroup.

As soon as the wall was down, he ran to Kayla. She turned to him, flying into his arms, sobbing. "Grady, you're okay!" She kissed him hard, long, and Grady forgot for just a second about the army of men about to descend on them.

Then he heard Justin yell behind him. "Mandy, now!" And suddenly he felt a forcefield erupt from Mandy, a translucent, flickering shield that surrounded their group and cut off the sound of the pursuing army abruptly. Grady breathed a sigh as the world seemed to get quiet.

"Thank you, Mandy. I owe you."

She simply nodded, struggling just as he had to keep the shield up as the front line of the army came up against it and fell away. Then one took his sword and jabbed it into the shield.

Mandy cried out, her arm suddenly bleeding, but she kept her hands out and the shield up. Justin ran over to her. "Grady, do something! They're going to kill her!"

Another jab, a knife this time, and Mandy screamed, falling to her knees, blood spreading under her shirt on the left side of her torso. "GRADY!" Justin screamed.

"Wait." Yatzil's soft word froze them all in place. Grady looked back at her as she stood up and walked forward. Holun stirred beside her but didn't wake up. "I can do this."

Grady blinked at her. "Do what?"

She placed her hand on Grady's shoulder. "I have got this. Mandy"—she looked back at her new friend—"lower the shield."

Mandy blinked at her then nodded. "You ready?"

Yatzil nodded solemnly.

Just as Mandy raised her hands, preparing to lower the shield, Grady heard Holun stir again behind them. And as the others stepped back and the shield went down, Holun screamed out a long "Nooooo!!" as he watched the woman he loved stand and face the ferocious army alone.

Yatzil stared at the men in front of her, only yards away, who were just staring right back with wide eyes, frozen. She knew she didn't have much time before they attacked.

She held up one hand and spoke in their native tongue, calling her power to enhance the volume of her voice, which boomed in the large space. "Men, please listen to me! You have been deceived." The men exchanged confused glances, started murmuring. "The Elders are not who we were taught to believe they were. They brought you all here to fight the true keepers of the Codex and its Power! They brought you here so you would kill them and they could take the Power for themselves!"

Yatzil knew that talking like this was liable to get her killed. She could sense the glares of the Elders as she planted doubt in the men's minds. She had to hurry.

The room was nearly silent as she continued. "Please, listen to me! The globe these four discovered last year at the First Site—it was *meant* for them to find. It has changed several of us, given us powers. The Codex was found to help the globe carry out its purpose on this earth, and these Four have been given the Power to ensure the globe is successful!"

She glanced around at the army, worried she might not be holding their attention, worried they might not believe her. "I know this is true, because it has happened to me." Yatzil took a deep breath as the murmuring continued. "I have power as well, power I was given to stop the Elders from obtaining the Power of the Codex." She steeled herself then closed her eyes and leaned down on one knee, her opposite fist on the ground. Then she called the full force of her power to her, feeling the lightning rod shoot through her again, and she exploded into the air.

Tohil stared up at the girl who was trying to turn their army against them and felt the blood drain from his face. The other Elders' thoughts began to jumble in his head.

No, it can't be . . .

The prophecy . . .

Not . . . no . . .

Zotz seemed to be the first to come to his senses and silenced the others. He looked over at Tohil, caught his gaze, then resolutely issued his command. "The time is now."

Holun watched as Yatzil launched herself into the air, her awe-inspiring, swirling, ebony wings shooting out on either side of her. The dim light and enclosed space in that tiny cabin hadn't done them justice. Now they were fully extended, easily seven or eight feet on either side of her, dazzling and expansive in the wide open space. Holun froze, awestruck. They all were. The army stared into the air above their heads, staring at her, every eye wide and mouth open.

Holun heard the men murmuring, their mouths still open and staring, and heard a few of them mutter "*b'alamax*" as they stared. *Butterfly?* Holun wondered why they would call her that. The wings looked more like an angel's to him.

But then something came to him, a memory that seemed like a lifetime ago, and all the pieces fell into place. Holun's stomach dropped, then his mind started swirling.

Her powers.

She could float, could fly.

She could call any power to herself, give herself any power she desired.

She was beautiful, breathtaking. She was basically unstoppable.

Important, vital to their cause.

The Codex. The prophecy.

The *prophecy*.

And he realized he hadn't remembered that word's full translation correctly: The men weren't talking about just any butterfly—they were talking about a *monarch* butterfly.

Holun swallowed hard, realizing in this moment that everything in his life, everything in the *world* had changed.

Yatzil was the Monarch.

Shani watched Yatzil's wings expand, and, as she did, something gnawed at her subconscious, a distant memory. Something she'd studied in the Clan's histories . . . what was it? An ancient prophecy?

Yes.

Shani staggered and fell to her knees as she remembered the exact prophecy, the one about the Monarch, the One who would save the world.

Then she heard a noise to her right and looked up. She first saw Chac, smiling ever-so-kindly at her, then her eyes grew wide as she recognized the man beside him.

Her face went white. Alex was here.

"A-Alex? Shani stuttered tentatively, staggering to her feet and walking toward him, the artifact still in her hand. Though at this point, with the Four back together and Yatzil's powers on full display, she suspected it would be utterly useless against them. "What . . . what are you doing here?"

Alex looked over at her briefly then turned back to the obvious focal point in the arena. "I—what is *that*?"

Shani followed his gaze to the young woman floating in the air, addressing the army of their Clan. An inexplicable pride filled her, and Shani almost smiled. "That is Yatzil."

Alex gasped, and Shani noticed Chac's eyebrows furrow. They really didn't know, did they? The Elders truly didn't know who Yatzil was.

Then Chac's eyes grew wide, and Shani knew he'd figured it out. His mouth was moving, but nothing came out. Shani didn't think any Elder had ever been rendered speechless.

But it didn't last long. "Shani, is she . . . ?"

Shani nodded, crossing the distance to Alex's side and slipping an arm around him, loving the feeling as she did. "Yes, Chac." She paused, looking over at Yatzil, then glancing

up at Alex before turning back to Chac. "Yatzil is our daughter."

CHAPTER 39

The Battle to End the War

KAYLA WAS SPEECHLESS.

Yatzil had wings?! When did that happen? She was grateful that she'd calmed the men down, caused them to doubt their leaders, but how had she been hiding this?

Perhaps it was a new development. She glanced over at Holun, who was staring at her but didn't really seem surprised at her appearance. Though something else seemed to be bothering him . . .

Grady, she tried, not certain it would work, but thought it couldn't hurt to try. She hadn't heard him in her head since Shani'd whisked her away, and she hadn't tried since she'd been back.

Kayla? His voice reached her. *Oh, thank God. I thought I'd lost you again.*

Never again. She smiled. *What's the plan?*

Yes, what do we do? Mandy's voice broke into their thoughts.

Mandy! Kayla exhaled. *Is Justin here, too?*

Of course, my lady.

Kayla rolled her eyes. *We need to plan our next step now, while everyone's still in shock. Yatzil can't hold them off forever.*

Or maybe she can. Grady's words froze them in their tracks.

Really? Mandy was staring up at the girl.

Grady sighed. *Guys, remember the second prophecy?*

Kayla blinked, thinking back, then she froze as she remembered it. She felt the blood drain from her face. *The Monarch . . .*

She felt the realization shoot through her chest again when Mandy and Justin figured it out.

What does this mean? Justin asked.

Grady glanced over at Kayla. *It means we cannot let her die.*

Of course, Grady! Mandy yelled. *That was a given from the beginning.*

But it also means that we might.

Justin's words made Kayla's blood run cold. If Yatzil was the Monarch and was revealed now, right now . . . the third prophecy came to her in an unwanted rush. *"The Four will be substantially and irreversibly transformed as a result of the Battle, and survival is unlikely."*

Kayla grabbed Grady's hand as they all turned to stare at the girl who'd stolen Holun's heart, the sixteen-year-old girl who now held their fate—and the fate of the entire world—in her hands.

Yatzil wasn't sure what came next. The army of men below her seemed to believe her, or seemed to be willing to, at least. She lowered herself to the ground slowly, her wings disappearing as her feet touched the ground.

"Please, go back to your homes. Enough people have died here tonight."

For a moment, she thought they might actually listen to her. But then she heard a voice from the side, a voice she recognized as Bacob's though she couldn't see him any longer. "No, my dear, not nearly enough."

Yatzil froze, ice flowing through her veins. Holun came up beside her and grabbed her hand.

The men in front of them parted as Bacob and three other Elders came toward them. Yatzil kept an expressionless mask on her face, the one she'd perfected in that cave with Shani just last night. Holun squeezed her hand.

"Hello, you two. So nice of you to join us all here." Bacob waved a hand around the wide space. "But I'm afraid your claims have fallen on deaf ears. The men here want to serve us." Yatzil eyed the army, looked into their eyes. They didn't look like they wanted to stay and fight. What was Bacob talking about? She looked over at Holun, who caught her gaze with a confused look in his eyes that she knew matched her own.

Then Zotz and Chac came forward together from where they stood with Shani and the man who'd just arrived, splitting the crowd and standing beside the other Elders. Zotz lifted the amulet from his neck and returned it to Chac, who draped it over his head.

Chac looked over at the Four, who stood just off to the right. "I know you all were looking for this," he touched the amulet around his neck, "and you were right to want it. It would have stopped Shani's mind control, helped Grady get his memories back." He smirked at them. "But it's so much more powerful than that." He picked up the amulet between his thumb and forefinger and pressed the sides together. A bright white light shot out from the front, and the Four, Yatzil and Holun, Paulo, and Shani's crew all shielded their eyes from it. Chac turned toward the army, letting the light wash over them as Yatzil looked up.

She watched as the men's expressions all changed as soon as the light passed over them. Suddenly they were angry, ferocious, eyes hungry and teeth gnashing, eager to rip apart whatever stood in their way.

"Yatzil, we need to go *now*," Holun whispered beside her.

He saw Yatzil squint at him out of the corner of his eye. "But the Four . . ."

Holun glanced over at the group in question. Kayla caught his eye and nodded at him. She clearly knew, as he did, that protecting Yatzil was their number one priority. "They've got this. Any way you can get us out of here?"

Yatzil just nodded. She leaned down again, placing one knee and the opposite fist on the ground, her other hand still gripping Holun's . . . then Holun felt himself disappear.

What's the plan, guys? Mandy was staring wide-eyed at the now-bloodthirsty army in front of them.

Kayla reached for her hand, reached for Grady's on her other side. Mandy sensed what she was trying to accomplish and grabbed Justin's hand.

Now.

The Four called the Power of the Codex to them, closing their eyes and opening themselves up to the Power like never before, as one. Anything their minds conjured up to doubt the Power dissolved in the force of their will. Any personal issues, problems, questions they had melted away. And all that was left was the Power of the Codex, pure light and energy swirling through the air in yellow, glowing arcs, flowing through their veins.

It took them over, filled them up, consumed them entirely. Their thoughts coalesced as one, one mind, one consciousness.

They faced the army, faced the Elders, and their eyes opened simultaneously. They all heard the thoughts of the army facing them, heard the thoughts of Shani's crew behind them, heard Shani and Alex and even the Elders as they stared wide-eyed at them.

They heard in those thoughts that their eyes were consumed—Kayla's with sand, Grady's with water, Justin's with fire, and Mandy's with wind—as they now glared, their vision clearer than it had ever been, at the people who stood in their way.

No longer.

"ATTACK!" Bacob yelled, and suddenly the room exploded. The men charged the Four, hundreds at a time. Some fell with Kayla's blast of earth, some in Justin's rain of fire. Some drowned in Grady's torrent, some of their throats collapsed under the force of Mandy's wind. The army was losing men quickly. Again.

Shani could not let this stand. The Power of the Codex now being displayed so fearlessly terrified her. She was supposed to be the all-powerful one, the one who deserved the Codex's Power. It was rightfully hers. Forget Na-um—he wasn't even here to help. This was her birthright alone.

"Shani, what's going on?"

She ignored Alex's question—she didn't have time for him at the moment. She knew that what he saw here tonight would be hard to erase from his mind, but she couldn't think about that right now. She needed to survive, needed to get the Power for herself. He could wait.

But to do that, she had to separate the Four. And she knew how.

She pinched her necklace between her fingers, watching it glow red and shield her from view, and she ran toward the girl, toward Alexia. This was her only shot.

Kayla shot a missile of earth from her right hand into the closest Elder as another screamed his name. "Bacob!" He went flying across the room, his white robes flowing around him. He flew into a mountain she'd created, smacking it hard at about two stories up, then crashed to the earth with a sickening snap. She felt Grady beside her, flowing a constant stream of water into Justin's torrent, creating a liquid fire, lava that sucked the men in and quickly silenced their screams.

She saw Mandy abruptly squeezing her hands in front of her, again and again, and Kayla realized she was cutting off air, crushing windpipes of those she'd set her sights on.

The battle was vicious, brutal. But Kayla couldn't stop. She didn't want to. The Power was all-consuming, and it was *theirs*. No need to hold back now.

But a small yet persistent voice sounded in the back of her head: Were they taking this too far?

Shani didn't let down her shield until she was right in front of Alexia. The girl yelped when she appeared in front of her, and Shani clamped her hand over her mouth. No time for niceties now; the Four couldn't figure out her plan.

"Alexia, you will help me now."

"No, Shani, I won't! I can't!"

Shani reached for her insurance, the gun sheathed at the small of her back, and shoved it in Alexia's face, pressing it to her forehead. "You. Will. Help. Me. Now."

Alexia, eyes wide and full of sheer terror, nodded frantically.

Mandy telepathically held the throat of Zotz, the one she now knew was the oldest, the most respected. She held him above the ground, several feet in the air, ready to drop him in the next instant.

Then Kayla yelled out. "STOP!"

Mandy froze, and she sensed Justin and Grady do the same. "What?!" Grady yelled back. "Stop what?"

Kayla shot a stream of earth at Grady and Justin's lava, cooling it instantly, stopping it from reaching a group of men anxiously scurrying away from it.

"We have to stop this!" Kayla yelled again, and Mandy set Zotz down—not pleasantly, but not fatally, either.

"Why, Kayla?" Mandy asked, walking over to her, eyeing the army who was still struggling to regroup.

Kayla was crying, tears staining her cheeks. "The Power has taken us over. We are being cruel, merciless, ruthless. No one deserves to die like this."

Justin crossed his arms near her. "I disagree."

Kayla was pleading now. "Please! This is how I felt earlier, when I killed all those men." She wiped away a stray tear. "I think this is what the prophecy was about."

Grady walked over to her, sighing, clearly impatient. "What prophecy, Kayla?"

"The one that talked about our survival! This is what it meant! It meant our true selves—our good, human selves— would not survive! If we continue like this, we will lose ourselves in the Power. It happened to the Old Ones so long ago, when they let the Power take them over, when they destroyed their people. And it could happen to us."

Mandy looked around, blinking. Then suddenly she felt herself jolted out of it. Abruptly, she felt the force of the pain of everyone she'd killed, everyone whose life she'd choked right out of them. She'd heard their thoughts as they died, as much as she'd tried to ignore them.

The weight of what she'd done came down on her with crushing force, and she fell to the ground, gasping for air.

Then she was back in the Stanfords' home, back in their kitchen, staring at Justin's lifeless body in the face. Only it wasn't Justin anymore.

It was her.

CHAPTER 40

Death Is Not the End

MANDY RAN; SHE DIDN'T KNOW what else to do. She ran from the house, out the front door, down the porch steps, out to the lawn. She ran until she didn't recognize anything any more, faster than she'd ever run.

Mandy! Come back to me!

She froze, confused. What . . . ?

But Justin's voice had broken through her vision, and suddenly she was back in the warehouse, surrounded by bookcases filled with ancient artifacts, Justin at her side. He must've followed her, stayed by her side as she ran away from the effects of her vision. She pulled him into a hug, holding him tight.

Then a shot rang out, and Mandy slumped in his arms.

"Mandy!" Justin screamed, following her to the floor. The woman he loved more than anything else in the world lay on the ground, a pool of blood forming beneath her. Her face was contorted, her lips moving noiselessly. She stared up at Justin, and he saw the pain there, the misery that was gripping her.

But he noticed something else, too. Something that was tearing into his chest and ripping his heart out piece by bloody piece.

The light in her eyes was going out. Slowly, so slowly, but definitely disappearing. "NOOO!!" Justin anguished, his cry piercing the silence the gunshot had left in its wake. He grabbed her hand. "Mandy, baby, no! Stay with me. Please, baby . . . I can't . . . please don't make me do this without you. Please stay. Please fight. I can't do any of this without you."

Mandy's eyes held his, and Justin saw a strength there he'd never seen before. A will to live, a will to fight. Her thoughts were jumbled and incoherent as Mandy fought the wound, fought the ensuing death.

But she was losing the battle, and there was nothing Justin could do to stop it.

Shani walked up the aisle toward Mandy and Justin, toward where her gunshot had hit its mark, the gun still smoking in her outstretched hand. The smile on her face spread as she closed the distance.

The shot had done just as she intended; her plan had been executed almost perfectly. Mandy was on the ground, blood leaking from a gaping wound, minutes from death.

She hoped it hurt. She hoped Mandy felt all the pain Shani'd felt over the years, the pain of loss, the pain of struggle. The pain of death.

She walked up to Justin, sneering, and pointed the gun at him. "Hello, Justin."

Justin slowly lifted his head up, his red, tearstained eyes staring daggers into hers. "Shani." He clenched his teeth, grinding her name out between them. "You will die for this. I will kill you myself."

Shani just nodded once. In the next instant, Justin's head fell backward, followed by the rest of his body. He howled at the pain.

She grinned as Steven invisibly grabbed his shirt, pulling him to his feet just so he could punch him again, forcing him again to the cement floor.

Satisfied Justin wouldn't be a problem, Shani turned her attention to the woman on the ground, the woman she'd spent years working alongside.

Mandy was struggling to breathe against the hole in her torso. "Wh . . . why, Shani?" she sputtered.

Shani stomped her foot on Mandy's wound, and Mandy cried out, an agonizing scream that she knew Justin felt to his core. She saw him lurch toward Mandy from her right, but Steven caught him with a right hook before he could get far.

Shani grinned down at Mandy as she saw the light start to leave her eyes. "Because you have what I want."

"Wh . . . what do you want?" Mandy coughed, wincing as a fresh flow of blood poured from her wound from beneath Shani's foot.

"Your power. All of it. I deserve it. It should have always been mine."

Justin shouted beside her where he strained against Steven, who was holding his arms roughly behind his back.

"Shani! You can have all of it! We don't want it! Just let her live!"

Shani stomped down on the wound again, but Mandy didn't respond. Just as well. She looked down at Mandy where she lay motionless on the ground.

"Noooo . . ." Justin's strangled words met her ears as he fell to his knees on the cement, several feet away from the woman he loved, Steven's arms still holding his captive.

Shani lifted her foot, wiped it on the cement, and nodded to Steven, who promptly dropped Justin. Shani walked back down the aisle, leaving behind the man she'd successfully taken everything from. She grinned, cocking the hammer of the gun she still held, speeding up into a run. Kayla was next.

Yatzil had taken Holun back into the dark room, the room that held the globe. She didn't know why; it was just the place she'd thought to go first. And something had been nagging at the back of her mind, something that told her she needed the globe. For what, she didn't know.

But it had just started glowing, different than before, and she just stared at it. Why was it doing that? Perhaps this was why she'd felt drawn here.

Then she had another vision, but this one wasn't like her others, those that had come to her in a dream or those that she'd called. This one came from the globe; she could sense it. And it told her that Mandy was dying.

She gasped, staggering backward against a wall of empty shelves.

"Yatzil?" Holun called, reaching for her.

"I have to go, now. Mandy needs me." Yatzil got down on one knee, one hand touching the ground. She grabbed Holun's hand and squeezed once, quickly letting go. Then she was no longer in the dark room.

She was kneeling beside Mandy's unmoving body, beside Justin's crumpled form next to her. She blinked from the shock of it but then quickly jumped into action. She didn't have much time.

Steven staggered up the aisle, fighting the nausea that threatened to overtake him, biting back the tears. She'd gone too far this time. He'd been all about the fighting, all about revenge, but Shani had taken it too far. She'd killed that lady, Mandy, in front of the man she loved. He'd killed Hannah, sure, but he *never* would've done it in front of Simón, no matter how much he hated him. It was too cruel.

But . . . he wasn't much better, was he? The lives he'd taken, the things he'd done in the past several weeks . . .

Mandy didn't deserve what she'd gotten, and that man who loved her, Justin, didn't deserve it, either.

Steven sighed, suddenly realizing what he had to do, finally figuring out the only logical end to this scenario. Shani was too powerful for him to take out, but he sensed her day was coming soon. He would leave that to someone more powerful than he was.

But it really didn't matter, whatever happened to her. She was someone else's problem now. He'd control what he could, make his last act the right one, the courageous one. After all, *he* was the one that deserved to die.

He sped up, running toward the arena at full speed.

Holun just stared, the sudden absence of Yatzil shocking but not surprising, considering how they'd gotten here. But where did she go?

Then, in one horrible moment of clarity, he knew exactly where she was. Something had happened to Mandy, and Yatzil had gone to help her. He felt a knot form in his stomach.

Holun wasn't sure what to do next. He was alone in this dark room and wasn't sure when—or even if—Yatzil was coming back.

He closed his eyes and quickly saw a vision of Mandy and Justin, saw Yatzil at their side, confirming what he'd thought. What he'd said back at Lamanai still stood—he had to take care of Yatzil. If anything happened to her, he didn't know what he'd do. But he didn't want to find out.

So he slowly opened the door to the small, dark room, tentatively sticking his head outside before making his way out. Then, as quietly as he could manage, he made his way back up the aisle, looking for any way to get to Mandy and Justin. To get to Yatzil.

The Four had split up, stopped their attack for now, but who knew how long that would last? Tohil ordered the remaining army to retreat, gathered Shani's remaining recruits—Tyler and Akna—and ordered them back to the entrance, back outside, away from this fatal place. He even ushered Paulo out in a hurry. They all left without argument.

Now on to his assignment. Mandy and Justin had disappeared, Shani was gone, Alex was staring—clearly dumbfounded at everything that had transpired—and Kayla and Grady were just standing there, trying to catch their breath.

Who knew where Steven and Alexia had gone? Probably with Shani.

He nodded to the other Elders—worse for wear but still accounted for—who were collecting their injured and heading out as well, hoping to live to fight another day.

He supposed the time had now come, as Zotz had said; there was no delaying it any longer. They could still salvage this mess.

He sighed deeply, gathering his robes around him, and headed up the aisle to where he knew Holun would be.

Justin blinked up through his tears at Yatzil, who seemed to have appeared out of nowhere. What could she do? He simply looked back at Mandy's lifeless form, squeezing the hand he already held, tears still pouring out of him. It seemed allowing himself to mourn his parents this past summer had opened the floodgates, and now he couldn't make himself stop.

He wanted to curse Mandy and her hubris. Hadn't she just said how she couldn't die, how she'd felt invincible?

He wished he could go back in time, say something different. He wished he could stop them from entering this warehouse, stop them from coming back here, stop them from discovering the Codex at all. If this was where it all ended, what was the point of any of it?

He'd lost everything. Everyone he loved. First his parents, now Mandy . . . would life ever stop taking away everything he held dear? He'd had to wait three long years for Mandy to notice him, and now he only got three years with her? Life wasn't fair, not in the least.

Yatzil held Mandy's hand, felt her faint breath as she exhaled. There was still time, but not much.

Yatzil knew this would hurt, would cause her worse pain than she'd ever experienced, and may even kill her. But she knew, as she called her power to her, that she would never make a different choice, *could* never make a different choice, even if it did end her life.

As she felt the gunshot rip through her torso, Yatzil heard Holun start to scream before her world went dark.

Justin couldn't believe his eyes. Mandy was waking up.

She blinked up at him then sat up abruptly.

Justin pressed on her shoulder, urging her back to the ground. "Mandy, no! You've been shot—you're bleeding." He nodded to her side.

Mandy blinked up at him, her eyes searching. Justin supposed almost dying would be disorienting, confusing. She'd probably need a little time to adjust.

Finally, his words seemed to sink in, and she looked down at her bloody shirt. Then she reached for the bottom hem and lifted it up. And Justin's mouth dropped open.

The wound was completely gone.

Holun saw a flash of red from Justin's shirt come into view just before Yatzil's agony-filled eyes met his. He sped to Yatzil's side, cursing her powers, cursing the Codex. He grabbed her hand and held it tight, pushing his power to soothe her pain through his fingertips while begging it worked. He had found the love of his short life, and he knew he'd never love another like her. If she didn't recover from this . . .

Then he heard a familiar voice, one he hadn't heard directed at him in what felt like forever, one that sickened him as it approached. "Hello, Holun."

Holun glanced up. "Tohil." His eyes shot daggers at the man who raised him, the one who he somehow knew was here to hurt him.

Tohil sighed, his face solemn as he lifted his hands in front of him.

Holun knew what that meant—he'd unfortunately seen his adoptive father's powers in action. "Really, Tohil? Are you going to kill me now?" Holun almost rolled his eyes.

"No, Holun." He paused, looking over at Yatzil who was still lying motionless on the ground. "I'm going to kill *her*."

Holun froze, his body suddenly ice cold. He just stared as the words fought to sink in. Then they did, and he couldn't breathe; he felt like someone had reached into his chest and was cutting off the blood flow to his heart. "No . . ." he choked out.

Tohil shifted his outstretched arms her direction, and Holun sensed his power building. "She must die, Holun. I am truly sorry for this, but she cannot survive. And only now, when she is weakest, is death truly possible." He lowered his hands, pointing to her chest, and Holun knew his power was about to be released.

Holun's mind went into overdrive, sped up, started moving so quickly that the flurry made him lightheaded. The man who raised him was threatening the woman he loved.

Suddenly, the second prophecy came to him, the part that he'd forgotten until this very moment. *The Monarch must not die or the world will not be saved.* And Holun realized that although he didn't want to die, he'd take the brunt of Tohil's fatal power for her. He'd die so she didn't have to, so the world would be saved. So she would live.

Just as a bright, stark-white lightning bolt shot from Tohil's hands, Holun leapt in front of Yatzil's body still on the ground, unmoving. He watched Tohil's eyes grow large as he realized where his lightning strike would hit. And in that instant, just as Holun felt the bolt sear through his chest, he called out to her, praying that somehow she'd hear him, somehow she'd understand.

Yatzil, I love you. Please forgive me.

Then the world disappeared.

As soon as he'd realized what he'd done, Tohil started running. He sped past the girl, Yatzil, past Mandy and her boyfriend, Justin, and back toward the entrance. He felt the sting of tears threatening his eyes, but he didn't have time for that now, the luxury of showing his emotions.

He was an Elder, the most revered in his Clan, one of five of the most respected and feared men in their . . . Brotherhood. Yeah, that was the right word.

So he couldn't afford to show weakness. He had to stay strong, at least appear to be, and pretend that he didn't just kill the only person he'd ever truly cared about.

The Elders weren't forbidden from having families, and they certainly enjoyed companionship on a regular basis—an undeniably enjoyable side effect of their position—but most stayed unattached. Perhaps it was an unwritten rule that they willingly followed because they all sensed the potential for disaster.

And Tohil had followed it religiously, until the day that small orphan boy had shown up. The day Holun entered his life.

And he'd never been the same.

Raising Holun had been the most challenging and rewarding task of his admittedly long life. And no matter how many times he'd tried to deny it—so many times over the years he'd lost count long ago—Holun had changed him. He thought it was for the better, but he knew the other Elders wouldn't share his sentiments.

Holun had taught him to care, to love, to be human. He had that effect on everyone he met. He'd learned more from Holun than he'd ever been able to teach the boy.

He'd be forever indebted to that young man, the one who was now lying on the cold, hard, cement floor of this underground warehouse, a hole in his chest. The one who'd died too young, the woman he clearly loved undoubtedly weeping at his side. Holun would've given his life for another in a heartbeat, but Tohil had seen the importance of this one in his eyes. How much she meant to him. He'd loved her, sacrificed himself so she could live.

As Tohil ran up the steps and into the crisp, night air, he stopped to catch his breath, thankful that the others were already out of sight. He stared out into the rainforest, the lights of Lamanai a blip in the distance. Holun was a much better person than he ever deserved. He saw that now.

He'd never forgive himself for this. Not if he lived another hundred years.

Kayla reached for Grady's hand, pulling him close and wrapping her arms around him. With the others gone—at least for the moment—she felt she could afford herself this luxury, this *necessity*. The need for her to show Grady just how much he meant to her, how sorry she was. Her body started shaking as tears began flowing.

Grady held her tight. *You have nothing to apologize for, my love.*

Kayla sniffed. *That couldn't be further from the truth, and you know it. I have a lifetime's worth of apologies to give.*

Grady pulled away, putting his hands on either side of her face and making her look at him. *No, Kayla. All is in the past, all is forgiven.*

But Grady . . .

As if to stop her protest, Grady swiftly crushed his lips to hers, kissing her hard. Kayla pressed closer to him, needing this feeling again. He had come back to her, had forgiven her. And everything would be okay.

Except . . .

A small, nagging voice in the back of her head—the one that had checked her with the Power, the one that had kept her honest, the one that had begged her to stop hurting people—told her things weren't quite over just yet. There were too many unanswered questions, like where Justin and Mandy had gone, what Holun and Yatzil were up to, why the army had just retreated, and where . . .

Then she heard a *click, click* of the hammer of a gun sliding into place at her right, and she froze, overwhelmed with déjà vu. She instantly and vividly remembered that cavern this summer where Shani had captured them, threatened them with a gun, shot at Kayla's chest. And she instinctively knew it was Shani once again.

Kayla held Grady's arms tightly, facing him, holding his gaze like her life depended on it.

Grady, just look at me.

There was nowhere to run.

Grady, my love, don't look at her, just look at me.

Kayla, please, we need to fight. But he kept his gaze locked on hers.

Kayla nodded once. *We will. But Grady, in case this doesn't work, I just wanted you to know that I love you, more than you could ever know.*

I love you, Kayla, forever and always.

Kayla took a deep breath. *Ready?*

Grady nodded quickly, listening in on her plan as it flashed through her mind. Kayla was smiling at him as the gun went off.

Yatzil woke slowly, her head aching but feeling otherwise okay. She glanced over at Mandy, who seemed to be crying, but she appeared unharmed save the drying blood on her shirt. Justin was beside her, holding her, tears streaming down his face. She wanted to tell them she was alright, tell them not to cry, that everything was going to be okay.

But they weren't looking at her.

Suddenly afraid of what she'd see, Yatzil turned around, ever so slowly, knowing something was terribly, dreadfully wrong.

Then she saw him, a burning hole still sizzling in his chest, and it knocked the breath right out of her.

"Holun!" she screamed, lurching to his side. The cauterized edges encircled a hole as large as her palm, and the sight of the gaping hole in Holun's chest made her feel as though she had a matching wound. She couldn't breathe.

"What happened?" she yelled over at Mandy and Justin, tears streaming down her face, already staining her cheeks. "What happened to him?"

Mandy and Justin weren't answering her, so she turned back to Holun. "Holun, my love, can you hear me?" She started sobbing, her hands on his shoulders, shaking him gently. "Please . . . Holun . . . love, come back . . ." She sniffed. "Come back . . . to me. I . . . need you. I love you."

Sobs wracked her body as she cried over him. She leaned in, tried to see if he was still breathing. Then she called her power, but nothing happened. No! Not now! Not when she needed it most! She tried again, but something was blocking her. Maybe she'd used too much of it to save Mandy. Maybe she had to somehow recharge. How was she supposed to know how this worked?

But Holun could not die. Not now, not ever.

No . . .

CHAPTER 41

Death Is Only
the Beginning

YATZIL LOOKED UP AT the ceiling and screamed in K'iche, "Why?! Why now?! He was INNOCENT! He did not deserve this! He was kind and good and loving! Why would you take him now?!"

She was still struggling to breathe, and she fell to her hands and knees, gasping. Sobbing. Holun, the boy she fell in love with mere days ago, was lying here moments from death, if he hadn't breathed his last already.

It wasn't fair.

She hadn't lived a long life, but it'd been a hard one, though she knew she had plenty to be thankful for. And she was. But growing up without her birth parents—a real family—had left a hole in her she hadn't realized she'd had until Holun had begun to fill it back up.

He was her heart, her soul, her *everything*. He'd loved her, more completely than she'd thought would have been possible in such a short time. He'd brought her into this wild adventure of his, taught her how to speak English, gave her confidence to use her powers. Taught her never to be ashamed of them.

But now she was. She *was* ashamed. That her powers, ones she considered so miraculous just moments before, were failing her. She'd never forgive herself until the day she died that she couldn't save him. That her powers had given up on her when she needed them the most.

Then she saw movement beside her out of the corner of her eye. She blinked away the tears, searching the area around her for confirmation of what she thought she'd seen, what she *hoped* she'd seen. *Was that . . . ?* "Holun?" Her voice was breathless, eager. She didn't want to let herself hope, though she felt it coursing through her veins anyway.

She stared down at the substantial hole in Holun's chest, and her eyes grew wide as she watched the skin slowly heal itself with a light crackling, fluttering sound. Muscles, veins, bones, and organs knitted back together before her eyes.

Then Holun stirred, and Yatzil's heart stuttered. Holun blinked then sat up. "Yatzil? What . . ." Then he seemed to notice her panicked expression. "My Yatzil, I am fine! Please, do not cry." He reached for her, pulling her close to his now-whole chest.

Yatzil hugged him so tightly she thought she might burst.

"My Yatzil, have you no faith?" he asked in their language, his voice breathless.

She was still crying, but they were no longer tears of sadness; Holun was back, and she'd never felt more joy. "What happened?"

Holun stood up, reaching for her hand and pulling her up with him. Mandy and Justin rose as well, their expressions frozen on their faces as they just stared. "My beautiful, wonderful Yatzil, you healed me."

Yatzil blinked. "No, Holun, I did not! My power was not working!"

Holun smiled at her, wiped her tears from her cheek with his thumb, tucked her hair behind her ear. "But it did work, my love. You healed me, without even trying. I felt it. I felt *you*. You were all around me."

She smiled at him, at the man she loved, the one who'd miraculously come back to her. But she still didn't understand. "But *how* . . ."

Holun kissed her lightly. "It doesn't matter. What matters is that we're both okay."

Then a gunshot sounded in the distance. "Uh, guys . . ." Justin spoke up from behind them. "We may all be okay, but Kayla and Grady are in trouble. Yatzil, a little help?" Justin reached out his hand to her.

Yatzil nodded, and they all clasped hands. Then they were back in the arena.

What was going on? Mandy was staring at the scene in front of her. Shani's gun was pointed at Grady and Kayla, and Mandy'd heard the gun go off, but what she was seeing didn't make sense. If the bullet hadn't hit her friends, what had Shani shot at?

Kayla and Grady were facing each other, their arms around each other, clearly accessing their powers . . . but now they were staring in Shani's direction, their powers unneeded.

What had happened?

Then Mandy saw it, a pool of blood seeming to gather out of nowhere and spread at Kayla and Grady's feet.

Steven.

The man who'd tried to stop them all this time, Shani's right-hand mercenary, had stepped in front of a bullet for her friends.

She couldn't tell if he was still alive or not, but given how fast that pool of blood was spreading, if he wasn't dead now, he soon would be. As Mandy crossed the arena to go to her friends, the others just behind her, she looked down to the empty space, praying he'd hear her before he slipped into unconsciousness. She whispered a quiet "thank you, Steven" and could've sworn she heard a very quiet, final breath.

Shani cursed under her breath. Would these people not *die*? She started stalking toward the circle—the Four plus Holun and Yatzil—prepping her gun for another shot. Mandy threw up a shield but it quickly came down. Shani grinned. She must still be worn out from almost dying. Pity it hadn't stuck like she'd hoped.

Shani kept going, walking to increase the tension, the anticipation. She could've sped to their sides in an instant, probably taken most of them down before they stopped her, but that would be a suicide mission. And Alex—the man who still stood off to the side just staring—was waiting for her.

Then she was back at Lamanai, just outside that work trailer, Alex at her side, the Elders and the Clan in front of them. They were jeering, sneering at her.

She turned to Alex, crying now, begging and pleading with him to understand, realize that she'd done all this to protect him, to save him from her dangerous life, to create a life for them so much better than the one she'd had to offer him all these years.

"Shani," she heard him whisper, but his mouth hadn't moved. What . . . ?

"Shani, wake up."

Alex, her Alex, was at her side, back in the arena, pulling her out of Alexia's terrible vision. She blinked then looked over at him.

"Shani, my love, you need to stop this."

She just stared at him. What was he talking about?

He tried again. "All this killing, this fighting . . . you need to stop, love. It is killing you."

The killing and the fighting was all she'd ever known. And the loneliness it brought had been her companion for years, despite knowing she'd eventually go home to her love, home to Alex. But he'd gotten it wrong. It wasn't killing her; it was what made her strong.

Then Alex's next words broke her heart into pieces. "Shani, please stop. For me. For our daughter." He looked over at the group of wide-eyed strangers, and Shani watched them put the pieces together.

Yatzil took one half step forward. "D-daughter?"

Alex nodded, moving toward her. "I am your father, and Shani is your mother."

Yatzil's face went white. "No, it cannot . . . I cannot . . ." She turned away and stepped back to Holun, grabbing his hand and burying her face in his shoulder. Shani watched her body start shaking.

"Yatzil," she tried, reaching out for the only good thing she'd ever done, the only thing that had ever made sense in her crazy world.

The girl whipped around, her tear-lined eyes on fire. "You will *never* be my mother, Shani. You are evil. You hurt my friends, hurt the man I love. You deserve to die for that." Shani's heart broke again as Yatzil sighed. "But I will not kill you. No one deserves to die, not even you. You are not worth it."

Shani just stared, her world crumbling. Alex was finally here with her and knew everything now—everything she'd spent nearly a lifetime keeping from him—but the one girl in the world she loved, her own flesh and blood, had summarily rejected and disposed of her.

That hurt worse than anything else.

She stared down at the artifact in her hand, willing it to activate again. Perhaps she could somehow take over Yatzil's mind, make her forget everything she'd done so the girl would come to her and Alex, and they could finally be a family.

But as she sent her power to the artifact, she realized the ancient stone was no longer working. The artifact had done its work, enhanced her powers so she could capture the Four, but now it seemed its power was exhausted. And Shani realized, with a growing pit in her stomach, that no matter how much power she amassed, no matter what artifacts she stole and used to increase her abilities, she'd always be weaker than the Four, weaker than the Power of the Codex. Nausea threatened to consume her as she realized their Power was exponential, that their strength was in their bond. They were a family—something she'd never have.

So Shani stood up straight, lifting her gun again and pointing it at the Four, at Holun, at *Yatzil*—she thought her name with distaste. If that's how she was going to play this . . .

Shani cocked the hammer of the gun, set her stance, and aimed down the barrel at Kayla.

Kayla stared as Shani woke from Alexia's nightmare. She gave Grady a quick smile before releasing him then turned to face the woman who had repeatedly tried to kill them. Slowly, secretly, she started calling her power to her. It grew as Yatzil told Shani that she wasn't worth it, that she wouldn't kill her.

But someone had to.

Kayla felt her power build inside her until it was begging to be unleashed. She raised her hands toward Shani, praying Shani would see the movement as defensive instead of offensive as the other woman straightened and pointed the gun directly at Kayla's forehead.

Kayla tensed, ready to release her power . . . then stopped.

In the split second before Shani pulled the trigger, everything she and Grady had been through the past few weeks raced through her mind. Grady had forgiven her, for everything. For every unspeakable thing she'd done, every horrible act she'd committed. The kiss with Na-um, murdering much of the army—the man she loved had forgiven her for it all.

Didn't Shani deserve the same chance?

Maybe *deserve* wasn't the right word, but Kayla suddenly understood why Grady was always telling her to keep her anger in check. If she gave in to it, if she let it control her, she would keep doing things she'd regret, things that hurt other people.

So even though Shani mostly assuredly did *not* deserve it, Kayla realized that *she* did. She owed it to herself to stop.

So she did, letting the Power fizzle out.

But there was still the small matter of Shani's loaded gun pointing directly at her head.

Alex saw something move out of the corner of his eye just before the gunshot sounded. He screamed as he launched himself toward the woman he loved.

But he was too late.

Shani crumpled to the ground, a red stain spreading on her chest. Alex flew to her side and crashed to his knees.

"Shani, my love . . . nooo . . ." His voice caught as he cradled her head in his lap. He searched her face, her eyes, her entire body for signs of life, but she'd already breathed her last. He hadn't had any final moment with her, hadn't told her one last time how he felt.

Funny how life could change in an instant. One moment, his family was united for the first time, then in the next moment, the person he loved the most was gone—and he didn't even get to say goodbye.

Alex felt like he was being strangled. He slowly lifted his eyes toward where the shot had come from, and his eyes narrowed.

There in front of him, dressed in a modern, light-blue t-shirt and khakis but with the distinctive build and features of Shani's Clan, stood the man who had shot the woman he loved more than anything. He glared, wishing his looks alone could kill. Whoever this guy was would pay.

But not today. The man with the gun—the man who seemed oddly familiar but who Alex just couldn't place—always had the upper hand. And suddenly Alex saw another option, one that would rid him of this incomparable grief forever. He carefully, deliberately rose to his feet, setting Shani's lifeless head gently down on the cement floor. He closed his eyes for a moment, taking in a deep breath.

Then, in the next second, he closed the distance between Shani's killer and himself and pushed up against the gun, pressing it to his chest.

"Go ahead."

The man furrowed his eyebrows.

"You have taken everything from me. I have nothing left. So do it."

The man's eyes softened, and Alex almost thought he saw pity in them. And he felt his blood pressure shoot up.

"Do it! Now!"

The other man dropped the gun to his side, shaking his head. "Alex, I will not kill you. I regret killing Shani—I loved her as well. More than you know."

Alex's eyes grew wide. "You're Na-um?"

The man nodded solemnly.

Alex just stared. So that's why he was so familiar. His mind briefly went back to that fateful day all those years ago, when Na-um had found him and Shani together, the day she was banished from her Clan . . .

He shook his head to come back to the present. What now? Na-um refused to kill him, and he didn't know how he'd live without Shani. He took a step back as he saw his options flash before his eyes.

And he realized he really only had one.

With all the powerful people in the room, including the ones standing silently behind him who would no doubt jump into action at any moment—and the daughter who'd summarily rejected Shani and, by extension, him—Alex didn't stand a chance. And he found within him the slightest will to live.

He would get his revenge on Na-um. He would eviscerate him, tear him apart limb by limb. But to do that, he'd need help. And he knew exactly who would help him.

So, for now, he'd run. Run and find the people who would help him avenge Shani's death. Run and find the people who would be eager to help him get revenge on Na-um, especially once they heard what he'd done.

As he sped around Na-um and sprinted toward the warehouse's entrance, Alex let the burning in his lungs from the run spread throughout his body and give him strength. He focused that burn and fed his hate, his anger, until it completely consumed him.

As he stepped out into the night air, Alex took a deep breath, calming himself until he was able to breathe a little more normally. He looked up to the stars and vowed that Shani's death would not be forgotten.

He headed back to the Clan's camp, running as fast as he could. The Elders were foolish for working with someone as volatile as Shani—now that he knew the whole story, he understood just how dangerous she'd truly been. So he'd offer himself, someone steady and sure, to the cause of ending Na-um and those Americans. They'd have to listen to him, have to accept him. He'd make sure they did.

The hate consuming him now was unfamiliar but not unwelcome. And he would let it make him strong.

Kayla just stared at the scene in front of her. She couldn't even make sense of everything that had just happened. It was too much. This was all too much.

She fell to the ground, barely holding herself up with her hands, her breath ragged and shallow. Grady knelt down beside her, wrapped an arm around her, pulled her close. "It's going to be okay, Kayla. We're safe now," he whispered in her ear.

Kayla nodded, but she felt the tears start coming. She sobbed, feeling all the emotions of the past few hours, the past few weeks finally come crashing down on her. She held Grady close, grateful he was still here, still by her side. Beyond grateful that he'd forgiven her for all her mistakes.

I love you, Kayla. Just had to say it again. She felt him smile.

And her tears quieted, the sobs lessening until she could breathe again. She looked up into Grady's face then looked around at the mess surrounding them. "Is it finally over?"

Justin pulled Mandy to him as Kayla and Grady stood up to meet them. Justin looked around at the destroyed but largely empty arena, then he nodded. "I think so."

Na-um stared at the woman on the ground, the woman he'd killed, the only family he had. He bent his knees, lowering the gun to the ground, leaning down to set it on the cracked cement floor. Though he was grateful he'd thought to snag one from Lamanai before coming here, he didn't want to touch that thing any longer.

He could feel the shock wearing off, feel the tears threatening. He had to get out of here before it all came crashing down on him.

But then Mandy walked over to him, putting a hand on his shoulder. "I'm so sorry about your sister, Na-um. We all are."

The others walked toward him and surrounded him, nodding their assent.

Then Yatzil stepped up to him, her eyes wide. "Shani . . . she was your sister?"

Na-um glanced up at her quiet question and nodded slowly.

Yatzil swallowed hard, glancing down at the body of the woman on the ground then back at Na-um. "I am her daughter."

And the tears that Na-um had been holding back for what felt like a lifetime finally spilled over like a dam breaking, and he fell to the floor, sobbing.

Alexia watched the scene in the arena from behind a bookcase, careful not to be seen. She'd given Shani a taste of what she'd made her do to the others, to the Four, the ones who didn't deserve any of it, and she hoped it had helped the others take her down. She didn't fully understand the reunion going on in the middle of the room right now, but she hoped it meant something good, hoped it meant this whole stupid thing was over.

Then she heard a rustling behind her, and she jumped.

"Shh!"

She sighed when she recognized Tyler behind her. "Tyler! I thought you left with Akna!" Alexia whispered, though not quite certain why.

Tyler smiled at her, reaching for her hand. "I came back for you."

Alexia's heart leapt in her chest. "Why would you do that?"

Tyler looked at the ground, his fingers playing with hers. "I just . . . didn't want to see you hurt."

Alexia grinned up at him. "I think you just liked me too much."

Tyler froze, and Alexia thought for a moment that she'd said the wrong thing.

Then Tyler leaned forward, drew in closer, and touched his lips to hers. Alexia kissed him back gently, carefully, but tried to make it good. She didn't want to let this one get away.

Then she heard Akna yell at them in her own language, words Alexia couldn't understand, and she jumped away from Tyler suddenly, shushing her.

But it was too late—the group in the center of the arena turned toward the sound, toward where they were hiding. Alexia pulled Tyler out from behind the shelf.

She raised one hand, waving it in the air, her shoulders hunched, her tone apologetic. "Hi, sorry."

Mandy ran over to her. "No, Alexia, we're just glad you're okay!" Mandy pulled her into a hug, ignoring the fact that she still held Tyler's hand. Then Mandy pulled away, eyeing the young man beside her. "And who's this?"

Alexia smiled shyly, her heart in her throat. "This is Tyler. He's from UCF, too," she stated quietly.

Kayla offered her hand to him. "Hello, Tyler, it's nice to meet you. I'm Kayla."

Tyler took it, releasing Alexia's hand, and Alexia exhaled. "Hello, Kayla. I'm sorry about earlier . . ." He looked away.

Justin came up beside him, actually putting an arm around his shoulder. "Hey, man, it's okay. We get it. Shani was a little . . . crazy. But she can be convincing."

Tyler just nodded, and Alexia smiled up at him. "So what do we do next?" she queried the group.

Her professors and fellow students exchanged glances for a brief moment before Grady answered. "Well," he started, rubbing his chin, "I think we need to get out of here, but . . ."

Kayla nodded at him, and Alexia thought she was missing something. "Yes, Mandy—perhaps you can help?"

Mandy just nodded as the four of them walked away. Alexia leaned over to Tyler and asked a quiet "help with what?" but Tyler just shrugged.

We need a way to seal off this warehouse, protect it from the Elders. We need to contain the artifacts here, keep them under guard. Kayla was surveying the aisles of bookcases surrounding the arena on three sides, grateful that everyone had left but not entirely convinced they wouldn't come back, and soon.

Grady nodded beside her. *I agree. The Elders cannot be allowed access to this treasure trove any longer.*

Okay, sure, but how do we protect it? We can't stay here forever—we live in Florida, for heaven's sake! Mandy crossed her arms.

Justin reached an arm around her. *It's okay, babe. We'll figure this out.*

Um, hello?

Kayla's head snapped up, her eyes scanning the area surrounding them. *Who was that?*

Then she saw Yatzil heading their way, Holun's hand in hers.

Yatzil? How are you hearing us? And talking to us?? Kayla felt her eyes widen.

Another one of my powers, maybe? Yatzil smiled at them as she and Holun approached. *I was thinking I could help you protect this place, that we could help*—she looked over at Holun and smiled—*and then I could hear you!*

Mandy glanced over at her. *Is that how all your powers work? You just think of something you want, and it happens?*

Yatzil smiled then shrugged. *Yes, I think so.*

Holun was frowning, so Yatzil leaned over, and Kayla heard her whisper an explanation in his ear through her thoughts. Holun just smiled and squeezed her hand then kissed her cheek. "Let me know what I can do to help. I will go sit with him." He dropped her hand and walked toward where Na-um was sitting on the cement floor beside Shani's lifeless body.

So what's your idea, Yatzil? Grady asked as Holun walked away.

Holun and I will stay here in Belize. We can watch the warehouse, guard it against intruders, the Elders.

Yatzil, no! That's too dangerous for just the two of you! Mandy's eyebrows scrunched together.

Grady looked over at her, crossing his arms. *Mandy, I think she has a point. Holun can see if any attack is coming, not to mention his superhuman hearing and speed, and Yatzil is pretty much stronger than all of us put together. I think they can handle it.*

Plus, Yatzil began, *Holun and I no longer belong with our Clan. We have nowhere to go.* She looked around the warehouse. *So this seems like a good place to make a home.*

Yatzil, are you sure? Justin asked.

She just smiled, nodding. *I will ask Holun, but yes.*

Kayla smiled back, confident that this young woman—the woman she'd met only this morning—could handle herself. She'd already noticed her strength and courage, and she now could see her will. She and Holun would be fine; she could feel it in her soul.

"Okay, then," Kayla said aloud, breaking the silence by putting her arm around Yatzil and leading her back to the middle of the arena where the destruction was the worst. "Let's see if we can get this place cleaned up."

CHAPTER 42

The Brotherhood

HOLUN LOOKED AT NA-UM as he approached. He was still here, sitting on the cement floor mere feet away from Shani's lifeless body, and Holun couldn't figure out why. Was he just torturing himself?

He supposed he should say something to him, the man who'd trained him, the one who had a strange way of showing he cared, but the man who cared nonetheless. "Na-um?" he called as he approached his former commander, who looked up at his name. His eyes were red, his face blotchy. Holun had already known he'd been crying, but this man looked utterly broken. "Are you okay?" Holun sat down next to him, sensing this was the most important place for him to be right now. Anything else could wait.

Na-um hesitated, looking toward the wall of weapons that now lay scattered around the floor beneath their former resting place. "Sure, Holun. Or . . . I will be."

Holun nodded, not sure what else to say, following Na-um's gaze for lack of another place to look.

"Is Yatzil . . . is she really Shani's daughter?"

Holun nodded again, looking at Na-um this time.

"How old is she?"

"About sixteen, I think, same as me."

Na-um's eyes grew wide. "She . . ." He cleared his throat, and Holun didn't think his next words were for him to hear. "She was pregnant when I sent her away . . ." His voice cracked, and Holun just stared, his mind racing with the implications.

Then Na-um sat up straighter, and Holun's head almost started spinning from the abrupt change. "So what's your plan now, Holun? Are you headed back to Florida?"

Holun looked up at the Four, who were just coming over with Yatzil, and smiled. "No, I'm staying here."

Na-um followed his gaze then smiled back. "Oh. I see."

Holun's eyes flashed to Na-um's. "You do?"

Na-um's old grin was back, and Holun felt a wave of familiarity wash over him. "Of course. You love her. You cannot leave her."

Holun shook his head. "No, I do not suppose I can."

"Okay," Na-um said, jumping to his feet and offering Holun a hand up, "then I will stay to help you."

"Help with what?" Yatzil asked as she approached, a wide smile on her face.

Na-um shifted his weight but answered in a strong voice. "I will help you and Holun here, watch over you. Help you with whatever you need."

Yatzil smiled at him, and Holun thought she was making a nice effort given he was family to her newly discovered evil mother. "Thank you. Actually, the Four and I have a plan.

Would you both be interested in staying here, keeping this treasure trove safe?" She eyed Holun.

Holun felt a shock before her words sunk in. "We would stay here, protect these artifacts?"

Yatzil nodded quickly, eagerly. "Yes!" She waved her hand at the Four beside her. "They have to go back to Florida, but I would say we are well-equipped to handle things here. We can catalog the artifacts, figure out what they all do. Perhaps," she started as she glanced over at the young girl, Akna, "perhaps she would even like to help."

Holun was grinning ear to ear. "Yatzil, that is a brilliant idea!" He pulled her close, kissing her forehead. Na-um eyed him, and Holun pulled his lips away but kept his arm around her shoulders. Na-um couldn't tell him what to do, not now.

The corner of Na-um's mouth turned up, and the tightness in Holun's chest released. He thought that this new Na-um might actually be someone worth being friends with, someone worth looking up to. Finally.

Tohil reached the Clan's camp well before sunrise. He immediately went to his tent, hoping to clean up and take a very long nap. But as he approached, he realized that was not going to be the case, at least not in the immediate future.

"Tohil," Chac called, extending his hand as Tohil walked up, "we were worried you had failed when we didn't hear from you."

Tohil sighed, seeing no need to hide his exhaustion. It would make sense in the context of what the other Elders knew. The other explanation—the ones his counterparts could never know—was cloaked in the veil Tohil had many, many years of practice upholding. It was what kept them from reading his mind as he left the mountain and took a circuitous route back here to clear his head, figure out his next move. He suspected they all had a similar shield, though he could never prove it.

He looked up at Chac as he clasped his forearm tightly—their customary greeting—and released it. He had to be careful what he said and how he said it. "It is taken care of."

Chac nodded as the rest of the Elders came out from behind the tent. Zotz called out, "Tohil! I am pleased you have returned."

Tohil nodded in his direction. "Thank you. I am glad to see you all made it out mostly unscathed." He glanced at Bacob, who he knew had felt the worst of the Four's powers, and sensed his wounds were extensive and painful, but he would recover. They always did. "What's our next step?"

Bacob answered, his breathing ragged, and Tohil could tell they'd all already had this discussion. "We keep up appearances for the men." He nodded over his shoulder. "They are not happy that the woman, Kayla, killed several hundred of their fellow soldiers without cause. They will want retribution."

Tohil nodded, a knot forming in his stomach.

Chac continued. "No doubt the Four will have taken the warehouse, and we will not be able to return to it without a fight. It may be a lost cause at this point."

Kucumatz spoke up. "That is as we expected." He took a breath. "And it is a small matter."

The others nodded, voicing their assent.

"We continue with the plan. The Four may be close to discovering it, but it is unlikely they will find out in time to stop it." Zotz glanced toward the rainforest, toward the mountain.

"How close are we?" Tohil asked.

Zotz smiled. "Very. The Brotherhood has assured me that they are all in place, ready to mobilize when we give the word."

Tohil nodded absently, his mind on the Brotherhood and what they were planning, what they'd been planning for several years. He knew the Four would try to stop them, but the Brotherhood was large and well-prepared. The Four wouldn't know what hit them.

"And Na-um?" Tohil asked.

Chac sighed. "An unfortunate loss, but a manageable one."

Tohil knew Na-um would've been a helpful pawn in their game, but he was replaceable. They all were.

"Well, Brothers, I believe this day is catching up with me. I would like to clean up and rest." Tohil started to move toward his tent.

Kucumatz blocked his way, just for a second, his eyes concerned. "Are you sure you are okay, Tohil?"

Tohil placed a hand on his shoulder, stepping around him. "Yes, Brother. Today was just . . . difficult. The action I had to take was regrettable."

Kucumatz nodded knowingly and let him pass.

Once inside his large tent, Tohil dropped to the floor. He'd been holding it in, saving face for the other Elders, but killing Holun had broken him. He began to weep.

The Four, along with Tyler and Alexia, helped Yatzil, Holun, Na-um, and Akna restore the warehouse to close to its former glory. At least Kayla found it easy to disappear all the dirt she'd created. She actually found it kind of fun to use her powers for something good, something innocent for a change.

Tyler and Alexia, along with the Four, were getting on the next flight back to Florida later that day—since it was well past midnight at this point—though the long layovers meant they wouldn't get into town until Wednesday. Akna was going to stay at the warehouse with Yatzil, Holun, and Na-um, at least initially. Kayla noticed her persistent wide eyes and hesitant movements as they cleaned up, and she quickly understood how difficult this must be for that young girl.

Kayla and the rest of the Four promised to check in often. Holun had located a phone in the residential area—a hallway with a number of well-appointed bedrooms, a full kitchen, a large dining room, and even a comfortable living area and study—and found the number for the Four so they could keep in touch.

She noticed Na-um off to the side, avoiding eye contact as they got ready to leave. She squeezed Grady's hand with a smile before walking over to see their former enemy.

"Na-um, thank you for doing this. For staying and taking care of this for all of us."

Na-um gave her a half smile. "Of course, Kayla. You all have become like family to me." His face fell slightly at the word *family*.

Kayla nodded once. "You take care of yourself. And take care of those two." She nodded over at Yatzil and Holun, who were staring at each other lovingly, their hands clasped between them.

Na-um actually rolled his eyes. "I have my work cut out for me with those two, I see."

Kayla laughed then put a hand on his shoulder. "Thank you again. We'll be in touch."

Na-um nodded, and Kayla turned back to Grady, crossing the few feet to his side. "Ready?"

"To leave this rainforest and the Clan behind? Of course!" Grady grinned, and Kayla's heart squeezed in her chest. She'd never get tired of seeing his smile.

That was a long flight, Kayla thought as Grady pulled his SUV into a parking spot at her condo. She was grateful they'd parked it at the airport when they left—she had almost forgotten that Shani had stolen her SUV and subsequently crashed it until they'd landed.

Yes, it was, Grady answered back. He sighed, putting the car in park before reaching for her hand. "You ready?"

Kayla looked out the windshield at her condo's door then nodded, squeezing his hand before releasing it. "Sure."

She climbed out of the passenger side then sauntered to the back of the vehicle, reaching to open the back. She touched the handle just as Grady did.

"Oh . . . sorry." Kayla pulled her hand back as if a snake had bitten it. Ever since the final flight from Houston, things had been a little weird with Grady, but she couldn't put her finger on why. Even though she could hear his thoughts, she still had a feeling he was hiding something from her.

"No, I'm sorry—" Grady jumped back, too, then sighed. He reached again for the back latch as Kayla stood aside.

They wheeled her suitcases inside, stopping just inside her front door in the oak kitchen with dark granite countertops, neither saying much. Kayla wished she knew what to say, what to ask to make this okay. She watched his back as he looked around her small condo—the eat-in kitchen, the staircase to the left, the living room beyond—like he was seeing it for the first time.

"Grady . . ." she started.

He turned back toward her, his forehead creased. "Yes?"

Kayla bit her lip, fighting back tears. "Is something wrong?"

Grady crossed his arms, a sure sign his next words wouldn't be altogether truthful. "No, nothing's wrong."

Kayla felt her anger flare and stepped closer to him. "Grady, please! Tell me what's wrong! I know you're hiding something from me."

Grady's eyes widened a little as he uncrossed his arms, raising them in the air, palms up. "Kayla, I promise, it's nothing."

"It's not nothing!" Kayla was shouting now, unable to help herself. She was glad the residence next to her had been vacant for the past three months. "You *are* hiding something from me."

"Kayla . . ." Grady began.

"No!" Kayla pointed a finger at him, feeling the rage coursing through her body now. "I know you too well. We've been together for several months now, and I think you know how well I can read you. Tell me what's wrong! Tell me what you're thinking! Tell me now Grady, before I send you home."

Grady looked like she'd slapped him. She supposed, in a way, she had.

She felt bad about that. "I'm sorry, Grady. I didn't mean to get upset. I just . . . we've just been apart for too long."

He nodded, biting his lip. "Kayla, I . . ." He sighed. "There *is* something I've been keeping from you. Something . . . something I've wanted for a very long time. But I'm not really sure . . . I don't know what you want."

Kayla felt her anger rising again. "What do you want, Grady?"

Grady's gaze caught hers and held it, his eyes suddenly fierce. Kayla's heart jumped into her throat, and she started to worry she didn't want to know. Then his next words came in a whisper: "I want to be married to you."

CHAPTER 43

The Moment

KAYLA'S HEART STOPPED, all anger dissipating in an instant. She blinked. "Wh-what?" she managed. Had she heard correctly?

Grady's eyes softened, watching her carefully. Kayla wondered what he saw on her face. Then he nodded slowly, answering her unasked question in a stronger voice. "You heard right. I want to marry you, Kayla."

Kayla blinked, her feet still frozen to the floor. She didn't know what to say. She blinked once, hard, then shook her head to clear it. "What . . . are you . . . what would make you say that?"

Grady, ever patient with her, smiled kindly, reaching for her hand. Her left hand, she noticed. Then he dropped to one knee, and Kayla gasped.

"Kayla, you know how much I love you. You know how perfect we are for each other, how we were destined to meet, fall in love. Destined to be together forever."

Kayla gulped, convinced it was audible.

"Everything that happened this summer, these past few months—it only solidified how I felt about you, about us. I'd already been considering this before we left Florida—what happened in Belize only confirmed how I felt—how I feel."

He paused, then he reached his free hand into the pocket of his khakis. What . . . how'd he get that? Did he have it with him on the plane?

"Kayla, I've wanted to be your husband for some time now. Because you deserve someone who will love you, commit to you fully before asking anything of you. You are my whole life, my whole world, my everything. I would be lost without you, and even if you never used your powers again, you would still be the strongest woman I know."

Kayla saw a tear well up in his eye as he let go of her hand for a brief moment to open the dark-blue box he'd pulled out of his pocket. *The* box.

"I've loved you since I've known you. Our love is astonishing, the kind of love they write stories about." He smirked as Kayla recognized her own words to him, what seemed like a lifetime ago. "You have my heart forever, Kayla, and I will love you the rest of my probably very long life." His smile widened, and Kayla felt a smile spread across her face at his words that echoed her own from just a few days ago.

Grady took a deep breath then swallowed hard. "Kayla Harrington, will you please marry me?"

Instantly, tears welled up in Kayla's eyes, and she had a hard time seeing his face. She blinked quickly, trying to clear her vision, desperate to see the beautiful face of the man who'd stolen her heart. Forever.

She nodded quickly, laughing through her tears. "Of course, Grady. I would love to marry you." He pulled the ring out of the blue satin box and slid it on her finger. It was a small, oval solitaire set in a dizzying array of tiny diamonds swirling around the center stone like waves with a thin, platinum band. It was so her and so Grady at the same time. Kayla gasped when she saw it on her finger then looked up.

Grady leapt to his feet, pulling her off the ground. Kayla wrapped her legs around his waist as she pressed her lips to his. She wrapped her arms around his head, twisting her fingers in his hair, convinced she had never felt this much joy in her life.

Uh, Mandy?

Kayla's voice broke into her thoughts. *Yeah—what's up?*

Kayla hesitated. *Well . . . I kinda have something to tell you.*

Mandy sat up straight on her couch, tossing her phone aside. *What is it?*

Grady . . . kinda . . . proposed.

Mandy screamed, her voice piercing through the apartment, and Justin came running from the bedroom.

"What on earth happened, Mandy?"

"Kayla and Grady got engaged!" Mandy was on her feet, bouncing up and down.

Justin jumped into the convo. *I just heard the news, guys—congratulations!*

Thanks, man, Grady answered, a smile in his voice.

And sorry for Mandy blowing out your eardrums. You know, metaphorically.

Mandy shot him a look. *Seriously—we're so happy for you guys!*

Thank you! Kayla's joy was evident in her thoughts.

How about we take you guys to dinner? Justin asked. *Our treat?*

Mandy nodded as Kayla's answer came back. *That sounds really nice—thanks, Justin!*

Meet us at Palermo's. Twenty minutes? Justin asked. Mandy was already following him back to their bedroom to change.

Make it an hour. I'd love to get the airplane smell out of my hair, Kayla joked.

Of course. Mandy chuckled. *See you soon!*

After a nice dinner at the swanky Palermo's restaurant across town, Kayla and Grady said their goodbyes and headed to Grady's Jeep. Mandy hadn't been able to stop asking Kayla questions about the wedding the entire meal—she knew it was too soon and that Kayla wouldn't have any of the details figured out yet, but she just couldn't seem to help herself.

Justin paid the bill and reached for Mandy's hand as they walked out to his car. "Uh, Mandy?"

Mandy stopped and turned to him just as they reached the vehicle. "Hmm?"

Justin swallowed hard. "I had an idea. Do you want to go somewhere for Christmas? Get out of town for a while?"

Mandy blinked but then smiled. "Sure!" Mandy could hear the fleeting thought about this being his first Christmas without his parents pass through his head. "Where should we go?"

Justin smiled serenely, leaning in to kiss her forehead. "Our place."

Mandy's eyes widened a little. "Is it even available on such short notice?" She started to reach for her phone, but Justin put his hand on her arm.

He just grinned at her when her eyes caught his. "I already booked it starting the weekend before Christmas. For a week."

Mandy grinned back. She pulled him into a hug then kissed him hard.

Justin blinked. "What was that for?"

Mandy smiled as she walked around to the passenger side, tossing the car keys over the hood before climbing inside. "I'm just ready to go on a vacation with you. Relax. Take in the salt air." She dreamily stared out the windshield as Justin started the car.

"Your wish, my command, my dear," Justin quipped as they headed home.

Where to, sweetie? Grady asked once they got on the highway.

Kayla smiled, marveling at the way this day had turned out. Only a few hours ago, she'd been mad at Grady for hiding something from her. Now they were headed to . . . she interrupted that train of thought to answer him. *Let's go back to my place. That okay?*

Grady reached for her hand across the center console and brought it to his lips. *Of course, my love.* He kissed her hand gently then held it between them for the rest of the ride.

When they walked in the front door, Grady pulled her to him and kissed her hard then quickly let her go. "So . . . what should we do?"

Kayla had some ideas—ideas she suspected Grady was having, too, given his playful tone—but she wasn't quite ready for him to know that just yet. She swallowed hard, carefully masking her thoughts as she noticed that her throat was bone dry. "I think I need a drink of water." Kayla walked over to the sink, pulling a glass from her cabinet on the way and filling it. She drank it slowly, turning to lean against the counter and eye Grady as she did.

And she noticed something change. Suddenly, Grady was no longer teasing, and his eyes now held a hunger in them she'd glimpsed before but never this intensely.

Kayla swallowed again, thankful for the water, then turned and poured the rest out in the sink, setting the glass on the counter. Slowly, deliberately. Trying to calm her racing heart.

Then Grady was right behind her, his arms wrapping around her waist. "Kayla . . ." he whispered in her ear, voice low and enticing, and Kayla shuddered. Yes, the teasing was definitely gone.

She slowly, so slowly, turned around to face him, his body so close she was pressed up against the sink.

Kayla stared up into his eyes, and Grady noticed the hunger increase exponentially in hers. She spontaneously pulled him into a hug, wrapping her arms around his neck and putting her lips to his ear. "Make love to me."

Grady's breath caught. How could he be this lucky? He took a step back, lifting her off the ground much as he'd done when they'd come here just a few hours before, and he smiled as she wrapped her legs around his waist again. He leaned in for a kiss, feeling her comb her fingers through his hair. He carried her through the house, past the dining room, the living room . . . and found her bedroom. Finally.

The bed was perfectly made, her comforter warm and inviting. Grady suddenly wanted nothing more than to take her right here, right this second.

But he had to remind himself that they'd been waiting for this for *forever*, and that Kayla deserved more, better. She deserved for him to take his time.

He set her down on the floor, near the door and facing the bed, then took a couple of steps back, wanting to look at her, all of her. He was amazed at how this night was turning out, amazed that this incredible woman had agreed to be his wife. He was the luckiest man in the world.

And as he looked at her, *really* looked at her, his breathing sped up. He couldn't seem to help it; as much as he'd wanted Kayla before, the feeling was so much stronger now. Intense passion flooded through him, and he had to physically restrain himself.

"Come here, my love." Grady held out his arms to her, beckoning her closer while keeping his feet firmly planted on the ground. He needed her to close the distance, needed her to make the first move. "I've been waiting for you forever."

Kayla took one tentative step closer, knowing the truth of his words but suddenly feeling unsure. This was Grady; why should she feel unsure?

"Kayla," Grady breathed, less than a foot away now, taking what appeared to be a much more certain step forward, matching hers.

The sound of her name on his lips melted her concerns away. She stepped into him confidently, inches away now, and found his gaze, locking onto it like her life depended on it. In this moment, it probably did.

Kayla reached for him, placing the fingertips of her left hand on his waist. Grady's sapphire eyes tightened infinitesimally as she blindly felt the softness of his dark-gray t-shirt beneath her touch, the subtle strain of his muscles beneath his shirt.

She slowly trailed her fingers down until she found the edge of his shirt, never breaking their gaze. She could always read him, but it was different now. Better. Any walls they'd ever had had fallen, and she could see exactly what her touch was doing to him. He was aching for it, begging for it, just like she was. She didn't need to hear his thoughts to know that.

Kayla slid his shirt up with her hand, and her fingertips found his skin. Grady's eyes fell closed for an instant then opened to once again catch her gaze. The want, the need in them had increased exponentially.

But she wanted to take this slow. She had to take this slow. It felt like she'd been waiting—they'd been waiting—forever for this, and she was going to savor it. Even if it killed her.

Kayla slowly trailed her hand up, grazing his stomach, finding his chest. She drew in a sharp breath as her hands felt chiseled muscle. When on earth had he found time to work out?

The corner of Grady's mouth turned up as he heard the thought pass through her head. She would've been embarrassed, but this was Grady, and they were way past that.

She reached her other hand under his shirt and pulled the fabric up slowly, dragging it toward his neck.

Gazes still locked, Grady pulled his shirt over his head, dropping it to the carpeted floor. Kayla stole a glance at his chest and felt herself reaching for him again, letting her hands trace over the perfect contours of his body. She watched her hands explore, felt the warmth of his skin beneath her fingertips, felt the reckless beat of his racing heart.

Grady reached for her, his hands cupping her face and drawing her gaze back to his. He leaned down and pressed his lips to hers, more gently than Kayla would've thought possible in his current state of mind. It seemed he was willing to take this slow as well, which pleased her very much.

Kayla let his lips linger for a gloriously long moment before she pulled away and reached up to take his wrists in her hands. Finding his gaze again, Kayla guided his hands to her waist.

Instantly, she could hear all the thoughts in Grady's head, the ones that she now realized he'd been holding back. The ones that told her just how much it was killing him to wait for this, just how much he wanted her.

And she loved him even more for it. If she would've known how he felt, she may have given in before she was ready. Grady had given her the greatest gift, and she'd love him forever for it.

With a featherlight touch, Grady slowly dragged the hem of her flowy, emerald-green blouse up, exposing her stomach. He traced the lines on her bare skin, watching himself do it much like she had, before reaching a hand up to caress her cheek, tucking her hair behind her ear.

Then, it seemed, he was ready. He pulled the sleeveless shirt up and over her head, dropping it on top of his. Then he looked down, taking in the sight of her.

Kayla would've felt self-conscious, had it been anyone else. She might've been nervous, even just a few weeks ago. But now, in this moment, in this perfect, amazing timing, she welcomed his gaze, ached for it, pleaded for it. She needed him to finally see her, all of her, to unwrap her then devour her.

She reached for the top button of his jeans, unbuttoning them quickly. She helped him slide his jeans down just before he reached for hers, quickly pulling them around her curves and pushing them down to the floor. Kayla slid her own jeans over her heels, and Grady stepped out of his as they inched closer to the bed. Kayla stopped breathing.

Her thoughts were so chaotic, she wasn't sure what Grady would actually be able to hear in them. Her mind was swirling with love, lust, admiration, respect, anticipation, need. And she couldn't get enough.

"Grady, I love you," she whispered, her eyes sliding shut as his hands explored her stomach, her waist, her hips. She moved closer to him, wanting more but enjoying this moment, too.

"I love you, Kayla, more than anything," Grady breathed as his hands trailed up her back, stopping at her bra. She leaned against his chest, grateful she'd chosen her lacy black bra for this very moment. She heard the clasp unsnap and felt the elastic release.

Still against his chest, she gazed up into his eyes. Oh, she could see he wanted her, very much, but she could see all the love he had for her in them as well.

And in an instant, everything was okay. Better than okay. It was downright perfect. Grady kissed the top of her head before Kayla stepped back, helping her bra to the floor. Grady's eyes took her in, then he reached for her suddenly, pulling her toward him with a force that took her breath away. His lips were hard on hers, their bodies pressed together, and the thin fabric remaining between them left little to the imagination.

And then the fabric was gone, and absolutely nothing stood between them.

Grady picked her up, turned around, and set Kayla gently down on the bed. He stood over her for a brief moment, his love-filled eyes gazing into hers until she reached for him, pulling him down on top of her.

The Beginning of the End of the World

Three Weeks Later, The Underground Warehouse in Belize

"YATZIL?" HOLUN CALLED. "What should we do with this?"

Yatzil frowned then came over to where he was standing, not knowing what he was referring to. Then she saw it.

The globe.

"Oh, yes. We should . . . how do we even catalog something like that?"

Holun smiled at her, grabbing her hand and pulling her in for a quick kiss. "I am sure you will figure it out, my Yatzil."

Yatzil smiled back, but she was getting an achy feeling in the pit of her stomach. This was a dangerous piece, and in the wrong hands . . .

She remembered all too well how Shani—her *mother*, the thought feeling like poison in her mind—had used it to manipulate those poor people.

Yatzil reached for the globe, taking a breath as she did, knowing it had given her powers once, assuming its work was done.

She was wrong.

The instant her hands touched the globe, it lit up, brighter than she'd ever seen it. Lightning bolts shot out from beneath her hands, and she screamed though she felt no pain. She held it out in front of her, terrified of what was happening but unable to put it down.

"Yatzil!" Holun was screaming her name beside her, but she barely heard him. She was just staring at the lightning shooting out from the globe's center.

Something was coming. She could feel it. The globe was building up to something, something big. Yatzil just stared, hoping that she'd survive.

She didn't like that feeling.

With a force that she knew the world had never seen—a dozen atomic bombs going off at the same time, perhaps—the lightning from the globe suddenly became a razor-sharp band of blinding yellow light, one that emanated from its center and shot out in all directions. She dropped the globe and was shoved backward, and she saw Holun forced backward as well. She didn't even feel herself hit the ground.

Kayla couldn't believe she was so lucky. She was engaged to the most wonderful man in the world, and their powers were growing stronger every day. She couldn't help but think that her life was finally coming together.

She turned at the sound of the front door opening. Grady came in the door with shopping bags crowding his arms. She chuckled at his tendency to try to get everything in one trip and ran over to him. "Need some help?" She snagged a few bags as he dropped the rest to the kitchen floor and leaned over for a kiss.

"From you, always." He flashed her the grin that always made her breath catch then closed the front door behind him. "But no snooping!" He snatched a bag away from her, and Kayla knew he'd heard the plan in her head the second before. "You'll get this later." He smirked, one side of his mouth turning up.

Kayla pretended to pout before smiling then glanced around her increasingly crowded condo.

"You know, we should have everything else from my place moved in here today." Grady was following her gaze, and Kayla knew what he was thinking. Of course she did.

She was just as frustrated with the lack of space in her small condo, though it was somehow bigger than his, and they both thought simultaneously—again—that they needed to start looking for another place.

Then Kayla felt something, a small twinge in her subconscious that told her something was coming. Grady felt it, too.

"What is that?" she whispered, freezing in place, the shopping bags at their feet forgotten.

Grady turned wide eyes to her. "I don't know—" But his words were cut off as they saw a band of light approaching out the window, a thin, yellow arc slicing the world in two.

He reached for Kayla's hand, and she squeezed it tight as the wave washed over them.

Then the world went black.

LOVED THE BOOK?
LEAVE A REVIEW!

Independent authors like me rely on online reviews from our readers to help others find our books. Please take a few moments to visit Amazon or Goodreads and leave a review of *The Prophecy of the Codex*. I would really appreciate it!

www.melissafrey.com

Acknowledgments

My first thank you always goes to my husband, Andrew. Thank you for going over my manuscript fifty bajillion times while formatting and catching the errors I missed. You make my words beautiful on screen and on the page, and you're always my biggest fan and a true partner both in business and in life. You're my anchor, my rock, my support, my encouragement, my love . . . and forever my Grady. I love you.

To Meghan, my fabulous critique partner! Your comments got me through the hardest days of editing (because self-editing is always the hardest part of writing and publishing a book) when I doubted myself and my story. Your encouragement and suggestions helped me make this book the best it could possibly be, and I can't thank you enough.

To Eve, who has quickly become one of my best author friends. Your support and encouragement as I finished this book was invaluable, and I'm so glad we *virtually* met! Here's to meeting soon in person!

To the Badass Author Babes, who gave me a community of fellow indie authors to bounce ideas off of, get advice from, and always give me someone to talk to when I'm having a rough day. You ladies are the best, and I have made lifelong friends (and discovered some amazing authors!) in this group. I love you all!

To the Instagram writing community, I am so glad I found you! Thank you for all your support and kind words. I'm so lucky to have stumbled onto this amazing group of indie authors and voracious readers and have made so many friends in this community that it's crazy! My Insta friends have seriously gotten me through a lot of hard things. Keep being your awesome selves.

To my beta readers, thank you for taking the time to read my book. Your notes helped me make my story better—I appreciate you so much!

To my readers, THANK YOU from the bottom of my heart for choosing this book among the millions out there and reading it. I wouldn't be here without you all cheering me on! So I'll say it again: THANK YOU.

And to all the writers out there, keep being amazing and writing the stories that need to be told. Don't listen to anyone who says you can't do it—they are always wrong. The only person's opinion that matters is your own, so tell yourself you can do it, and you will.

Most importantly, keep doing the brave things. Life is much too short to stay small.

Also by Melissa Frey

The Codex Series
The Secret of the Codex

Non-Fiction
How to Work from Home (with Andrew Frey)

WANT MORE?

Find out what happens
next in Book Three of
the Codex Series,
coming in 2021!

For the latest news on the release, writing
advice, and random life updates, follow me on
Instagram at @melissafreyauthor or sign up
at melissafrey.com to stay up to date!

#theprophecyofthecodex
#thecodexseries